# Daughter of Water

## A. S. DAMPT

# Daughter of Water

## A. S. DAMPT

The Verdélian Chronicles

I

YEAR 4020

Grisdon ◇

Brédisse ◇

Vivess ◇

Mistralle Peninsula

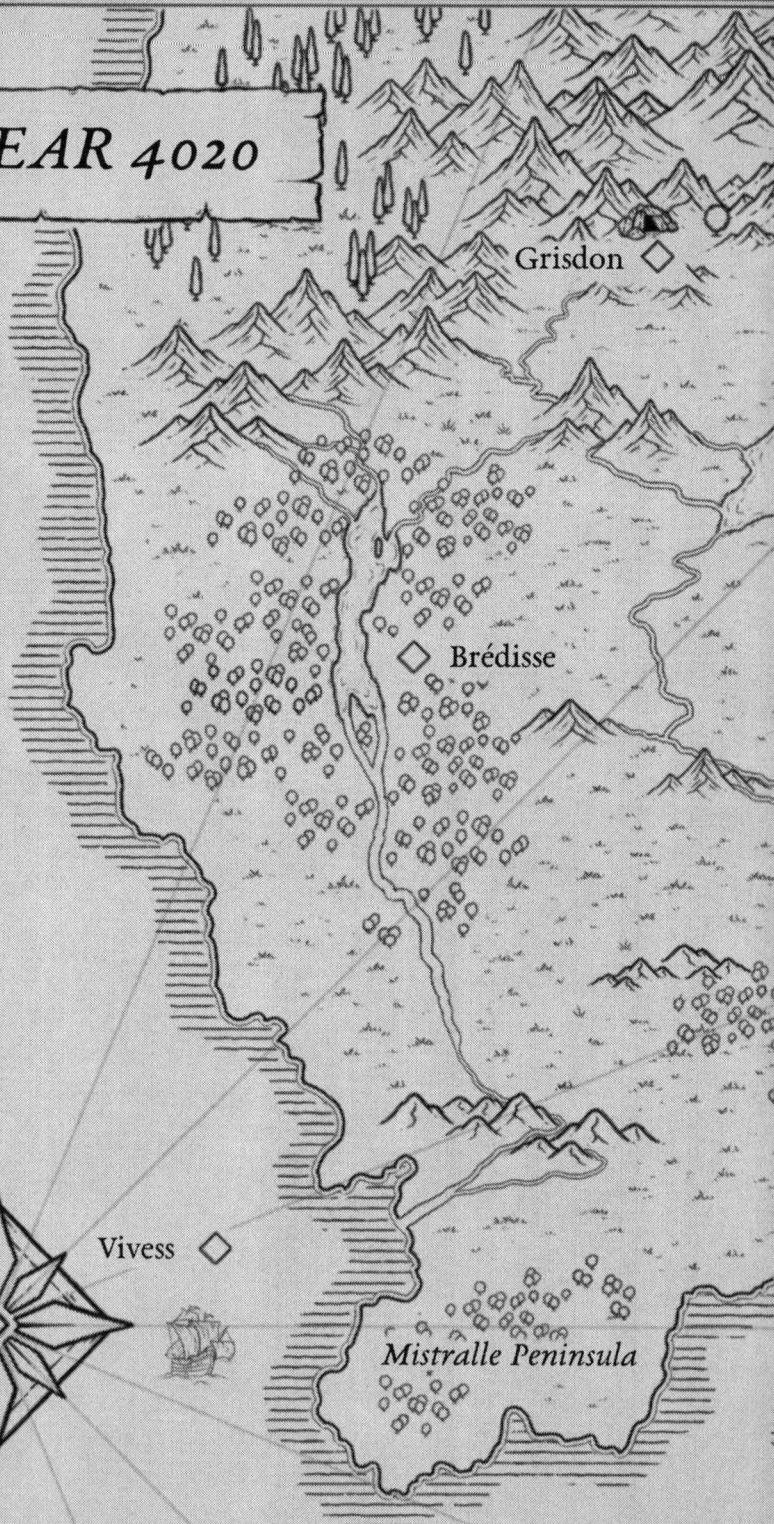

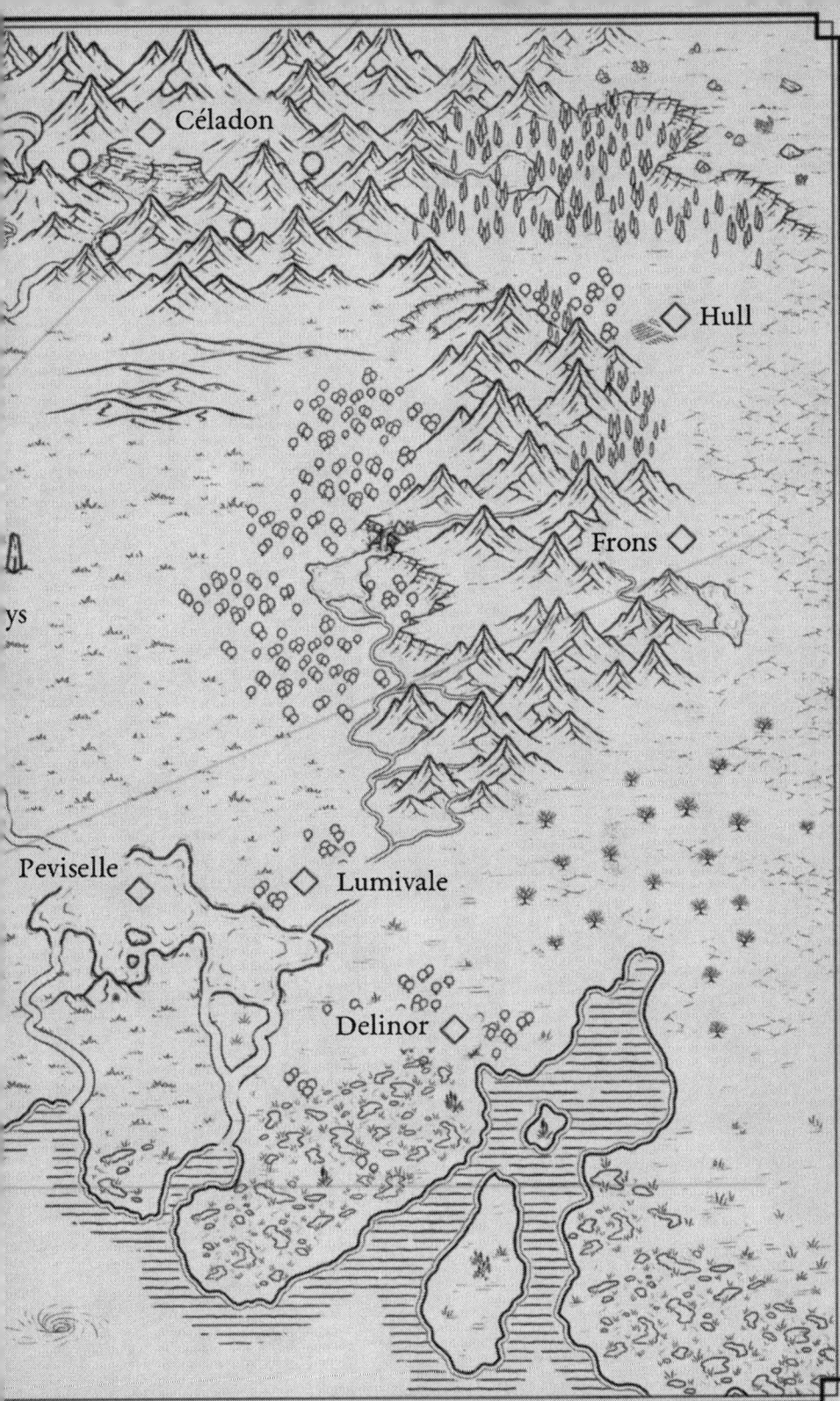

Céladon

Hull

Frons

ys

Peviselle

Lumivale

Delinor

# Spring | First Moon

| Aprél | Hitrovère | Livan | Simphron | Vildrèd |
|---|---|---|---|---|
| 1<br>Birth of Spring Celebration | 2 | 3 | 4 | 5 |
| 6 | 7 | 8 | 9 | 10<br>Celebration of the Firstborn |
| 11 | 12 | 13 | 14 | 15 |
| 16 | 17 | 18 | 19<br>Candlelight Celebration | 20 |
| 21 | 22 | 23 | 24 | 25 |

# Spring | Second Moon

| Aprél | Hitrovère | Livan | Simphron | Vildrèd |
|---|---|---|---|---|
| 1 | 2 | 3 | 4 | 5 |
| 6 | 7 | 8 | 9<br>Water Creature Carnival | 10 |
| 11 | 12 | 13<br>Baking Feast | 14 | 15 |
| 16<br>Day of Remembrance | 17 | 18 | 19 | 20 |
| 21 | 22 | 23 | 24 | 25 |

# Spring | Third Moon

| Aprél | Hitrovère | Livan | Simphron | Vildrèd |
|---|---|---|---|---|
| 1 | 2<br>Festival of the Heart | 3 | 4 | 5 |
| 6 | 7 | 8 | 9 | 10 |
| 11 | 12<br>Water Energy Display | 13 | 14 | 15 |
| 16 | 17 | 18 | 19 | 20 |
| 21 | 22 | 23 | 24<br>Floral Parade | 25 |

# Spring | Fourth Moon

| Aprél | Hitrovère | Livan | Simphron | Vildrèd |
|---|---|---|---|---|
| 1 | 2 | 3 | 4 | 5 |
| 6 | 7<br>Day of Mothers | 8 | 9 | 10 |
| 11 | 12 | 13 | 14 | 15 |
| 16 | 17 | 18<br>Water<br>Wildlife Jubilee | 19 | 20 |
| 21 | 22<br>Flower Fest | 23 | 24<br>Royal Philharmonic | 25 |

# Summer | First Moon

| Aprél | Hitrovère | Livan | Simphron | Vildrèd |
|---|---|---|---|---|
| 1<br>Birth of Summer<br>Celebration | 2 | 3 | 4 | 5 |
| 6 | 7<br>Day of Fathers | 8 | 9 | 10 |
| 11 | 12<br>Cultural<br>Consideration | 13 | 14 | 15 |
| 16 | 17 | 18 | 19 | 20 |
| 21 | 22 | 23 | 24 | 25 |

# Summer | Second Moon

| Aprél | Hitrovère | Livan | Simphron | Vildrèd |
|---|---|---|---|---|
| 1 | 2<br>Jewel Festival | 3 | 4 | 5 |
| 6 | 7 | 8 | 9<br>Earth Creature<br>Carnival | 10 |
| 11 | 12 | 13 | 14 | 15 |
| 16 | 17 | 18<br>Day of Chance | 19 | 20 |
| 21 | 22 | 23 | 24 | 25 |

## Summer | Third Moon

| Aprél | Hitrovère | Livan | Simphron | Vildrèd |
|---|---|---|---|---|
| 1 | 2 | 3 | 4 | 5 |
| 6 | 7 | 8 | 9 | 10 |
| 11 | 12 <br> Earth Energy Display | 13 | 14 | 15 |
| 16 | 17 | 18 | 19 <br> History Celebration | 20 |
| 21 | 22 | 23 | 24 <br> Day of Recreation | 25 |

## Summer | Fourth Moon

| Aprél | Hitrovère | Livan | Simphron | Vildrèd |
|---|---|---|---|---|
| 1 | 2 | 3 | 4 <br> Fest of Construction | 5 |
| 6 | 7 | 8 <br> Family Day | 9 | 10 |
| 11 | 12 | 13 | 14 | 15 |
| 16 | 17 | 18 <br> Earth Wildlife Jubilee | 19 | 20 |
| 21 | 22 | 23 | 24 <br> Royal Theater | 25 |

# Autumn | First Moon

| Aprél | Hitrovère | Livan | Simphron | Vildrèd |
|---|---|---|---|---|
| 1<br>Birth of Autumn Celebration | 2 | 3 | 4 | 5 |
| 6 | 7 | 8 | 9 | 10 |
| 11 | 12<br>Feast of Faith | 13 | 14 | 15 |
| 16 | 17<br>Day of Friendship | 18 | 19 | 20 |
| 21 | 22 | 23 | 24 | 25 |

# Autumn | Second Moon

| Aprél | Hitrovère | Livan | Simphron | Vildrèd |
|---|---|---|---|---|
| 1 | 2 | 3 | 4 | 5 |
| 6 | 7<br>Martyrs' Day | 8 | 9<br>Fire Creature Carnival | 10 |
| 11 | 12 | 13 | 14 | 15 |
| 16 | 17 | 18<br>All Creatures' Day | 19 | 20 |
| 21 | 22 | 23 | 24 | 25 |

## Autumn | Third Moon

| Aprél | Hitrovère | Livan | Simphron | Vildrèd |
|---|---|---|---|---|
| 1 | 2 | 3 | 4 <br> Healers Harvest | 5 |
| 6 | 7 | 8 | 9 | 10 |
| 11 | 12 <br> Fire Energy Display | 13 | 14 | 15 |
| 16 | 17 | 18 | 19 | 20 |
| 21 | 22 | 23 | 24 <br> Festival of Familiars | 25 |

## Autumn | Fourth Moon

| Aprél | Hitrovère | Livan | Simphron | Vildrèd |
|---|---|---|---|---|
| 1 | 2 | 3 <br> Day of Peace | 4 | 5 |
| 6 <br> Day of Prosperity | 7 | 8 | 9 | 10 |
| 11 | 12 | 13 | 14 | 15 |
| 16 | 17 | 18 <br> Fire <br> Wildlife Jubilee | 19 | 20 |
| 21 | 22 | 23 | 24 <br> Royal Ballet | 25 <br> Festival of Flowers |

# Winter | First Moon

| Aprél | Hitrovère | Livan | Simphron | Vildrèd |
|---|---|---|---|---|
| 1<br>Birth of Winter Celebration | 2 | 3 | 4<br>Celebration of Unity | 5 |
| 6 | 7 | 8 | 9 | 10 |
| 11 | 12<br>Forebear Festival | 13 | 14 | 15 |
| 16 | 17 | 18 | 19 | 20 |
| 21 | 22 | 23 | 24 | 25 |

# Winter | Second Moon

| Aprél | Hitrovère | Livan | Simphron | Vildrèd |
|---|---|---|---|---|
| 1 | 2 | 3 | 4 | 5 |
| 6 | 7 | 8 | 9<br>Air Creature Carnival | 10 |
| 11 | 12 | 13 | 14 | 15 |
| 16 | 17 | 18 | 19 | 20 |
| 21 | 22<br>Astronomy Fest | 23 | 24<br>Festival of Enlightenment | 25 |

# Winter | Third Moon

| Aprél | Hitrovère | Livan | Simphron | Vildrèd |
|---|---|---|---|---|
| 1 | 2 | 3 | 4 | 5 |
| 6 | 7 | 8 | 9 | 10 |
| 11 | 12<br>Air Energy Display | 13 | 14 | 15 |
| 16 | 17<br>Prophets Day | 18 | 19 | 20 |
| 21 | 22 | 23 | 24 | 25<br>Inheritance Day |

# Winter | Fourth Moon

| Aprél | Hitrovère | Livan | Simphron | Vildrèd |
|---|---|---|---|---|
| 1 | 2 | 3 | 4 | 5 |
| 6<br>Day of Rest | 7 | 8 | 9 | 10 |
| 11<br>Wishes of Winter | 12 | 13 | 14 | 15 |
| 16 | 17 | 18<br>Air<br>Wildlife Jubilee | 19 | 20 |
| 21 | 22 | 23 | 24<br>Royal Art Gallery | 25 |

# *Prologue*

The frigid wind carried an ominous silence as it glided along the street. The dark, foreboding night lay like a heavy yoke over the shoulders of a young couple. They huddled over a porcelain vessel, from which sprung a delicate flower.

"Have we been blessed?" the woman asked her husband.

The man, his fair features reflecting the dim moonlight, grimaced.

"Under other circumstances, I would say so."

Couples would sacrifice everything for a child in a year like this. They carried the hope that Solaidi, the great creator, would choose them to bring the next generation of royalty into the world. This miracle transpired every two hundred years. For many, the event would not occur at all during their lifetimes.

Things were different this cycle. Malevolent forces were present in Verdélys, the City of Blooms. Mourning replaced celebration. Even now, the young woman could hear the cries of her friends and neighbors as they lamented the loss of their loved ones.

Beneath the couple's loving eyes in the dark, the little flower opened. It revealed shimmering golden petals as it stretched itself in the cold. As her husband looked on, the mother cupped the bloom gingerly in her hands. There, amid the petals, lay a beautiful baby boy.

The mother gasped in amazement.

"He's perfect."

The father nodded, grim but proud, his eyes shimmering in what little light the night provided.

The mother gently picked up her baby, enveloping him in a loving embrace. Her two hands cradled his meager frame.

The child cried out.

The father's features grew somber and sad.

"We must get him to the palace," he instructed.

"Must we say farewell so soon?" his wife asked, tears in her eyes.

"They will come for him, and we cannot guarantee his safety," the father said. "Come, we cannot delay."

The mother grabbed her husband's hand.

"Not before we name him. Look at your son," she invited. "What shall we call him?"

The father looked down upon his family, trying for the sake of his wife to quell the despair he felt growing inside of him.

After a brief pause, the father said, "Gaëtan."

"Gaëtan," the mother repeated as she gazed lovingly at her precious infant. "He will hold the same traits as his father: strength, bravery, and above all, kindness."

The father clenched his jaw to steel himself against overwhelming emotion.

"We must go," he choked out. "You take him to the gates. I will follow close behind. A couple traveling together will raise suspicions."

The father helped his wife bundle the child within his mother's cloak, out of sight of prying eyes.

"Go now. Get to the palace. Don't turn back."

The streets, once lively, were now empty as they walked in silence. The parents' eyes scanned the surroundings. Every shadow was a potential threat.

The infant cooed quietly from his place in his mother's bosom.

From the darkness beneath the eaves of a wood-framed house bordering the street, a shadow stepped out towards the young mother.

The stranger menacingly approached the cloaked woman, "Late night for a stroll; you wouldn't have a child on your person, would you?"

"No," the mother said, quickening her pace.

"If you speak true, you won't mind showing me what you are carrying, then." The stranger grabbed the mother's cloak.

The stranger grunted and fell to the ground as the father struck him.

"Run to the palace!"

As he begged, she fled. Men were shouting from behind.

"A child! She has a child! Stop her!"

She glanced over her shoulder. Her husband was fighting half a dozen men. An unseen force overrode her instinct to run back and fight by his side. On she dashed. The palace walls towered above the rooftops.

"Help! Help us!" she cried as she ran.

Suddenly, she felt a heavy blow on her back. Her breath left her in an instant, and she collapsed. She hardly cushioned the baby as she fell and struck the stony street. What had felt like a blunt strike a moment ago was now a sharp pain below her left shoulder, and she felt her dress and cloak saturate with a warm, wet sensation. She was bleeding heavily.

She heard strangers jeering and shouting from where she lay on the ground.

"I got her!"

She turned her attention back to the palace. Would anyone come?

Her foes were approaching.

Mustering her strength, she gathered her child in her right arm and got to her knees. Already, her assailants were upon her.

In a flash, an enormous shadow flew over the mother and crashed into the nearest attacker. The man's body shriveled and shattered, caught between the cobblestones and four heavy hooves. Two additional brigands were cut down by the newcomer's long sword.

An imposing centaur turned to the mother.

"Come, let us get that child to safety!" he beckoned.

The mother stretched forth her hand, offering her precious cargo to her rescuer.

"Take him to the palace!" She rasped. "He is a Firstborn."

More and more enemies approached.

The centaur beckoned her, "There is still time for you, madam,"

The mother shook her head.

"I will only delay you. The child must be safe. I will buy you time, and then I will join my husband. Promise me you will see him safe."

"I swear it," the centaur said with a bow. He took off at a dead sprint towards the palace, but not before another assailant lunged at him from the shadows, shearing a long gash along his flank. Bellowing, the centaur kicked, sending his attacker sprawling back before landing motionless on the ground. In an instant, the centaur and his new ward were bounding towards the palace.

The mother stole a last glance towards her child. Then she turned to the men rapidly nearing her. Before their eyes, her petite form surged and writhed for a moment. Then, from beneath her cloak, a savage beast, a tiger with fangs and claws, bared as she launched herself recklessly at her attackers. Men screamed as their prey became the predator. After several violent moments, numbers overwhelmed the mother's ferocity, and she fell lifeless on the ground. Her child was safe.

*The First of Four.*

Amidst a field of corn, a flower bloomed. The brittle stalks of corn muffled the cries of the tiny child. As the petals had opened into the night, the harsh cold tensed her body.

A dark-haired woman with eyes of gold stopped mid-step as the wind carried an unexpected sound to her ear. She followed the noise through the corn, and alone on the frigid earth, she beheld a sight never seen.

There, hidden beneath the tall corn, was a single flower, its petals the color of coal. Within, however, the flower radiated a unique golden light, and at the center of that light lay a tiny infant with striking red hair.

"How can it be?" The woman gasped. Shaking herself from her stupor, she quickly unraveled her scarf from around her neck and bundled the newborn inside of it, rocking back and forth to soothe the abandoned baby. The baby, exhausted from its wailing, soon fell asleep.

The woman started for the road. She strode purposefully towards the center of the city, careful to keep the baby tucked well inside her cloak. Soon, the palace walls were in view. She approached the guards at the gate.

"I'm here for work," she said.

"At this hour?" The guard replied with gruff skepticism.

"Please, you must let me in."

The guard was unmoved.

Stealing a glance over her shoulder, the woman parted her cloak and brushed aside the end of her scarf, revealing the babe.

The guard's face softened with comprehension.

The guard promptly allowed the woman to pass. "Alfric!" He called out after her.

A man exited the guardhouse beyond the gate. He was broad and tall and wore elaborate golden armor. His breastplate bore an emblem of a sun-shaped flower atop a four-leafed stem.

"What is it?" Alfric asked.

Instinctively, the woman revealed her cargo to the ranking officer. The baby cooed, then opened its eyes as it woke.

Alfric's eyes narrowed. "An imp?"

"Yes, but look," the woman said. She pulled the petals from her pocket and into the dim night light. She had plucked them from the child's bloom. The glint of gold was unmistakable. "I found her in a field on the outskirts of the city."

Alfric showed visible surprise, but he furrowed his brow and nodded.

"Very well. The palace will be her protection. You did well to bring her here."

"They will not accept her...," the woman said, relinquishing the child into Alfric's powerful arms.

"They will have no choice. Solaidi has chosen her," Alfric said.

*The Second of Four.*

꽃

Far south of the City of Blooms, a Verdélian family gathered around. A flower bud sprouted from a small pot set on the dining room table.

"Mama, Mama!" a little brown-haired girl called out excitedly. "Tonight he be borned!"

The kind face of a petite woman gazed affectionately at the toddler.

"Yes, dear, tonight is the night. Are you ready to meet your sibling?"

The girl nodded vigorously, a toothy grin on her face.

"Mama," she said, "Girl or boy?"

"I don't know," the mother said. "What do you think?"

The little daughter smiled, remaining quiet.

"Papa, girl or boy?"

The father smiled at his little girl.

"How about boy?" He proposed.

The little girl nodded again.

"Yes, Papa. A boy. He my brother. I know."

The parents laughed together.

The little girl shrieked in anticipation.

"Look," she shouted, "it moved!"

The mother shushed her daughter.

"We don't want to frighten him, dear. Look, it's time now."

The petals parted. Before the bloom could open, a tiny hand stretched itself skyward. The little girl squeezed her mother as tightly as she could, doing everything she could to stop herself from letting out another excited scream.

"I'll get him," the father said.

"If indeed it is a him," the mother said.

The father slipped his hand beneath his infant and pulled him from the comfort of his little bud.

"It is indeed a him," the father confirmed. He lowered the tiny baby towards the little girl. "Say hello to your little brother, dear."

The girl stared at the little child.

"Hello, brother," she whispered.

"Here," the father said. He handed the child to its mother. "Watch over him for a moment. I'll take care of the bud."

The man turned to the flower, a beautiful golden bloom, and plucked it from its pot. He placed it into a glass bottle prepared for this purpose. He stoppered the bottle with a cork before placing it into a wooden chest full of straw. He closed the lid and secured it with a heavy iron lock before returning his attention to his newborn son.

The father and mother exchanged a knowing glance before directing their gaze towards their children.

"Would you like to hold him?" The mother asked her daughter.

"Oh, yes!" the daughter said, wide-eyed.

"Gently now," the father said. He placed the baby in the child's arms.

There, in that quiet cottage, a sister held her brother, and a golden flower lay secreted away from the world.

*The Third of Four.*

"We've no child! No bloom!" She screamed. They had killed her husband all the same. Before she realized what she was doing, she had taken their lives in return. She awakened the Celestine glass that lay beneath her feet, the glass she had crafted for her little family's home. Now, it would be the tomb of those who had torn her family apart. Before her husband's killers could reach her, they staggered into a daze, and she thrust her husband's sword through each of their hearts. In a mad scramble and through tears, she had gathered her things, clutched her precious bloom to her chest, and ran, leaving behind her what should have been a home full of happiness, but that was now a memorial to her endless sorrow.

She had left word. A loyal friend of her husband's, a soldier, had promised to meet her far to the east. There she lived now, alone with her bloom. Not alone, though, as the creatures of the wood had welcomed her with open arms and rejoiced as they watched her precious bloom grow. The days beneath the boughs were almost happy. Then, one day, the bud opened. The forest creatures gathered in awe as the mother held the bloom, ready to welcome her child into the world. The mother hummed a song she and her husband had sung together as her babe came into view.

Beneath it all, however, lay a darkness like a canker. Darkness soon reached the secluded woods where a mother and her child hid.

"Hide her away!" A dying mother begged the forest. "A friend will come for her. Watch her until then!"

A tall, slender nymph solemnly took the small child into her arms.

"She will forever be a child of this forest," the woman promised.

The mother had passed on, and soon, the promised friend, a tired but determined soldier bearing the tokens of the Verdélia, arrived.

He gritted his teeth and said, "Too late. I have failed them."

"Honor the request of this child's mother and see the babe to safety, and you will have filled your duty," the nymph encouraged as she entrusted the child to the soldier. "Be swift now. Not even the woods could conceal her from the growing darkness."

The soldier set out resolutely, his charge nestled in a sling that hung close against his chest. On he went, searching for safety for the child.

*The Fourth of Four.*

# I

## A Naturally Unnatural Morning

"Yes, why don't you join us?" Heidi asked.

A radiant white rose stretched its petals and yawned in the breeze. Heidi imagined the blossom taking a deep breath of air as she held it up to face the early morning sunlight. The flower's golden center revealed itself to her as the final petals unfurled. She turned her attention to the next flower bud. It bloomed as miraculously as the first as she coaxed it awake.

The rising sun drew her eyes to the horizon. Flocks of birds added their song to Heidi's hummed melody. The garden flooded with crisp morning light, gleaming and dancing on a thousand colorful blossoms. She smiled and walked dutifully to her family's extensive garden behind the house.

Heidi worked best in the early hours when she could hide from the eyes of her distant yet nosy neighbors. She wished she could tend to her plants on a more regular schedule; unfortunately, the town's wandering eyes would catch on that something *unnatural* was afoot. Her father warned that would only mean trouble. For now, this was the only solution Heidi had devised. This allowed her a few hours to be completely herself.

The neighbor's rooster crowed heartily into the brisk morning air as Heidi pulled up two small sprouting weeds. The garden was vast but not unmanageable, and this morning, she weeded the pumpkin patch. With that chore complete, her attention returned to the pumpkin plants. She twisted her hands in the air over the vines, almost caressing them to help them lengthen and grow. Leaves sprouted on the vines, followed by small flowers that turned into tiny green fruit as Heidi poured her energy into the plants.

"I think *you* have a grand purpose. You could feed a weary traveler or a starving child," Heidi said. "More likely a starving child since we don't get many weary travelers around these parts."

Each plant grew with prodigious ease. Heidi hummed, her eyes alight as she released her energy into her crops and flowers. From where she knelt next to the garden plants, Heidi let herself sink her knees into the dirt as she finished tending to the last stalk of squash. Her work in the garden, though easy, grew taxing. She took a deep breath of the cool morning air and reached a dirty hand up to wipe the beads of sweat on her hairline. Heidi huffed, stood, and swiped at the dirt on the front of her skirt.

She squinted and looked towards the sun. *Two hours*, she thought, *then breakfast*. If she hurried, she could finish gardening and venture to the pond.

Heidi worked briskly through the tall rows of corn, regularly stealing glances at the nearby tree line where the pond hid. The stalks were already tall, and on them, the ears of corn grew to a ripe, healthy size and even beyond as Heidi carefully and quickly tended them.

"You and you and you. Go on, race to the sky! Who will be the tallest?"

Finally, her heart pounding and dress damp with sweat, Heidi emerged from the other side of the cornfield onto a vast, brushy plain. Heidi closed her eyes and felt the sun's warmth on her skin. As much as her work in the garden drained her strength, the sun's rays rejuvenated Heidi.

She stood for several minutes on the edge of the garden, the last bit of earth touched by mankind before the wilderness before her. She kicked off her shoes. Eyes closed, she buried her naked feet into the earth, feeling the moist soil between her toes. The dry, cool breeze hinted these were the last warm days of autumn.

Reoriented, Heidi opened her eyes and locked them onto the woods ahead. The forest appeared suddenly out of the otherwise barren plain; large, twisting trees created a wall of dark green, hiding a mysterious shadow behind them as the forest grew thicker. Heidi always imagined the tree line looked like the ranks of a formidable army, each tree a disciplined soldier holding its position in the line. Protecting some secret, perhaps. The thought sounded more intimidating than she intended; the forest had always beckoned to her. Heidi had lost track of how often her mother had searched for her and called in exasperation for her to come home.

Glancing back at her family's small cottage, Heidi headed across the field between her family's crops and the forest ahead. She skipped, tossing her arms through the air and lightly swatting the crisp, wild grass surrounding her. The occasional shrub grabbed her skirt's hem as she walked over the quarter-mile field preceding the forest's border. She didn't stop at the tree line, pushing directly into the emerald darkness created by the foliage of the wild and ancient trees. Nor did she wait for her eyes to adjust to the darkness; her feet knew the way.

After five minutes of navigating the gnarled roots that crawled over the forest floor, Heidi heard water gurgling over rocks. She rounded a twisted oak tree and smiled as the rippled surface of the pond reflected the few rays of sun that penetrated the canopy. She eased herself down onto the water bank and slipped her feet in as she caught her breath. The water cooled and soothed her scuffed feet.

She found the pond when she was young. It became a favorite place for her to find solitude. Everyone in the village avoided the forest; the local legend swore it was a cursed place full of *unnatural* creatures. The trees bore nothing but spite towards any fool unlucky or unwise enough to wander among their branches. For all her time in the forest, Heidi never saw a hint of any such stories being true. Well, perhaps one hint. If the entire village wanted to believe they should avoid the forest, Heidi wouldn't argue. This made the forest hers.

As for the pond, it was a small thing; it ran about twenty feet wide in any direction. Trees grew right up to its edge in most places, their roots dipping into the pond like long tongues drinking up the water. On one side, wedged between two trees, an enormous rock bordered the pond. The base of the rock was split, and where the crack met the water, the surface churned softly; a natural spring filled the pool with pure water from somewhere deep in the earth.

Heidi stood and found a sizable straight stick, which she propped against the nearest tree. She undid the lacing on the back of her dress and shrugged it off, leaving her in her long green tunic, which fluttered just above her knees. She hung her dress over the branch of a nearby tree and, grabbing the stick, beat the dust and dirt off the dress. Finished, she tossed the stick aside and turned to face the water. Heidi breathed quickly in through her nose and dove headfirst into the water.

Although small, the pond was deep. Heidi swam down towards the bottom of the pond; the water grew darker as she went. Her fingers brushed the rocky bottom, and she stopped momentarily. This was the darkest, coolest part of the pond. She couldn't explain it, but surrounded by this much water, Heidi felt almost more alive than when she was breathing air. She felt that the water lived, and she was a part of it.

Heidi's head burst out from underneath the water, her long blonde locks floating like fallen golden leaves on the surface. She let herself sink back down, gazing at the trees draping across the sky, fully embraced by the clear water. There, Heidi's vision changed; the present vanished from view. In front of her, she watched a vision that hinted at another time. Heidi watched. The pool replayed the same memory she had seen time and time again. She recognized the outline of the pond. As she gazed at its surface, she saw the trees bordering the pond swaying in the wind. Moonlight glowing around the edges of every leaf. She watched the events of some historical night: a pair of birds flying, then a pair of boots splashing into the pond's surface. A man. A man in a worn but splendid cloak, a glint of mail underneath his tunic, carrying a bundle that she couldn't quite make out. And as quickly as he had appeared, he vanished.

This was why Heidi loved the pond. She didn't know how or why, but the water shared its memories with her. Like her work in the garden, this bond felt more personal to Heidi. The water rushed about her mind, showing and sharing all it had witnessed in the forest's secrecy. The sensation was both relaxing and exhilarating.

Heidi let her face break the water's surface and took a deep breath through her nose. This hinted that not all was entirely normal in the forest. The *unnatural* creature was, in fact, Heidi. Heidi and visions. Heidi and her garden. Heidi... and her mind. And the villagers didn't know.

She knew she couldn't afford to linger. Her parents would want her to join them for breakfast soon. With a few sure strokes, Heidi swam to the water's edge.

On the bank stood Heidi's feathered friend. She rested her forearms on the edge of the pond and winked at the soft red bird.

"I see you're joining me for my morning dip."

It whistled a sweet, gay tune in her direction.

"Sure you don't want to join in?"

It whistled three cheerful notes while hopping closer to Heidi across the wet soil. Heidi imagined she heard the phrase *can't join in.*

She laughed and flicked water in the bird's direction. The bird jumped back with a sharp note and fluffed its feathered body, shaking off the drops. He twittered and took off overhead, circled quickly, and flew away. Heidi used a knotted root to pull herself onto the grassy bank.

She twisted her long golden hair into a rope over her right shoulder and wrung out as much water as possible. Heidi reached down and did the same with the hem of her tunic. Then she slipped her dress back over her head and cinched it into place. She arched her neck, shook out her hair, and let it fall in messy waves down her back. She grabbed as much skirt as she could manage in one hand and began skipping over roots on her way back home.

Heidi's brow furrowed deeply as the sunlight hit her face. She let go of her skirt and placed her hand over her eyes as she marched briskly towards the house. Without the trees' protection, Heidi shivered as the wind on the plain buffeted her dress, which showed signs that her tunic underneath was soaked through.

She had almost made it through the cornfield when she halted. A large woman, in both height and girth, made her way towards the wooden gate. The gate let out from Heidi's home onto the village road. Donna Venterra: officially the wife of the town tanner and, unofficially, the town gossip. Heidi stayed behind the hedge of corn. She preferred avoiding Mrs. Venterra.

*I wonder where that odd child of theirs is. She's normally out with the plants in the morning.* Heidi heard Mrs. Venterra's thoughts as her meaty hand thumped at the front door of her family's house. Another gift, or curse, Heidi was born with: the thoughts of others were no secret to her. Noise from within the house implied that Heidi's mother had stopped her work in the kitchen to tend to the visitor at the door.

The old wooden door croaked discontentedly as it opened, and her mother's voice stated matter-of-factly:

"Oh. Mrs. Venterra. I'm tending to breakfast now. Do come in and have a seat. We can talk while I finish in the kitchen."

"Thank you, Taffy," said Mrs. Venterra, who likely would have entered, invitation or not.

Heidi ran quietly along the house's perimeter, then crouched among the flowers underneath the kitchen window. Although she didn't like Mrs. Venterra, her rumors were usually entertaining. They always gave her something to talk about with her parents.

"Believe it or not, Tafetta," Mrs. Venterra said, "I have it on reliable authority that a stranger is wandering about in Hull."

"Well, it's not uncommon for the occasional trapper or wanderer to stop a few days in Hull for provisions."

Mrs. Venterra snorted. "This is no ordinary wanderer, believe me. An odd fellow, that's what I heard." She paused. Then whispered, "Possibly not even human. An *unnatural* creature from beyond the mountains."

Heidi raised an eyebrow. From her limited knowledge, only a few creatures could be mistaken for humans. In fact, only one such creature came to Heidi's mind: Verdélia.

Verdélia were creatures of myth and legend in Hull. The stories handed down through oral tradition spoke of creatures: creatures with *unnatural* connections to the arcane things of the world. As the legends were told, the Verdélian armies had appeared from the West nearly six hundred years ago. The golden armor of their soldiers was as beautiful as it was terrible. They descended on the coastal city of Burne, a key trade port of the humans far to the South, and burned it to the ground. The humans did all they could to slow the Verdélian advance; however, the gifted Verdélia had strength and dexterity, sorcery and magic. They drove the humans north to the stronghold of Frons, where the humans finally surrendered. The human nobles delivered their oaths to the Verdélia, saying they would give up all their riches in the southern waters. Only then did the Verdélia leave as suddenly as they had come. No Verdélia had ventured east of the mountains since.

The opening of the front door roused Heidi from her thoughts, and she instinctively lowered herself further into the bushes.

Mrs. Venterra's heavy voice rang out, "Thank you for having me, Taffeta. It's time I be on my way. No, I've no stomach for breakfast at this moment. The stress of the morning and a mysterious vagabond have given my heart quite the palpitations—well, if you insist, I'll take a muffin. For the nerves, you know."

"Glad to have you, Donna. Have a nice day." Heidi's mother said in a strong yet airy voice that starkly contrasted Mrs. Venterra's gruff tones.

Heidi waited until Mrs. Venterra's figure was well down the road before she rounded the house and walked in through the front door.

"Morning, Mother," Heidi said as she entered the kitchen. Heidi watched her mother's dark brown curls bounce down her back. Her tan skin and brunette hair stood in steep contrast to Heidi's complexion and coloring. And yet, here was the mother who birthed her.

"Hello dear—oh Heidi, your feet—" Taffeta said as she glanced over her shoulder. She continued to tend to the meal over the hearth.

"Sorry, ma," Heidi said, wiping the soles of her feet on her calves just outside the front door. She saw her mother's eyes glance at the water marks on her dress.

"Been out roving the forest again, have you?"

Heidi said, "Yes, but don't worry, the work in the garden is done."

"I'm not worried about the work not getting done," her mother said. "Every once in a while, I wish you'd spend more of your free time outside of that wild place with some young people your age in Hull. Find yourself a nice boy, perhaps."

Heidi's shoulders drooped. "Mother...it's...well, you know. Everyone already thinks I'm strange. I don't want anyone's friendship extended to me out of pity. And a boy? What for?"

"Mrs. Venterra never forgets to mention how fond Ardulos is of you. He's always mentioning you," Taffeta said.

Heidi grimaced and said, "Don't worry about me, mother. I have you and Father, and I'm not interested in Ardulos. He's so..." Heidi's voice trailed off.

"Oh, Heidi..." her mother stated. She decided against her comment and called to her husband, "Breakfast!"

Heidi's father limped in from the other room, his frame filling the doorway. His skin was tan with olive undertones, and his head covered with dark, thick hair that was parted roughly on his head. Graying stubble adorned his face.

"Good morning, ladies," Heidi's father hummed in his gravelly baritone as he made a bowing gesture with his hand.

"Good morning, father! Let me help you to your seat."

Heidi let her father lean against her as he hobbled to the table. Heidi could feel his leg shaking with every step.

Heidi's father, Remi, had been born far from Hull to the south. As a younger man, he had spent years on an errand beyond the western mountain ranges and adventured far from any lands their neighbors would recognize. He never spoke of it, and many in the town avoided him for it, believing the dark and accursed things that they were sure lay beyond human lands had touched him. Though his body remained unnaturally strong, his journey had left him with a crippled leg. His aging didn't affect his strength, either. Heidi had always suspected that there was knowledge untold hidden behind his dark brown eyes.

The three of them sat at the table and ate their breakfast of eggs, cooked vegetables, and apple muffins. As the meal drew to a close, Heidi chimed, "So, Mother, tell us what the town's daily rumors are."

Her mother chided, "Young lady, where are your manners?"

"Oh, come now," her father intervened, "When has that woman ever had anything to say that wasn't gossip and half-truth?"

Heidi giggled.

"Remi!" her mother scolded, but with a smile on her lips.

"Well?" her father smugly asked.

"Alright, alright. You two are insufferable." Heidi's mother shook her head. She took a bite of her breakfast and cleared her throat. "According to an unnamed yet credible witness, they saw a stranger wandering Hull."

"That's hardly news," Heidi's father pointed out.

"Except," her mother said, "Some in the village are saying he isn't human."

*Could it be?* Heidi heard her father think.

Something flashed across the eyes of Heidi's father, and she saw him suppress his reaction.

Instead, he casually offered, "Oh? Well, what kind of stranger could appear human yet not be? Hmm?"

"That's what I said," her mother said.

"Maybe he'll come to call!" Heidi said.

"Why on earth would he come to call?" Remi asked.

"I don't know. Do you think he's handsome?" Heidi asked.

"How should I know? It's not like the rumor came with details, did it, dear? As usual," her father said, leaning back into his chair and raising his eyebrows at his wife.

Heidi's mother stood, gathering her used dishes. "Well, there's another more important rumor we should discuss. A certain young man in the town has saved up for a courting band and is expected to come calling here on account of a certain single young woman."

Heidi and her father were grimacing now, but her father spoke first. "Don't do that to her. She deserves better."

Taffeta gaped at her husband. "It's not as if Hull is full to the brim with eligible bachelors, Remi."

"Mother, he's so young," Heidi said.

"He's a year your senior, Heidi!"

"Well, he doesn't look it...or act it," Heidi grumbled.

"You're twenty, darling. You're bound to lose prospects the longer you wait. And we won't be around forever."

"Ma. I would die if Donna were my mother-in-law." At this moment, Remi was laughing, and Taffeta was smiling stubbornly.

"Leave the girl be, love." He grabbed her hand. "She'll find better. I'm sure of it." With that, Heidi stood and helped her mother with the dishes.

Heidi mindlessly worked through her list of daily tasks. It was hard work, and there was much of it. Her parents had hoped for a large family, with at least a few sturdy boys, to help around the farm. Heidi was not the first child born, but she was the first and last born alive, and Heidi's birth had nearly killed her mother. Heidi did not mind doing the work alone. It had made her strong. Though thin, one could see her muscles toiling underneath her fair skin as she hauled and cut the wood her family would need for the coming fall and winter.

Heidi let her mind wander as she forced her body to press through the day's labors. Her thoughts turned to her future, as they often had of late. Ever the optimist, Heidi was not blind to the reality of what lay in store for her. Probably, she would wed a boy from the village—Ardulos, if some other prospect didn't show himself—and settle down to a life very similar to that of her parents. Though without the same affection. Though she loved her parents and found joy in her life with them, this thought cast a shadow over her spirit. The thought of leaving Hull to find a love that stirred her heart, as she'd witnessed in her mother, caused her no slight apprehension. And so, as if by habit, her mind revisited the same dead end.

A strand of Heidi's light hair danced over her face, buoyed by the wind. She brushed it gracefully out of her eyes and tucked it behind her ear. Night was fast approaching, the bottom of the sun's disc already retreating beneath the Western horizon. Heidi leaned her chest on one of the solid oak fence posts surrounding her family's farm. She wrapped her arms loosely around the rough wood. Heidi enjoyed the beauty of the sun and embraced its warmth on her face; however, the shadows that appeared at day's end held a mysterious beauty in Heidi's eyes as well.

"Heidi! Dinner!" her mother's fluid tones drifted in the breeze.

Heidi turned to head inside. As she unwound her arms from around the fence post, she noticed a golden shimmer on her fingertips that caught the warm glow of the receding dusk. She stared at her fingers, wondering what could have caused such a sheen on this drab farm. The residue was far too beautiful to be sawdust or any other form of garden grime. Another call from her mother interrupted her thoughts and Heidi brushed her hands on her apron before making for the cottage.

# II

## *The Stranger*

A sweet silence settled on the cottage as Heidi and her parents sat around the small dining table. Her mind foggy from a long day's work, Heidi mindlessly spooned her mother's soup into her mouth.

A knock at the door called everyone's attention from their meal.

"Who on earth could that be?" Heidi's father asked.

It was unusual to have visitors this late in Hull. Families had dinner near the same time, and everyone kept to themselves after dark.

Another knock sounded at the door, more insistent this time.

"Heidi, would you fetch the door, please?" Remi asked.

Heidi pushed herself up from the table, walked to the door, and opened it.

She raised an eyebrow. On the other side of the open door stood a man. He looked like no one she'd ever seen before. Heidi remembered Mrs. Venterra's morning gossip. Perhaps the woman had been right after all. The stranger stood taller and thinner than the average man in Hull. His hair was brown, although lighter than the dark locks common to the people of Hull. His angular features and taut, fair skin reminded Heidi of her father's sculptures.

His clothing signaled to Heidi that this visitor was from nowhere near Hull. He wore an immaculate, vividly green short coat over a beautifully embroidered ivory tunic. His spotless boots bore intricate patterns in the leather like no human art she'd ever witnessed. And as Heidi wandered into his mind, she found it *utterly barren.*

The stranger smirked at her, noticing the bafflement on Heidi's face. Heidi, flustered, said, "Hello, sir; how can I help you?"

"Oh, I need no helping," the stranger said.

Amusement exuded from his expression.

Remi's voice echoed firmly inside the house. "Well, what's this then? Who is it?"

"I..." Heidi said, unsure of how to introduce the visitor.

The stranger intervened.

"If I may come in, sir, I'd be happy to introduce myself properly."

Remi said, "Very well, but be quick about it. The day's no longer young."

The visitor's face showed gentle delight as he walked through the open door, which Heidi closed behind him.

Heidi's mother's eyes widened as the stranger stepped into view. She looked at her husband. Heidi's father seemed equally intrigued, although his eyes had a look of recognition. It was as if this was a sight long forgotten but not unfamiliar to him.

"My name is Ancelin," the stranger said, "And I have some rather serious business to discuss with you and the young lady."

"And you are here because?" Heidi's father responded.

"Because..." Ancelin said, then asked, "May I sit?" pointing down.

Heidi's father gestured to a chair near the fire.

"Please."

"Thank you," Ancelin said.

He brought the chair up to the table.

Turning to Heidi's father, Ancelin said, "Now, before I commence, how much have you told the girl?"

Heidi's eyes fixed on her father, her face twisted into an unspoken question. Not only wondering, *what do you know?* But *why can I not read his mind?*

Heidi's mother interjected for the first time tonight, "Told her what?"

"Ah. This may be more difficult than I anticipated."

"What are you talking about? Will you tell us plainly why it is you're here?"

"I believe," said Ancelin, "That it would be best if the beginning of this story came from your husband. I will tell my tale when his is complete."

Now, all eyes focused on Heidi's father. He stared at the table, his eyes lost in thought, a mixture of sorrow and amazement in his gaze. He seemed to recognize something lost on the women in the room. Then he studied the stranger.

"Is it time? You come from Verdélys?" Remi asked him.

The stranger only nodded. "I come to *return* to Verdélys."

*Verdélys*, Heidi's lips repeated silently before glancing at her mother.

Heidi's father turned his gaze back to his hands, which he wrung together anxiously as he addressed Heidi and his wife.

"I should have told you both long ago," Remi said, "But I just couldn't find the heart to do so. It would have endangered us had I muttered the words. Heidi, I'm going to tell the story of how you came to our family."

Taffeta asked, "Remi?" Her eyes were wild with uncertainty.

"Heidi did not come to us in the way that you think," Remi said.

Heidi's father took a deep breath. His eyes watched his interlaced fingers as if looking into his memories.

"That night, when you began your labor, my love, was a terrible night. The midwives had been here for the better part of two days, and no one was sure if either you or the baby would make it to see the next sunrise." Remi's voice caught, and in a choking tone, he said, "Thank the heavens you did." He paused again, and a tear fell from his face, soaking the wooden table. "Our child did not."

Heidi's mother gasped, a hand over her mouth as tears flowed down her face.

Bewildered, Heidi glanced towards the stranger, Ancelin. That child was supposed to be her. If she wasn't her mother's child, who was she?

Heidi's father said, "Exhausted from your labor, you fell into a sickly sleep. The midwives helped me dress the baby's body and place it in the crib. Then they left, leaving me alone in the dark of that miserable night."

The house was silent. The darkness of Remi's story seemed to close in around the table. As her father's story continued, images appeared in Heidi's mind, portraying the events Remi described.

꽃

Remi sat crying at the table in the cottage. His head rested in his hands as his tears fell one by one onto the round wooden table, leaving their mark.

Delirious in his grief, he glanced towards the far bedroom where the midwives were toiling with his wife. They changed out the bloody linens, laid her on her side, and placed food on the bedside table.

As they toiled, he trudged toward the closer bedroom. He had already buried four children and was now preparing to bury a fifth.

He peered within the bassinet at a small body wrapped in white linens. The baby was silent, save for labored breathing. He wiped his eyes again, seeing the little girl his wife likely would never know.

The midwives shuffled out of the front door. One touched his back, offering an unspoken—or unspeakable—apology, and then it was silent.

Less than an hour passed, during which Remi held his precious daughter, watching as the vitality drained from her meager body. He sat powerless, yearning with all of his will to reach out and prevent the life from leaving his daughter. But it was no use. Suddenly, the baby inhaled raggedly, then let out her last breath. In stunned silence, Remi wept bitterly.

After a few minutes, there was a knock at the door. Remi dragged himself to the door, confused and angry that anyone would dare show themselves to this house during such a time. He cracked open the door and barked at the uninvited stranger who stood on the doorstep beneath a dark, hooded cloak.

The stranger didn't reply, and Remi lifted his eyes to glance into the visitor's eyes. When the hood was pulled back from his face, he recognized an old friend.

"Cédric," Remi croaked through tears. "How have you come here?" Upon further inspection, he noticed that his friend's body was haggard and spent. His boots were muddy. His face bore several cuts, and his cloak was dirty and torn. He cradled something underneath his robe, which he held as if it were a priceless treasure.

Cédric responded immediately and urgently, "Remi... please, old friend, I'm sorry I haven't the time for a proper reunion, but my errand is urgent. I must speak to you inside."

Remi turned to accept him into the cottage, eyeing the darkness behind him and hoping for no prying eyes. Cédric made his way to the fireplace. He noticed first Remi's sickly wife asleep on the bed, then the silent child in the closer bedroom.

"It would seem this is a dark night for both of us," he said before returning to Remi. He straightened up, taking on an air of responsibility. "As captain of the Verdélia's easternmost outposts, I must charge you with the care of something precious to our people."

Almost out of habit, Remi straightened himself up as well in response to the order, "I serve Solaidi."

A rush of relief crossed Cédric's face, and Remi stepped forward to meet him. As he approached, Cédric removed the bundle from underneath his cloak. "There isn't a proper way for me to explain this to you, and even if there were, there isn't the time. The child is one of four Firstborn of the Verdélia. She was entrusted to my care when her mother was killed not long ago, west of the mountains. There is a great war among my people as we speak."

Remi's face, still streaked with grief, looked at the bundle of cloth the visitor held in his hands. Among the folds of the navy fabric was the face of an angel.

"She has fallen under my care in a horrifying turn of events. I gathered a band of soldiers to help me reach her mother, who had contacted me for help. We made it in time to save the child, but not her mother. Her father was among my ranks and died to dark treachery a season before her birth. My little band, loyal to the Verdélian Firstborn, was hunted and tracked by our enemies. They will stop at nothing to destroy her." He handed the bundle to Remi and continued, "I've wandered the mountain ranges for a moon longer now, I suppose. I dreamed of this cottage and your face. A blessing from Solaidi, can't you see? He has something in store for you, my brother. Take her, Remi. Raise and care for her as if she were your own daughter."

As Remi searched the face of the tiniest newcomer, Cédric entered the spare bedroom to study the motionless child. The air in the cottage was now heavy, draining, and silent.

Cédric's hands brushed the folds of fabric that bore the child and whispered, "I can offer her a proper burial if you wish."

Realization dawned on Remi, "You must. Everyone must believe that our child never died. That she lived. There can be no worry or wonder surrounding this child. They must believe she is, in fact, our own, or she will not live here. She will not survive."

Cédric carefully gathered the bundle in his arms and bowed to Remi as he drew his cloak about him again. "I must be on my way. Those who would harm this child are still searching, and I will draw them from here."

He placed an arm on Remi's shoulder. "May we meet again, brother." And with that, he opened the door and disappeared into the night.

Remi sat and gazed at the sleeping infant in his arm. She wriggled, and he choked back tears as he witnessed the movement. He walked closer to the fire to take in every detail of her face.

Then his thoughts turned to his wife, and he smiled. Walking towards their bed, he knelt at her side and softly rubbed her arm. "My love," he whispered.

She took a deep breath, her eyes opening for only a moment to take in her husband's face, then scrunched her eyes closed and spoke instantly, "I'm so sorry, dear. I couldn't bear to bury another. I never wanted that for you. Please forgive me."

"No, no, no," Remi shushed, touching her lips, "Open your eyes, my love. Look at your daughter."

As if on cue, a little coo erupted out of the bundle of navy fabric. Taffeta's eyes shot open in shock, and she breathed heavily. "Remi— is it?" She couldn't form a sentence and instead used the energy to sit herself up in bed.

Remi reached for pillows to prop up behind her and laid the little girl in her lap. "Remi..." she sighed. "She's so beautiful. She's alive. But how—she wasn't breathing."

"Just a few moments ago, she coughed up and cried out. I couldn't believe it myself and waited a little longer before bringing her to you. I couldn't bear to give you false hope." He cringed at his lie but saw no other sure way to protect his wife and this small Firstborn child.

"Heidi," she said at his side, then glanced towards him for reassurance, "Yes?"

"Heidi," he repeated.

茶

The implications froze Heidi in place. She could do nothing more than stare wide-eyed at her father—or who she had thought was her father—mouth slightly agape, tears trickling down her cheeks.

Remi dried his eyes with the backs of his rugged hands. He said quietly, "And that brings us to where we are tonight and the end of my part of this story."

Heidi spluttered as she tried to put together any question that might get her answers.

Ancelin interrupted, "If I may, I believe your father's night has been demanding enough. I shall endeavor to answer your questions, although I may withhold certain answers which might be best received at another time and in another manner."

From Heidi's churning emotions, discomfort and uncertainty surfaced. Heidi was unfamiliar with spontaneous emotion. Her emotions had always been built from pieces and likenesses of others' inner thoughts and feelings— an inevitable result of her *unnatural* gift. But at this moment, she couldn't bear to pry into her mother's feelings for fear of what she would find.

And her father, her dear father. So she turned her feelings to Ancelin.

"You—" she paused and wrung her skirt with her hands, "Who are you?"

Ancelin spoke clearly. "I am Ancelin of the Awakening. I am the summoner of spring, the embodiment of the turn of the seasons after the cold of winter. Solaidi gave me to this world through the joining of the earliest of the Verdélian Firstborn."

Ancelin's answer did nothing to ease Heidi's concerns; he might as well have been speaking an unfamiliar language.

"But why are you here?" she asked accusingly. "Why did you come to our home? And what do you want with me? Just to turn my world upside-down?"

Heidi had listened to her father's story. She suspected Ancelin's answer, though she did not want to accept it.

"I am here to turn your world right side up, Heidi," Ancelin said. "As your father said, a time would come when you would be called back to your people, back to the Verdélia. That time is now."

"But the Verdélia aren't my people!" Heidi exclaimed. "I know nothing about them! They're a fairytale—a legend—scary stories told by the older generations to frighten children! Everyone I know and love is here, very human and very real."

She looked at her parents, Remi and Taffeta, who sat at the humble cottage table, hands clasped together tightly as they gazed at each other. *These twenty years,* her mother was whispering to her husband, *how have you hidden this from me?*

"I'm so sorry, my love," Remi whispered into her ear. He answered a question carefully. "I couldn't risk the danger that could come upon us. I believed I should carry the burden of the secret alone. What would they have done to her?"

Recognition seemed to dawn on Taffeta's face, and she looked towards Heidi, her eyes fearful now.

"The Verdélia are not real," Heidi said, trying to convince herself. But even as she said it, she remembered her pond and the memory she had returned to for years. The man and the hidden bundle under his arm. If the story was real, then there could be no question.

"Heidi," Ancelin said, "Humans are and always will be your people. That is more than many Verdélia can say. But you have suspected for some time that you are more than an ordinary human girl from Hull, have you not?" With a swift motion that caught Heidi off guard, Ancelin swiped two fingers against Heidi's right temple. He brought his hand back in front of everyone, a light coating of gold dust glistening in the flickering firelight. "Soon enough, it will also be obvious to everyone else in this sleepy little village."

Heidi's voice caught in her throat. She wanted to respond, to silence Ancelin and prove him wrong, but he was right. Her connections to the earth and unnatural abilities were no ordinary human features. She had wondered who, or even what, she was.

Ancelin continued, accepting Heidi's silence as permission to carry on. "Heidi, as your father rightly stated, you are no ordinary Verdélian: you are a Firstborn. Every two hundred years, four special Verdélia are born, leaders, kings, and queens who rule the kingdom of the Verdélia and all who live in it. Although the Verdélia have managed to, more or less, govern themselves in your absence, it is time you take your rightful place among them. That is why I am here."

Heidi fought against what seemed to be an increasingly inevitable fate as the evening continued. "Do you just expect me to pack my things and leave my family, the only family I've known? And, supposing I did go with you, I can't do what you ask. I know nothing about the Verdélia; until tonight, I wasn't even sure they were real. How could I ever guide them, rule over them like you say?"

Undisturbed, he said, "The demand is significant, I understand. Your family here will always remain your family, no matter who you become or where you go. But yes, I have been tasked with returning you to the Verdélia so that the four Firstborn may be reunited, as they should be. I also understand that you do not feel qualified for the fate that has befallen you. Few ever do. However, there is much I can teach you on our journey, and I am confident you will learn the lore of the Verdélia quickly."

"Besides," Ancelin said, one corner of his mouth lifting into a grin, "I have seen your handiwork out in the garden. For that, you needed no teacher but yourself, and it is rather impressive work for one who is self-taught."

"My abilities aside," Heidi said, "you ask me to leave my parents on an unknown journey, trusting to fate that they will get by without me."

Ancelin said, "Yes, this is true. But do not be so quick to judge fate a cruel mistress. I am confident she will be kind to your family."

Ancelin's eyes glowed intensely as he spoke. Heidi felt herself agreeing with him, trusting that her parents could care for themselves should she leave.

Ancelin stood and said, "I have delivered my message. I think it will be best if I leave you to discuss the matter amongst yourselves. I will return on the morning of the third day, ready to travel. If, Heidi, you have agreed to join me, as I am confident you will, we shall depart before sunrise." With that, Ancelin lowered his slender form in an elegant bow and left for the night. The door closed behind him. The house was silent.

Heidi stared at her parents through eyes made hazy by unshed tears, longing for either of them to speak first. Taffeta sat in her chair, one hand over her mouth, crying quietly. Her father's gaze was fixed on the table in front of him. His eyes, already dark, were an endless void, a gateway to the past.

Heidi reached out with her mind, seeking to understand her parents' thoughts on the night's events. Tentatively contacting her mother's thoughts, Heidi entered a fog of sorrow and confusion. Heidi's head seemed to spin, and she withdrew quickly. Heidi's heart ached; her mother didn't deserve this.

Heidi cautiously approached her father's thoughts. She soon found herself in a shocking stillness. She observed, as if from an enormous distance, scenes that seemed to have come from the narrative her father had just recited that night. Her father's thoughts, ever as composed, then turned to duty, love, and family. Heidi felt her father's mind weigh the implications of the night's events.

Finally, Heidi broke the silence.

"Mother? Father?" she offered quietly.

Heidi could see her father's eyes returning to the present. Her mother used both hands to wipe her eyes.

For the first time that night, Taffeta spoke to her daughter.

"Heidi," she said hoarsely, "it seems fate has set a fork in the road before us. I always wondered if you were something special and feared that a day would come when you would be called far from our home, even if in a less unexpected fashion."

She continued, "The words that have been said will certainly change things in this little cottage. However, they change nothing of what has been. You are and always will be our daughter, for we have raised and loved you as such..."

Taffeta's voice caught, but she pushed on, "Never forget that a part of who you are stems from this small home in the little-known village of Hull."

Tears streamed down Heidi's face. Taffeta seemed like an ordinary woman from a small farming town; however, she had an inner resilience that inspired and guided Heidi. Heidi was unsure if she was ready to leave the safe shelter of her mother's strength.

# III

## *Tales of Truth*

The next morning, Heidi's eyelids were heavy as she dragged herself to the kitchen. She had woken to the sound of the neighbor's rooster, realized the hour, and then dug herself deeper into her covers. The garden could wait.

She had stayed up late with her parents—or those she had always considered her parents—the night before, shaken by the revelations of the stranger Ancelin. She and they had sat in silence deep into the night. Finally, Remi had suggested they all try to get some sleep.

"We all have much to discuss, but I think these matters will be best addressed with rested minds."

Heidi had been sure she would be unable to sleep, but the turmoil in her mind had dragged her down into a troubled slumber. With the daylight now poking into her bedroom, she groaned as she realized she had not dreamt the entire scene from the night prior.

Before long, she heard her mother shuffling about in the kitchen. Her father hobbled into the kitchen after her, insisting he help with something, "Give me something to chop; I can help."

Heidi made her way timidly to the kitchen.

"Morning," she forced out, clearing her throat as she searched for a cup of water.

Remi and Taffeta turned to her, expressions full of unspoken words and apprehension.

Taffeta replied first. "Good morning, dear," she said, wringing out her worn kitchen apron. "Why don't we just take the day to rest and enjoy each other's company? No chores. Just family time."

*Family time.* Taffeta—her mother—was right. Remi, Taffeta, and Heidi were as much family as any other in Hull, regardless of how Heidi became her parents' child. Hearing her mother confirm this warmed Heidi's heart.

Heidi smiled and sat down at the table with her father, who was chopping apples for the porridge that her mother was cooking over the fire. "I'd like that," she said.

They ate breakfast together, though the conversation was sparse. Heidi's family wasn't the talkative sort. Even by their standards, the weighty news of Heidi's origin hung over the humble kitchen like a cloud.

As the last of the food was being eaten, Taffeta cleared her throat.

"Heidi dear," she said. "Your father and I spoke at length last night. I won't pretend to understand everything shared yesterday at this table. It is all foreign to me. But I believe your father, and I know you are special."

Heidi could see her mother was struggling to keep her composure.

"From what I understand, you were always destined for things greater and grander than this little village." Taffeta's eyes shimmered at this, and Heidi caught herself in her mother's emotions.

"What you decide to do with the news you learned last night is your choice. I just want you to know that I encourage you to fulfill your highest calling, even if that takes you far from our home."

Taffeta was not the only one crying, and Heidi brushed a tear from her cheek with the back of her hand.

"Oh, Mother...," she breathed through tears, "what am I to do?"

Taffeta sniffed, then smiled.

"Well, you were complaining just yesterday about Ardulos and his ongoing efforts to court you. This would solve that problem."

Heidi giggled through sobs.

"I guess that settles that then," she said, returning her mother's smile.

Taffeta looked at Heidi, then continued in a more serious tone.

"Jest aside, from what your father says, you cannot stay and court a..." she stopped, uncertain how to communicate her thoughts.

*A human boy*, Heidi heard her mother think.

"A human boy?" Heidi offered. After last night, there was no point in keeping the matter a secret.

Taffeta looked at Heidi in shock.

Heidi had never revealed her ability to access the minds of others to her mother. Her father discovered this power early in her life. He had been very clear that she was not to share this ability with anyone, not even her mother.

"How did you...," Taffeta asked.

"Since we're all sharing secrets now...," Heidi began, "I can access others' minds. I heard what you were thinking."

Taffeta sat wide-eyed, obviously struggling to believe Heidi. She turned to her husband.

"Is that a Verdélian ability? You didn't tell me about that."

Remi rubbed the back of his neck awkwardly.

"Well, no, actually, not that I'm aware of," he replied. "I'm assuming it has to do with the fact that she's a Firstborn, but honestly, I don't know."

Taffeta looked back at Heidi in fascination, then turned back to Remi.

"Did you know about this?"

Remi drew in a breath through clenched teeth.

"Yes."

"And you've kept it a secret all this time?"

Heidi and her father shared a long look.

"It was for the best. I couldn't tell you—how could I explain? Besides, if news had ever gotten out, we could have ended up on the pyre."

Taffeta remained silent as she processed the information. She nodded slowly as she grasped the necessity of secrecy.

"Still," she said finally, "how did you manage to keep it secret for so long, Heidi?"

"Father told that fairytale, the one about the sterling maiden. You remember the girl who sings to things and turns them to silver. He told me, 'Heidi, you're just like the sterling maiden; you have wonderful gifts. But you must keep them secret, because what will happen if you don't? Do you remember what happened to the sterling maiden?'"

"She was kidnapped by the king and locked away in his castle, of course," Taffeta smiled as she completed the tale.

Heidi nodded. "As a child, I was so afraid that if I let anyone discover my ability, they would take me away from you. It wasn't until I got older that I realized why the others couldn't know about my abilities and how our neighbors viewed that sort of thing. Besides, I did want to fit in—at least when I was a little younger than I am now."

After a pause, Taffeta continued with another question, "So how does it work? Mind reading. You just hear everything?"

"In some ways, it's a lot like regular conversation. I can differentiate between voices in someone's head and their speaking voice. Almost without fail, if somebody thinks something towards me, I'll hear it whether I want to or not—and proximity matters. If you're speaking in your head, but you're in another room, then it's just jumbled sounds unless I'm focusing.

Heidi continued. "In other ways, it's nothing like regular conversation. There's a dream-like quality to most people's thoughts, and it can be a little disorienting if the person is lost in their thoughts—almost like the mind is a place tailor-made only to be understood by that individual. I can usually block out the thoughts of others to a certain extent, assuming the thoughts are passive and not directed towards me. Besides, listening in is strangely draining if I stay at it too long."

"Is that why you never like leaving home?" Taffeta wondered.

"Yes!" Heidi confirmed, "It's awful. I mean, think of even ordinary holiday gatherings. There's commotion and noise everywhere; for me, there's an added layer of unspoken thoughts and emotions. As if the drone and bustle of many ongoing conversations weren't enough, with all the extra stimulus, it gets overwhelming fast."

"You feel emotion?"

Heidi nodded, "Emotions, thoughts, words, pictures. Sometimes, sounds or visions. Anything in your mind. It largely depends on the person—people think and feel differently."

"Is it difficult to manage, having access to all that?"

"Not at home. Out there, though... yes. Interacting with someone—or at least the costume they put on for the world to see—while being privy to their true thoughts, feelings, and intentions can be hard. Some people aren't as kind, honest, and patient as they let on. You two luckily don't fall into that category," Heidi complemented, and then, a little worried, whispered, "I try to give privacy where I can."

There was another moment of silence in their little cottage. Then Taffeta spoke.

"You are something special, aren't you?"

Remi beamed as he nodded. Heidi felt a little embarrassed.

"I...I suppose," Heidi replied, "though I'll bet our neighbors would have different words for it."

"Sure enough," Taffeta affirmed. "Which brings us back to my original thought—you must leave here and return to Verdélys." Again, Taffeta's eyes filled with tears at the thought of Heidi's departure.

"You have no prospects of a future or family in this little town. Clearly, you were meant for greater things, and even if not, I won't watch you waste your life alone in Hull."

"Oh, Mother," Heidi said hoarsely, "I'm not alone; I have you two!"

"For now, yes," Taffeta replied, "but the time is already here for you to consider courting and finding a husband of your own. Someday, your father and I will no longer be here, and then what will you do? Besides, as a Verdélian, your father tells me you will age much slower than the rest of the inhabitants of Hull. You'll be discovered eventually, and then what?"

The inevitability of a departure crashed down on Heidi like an avalanche. An indescribable internal sensation during the stranger's visit the night before had already assured her she would not stay in Hull, but to hear her mother state why a departure could not be avoided made the situation more real.

"Your mother's right," Remi said. "You cannot stay here. You must go with Ancelin."

"I know," Heidi said slowly, "There's just a part of me—maybe even the bigger part of me—that wishes it wasn't so."

"For us as well, dear child," her father replied, taking her hand in his. Taffeta put her hands over her husband's, and the three of them sat at the table, holding tightly onto one another.

"I suppose that leaves us with today and tomorrow together before you depart," Remi said. "We'll need to pack for your journey."

It was silent momentarily before Heidi turned to her father in curiosity, "Father, what can you tell me about the Verdélia?"

Excitement crept onto her father's face, breaking its way through the somberness of their farewell. He didn't immediately speak, but pictures flashed across his mind quicker than Heidi could take in. "The world beyond the mountains.... Heidi, even with my limited knowledge, there's too much for me to tell you before you leave. But it's wonderful. Truly miraculous. Where to begin?"

Heidi began, "What are they like, the Verdélia?"

He nodded his head and gathered his thoughts.

"In appearance, the Verdélia are not so different from humans, though they are more graceful in a way that makes them appear much more connected to this earth than humans. The Verdélia are separated into four kinds, one for each season. They each have unique abilities and different strengths. The Verdélia of Spring, for example, have abilities primarily dealing with flowers. I don't know much about the details, but certain flowers have inherent magical abilities or properties that these Verdélia can harness to great effect."

"What kind of effect?" Heidi asked.

"Some form of emotional influence or manipulation, from what I understand."

"So that's the spring Verdélia. And summer?" She asked.

"Yes, those born in summer are the next most common. They're more powerful. They deal primarily with wood, metals, and stones. But they don't grow them; they mold them. They don't use tools to create sculptures or furniture like I would, either. They simply use their hands to mold the material into whatever shape or form they wish. Just like the Spring Verdélia, the Summer Verdélia also have control over inherent magical properties in stones and woods that we know nothing about."

Heidi sat mesmerized—not only by her father's story but especially by the vivid scenes dancing across his mind as he explained.

"Now the autumn Verdèlia. Less common. More powerful. They have power over every plant—but not floral essences, which are the purview of the Spring Verdélia—and animal. They're farmers, cooks, tanners—but not like you would find here. As I'm guessing you can guess by now, they, too, can engage with magical properties within plants, fruits, vegetables, hide, and other animal products. Food becomes more energizing and more flavorful. Herbs and animal products get turned into powerful medicines. The applications are beyond imagining and frankly not well known to me."

"Father, you sound like a lunatic... like you're making all of this up."

"I assure you, Heidi. You will see, and likely more besides. You are headed for the heart of the Verdélian realm, Verdélys itself. I only ever ventured on the outskirts of these lands. Besides, I haven't even gotten to the most unbelievable part yet. The winter Verdélia."

"What of them?"

"There are far fewer of these, but they are far more powerful. One of the most common things they do is create bottled solutions. They can capture gases, liquids, and solids within a glass container and give it another purpose. They can create something totally new."

"How do you mean?"

"Well, for example, when I traveled, we would have to set up camp, and we had a shelter solution—a tent. Where you and I would think of a tent as bulky—requiring a traveler to carry the canvas, frame, and rope needed to set it up—the Winter Verdélia used their solutions. Some wood, a bit of canvas, and a few other ingredients were all encapsulated into a little bottle. The whole thing could be summoned out of the bottle, creating a tent."

"But I don't understand. How can a few scraps in a bottle make a tent?"

Remi shrugged through a chuckle. "I don't know how it works. That's why humans call it magic, I suppose. Talking to them—the Verdélia—it is both art and science. But I couldn't tell you the first thing about the rules other than that each solution has a recipe."

"Like cooking?"

"Somewhat. Certain ingredients give you certain solutions. They can do more, too," her father smiled at her, sitting back. "They're powerful. Leap into your dreams. Shapeshift. Grant wishes." Heidi's eyes grew wider and wider with every claim. "Of course. There are rules to all of this, too. And they aren't simple things to learn. Most Verdélia specialize in one magical ability and spend their lives perfecting it."

"And me, father, which one am I?"

"All and none. You are royalty. A gift from Solaidi," he said.

"Who is Solaidi?"

"Your creator."

"What, like my father?"

"No, no… well, in a way. Your first father. He created your kind. The Verdélia. All the Verdélia are descended from the original Firstborn, four special Verdélia with unique gifts and abilities. Every two hundred years, the Firstborn die, and four more are born to take their place."

"Is Solaidi still alive?"

"The Verdélia believe Solaidi has always lived and always will live, though he doesn't walk this world. It's a religious tradition of the Verdélia. I'm afraid I'm not all that familiar with the details."

"Oh," Heidi paused and tapped the table, "So what can I do? What are my abilities?"

"What all the seasonal Verdélia can do and more, I suppose," Remi shrugged. "One more reason for you to return to Verdélys—your potential is squandered here. You're like a caged bird here—safe, maybe, but certainly not free."

Remi's stories had filled Heidi with curiosity about the world beyond Hull's borders. Still, Heidi's cage was familiar and comfortable to her. Out there, who knew what was waiting for her? She would not have her parents to rely on.

※

The next morning, Heidi made her way out to the garden. She picked and pruned. Despite her mother's protests, Heidi insisted she spend her last day working on the farm so that the crops would be left in the best possible condition for her parents. She grew the bulk of fruit before the sun revealed her. In the afternoon, she found everything she could and filled a large cart with all the produce she had grown that morning. Her mother prepared and packed her a bag for her journey.

As the sun fell in the sky, she returned to the cottage and stepped into the home to smell a wonderful spread of food on the table. "Mum…" she sighed. But her mother was out of sight, and she could hear her sniffling behind her bedroom door. Her father was consoling her.

There was a knock at the door, and Heidi turned quickly to open it.

"Heidi," a boy stated. He nodded an acknowledgment towards her.

"Ardulos," Heidi responded, her eyebrows raising.

"How are you?" He asked politely.

"Exhausted. It's been a long day of gardening."

38

"Yes! I saw your cart," he leaned against the door and towards her. She leaned back. She could see herself front and center in the boy's mind, a role she neither asked for nor envied.

"What can I help you with, Mr. Venterra?"

"Well, Heidi, I've come to ask your hand to court. I've saved up, gotten a ring, but there's no need to leap into a serious courtship yet. I'd just like to spend more time with you. May I see you this week?"

"No, I'm afraid not," Heidi admitted, relief flooding her internally.

"Excuse me?" He asked, put off by her frankness.

"I'm leaving, you see," she awkwardly drummed her fingers on the back of the door. "I'm going to the city for an apprenticeship. I'm not sure when I'll return."

"The city?" He questioned, and his mind flooded with pictures of the city. He must've been a boy when he last went because everything in his memory towered above him. "May I call on you in the city? Where can I find you?"

Heidi stuttered, "To be honest, I'm uncertain. I'm afraid someone is coming to take me back, and I won't know the details until I've arrived."

"Will you write to me and let me know?" He pressed.

"If I can, perhaps." Heidi didn't want wholly to break the poor boy's spirit.

"It's disappointing," he admitted. "I was very much looking forward to becoming closer." He wiped something from her cheek—dirt, perhaps.

Heidi grabbed his hand and returned it to him. *Shy,* he thought. And a smirk crossed his face.

"Perhaps when I return," Heidi offered, "Would you do something for me?"

"Anything," he offered warmly, leaning in and gazing into her eyes.

Impatiently, Heidi pressed her hand against his chest and pushed him out into the autumn air, stepping out after him. "That cart," she pointed, "My parents won't be able to take it. My mother isn't strong enough; my dad has his injury. Could you hook it up to your horses and take it to town for them? I'm worried about how they'll do without me."

"I can do that," he nodded but glanced back at her, "It's too bad the burden you've been left with. The strongest of your family at your age. You shouldn't have to carry that alone."

"I'm quite capable and won't always be alone."

"Yes, I intend to see to that." His confidence was no longer amusing, and she rolled her eyes.

*She's cute when she does that.*

Heidi avoided rolling her eyes again and smiled back at him, "I appreciate your help. It will greatly help my parents, and I will be indebted to you."

At that moment, the front door opened behind them. It was Heidi's mother.

"Oh, there you are, Heidi. It's dinner. Ardulos! Nice to see you. How's your mother?"

"Taffeta," he bowed. "She's well. She's still fretting over the stranger my sister claims to have seen."

"Oh, was it your sister who saw him?"

"Yes, ma'am. It's been quite the family controversy." He laughed. Ardulos was much more charming outwardly than Heidi thought he had any right to be, and it made Heidi uncomfortable.

"Yes, well, goodnight," Heidi nodded, walking towards the front door, waving, and closing the door.

"Good night, Heidi," he waved back.

Heidi and her parents sat down for their meal. They exchanged memories, spoke of the journey and provisions, and spent many minutes quiet. Heidi wouldn't bring much, as she would travel on foot and could not shoulder too much weight. A change of clothes, some food, and a couple of water skins made up the bulk of the contents of her rugged pack, an old traveling bag that had belonged to Remi. As she stowed the final contents into place, Remi spoke. They sat around the fireplace now.

"There is one more thing," he said. "Heidi, under the rug there's a chipped stone. Lift it and pull out the box you find."

Heidi obliged and rolled back the heavy matted rug covering the cottage's stone floor. She looked to where Remi was pointing and noticed a slab of stone flooring with a piece missing, as if someone had intentionally cut it out. She bent down using her legs and pulled up, heaving the heavy rock out of place.

Underneath the flooring was a cavity of a fair size, inside which lay a dark wooden chest framed with aging yet sturdy ironwork.

"Pull that up, please," Remi asked. "It shouldn't be very heavy."

Heidi knelt to pull the chest out of the floor. It was wider than it was deep, and it took some maneuvering for her to remove it fully from its place in the ground.

"Thank you, dear," Remi said as he opened his fist to reveal an old iron key.

He bent slowly over the chest, his large hands deliberate as they inserted the key into the lock, fastening the chest shut.

"These," Remi said without taking his eyes from the chest, "came with you on the night you were brought to us."

He opened the chest, and Heidi had to squint to see what was inside. At first, it seemed to her that a dark cloth lined the inner walls of the chest. Upon further inspection, she noticed a neatly folded fabric of the most beautiful deep blue color. It reminded Heidi of the bluest of night skies right before the sun would rise.

Remi pulled the fabric out of the chest and unfolded it, revealing a stunning cloak. Heidi could see the embroidery now: a flowering vine crawling along the edge of the cape and its hood. The stitching was done with a thread so brilliant it seemed as if whoever had made it had spun it from solid gold. As it caught the firelight, Heidi noticed the golden embroidery gleaming with copper.

At the neck of the cloak was a large clasp of the same color as the beautiful embroidered thread, masterfully crafted into the shape of a wild rose. At the center of the flower lay a gem more exquisite than anything Heidi had ever seen. It was a deep blue stone, somewhat lighter than the cloak to which it was fastened. The gem glistened with a thousand hues of sapphires and rubies in the light of their humble fireplace.

Remi spoke, "You came to us wrapped in this. From what I understand, it belonged to your mother."

He stretched out his sinewy arms and handed Heidi the cloak. The fabric was incredibly soft to the touch, yet the cloak was heavy. Heidi found it strangely yet pleasantly comforting.

Something glistened from within the chest. Heidi had been captivated by the cloak and had not noticed something lying beneath it.

Remi reached in and, to Heidi's surprise, pulled out a sword sheathed in a dark scabbard.

He explained, "This was given to me by Cédric when he brought you here. He told me it might be useful when it came time for you to return to your people."

Heidi hesitantly took the weapon from her father's hands. The polished leather scabbard was perfectly straight and jet black, coated in a thin layer of dust. It was adorned with simple metalwork, which was more functional than beautiful. The sword's hilt fit snugly into the scabbard, the center of the otherwise straight cross-guard coming up to point in the center of the sword's blade. The grip of the sword was wrapped in leather, matching that of the scabbard, culminating in a metal pommel that was fashioned into a shape that somewhat resembled a leaf of sorts.

Heidi unsheathed a third of the blade. The years it had spent buried away had done nothing to diminish the shine of the steel. The blade's center was engraved with what appeared to be a perfectly straight stem, with four identical leaves, two on each side, reaching out and upwards. The stem grew into an ornate five-petaled flower. It reminded Heidi of the rising sun.

"That is the official symbol of the Verdélia," Remi explained. "You'll remember my friend was a Verdélian soldier. I believe this was his sword."

Heidi ran her fingers over the picture etched in the glistening metalwork of the blade. After a moment, she guided the sword gently back into its casing. "It is beautiful, though in a somewhat frightening way," Heidi said quietly. "I would not know how to use it, should I be doomed to need it."

"Do not worry about what might be." Remi said comfortingly, "In any event, it is better to go prepared. Besides," he continued, "should you have need, a sword is a tool, in many ways similar to those you have used here."

"I suppose," Heidi said, though she felt no more confident.

"You have quite the journey ahead of you," Taffeta stated softly from near the fire. "You will need your sleep, as much as you might still be able to get tonight. To bed with you."

Heidi stood and looked at Remi and Taffeta. Their eyes were fixed on her, full of tenderness, sorrow, and pride. She stepped forward slowly, then, exhausted from the unexpected events of that night, fell forward, embracing both of her parents. The three of them stood together in a long embrace for many moments. Shared memories of moments spent together over the years swirled through their minds.

Finally, after many minutes had passed, they separated. "We love you," Remi and Taffeta said in unison. They walked with her to her room, and Heidi slipped under her covers. Then it was dark.

# IV

## *Leaving Home for Home*

Heidi's mind wandered as she gazed monotonously towards the ground. The unruly grass yielded beneath every step of her scuffed leather boots. She replayed the events of that early morning to herself.

Still dark when she had risen, the night had seemed eerily quiet. She could hear not even the most precocious creatures stirring outside. It was just her.

She had forced herself to dress in her drab travel gear and thick boots. She had mindlessly stroked and clenched the fabric of the cloak her father had given her. This foreign fabric of hers felt like an introduction to Heidi's new life, and it seemed like a story too fantastic for her to be a part of—a dream. Ancelin appeared at their door as promised, and after a last embrace from her parents, Heidi followed the stranger west into the morning's mists and the shadows of the forest.

The snap of a branch beneath her boot roused Heidi from her daydream. She brushed a tear from her cheek and shook her head briskly, trying to sweep her homesickness from her thoughts. Heidi would have listened to Ancelin's thoughts to distract herself from her churning emotions, but her new companion's mind was an impenetrable wall. She could tell something lay within, but there was no way to access it as far as she could tell.

Heidi suddenly felt the warmth of the morning sun on her back and shoulders as it rose behind them. The morning light shot emerald beams through the canopy onto the forest floor below. They had been walking for some time and were now well into the old, thick growth of the forest. The going was slower, but the dark mystery of the surrounding woods was mesmerizing.

She heard a familiar twitter in the trees to her right and looked to see her feathered friend eyeing her, following her, and cocking his head left and right. He seemed to ask her questions. *Where are you going? Will I see you again?* All questions Heidi couldn't answer. She couldn't bear another goodbye and turned to watch Ancelin's back, avoiding eye contact with her little friend, who eventually disappeared into the forest.

As she followed Ancelin, Heidi noticed they were steadily turning north. From the little Heidi knew about the local geography, she understood they would make for the mountain pass a little ways north and west of Hull. What lay beyond that pass remained a mystery, even to the most adventurous humans.

"So," Heidi began, and Ancelin slowed his pace to match hers, "The Verdélia. You're one of them?"

"No," he smiled, "Not at all."

"No? Then what are you? You're not human, clearly."

"Clearly," he nodded, "No, I'm mostly just spirit. I was born in the earliest days of creation. I am Ancelin of the Awakening. A wedding gift, if you will, to the first two Verdélia who wed."

"How long ago was that?" Conversation distracted Heidi from what was behind her.

"Almost four thousand years now," Ancelin said coolly as if he were sharing his favorite color with her.

"Four thousand years?! Well, you look good." He grinned. "You must know a lot, then: history, people, places. Are there secrets of the world you know that no one else does?"

"Oh, at least one other person does."

"Who's that?"

"Ancelin," he grinned from ear to ear.

"Sorry?" Heidi was sure she'd heard wrong.

"My brother," he explained, "Ancelin of Rest. A gift to the second Verdélia couple to be married. We existed to usher in the first seasons. I had brought spring, then summer, and at his birth, he brought autumn and winter. And with the world prepared for seasons, soon the couples gave birth to seasonal Verdélia."

"So," Heidi tried to simplify, "You're nearly four thousand years old; you usher in spring and summer, and your brother of the same name ushers in fall and winter."

"Exactly."

"So you're off duty," Heidi stated.

"On the contrary, I'm fulfilling a sacred and important obligation. Probably as important as ushering in of seasons."

"Oh, you couldn't know that. You hardly know me," she argued.

"I know you are Firstborn. My coming into this world was and always has been intricately tied to the Firstborn, and will be for so long as this world exists." Ancelin looked at Heidi. "That means you and I know each other better than you realize."

"But I just met you," Heidi protested.

"Yes, maybe. But we've also met before, in a manner of speaking."

"Were we friends?"

"Yes, we were," Ancelin confirmed with a smile.

"Then we will be again," Heidi said.

※

Memories of Hull now seemed distant and vague as Heidi watched Ancelin stride energetically beside the jagged cliffs that jutted skyward on their left. He seemed utterly oblivious to Heidi's growing discomfort. An aching loneliness had been growing within her since they had left Hull. Heidi fought to silence herself more than once as thoughts of home sent tears tumbling down her face.

Even though Heidi was not traveling alone, Ancelin was not much company. Ancelin's mind was as communicative as the stony crags they were now hiking through, and the eerie silence of their march, punctuated only by their four feet and the sounds of nature, was almost too much for Heidi. She had spent her entire life surrounded by the thoughts of those around her. Now that she had spent some days without so much as a hint of any spoken or unspoken chatter, she realized the silence was just as deafening.

Not only that, but her inability to access Ancelin's mind made her wary. When dealing with every other person she had ever met, whether to extend trust had been a quick and simple decision. Honest folk said what they thought and thought what they said, and using her gift, Heidi could confirm that easily. Those less honest could say one thing but could not hide their deceit from Heidi. When dealing with these less savory individuals, she learned to operate based on what information they withheld. Ancelin was a whole other creature. Heidi had only his outward expressions to help her understand him. What he might hide, she could not tell. She wondered if this was how things would be for her among the Verdélia. The thought made her uneasy, and she shuddered beneath her cloak. Despite all of this, an inexplicable aura of calm in Ancelin's presence made Heidi want to trust him. To believe him. He felt like an older brother if Heidi had to imagine what having an older sibling would be like.

Heidi picked her eyes up and away from the chiseled rocky floor and noticed that the crevice in the mountain peaks they were traveling along turned abruptly to the west. The path, if she could even call it that, continued to climb. The little vegetation that had been growing now became even more sparse, limited primarily to imposing evergreens and the occasional shrub, dull and ragged in appearance.

"Come along," Ancelin's voice echoed from his place above her on a coarse boulder. Heidi struggled to keep up, clambering as best she could over the rough stones, regularly forced to use her hands to help her up.

The air was frigid as the sun descended in front of them. As they were still heading somewhat north instead of due west, the imposing cliff walls quickly hid the sun, casting heavy shadows on their already treacherous path. Before Heidi realized it, the night was upon them.

Ancelin and Heidi set up camp at the base of a giant pine towering along the cliff face. It looked to Heidi as if the tree was defying the very mountain, trying to show that it, too, could reach the sky. After a quick meal beside the fire, Heidi rolled herself up, exhausted, in her blanket and threw her mother's cloak over her for added warmth. The night air was already stinging her cheeks, and she knew enough to realize the night would not get warmer until well after sunrise.

From her position on the ground, Heidi tried to spot Ancelin, who perched above her in the tree, keeping watch. She thought she saw his leg dangling from a branch for a moment, but she realized it was only the pine needles swaying in the breeze rushing between the canyon walls. Listening to the wind dash itself on the rocks, Heidi drifted to sleep.

※

"Time to wake up." Confused, Heidi opened her eyes a sliver to see the pine tree towering over her, beckoning her to rise from her stony bed.

Heidi screwed her eyes shut and rubbed them hard. She opened her eyes again and saw Ancelin nestled in the branches above her like a curious bird. He called to her again.

"Wake up," he sang, "We have a long road ahead of us."

With that, he descended, bounding from branch to branch, finally gliding to the ground as if suspended by invisible cords. "At our current pace, we have approximately a moon's journey ahead of us."

"A moon?" Heidi repeated, propping herself up onto her elbows. "That will give you plenty of time to tell me all about the Verdélia," Heidi said.

"Telling anyone all about the Verdélia would take more moons than you will see in your lifetime," Ancelin responded, "but I will help you learn the foundations of what you will need to know in this new chapter in your life."

"Great!" Heidi beamed. "I learn best on a full stomach. I'll get breakfast started."

A few minutes later, Heidi crouched beside the small fire she had built and stirred a modest potful of oats boiling in the water she had collected from the nearby mountain stream the day before.

"So," she said, not taking her eyes off her pot, "how is it you know so much, even about me, that I've never heard in my life?"

"An unfortunate byproduct of your human upbringing, I'm afraid," Ancelin answered, his lips flattening in a grimace. "Humans are a fearful lot," he explained, "and as a result, they eschew things they do not understand. Instead of seeking to learn about them, they label them unnatural." With that, Ancelin looked up at Heidi with a grin. She knew all too well what he was talking about.

"As a result," Ancelin continued, "much of the world is unknown to them, a willful ignorance that has passed down for generations."

Heidi frowned, then said glumly, "Sounds like I'm coming in with a big disadvantage..."

"True," Ancelin admitted, "although humanity isn't just a big bag of flaws. Their inability to rely on magic has made them a cunning people, and strong and typically hard-working. Of course," he added, "this is not true of all humans, and these skills are not always put to good use."

Ancelin paused, and there was a silence, interrupted only by the sounds of Heidi mixing her food.

"As far as you are concerned, however, you drew as good a lot among the humans as you could realistically hope for." Ancelin looked up at Heidi with a gleam in his eye. "But you're still hopelessly clueless as to who you are," he smirked."

Heidi scowled, "Thanks a lot," she grumbled.

Ancelin laughed, "Excuse my frankness, but my point still stands!"

"A lot of good that does me," Heidi complained. "How about you teach me something about the Verdélia, then?"

"What would you like to know?" He asked.

"How many questions do I get?" she asked playfully, and he smirked.

"I'll give you three before we walk again. Give me your first."

"You said there are three others like me, Firstborn?—That's a statement, not a question," she corrected herself. Ancelin chuckled. "Could you give me an idea of who the others are? The people I share these responsibilities with?"

"Your companions, yes. I will let them introduce themselves by name, but I will give a simple description. The first to be born was a boy. A man now. He is extremely personable and sees the good in everyone. The woman is outwardly aggressive in defense of a deepfelt internal weakness. And the last, born moments before yourself, another man. Stoic and full of duty, sometimes to a fault."

"Are the men handsome?" Heidi asked in jest.

"Is that your second question?" Ancelin clarified.

"No," Heidi said, becoming more serious. "Second question: what brought me to Hull after my birth?"

"An uprising in Verdélys. Firstborn are born every two hundred years. That cycle began again twenty years ago, in the year of your birth. However, at that time, a faction of imps rose up, determined to break the Firstborn cycle by killing or destroying all blooms grown in that year. They failed, but they caused much chaos in Verdélys and set your parents on the path that saw you raised in Hull."

Heidi walked thoughtfully, digesting this new information. Although Ancelin answered her questions, each response seemed to generate more new answers than questions.

"Who is Solaidi?"

"What has your father told you?"

She shrugged, "My father mentioned him in his memory. I asked him about it, and he said Solaidi is my father or creator. It has something to do with religious tradition."

"You will be in for a shock upon entering Verdélys. The Verdélia are religious, unlike those from the town you were born in. There are ceremonies, rituals, and beliefs that are the building blocks of the society. You yourself are an important part of Verdélian theocracy. Solaidi is your creator. He created the Verdélia, who took part in creating all things living on this earth."

Heidi nodded, trying to feel a reverence for something Ancelin was speaking so solemnly about but that she understood little of.

Heidi hurriedly ate her morning meal and stuffed her few belongings into her packs before getting on with her journey. She knelt to whisper to a passing lizard before taking off after Ancelin. "Do you think the men in Verdélys look like you? Is that why Ancelin won't answer my question?" She chuckled a moment as the lizard scurried off up the rock face as if offended at her words. Heidi followed suit and scrambled after Ancelin. The road was still treacherous, though they were no longer climbing, which made the going easier.

Their road soon turned left again and led them due west. The sun was directly on their backs, countering the chill of the sharp mountain air. For most of that day, they walked through a ragged gap in the monumental peaks.

Finally, up ahead, Heidi saw an opening in the cliffs where their path began its descent on the western side of the mountains.

Ancelin reached the canyon exit first and stopped.

He turned to Heidi and exclaimed, "Come! See your new country!"

# V

## *A Name Remembered*

Heidi quickened her pace, still carefully choosing her steps over the sharp rocks of the mountain floor. She soon reached Ancelin's side; her breathing rushed and ragged.

"What?" Heidi huffed, looking up at Ancelin as she hunched over, hands on her knees, trying to catch her breath.

"See for yourself," Ancelin smiled, gesturing widely before them. Heidi turned to follow his arm with her gaze. Her eyes widened in amazement at the scene before her.

Despite how high they were above the lands below them, the colors were radiant enough to take Heidi aback. The fall colors were on full display, in tones more vivid than any she had seen in Hull. This land still had much green, a testament to the country's vitality before Heidi.

A little way before them and far below, where the stony feet of the mountain plunged into the earth, a sea of colorful treetops blanketed the earth. Many of the trees donned their autumn coats, some in reds, others in ambers, and yet others in different shades of gold. These stood in beautiful contrast to the stubborn few who kept their summer garb in various shades of green, from bright emerald to deep moss. Where the forest ended several miles away, an immense expanse rose and fell over hilly country, an ocean of wild grass buffeted by the wind.

Heidi's eyes rose to inspect the country far away, nearer to the horizon. Away to the south, the lands grew greener still, immune from the effects of the recent summer's heat. Here and there, she spotted the glimmer of water where rivers snaked across the land.

With her eyes still to the south and west, she heard Ancelin say, "You are looking directly at our destination and your new home. On that horizon is the country of the Verdélia, your people."

Heidi was mesmerized. This country was like nothing she was accustomed to. Although the lands around Hull were relatively fair farming lands by human standards, they still required hard work to produce what Heidi could only guess was perhaps one-third of the life and vibrance she was seeing before her. It was incredible.

But there was more. Heidi felt an odd pull, a sensation similar to one she had felt before whenever it was planting season in Hull. From each seed she would plant, she could feel a yearning to return to the earth, to be placed where it belonged and could grow. Now, she felt a similar desire within herself, something instinctual, subconscious.

"You'll have to do the remainder of your gawking on the go, I'm afraid," Ancelin teased. "We really must get going."

Heidi stood rooted as Ancelin started down the trail at his usual brisk pace. She shook herself after a few more moments and rushed to catch up.

"You told me you were going to teach me about the Verdélia while we walked!" she hollered at Ancelin, "And we are now entering Verdélian country, so start your teaching!"

Ancelin laughed, "We aren't entering Verdélian country and won't be for some time. Technically speaking, no one claims this land. The mountain pass is certainly unclaimed, but most considered the forest before us, the country of the nymphs and fawns. Though they certainly wouldn't consider this country as belonging to them any more than it might belong to any other tree in this forest."

"Alright, that's a start," Heidi answered, encouraged to be getting some information about the new life she was wandering into. "Is there anything about the Verdélia or the city I should know before stepping foot in it?"

He gave out a long sigh. "They love holidays, and there are traditions associated with each that you must understand to take part properly and publicly. There will be much to learn. You know how to read, don't you?" Heidi nodded. "Right. You will need to learn at least simple words in the ancient language that are used for greeting. 'Alondra' is the most common form of greeting. For the rest...well, like I said, there will be much to learn. For example, you play a significant role as an arbiter of the law in Verdélian society."

"Do I?" Heidi scampered down the rocky mountain path after her guide.

Ancelin continued without skipping a beat, "You must get used to wearing a headscarf in the autumn moons. Boots are common in cold weather, and bare feet are expected when warm, but it seems you are already in the habit of that. You will need to become familiar with the high councilmen of the districts. They will be highly involved in your life, and there will be much arguing and deliberating over their responsibilities and the direction the city and the Verdélia take."

Heidi tried to process the deluge of new information that Ancelin sent her way, but the downhill path before her required more focus than she had anticipated. She soon gave up trying to understand everything Ancelin was talking about. She hoped it would be enough foundation for her arrival in Verdélys.

❧

Getting off the mountain on the western side took Heidi and Ancelin the better part of a full day. The slope was gentler than it had been on the eastern side, and now they headed downhill. It was significantly easier going.

Ancelin had also been more talkative than during the first stretch of their journey. Although he was still much more cryptic with his responses than was to Heidi's liking, she was learning much about the Verdélia and their (or her, as she had to remind herself constantly) world.

Finally, the rocky path before her transformed into a soft dirt track, heavily overgrown with wild grasses and flowers, and burrowed itself beneath a mess of imposing trees.

Heidi wrenched off her boots and removed her worn socks, revealing impressive blisters. She grimaced, tied her boots and socks together, and hung them from her pack. The crisp grass felt like a luxurious carpet beneath her feet after the days of mountain trekking.

Turning her attention back to the road ahead, Heidi noticed Ancelin was no longer walking at his habitual rapid pace but fixed in place a little way ahead of her, his brow deeply furrowed and eyes fixed to their right on the treeline that opened out onto the grasslands not twenty yards away.

"What's so interesting?" Heidi asked as she caught up to Ancelin.

"Not the word I would choose under the circumstances," Ancelin replied in a low voice. "I believe danger has found us."

Heidi instinctively moved to a position somewhat behind Ancelin and turned to look at the scenery that was the focus of Ancelin's piercing gaze. She could see no apparent danger.

"What is it? What's after us?" She whispered to Ancelin.

As if on cue, under the shadows of the trees ahead of them to the north, Heidi could make out movement in the underbrush that was not following the breeze. A large shape was moving heavily.

"Make your way quickly south, deeper into the forest. It will guard you from harm. Leave the troll to me," Ancelin instructed.

"Troll?!" Heidi whispered hoarsely back to Ancelin.

"Yes, now run, Heidi!" Ancelin ordered.

"Go alone?" Heidi asked incredulously. "I'll never find my way out of there."

"I will be able to find you," Ancelin assured her, "and the forest will care for you. Now go."

The beast surged from its hiding place beneath the trees and barrelled toward Heidi and Ancelin. The troll was large, stout, and ugly. He rushed toward Ancelin, and Heidi watched as Ancelin disappeared, leaving behind a messy bouquet of fallen flowers.

Prompted into action by the sudden attack, Heidi took a few steps backward, then turned and plunged into the tree line. Heidi glanced back towards the path, looking for Ancelin, but she saw no sign of him. An icy fear overtook her, driving her legs into a worried run. Trusting Ancelin, Heidi could focus on only one thing: getting deeper into the forest. She dashed among the trees, leaping and bounding through the undergrowth like a doe fleeing a ravenous pursuer.

She fell to her knees, tripping over tree roots and bushes. Her hands were bleeding, and she noticed a scratch across her arm after scraping along a tree trunk. Her hair had fallen out of place.

Eventually, even the fear of the danger from which she fled could no longer power the muscles in her legs and feet. Heidi could do little more than plod along the forest floor, and gathering her thoughts, she realized she was far from the worn path she had been traveling with Ancelin.

With her wits somewhat more about her, Heidi took the time to consider the surrounding growth. Though some of the forest foliage was the same as that growing on the mountains' eastern slopes and familiar to Heidi, most of the plant life was foreign and strange. Heidi's fingers lingered on oddly shaped leaves and barks of unfamiliar textures, and she could only guess at the origins of and secrets held by these unfamiliar specimens.

Heidi's stomach groaned. Looking down with a frown, Heidi realized her frantic rush through the woods had depleted her. She would have had no problem finding a meal in the forest near her home in Hull. Painfully aware that this new environment presented a whole new dilemma, Heidi wondered what plants would be safe to eat. She could only guess.

She no sooner had the thought cross her mind than she saw, some fifteen feet in front of her, a tree bearing bright red fruit in the shape of a teardrop. She approached the tree and surveyed the selection of fruit, trying to identify which fruit looked ripest.

As she deliberated, she heard a rustling in the leaves above her. She glanced upward.

"I wouldn't look up if I were you," a mouth spoke inches from her face.

Heidi squealed and fell to the ground, clambering wildly backward to the cover of a nearby log.

From her hiding place, Heidi saw a beast jump to the ground from the branches of the tree she had just been inspecting. From head to hips, the creature looked human. Hips down, however, Heidi could have confused the creature for a goat.

Heidi drew the sword her father had gifted her. She held the hilt in a death grip, and her heart beat like a smith's hammer on an anvil.

Bursting up from her hiding place, she pointed the tip of her sword with both hands towards the stranger. "Don't come any closer!" She yelled as menacingly as she could manage.

The creature looked at her inquisitively but did not show any fear. "No need for that, friend," he said.

Heidi hesitated, her grip on her sword slackening. Catching herself, she kept the point of her blade at the stranger's chest. "Friend?" She asked.

"Sure," the beast replied, "mostly only friends are allowed in these woods. Besides," he continued, "I'm rather certain it's not the first time the trees have welcomed you into these parts." He continued to inspect Heidi with his eyes as if a farmer were inspecting the livestock he intended to purchase.

"You're mistaken," Heidi replied, keeping her guard up, "I've never been here before."

"No, I most certainly am not." The stranger replied, "That said, I cannot, for my life, recall who you are or when you were last here. But I am not mistaken. You surely have been beneath these leafy boughs before."

Heidi held her ground. "What—who—are you?" She asked.

"Ah, right, of course. How rude of me," the stranger responded. "How about you put that dangerous little thing," he pointed at her sword, "away, and we'll be properly introduced?"

"I don't think so!" Heidi retorted, "Not until I know who you are and what you want with me."

"Well, I don't particularly want anything with you. Although I sure wish I could remember what I know you from." He paused, his face showing the effort his mind was putting in to reach deep down the well of his memory. "That is going to bother me until I put my finger on it," he mumbled to himself.

"Although," he continued, suddenly remembering that Heidi was there, "I should say that a 'thank you' from you is in order. I did just save you from a lifetime of miserable blindness."

"Excuse me?" Heidi asked. "You did no such thing."

"I most certainly did," Responded the stranger. "That tree is the aveupoule tree. One glance up into those beautiful bulbs, and," he clapped loudly, "you're blind!"

Heidi hesitated. She had no way of knowing whether this stranger was telling the truth. Like Ancelin, she could not reach his thoughts. His odd, carefree temperament made her instinctively trust him, though.

"How do I know you will not trick or hurt me?" Heidi asked.

"You don't," the stranger answered, "but I can't think of any good reason to hurt you. Besides, you're the one with the pointy steel. As for tricking you," he continued, "to be honest, I may very well do so. I'm mighty fond of jokes."

Heidi lowered her sword. Though odd in appearance, this stranger's mannerisms reminded her of a child. She sensed no guile or threat from him.

"Ok, my sword is down. Can I at least get your name now?" She asked.

"It's Pemberley," he replied with a smile. "Now you tell me yours."

"I'm Heidi," Heidi replied.

"No, that isn't right." Pemberley shook his head energetically.

"What isn't right?" Heidi asked, perplexed.

"Your name. It sure isn't Heidi."

Heidi scoffed. "Yes, it sure is! It is my name. After all, I think I would know it."

"You most certainly would think so," Pemberley mused, "but that is just not right. Nope, not one bit."

Bewildered, Heidi said, "Well, it's my name as far as I know, and I've never been called any other name. You asked my name, and my answer is 'Heidi.' Take it or leave it, I suppose."

Pemberley stroked his chin, processing this conundrum. Suddenly, his eyes lit up. "I know!" He exclaimed, "The nymphs will know! Yes, of course! They'll know your name!" With that, he started on a skipping trot through the woods. "Come along then!" He shouted back at her.

Heidi hesitated but finally started after her new companion. She kept her sword in her hand, doubt still gnawing at her. She struggled to keep up with Pemberley's pace and haphazard meanderings through the forest's tangled growth. He seemed to go nowhere, changing directions randomly and often only to switch back to the opposite direction soon after.

Heidi reckoned she had followed Pemberley for the better part of an hour. In fact, the sky was darkening, and the shadows of the forest lengthened and grew thick and mysterious. Heidi quickened her pace, keeping closer to Pemberley, afraid that if she lost him from sight, she might lose herself in the woods forever.

Finally, Heidi noticed a flickering light ahead of her between the trees. As they grew nearer, she heard voices, which she recognized as songs, as the lights were now less than twenty yards away.

Suddenly, Pemberley and Heidi broke out into a small clearing. Trees covered the sky and bent inwards to create a leafy roof over the forest floor, covered in grass and wildflowers of every shape and color. Beautiful lamps hung from the tree branches, casting shadows and lights dancing and flicking about the leaves.

Several beautiful women were dancing among the grass, each wearing gorgeous, flowing gowns in various colors. They were each exceptionally tall, easily a head taller than Heidi, and incredibly slender. Their dancing made Heidi think of reeds blowing in the wind.

"Friends!" Pemberley said excitedly, "I've brought a no-name!"

The women stopped dancing and singing and looked at the newcomers. They approached Heidi with inquisitive looks in their eyes.

"She hasn't got a name?" asked a beautiful blue woman in a long gown the color of the summer sky. Although she appeared nearly human, Heidi couldn't help but notice that she looked like a snapdragon.

"I've got a name," Heidi protested, "it's Heidi."

"You don't look like a Heidi." said a rose-colored woman. Her dress was blush, nearly white, and comprised large flower petals.

"That's what I said!" Pemberley said eagerly, jumping up and down.

"She doesn't smell like a Heidi either." Said a woman whose face was just inches away from Heidi's. The woman smelled of hazelnuts.

"Is her mind lost?" Asked another voice belonging to a woman Heidi couldn't see over the faces crowding around her.

"I told you, she's a no-name," Pemberley insisted, visibly proud of his discovery.

"But she is..." another woman in a deep green dress started, "...familiar."

All the other women in the clearing nodded and hummed in assent.

"What's all this excitement about then, ladies?" A new, stronger voice came from behind the crowd. Although powerful, the voice was soft and comforting.

The crowd parted in front of Heidi, and a majestic woman, taller than all the others and in a shimmering white gown, walked towards her. Her golden-white hair gleamed in the firelight.

The woman approached until she was only inches from Heidi, then crouched until they were face to face. Her pale blue eyes gazed into Heidi's soul, searching for answers.

"But of course," she whispered, standing up straight.

"What?" Heidi asked, "What is it?"

"You certainly have grown since you were last beneath these branches, child," the regal woman said in a melodious voice, "but there is no mistaking who you are."

"Everyone keeps saying I've been here before," Heidi protested, "but I can assure you I have not."

"It's quite natural that you wouldn't remember your time here," the blonde woman said. "Your stay here was very brief, and you were quite young—newly born, in fact."

There was an audible gasp from the surrounding crowd. Heidi's realization was visible on her face.

"I was born here?" She asked, feeling more comforted as the conversation continued.

"Indeed," the nymph replied. "Your mother sought refuge within this forest some twenty years ago, during the struggle between the Verdélia and Imps that led to much suffering and loss between both peoples. She was being pursued by a dreaded shadow and evil and pleaded with us to hide her." She paused and looked squarely into Heidi's eyes, "and her most precious treasure."

She continued, "We agreed, and after a few days, you were born. What a miraculous event that was!" Her face darkened, "Unfortunately, those days of happiness were not to last. The shadow that sought you and your mother was—is—a relentless one. Its servants found you all, even within these woods, and despite our best efforts, not long after your arrival."

"But I don't understand," Heidi interrupted, "what is this shadow? And what would it want with me? Am I in danger here, then?"

"That shadow," stated the nymph, "is Rhys, agent of chaos and destruction." A heaviness made itself felt within the clearing as she spoke, the nymphs and fawns within the clearing cowering beneath its weight. "It would seem it is him who brings you here today. What are you running from, child?"

"I was walking with my companion, and there was a troll—he told me to run," Heidi stumbled through her words.

"Rhys' troll. His interest in you springs from your birthright. He seeks to destroy the Firstborn. This was the purpose of his attack on the Verdélia twenty years ago."

"Whether you are in the same danger now," the tall nymph added, "I do not know. But I would admonish against complacency."

Heidi felt overwhelmed trying to process this new information. Finally, she asked, "You knew my mother?"

"Yes, dear," the nymph said, "and the better for it, we all are."

Heidi held the nymph in her gaze, her unspoken question visible.

The nymph sighed, then spoke. "I am afraid your mother was pushed into making the ultimate sacrifice to protect you from the grasp of the shadow."

Heidi's heart sank. Though she had known that her parents were dead, hearing it confirmed directly shook her deeply.

"You should know, however," the nymph continued, "that your mother fell in battle against innumerable servants of the shadow, fighting valiantly to allow you to escape. The odds were against you ever making it out of this forest alive. Few are the tales of any Verdélia resisting the shadow as mightily as did your mother."

Tears welled in Heidi's eyes. Though she had never met her birth mother, in this moment, she felt her loss keenly, as well as pride at the recounting of her mother's bravery.

"Forgive me for interrupting, Maeva," Pemberley said for the first time in several minutes. "Would it not be right to give our new friend her name? It is, after all, a gift from her mother that has been lost to her."

"Right it would be indeed," said Maeva approvingly. She turned to Heidi. "Are you ready to receive the name given to you by your mother, child?"

Heidi nodded, emotion swelling within her throat and preventing her from speaking.

"Walk towards that pond there," Maeva pointed towards the center of the clearing, which was now lit only by the many lamps hanging from the boughs of the overhanging trees. "The forest will not soon forget your birth here. It will restore your name to you."

Heidi stepped reverently through the long grass, its touch soft and damp on her travel-worn feet. Finally, she reached the pond. Her feet dug into the mud below the surface. She stood, waiting for something unknown.

Then, as if the water had seeped into her skin, it traveled up her body and into her mind. It felt at once ancient and full of life, and Heidi could feel its immense power and wisdom, more imposing than anything her imagination could even conjure.

Finally, this new consciousness reached Heidi's mind from the soles of her feet, now dripping with dew. Then, from within the foreign enormity of this unfamiliar presence, a single idea crystallized itself into a form Heidi could understand. Clearly, Heidi heard a woman's voice call out in her mind.

"Sylvie."

# VI

## *Verdélys*

H eidi, *or I suppose it's Sylvie?* she thought to herself, sitting in the plush grass against the smooth trunk of a large tree. She watched as the fauns and nymphs danced and sang to celebrate her return to their woods. The soft firelight flickered in time with the music as the nymphs moved gracefully about the clearing like leaves in the wind. As she watched, mesmerized, the carefree nature of these creatures, so foreign to the laborious monotony of her human upbringing, astounded her.

Someone had lovingly carved rustic trees into long tables cluttered with food from the forest. Fruits and nuts littered the tables, an organized chaos of flavor. Heidi enjoyed food before resting beneath a tree in a soft grassy spot.

The entire forest, plants included, seemed to be moved by the music of the fauns. The nymphs appeared to take the growing things of the forest as their dance partners, swaying with the trees and brush. Heidi felt the magic thick in the air about her. Wrapped in the fantasy, she drifted to sleep.

When she woke the following day, she realized she had slept comfortably for the first time since leaving Hull. Looking around, she saw the fauns and nymphs asleep on the grass nearby or low-hanging branches in the trees surrounding the clearing. Then, not five paces away, she noticed Ancelin seated in the grass, twirling a leaf in his fingers.

"Good morning, Sylvie." He said.

"Good—" she paused, "I thought you said you didn't know my name?"

"I didn't say that." Ancelin chuckled, "I said I couldn't tell you."

"I guess you found me," Heidi said.

"As I said I would," Ancelin replied. He stood. "Now then," he said, "we'd best be on our way. We've some time to make up after our minor detour."

Heidi sat upright and stretched. "It would be nice to say goodbye before leaving." She looked around at her sleeping hosts.

"They know the prophecy," Ancelin responded, striding purposefully into the forest. Confused, Heidi followed, glancing over her shoulder at her newfound friends.

It took them a little while to reach the road again. Heidi's little detour had taken her deeper into the forest than she had thought. When they reached the road, Heidi asked, "You said they knew the prophecy. What prophecy?" Ancelin answered.

> *"When the fourth of the four blooms deep in the night,*
> *The fauns of the forest look on with delight*
> *The nymphs shower fits of the woods' tender heights*
> *Hiding the babe, safe for now, out of sight*
>
> *When, at last, she returns with a name on her tongue*
> *Known by none of the forest, both old and both young*
> *The fourth of the four will be renamed that night*
> *And be gone with the wind by the morning's first light."*

He did not elaborate.

Heidi marched with a renewed determination today, a bit of excitement in her step. Ancelin had told her that morning over breakfast that he expected they would make it to Verdélys, City of the Verdélia, in time for supper. She could hardly wait. Part of that was because of the twenty-six (*or was it twenty-seven?*) days of traveling that would soon end. Her romp through the forest had thrown off her count. Regardless, she could feel the distance in her tired legs all too well.

The other part, of course, was because of the excitement of finally seeing something that only one moon ago Heidi had believed to be nothing more than a myth. Real Verdélia, and not only that, their capital city, a place that she imagined was full of magic and mystery. She also had her apprehensions, but Ancelin had assured her she would be welcomed and well cared for in Verdélys. Heidi realized that during her journey with Ancelin, she had come to trust him, and so his words comforted her.

Questions drifted across Heidi's mind, each pushing out the previous thought before she could respond. Where would she live? Would she have neighbors? What would they be like? Would she need a job? What kind? She had tried to bring some of her questions to Ancelin, but he had seemed unconcerned by what he called "trivial mortal matters." Heidi thought to herself, to Ancelin, everything seemed like a "trivial mortal matter." Still, his nonchalant approach did little to settle her growing anxiety.

4020 | *Autumn* | *3rd Moon* | *23*

The two companions rounded a low hill, and the first signs of dwellings appeared. There, a ways away but not quite on the horizon, was what appeared to be a farmer's cottage. Heidi sucked in a squeal.

"Are we there?!" she blurted out.

Ancelin chuckled, "Not quite. We're on the outskirts of Verdélys, but the city is still a ways away."

Heidi's eyes shrank to their normal size, and her shoulders slumped slightly. "Oh." She said. Still, the promise of civilization (especially Verdélian civilization) prodded her to increase her pace instinctively.

"Farming, there's something I can do!" Heidi spouted to no one in particular.

Ancelin laughed again. "You won't be doing much farming, I suspect." He replied. "You'll have more pressing matters to attend to."

"Still," Heidi insisted, "if I get lost in the land of the Verdélia, there'll be at least one thing I'm familiar with." The idea was comforting.

Ancelin turned to her, a large green napkin in his hand.

"Here, tie this around your hair if you don't mind," Ancelin instructed, handing the napkin to Heidi.

Heidi took the cloth slowly, taken aback by the unexpected request.

"Why?" Heidi asked as she obediently tied the handkerchief about her hair.

Ancelin tugged at the napkin's edge, bringing it down until it touched Heidi's right ear.

"Just a precaution. I don't know if the other Firstborn will be ready to have your identity as the fourth Firstborn made public yet."

Heidi wasn't sure what Ancelin meant, but by the time she stopped thinking about it, she had noticed that Ancelin was already a way down the road. She ran to catch him.

They had walked for some time, and the farmhouses had become more numerous and the fields smaller. Heidi noticed voices floating in the air. Thoughts. It had been some time since she had heard these whispers, and the newfound noise took her aback momentarily. People—Verdélian people—could be seen bustling about in the fields. It enthralled Heidi.

Eventually, Ancelin and Heidi came upon a short stone wall about hip height covered in moss and overgrown by shrubs and long grass. The wall continued through the fields on either side of the road for as far as Heidi could see. The road went right through a broad opening in the wall, over which a wooden sign hung with a single word inscribed: Verdélys. Now, a beaten dirt path morphed into a patchwork of worn cobblestones.

The homes became more common as Ancelin and Heidi crossed this stone border. Many farm fields gave way to smaller yards, often still with good-sized garden plots. They crossed more and more Verdélia, many of whom were too occupied to give them even a sideways glance. Those who noticed them, however, stopped to stare at Heidi. She felt self-conscious, as she was sure she looked quite a mess, and Ancelin was not your average-looking travel companion either.

Heidi was soon walking through bustling city streets. The worn cobblestone patchwork had become intricate and smooth stone streets, laid out in such a fashion to create beautiful patterns and symbols beneath the feet of the Verdélia that walked the roads on their daily errands. The surrounding homes were stone and wood, demonstrating craftsmanship that mesmerized Heidi. Suspended on beautiful wooden arches, the second stories of some of the taller buildings leaned out over the streets, reaching for their counterparts on the other side of the road. Lamps littered the street, hanging from iron arches.

The city was surrounded by intense greenery, tossed about by the autumn breezes sweeping through the streets. Sylvie could find yellow arrangements of flowers on nearly every balcony and every corner of the street. The windows shone with color, and Heidi wondered if this was the glasswork her father had taught her about.

Heidi and Ancelin passed many metalworking and other crafting shops. Heidi watched intently as Verdélia worked metals of various colors and lusters, smelting and shaping them into tools, jewelry, and other items that Heidi could not identify.

Heidi noticed a curious pattern as she glanced from person to person in the crowd. Many women wore headscarves, just as she was, but embroidered, laced, and highly detailed. Fewer women, but many nonetheless, wore jewelry over the arch of their right ear. They were all different but placed in the same spot. The men—-again, not all, but many—often wore two metal bands, one around each wrist. Heidi made a mental note to ask Ancelin about it later.

"Come along now!" Ancelin prodded, catching Heidi as she gawked at a skilled craftsman working a shining copper metal into a set of beautiful cookware without the help of any tools other than his hands.

Heidi also saw several other workshops, all working with common or precious stones, wood, or glasswork. Ordinary glass was a luxury in Hull, and Heidi was astounded by the art being crafted in panes of all imaginable hues before her here in Verdélys.

Overwhelmed by her surroundings, Heidi suddenly noticed they were walking towards an enormous stone wall, which she could only guess was the city center. The wall was still quite far from them, but she could tell it was tall and robust. A broad and sturdy gate was built into the wall.

Ancelin walked along but was noticed by no one. He slipped between people as if he wasn't even there. "Ancelin," she began, "No one is acknowledging you."

"Most of them can't see me," he said.

A child wandering next to his mother glanced at him and waved happily. He waved back. "He can see you," Heidi mentioned.

"*He* is not *they*," Ancelin replied.

*Obviously*, thought Heidi, but he explained no further.

As she tried to take in the sights and sounds, a voice made itself heard clearly over the bustle of the city.

"Ancelin! You've finally arrived. We'd been expecting you today, and I came as soon as I got word someone had spotted you in Verdélys."

Heidi noticed the crowd part. Individual Verdélia stepped out of their way and nodded shortly in respect as a dark-haired man about her age approached them. He had a thick, square jaw and a very formal demeanor. He wore a deep red tunic overlaid with a dark leather jerkin, and a sword hung at his hip. A dark, formal coat flapped about his legs in the autumn breeze. To Heidi's surprise, like Ancelin, she could not perceive the newcomer's thoughts. *Why?* she thought to herself. The thoughts of other Verdélians they had passed had not been hidden from her.

"Master Loïc," Ancelin smiled, "It's good to see you." He turned to Heidi. "Meet Sylvie, the final element of your quartet."

Loïc's dark eyes looked intensely out from underneath his prominent brow. Heidi bit her lip awkwardly under the pressure of his gaze.

"Well," he said, "we'll make do. Which are you?"

Heidi, slightly indignant at Loïc's curtness, looked to Ancelin to answer the question.

"Morwenna," Ancelin stated.

Loïc looked at Ancelin, then at Heidi, then back at Ancelin.

"Is she mute?" Loïc asked, his face so stony that Heidi couldn't tell if he was being sarcastic.

"I am not." Heidi blurted out.

"Hm," Loïc vocalized, raising one eyebrow.

"Sylvie here was raised in Hull all her life," Ancelin explained.

At this, Loïc's face showed genuine surprise, a bemusement in his eyes.

Ancelin continued. "She has only recently learned of her Verdélian roots. She has only recently learned of the Verdélias' very existence."

"Solaidi provide," Loïc huffed under his breath, his head shaking back and forth, "if it weren't coming from you, Ancelin, I'd take it for an ill-advised joke." Heidi felt crushed but felt too out of place to say anything. Besides, he was right. What did she know about any of this?

"Though I know that none around us can hear your claim, I would rather continue our conversation somewhere private. Come along, we'd best get going," Loïc said, turning back towards the large gate.

When she wasn't staring at her feet shuffling over the cobblestone, Heidi observed the back of Loïc's dark figure. He cropped his hair just above his shoulders. He was taller than Heidi (taller than most other Verdelian men she had seen), and how he carried himself made him seem even more imposing. Heidi realized that was probably partly because the other Verdélia seemed to pause what they were doing as he passed to give a courteous and short bow. There would be a lot to learn about Verdélian culture.

As they neared the gate, Heidi noticed the homes had become larger and larger. Some buildings had even become joined, each multiple stories tall. Not only were the materials—stone, brick, and stained glass—beautiful, but the architecture was magnificent compared to what Heidi was used to in Hull. Beams and wooden arches decorated the fronts of the building with shapes and arches.

Upon reaching the gate, Loïc gestured to the guard.

"Good morning, Alfric. I'm sure you remember Ancelin," he said, "and we have a new guest of honor with us today. Meet Sylvie."

Alfric, a tall and well-built Verdélian in pristine armor, bowed low. Taken aback, Heidi—*Sylvie*, she tried to remind herself—curtsied back. "Hello," she offered.

"An honor," Alfric replied, standing back to attention at his post. He raised his hand in a strange gesture, and the massive doors slid open without a sound as if on wings.

"Thank you," Loïc said to the guard as he marched through the gate.

Heidi took a few hurried steps to catch up, and upon reaching Ancelin's side, she whispered, "Where are we?"

"Verdélys," he said with a smile.

Heidi gave him a look. "I can read, Ancelin. We crossed into the city miles ago. I saw the sign. The gate, what's inside—where are we now?"

"That would be the palace," Loïc answered over his shoulder, without missing a step or even turning his head, "or the palace commons. The palace is right ahead."

Heidi looked around. She wouldn't have thought it possible, but the surrounding buildings were far more detailed than those they had just left behind at the wall. Some were painted with botanical elements, while others bore detailed ironwork in the shape of trees and other nature motifs. Far more greenery and natural growth peppered the homes and streets, which was impressive considering the amount of trees and flowers she had already seen in the city. Her head on a swivel, she watched as the greens and yellows of the city turned into oranges, reds, and golds of fall. If there were a place that encapsulated the season, this would be it. Heidi was seeing, feeling, and breathing the autumn air; she felt so submerged in the season that she almost felt dizzy.

She giggled under her breath, avoiding the eyes of Loïc, who turned to glance at her. Ahead, an enormous structure rose above the tree line. As they approached, Heidi felt a powerful aura surging through the air. It reminded Heidi somewhat of her experience in the forest, though this was much more focused and clearer.

As they followed Loïc through a tunnel of trees overarching the stone walkway, they exited in front of the palace. The workmanship of the structure was detailed, and everything glistened in the sunlight, from the tall panes of multi-colored glass to the polished stone facades. However, something else caught Heidi's attention. In the courtyard in front of the palace entrance stood a sizeable golden pool, its surface a flawless mirror for the sky above, dotted here and there with golden oak leaves. Over this pool stretched an archway worn by at least hundreds of years of age. At the arch's peak, a stone etched with strange silver runes was humming. She didn't know how, but Heidi knew this was the source of the energy she could feel. Upon closer inspection, she could tell the stone was fissured with age. Silvery-golden tendrils seeped out from the cracks in the stone.

As intimidating as the structure was, Heidi was drawn to the pool. At first, there was nothing but water, but then she heard whispers—dark whispers— whispers she couldn't make out.

"The Keystone," Loïc offered. He had caught her staring, but his explanation was hardly satisfactory to Heidi. She exited her trance and followed the new stranger and Ancelin to the palace doors.

"Come," he continued, "let's meet the others."

With that, he pushed the ornate palace doors open and ushered Ancelin and Heidi inside.

# VII

*Firstborn Reunited*

U pon entering the palace, Loïc immediately turned his attention to a man dressed in an unassuming yet formal black uniform who was tending to an ornate plant in a beautiful brass vase.

"You there," Loïc ordered authoritatively, "summon the Firstborn to the study." Loïc turned as if to walk down the hallway to their right and then turned back to the man. "Oh," he added, "and tell the cook we'll need food for our guests." The man stood stiffly but couldn't help staring at the disheveled newcomer accompanying Loïc. "You are dismissed!" Loïc added forcefully. The man snapped out of his daze and scurried deeper into the palace.

Heidi heard Loïc mutter something under his breath as he turned right again and rushed down a long hallway. As she followed, she leaned towards Ancelin. "Is he always like this?" she asked, pointing towards Loïc with her gaze.

Ancelin chuckled, "The short answer is mostly yes, but I'll let you form your own opinions of your new companions."

"Speaking of which," Heidi added, "I asked if they were handsome. You could've just said yes."

Ancelin's grin widened. "Beauty is in the eye of the beholder, don't you know? For all I know, you may very well have found Master Loïc here to be rather hideous."

Heidi scoffed audibly as she followed Ancelin down the hall behind Loïc.

They passed under beautiful vaulted ceilings as they walked down a long corridor. On the wall to their right, the tall windows looked out onto the reflecting pool in front of the palace doors, underneath the aura of the Keystone. On their left, Heidi looked out of matching windows that revealed a gorgeous courtyard with an immaculately maintained garden of hedges, flowers, and intricate climbing plants on trellises and archways.

Ahead, Loïc opened a set of dark wooden double doors and invited Ancelin and Heidi inside with a gesture of his arm. The late afternoon sunlight cast golden beams through the windows that undulated on the velvet drapes. Heidi noticed the room was furnished with a couch and matching set of chairs, all beautifully upholstered, facing a fireplace built into the far side of the room. A good-sized sitting table sat between the couch and fireplace, topped with a few books and a vase of flowers. Against the room's walls were four matching desks, each with a bookshelf mounted to the wall above it and another bookshelf beside each desk. Several books sat on the desk furthest from Heidi, one book lying open on the desktop. From where she stood, Heidi thought she could also make out a map, a long knife, and other gear she couldn't identify. Heidi noticed the immaculately arranged contents of the next desk to her right. The first desk had been relatively neat, but this one was flawless. Someone perfectly arranged the few books on the bookshelf above it. A stack of paper and a quill in a pot of ink was on the desk. The rest of the desk's surface was bare.

To her left, Heidi saw an unruly mountain of books, papers, and other items, ranging from a goblet to an emerald necklace covering the third desk. Finally, in the corner away from Heidi and to her left, Heidi saw the fourth and final desk empty.

Loïc made his way to the first desk. He shuffled some papers around and closed the open book on the desk, careful to insert a bookmark at the open page.

"Make yourself at home, Sylvie," Loïc said without looking up from his desk. He continued to go through the contents of his desk, and from underneath, he pulled a large, half-packed leather bag. He rolled up the map and put it into the bag.

"It's Hei—" Heidi began, but quickly noticed Ancelin shaking his head at her. "What?" She whispered towards him, then noticed Loïc's eyes still on her, "Never mind."

Ancelin leaned towards her. "Not a common name. You will draw unwelcome scrutiny if you keep it."

*Sylvie*. Heidi was still not used to the name. There was nothing to it, though. Her Verdélian name—her birth name—was Sylvie. She would need to get used to it. *Easier said than done*, she scolded herself.

She settled into one couch in the center of the room, allowing her a view of Loïc and the door. The upholstery was softer and more beautiful than anything she'd ever seen or touched in Hull, even considering the most expensive goods she had seen passing through on merchant wagons.

Less than a minute passed by before a woman entered the room. With flawless posture, she strutted to the messy desk, her eyes fixed on Heidi with a disinterested and disapproving look. Her copper-red hair fell in rich, thick waves over her shoulders and down her back. Her irises were golden to match the autumn leaves—an evident tone of yellow that caught Heidi's eye for longer than she intended. The woman looked away.

"You had better have a good explanation for this, Loïc," she shot across the room, seating herself regally at her desk. Loïc ignored her. She turned to Ancelin, "Ancelin, welcome back."

"Always a pleasure, Margot," Ancelin replied with a grin.

Margot turned her eyes back to Heidi. "Is someone going to explain to me what's going on? Loïc?"

Loïc turned around, holding what appeared to be a half-folded cloak and a compass. His face barely betrayed his exasperation at being interrupted. "Margot, darling, as you can see, I'm rather occupied at the moment. I've had to interrupt my preparations for my journey to the Undines to welcome our guests because Gaëtan was busy with the Council, and you couldn't be bothered. So, if it's alright with you, we'll continue waiting for Gaëtan, and I'll return to my preparations." With that, he turned back to his desk and continued organizing its contents, packing some into his large leather bag. Margot huffed indignantly. Heidi glanced about her. Ancelin had a look of pure amusement written all over his face.

A dozen minutes passed in awkward silence. Margot had picked up one of the many books on her desk and was reading. Loïc had finished packing his bag and studied a map and other documents. Finally, a tall man, who Heidi assumed must be Gaëtan, walked into the room, followed by another, more petite man in a somber tunic.

"Yes, I understand that, Thibault. No, you make a fair point—" he stopped at the door, ushering the man out as he spoke. "We'll discuss this later. I'll only be a moment." With that, the man 'Thibault' left the room, and Sylvie heard his steps as he retreated down the hall.

"Sorry I'm late," he stated as he turned around. "The Council has many concerns."

"What a surprise," Margot retorted sarcastically, not taking her eyes off her book.

Gaëtan turned his attention to Ancelin and Heidi. "Ancelin, it's always a pleasure to have you in Verdélys," he said, extending his hand.

Ancelin took his hand and replied, "It's a treat to visit."

Gaëtan now looked squarely at Heidi. His eyes were blue, and golden locks hung loosely about his forehead and ears. His face was strong but soft and not nearly as angular as Loïc's. Looking into his eyes, Heidi could see he was piecing together the puzzle of her presence.

"If you've called us all here, Loïc, and she's here, that can only mean..."

"Hold your tongue for two seconds," Loïc interjected abruptly. Without Heidi noticing him, he had made his way to the doors and closed them quickly. He locked the door with a thick key. "Now is hardly the time for this to get out, especially considering something you'll discover momentarily."

"Time for what to get out?" Margot interrupted, looking up from her book. "Boys, will one of you tell me what's happening?"

"Of course, your highness," Loïc said in mocking reverence, "allow us to do all the heavy lifting for you, mentally and physically."

Margot glared at him coldly.

"That was unnecessary," Gaëtan reprimanded.

Loïc waved Gaëtan's words away with a gesture in the air as he took a seat opposite Heidi.

"Have a seat," he motioned to Margot and Gaëtan to take their places on the plush seating by the fireplace. Gaëtan sat in silence, his eyes on Heidi. Margot, visibly annoyed but still the picture of grace, stood from her desk and seated herself on the couch where Gaëtan sat, though at the far end with her ivory dress splayed out about her.

Loïc spoke. "As Gaëtan has so brilliantly deduced, I would like to introduce to you both the fourth and final Firstborn, Sylvie."

There was a brief moment of silence.

"An honor to meet you, miss," Gaëtan said with a short but courteous bow of his head.

"Welcome to our very select and oh-so-tedious inner circle," Margot said with a mocking bow of her own.

"Thank you," Heidi responded timidly, primarily to Gaëtan, who seemed to be the only one genuinely interested in meeting her.

"Right," Loïc interrupted, "under other circumstances, we might all sit down to dinner together and have much lengthier introductions, but as it stands, I have rather pressing things to attend to, as do you, Gaëtan, if I'm not mistaken, so we're going to have to cut this short." He opened his arm towards Heidi. "Sylvie here was raised in Hull." There were blank stares from both Gaëtan and Margot. Loïc continued, "Where—or what—is Hull, you ask? That is an excellent question. Hull is a tiny cluster of farms east of the Great Mountains."

"Wait," Margot cut in with a scoff, "it's a *human* town?"

"That's...unexpected," Gaëtan muttered.

"Right on all accounts, both of you," Loïc replied. "As I'm sure you've both supposed by now, this means that our newest friend knows approximately nothing about the Verdélia. Her run-in with Ancelin about a moon ago was the first time she realized they were real, let alone that she was one."

"You cannot be serious," Margot lamented, throwing her head back in exaggerated exasperation.

Gaëtan said nothing, but it was obvious that this surprise had left him deep in thought. Heidi felt awful, like the focal point of a poor farce.

Loïc resumed, "So, our newest Firstborn knows as much as Ancelin could and would teach her in her moon's journey here from Hull."

"And it's less than I'll wager you'd like," Ancelin added with a devilish grin. Heidi's heart sank.

Loïc turned to Heidi. "To be fair, Sylvie, none of this is your fault." Taken aback by Loïc's comment, Sylvie smiled at his first sign of empathy. His expression seemed genuine.

"That said," he continued, "your situation doesn't help us much, and having someone that knew something, *anything*, really, about what they were getting into would have been nice. As you'll find out all too soon, we've got plenty on our plate."

"Nice try sugarcoating this, Loïc," Margot smirked. "First, an imp, me, is determined to be a Firstborn—a first, might I remind you—and not a pleasantly surprising one at that. Now, it turns out our fourth Firstborn was raised in the wilderness by uncultured savages?"

Before Heidi could open her mouth to defend her human parents, Loïc exploded.

"You, of all people, should know better than to pass a blanket judgment like that on an entire race!" He was furious.

Margot was visibly stunned, her mouth agape. For a fraction of a second, Heidi seemed to catch her perfect facade waiver, revealing self-doubt and confusion. Heidi blinked, and the vision was gone, Margot's perfect porcelain face rivaling the statue of any queen etched in stone.

With as much composure as possible, Margot replied, but her voice wavered slightly, "You're right. My apologies, Sylvie."

"I'll have you know," Heidi replied, "my adoptive human parents were honorable people and certainly not savages," Heidi spoke with all the composure she could manage in this new and overwhelming setting.

"I believe you," Margot replied quietly, "I'm sorry."

"I think," Gaëtan interjected softly, "that everyone has their share of concerns that are making this conversation less constructive than it might otherwise be."

Loïc grunted in what seemed to be agreement. Margot was silent. Heidi was shaking. Ancelin, from his spot beside Heidi, seemed unaffected by the exchange.

Gaëtan took the silence as permission to continue. "Right then. Loïc, get on with your preparations. I'll take the orientation from here. Sylvie, I'll see that you're poured a hot bath, and we'll get you some clean clothes. Then we'll meet back together in the dining hall for dinner. I'm sure your journey has taken its toll on you physically, and your new life is an even greater one on your mind and emotions. Some rest and food will do you good." Gaëtan looked over at Margot. "Margot, would you accompany me in orienting Sylvie?"

Margot seemed to have gotten over her shock and was regaining her haughty demeanor. "Very well," she replied.

"Time and duties permitting, I'll meet you in the dining hall," Loïc stated as he hoisted his gear and other belongings onto his shoulder and walked out of the room. "And before you go, perhaps for now, we should introduce Sylvie as your long-lost cousin, perhaps Gaëtan. A simple excuse for having a stranger in our midst without putting too much pressure on her immediately."

"Very well," Gaëtan responded. He stood and extended a hand to Heidi, who took it gratefully. He helped her to her feet and picked up her pack. "Come, follow me," he said, turning towards the door. "Margot, are you coming?" he added.

Margot didn't answer but stood from her place on the couch.

"Well," Ancelin said, "it appears Sylvie has been conveyed into expert hands, so my work here is finished."

Heidi pivoted to face him, her heartbeat quickening. "You're leaving?" She cried.

"I am," Ancelin answered matter-of-factly. I have some other matters to attend to, and I have done what needed to be done here."

Heidi's back stiffened. "Don't worry, dear," Ancelin added. "They'll take care of you here, and I have a feeling we'll meet again before too long." With that, Ancelin strode briskly out of the room and disappeared from sight.

"Ancelin's right, Sylvie," Gaëtan said, "I can promise we will care for you here. Now come, let's get you settled."

Gaëtan turned towards the door, Heidi on his arm. Margot followed on Heidi's other side, a half-pace behind. They strode down the long hallway back the way they came.

"Margot will see that you're given a hot bath and some fresh clothes," Gaëtan repeated, "In the meantime, I'll make sure dinner's waiting for you when you're done."

As hungry as Heidi was, the thought of an actual bath was even more enticing. As they neared the palace entrance, she noticed the archway in the courtyard to her left. She pointed with her free hand and asked, "What's that?"

Gaëtan looked to follow her finger. "Oh, the Keystone," he said. "You'll learn plenty more about that soon, but for now, let me just say that it is a source of éthéra that protects the Verdélian realm."

"Protected from what?" Heidi asked.

"Chaos incarnate," Margot said, sarcasm dripping from every word.

"Well...true, though that's reductive," Gaëtan admitted. "The first Firstborn created the Keystone. The recorded details are limited and won't make much sense without the proper context."

The trio walked back into the large palace entryway.

"I'll leave you ladies here," Gaëtan said, handing Heidi's bag to Margot, who took it with an outstretched arm as if it were contagious. "See you soon," he said as he walked down the hall ahead.

"Come on then," Margot said, turning towards the lavish stairway to their right. Heidi followed dutifully.

Margot and Heidi made their way up the steps, beautifully carved out of stone and overlaid with ornate tapestry. The stairway turned at right angles twice, and they found themselves in a hallway directly above and parallel to the one just below on the ground floor. Margot turned right without hesitation and continued walking.

Margot started turning into one room that lined the hall, then stopped and turned towards a dark-haired woman walking down the hall with some folded linens.

"Dear, fetch up some hot water right away and get a bath on for this poor thing," she nodded towards Heidi, "and size her up and bring back a proper dress for her as well."

"Right away, ma'am," the woman answered, hurried back down the hallway, and disappeared around a corner.

Margot entered the room with Heidi behind her. Heidi's eyes sparkled as she inspected the beautiful bedroom she had just entered. The carpet beneath her feet was plush and silky. Decorated with intricate paintings of various flowers and plants, the walls stretched high overhead. A sky divided diagonally between night and day was painted on the ceiling above them. The details made the stars sparkle, and the clouds appeared to float in the air.

Pushed against the far wall, an enormous bed covered in golden-threaded linens held a mountain of pillows. To her right, Heidi saw the suite had its own bathroom, separated from the bedroom by a heavy velvet curtain. Behind it, a large brass tub sat atop beautiful marble tile. A large mirror adorned the far wall.

"Well, here you are," Margot said, placing Heidi's bag in a corner of the bathroom. "The palace staff will have hot water brought in momentarily, and someone will come size you for a more...appropriate...dress."

"Thank you," Heidi answered.

Margot seated herself on a large, comfortable day bed at the foot of the bed. Seconds later, several dark-haired women, all dressed in somber black dresses, lined into the room, each carrying a metal bucket full of steaming water.

As Heidi watched them pass and fill up the tub in the bathroom, another woman approached Heidi and began taking her measurements.

"Excuse me, miss," the woman said timidly as she ran a measuring tape the length of Heidi's back around her body. The process took her only a few seconds. "There, done," the woman said as she gathered her measuring tape and hurried out of the room.

"Your bath is ready, miss." Another woman said. "I'll take your old things."

The hot water seemed to soak at least half of Heidi's journey from Hull out of her sore and worn legs and feet. A hot bath was a luxury rarely afforded to Heidi back in Hull, and here, the palace staff had added soaps and perfumes to the water that seemed to transport Heidi to a place away from the wildness and stress of the past several weeks.

After what seemed to be all too short a time for Heidi (although she realized it had probably been nearly half an hour), the woman who had measured Heidi entered the room again, carrying a silky ivory dress. Another woman followed with a pair of shoes, jewelry, and other accessories.

After getting dressed, they escorted Heidi to a chair facing a vanity in the bedroom. One of the palace staff began brushing and drying her hair while another woman strung a delicate gold necklace around her neck. Tiny strands of gold flowed down from the chain, each culminating in a radiant but delicate light blue gem. Heidi touched the jewels carefully, stunned by their beauty. She had never seen much more than a silver chain about even the wealthiest necks back in Hull. What she wore now was fit for royalty, as far as she was concerned.

"Ummm..." let out the woman helping Heidi with her jewelry. She was unsure about something. Looking at the woman's hands, Heidi understood.

"Oh," Heidi said quietly, "I've never worn earrings."

Piercing her ears had always seemed like an unnecessary and frivolous luxury.

"We can take care of that for you if you'd like," Margot said, speaking for the first time since she'd sat in her spot on the daybed.

"I don't know..." Heidi said hesitantly.

"It won't matter for today, but the people will expect it," Margot said. "Here." She stood up and stretched out her hand to the palace staff. "I'll do it myself. This'll be fun."

Margot pulled up a chair and sat right next to Heidi. The woman holding Heidi's earrings handed Margot a velvet cushion and a long, thin needle with a smooth handle.

Margot looked at her tools and placed the velvet cushion underneath Heidi's ear. Without looking away from what she was doing, Margot told Heidi matter-of-factly, "This is going to hurt. But not too badly. Don't move."

With that, she brought the needle down quickly through Heidi's earlobe. Heidi winced. Margot repeated the exercise on Heidi's left side. "There," she said, wiping the needle on a handkerchief, "all done, and perfectly so if I may say so myself." The palace staff were already tending to Heidi's ears, applying mysterious ointments to the tiny wounds. Then, the woman with the earrings threaded the sparkling chains through Heidi's earlobes. The earrings bore stones to match her necklace. Heidi hardly felt like herself and was very out of place.

They adorned Heidi with a couple of bracelets and three rings. Her hair was now dry and braided into a crown by one of the attending staff, who had also placed a beautifully scented rose into the braid. Finally, they wrapped Heidi's head with a lacy scarf of ivory silk, something Heidi was beginning to realize was customary for reasons she had not yet been taught.

"Much better. You clean up rather nicely," Margot said with a smile. She paused and added, through a smirk, "Almost as nice as me. Come along then; let's go meet the boys." With that, Margot stepped confidently out of the room. Heidi followed awkwardly, self-conscious of her new appearance and struggling to master her new shoes.

Margot led them back down the hall and the stairs. They rounded the corner and approached where Gaëtan had left them. Heidi followed Margot through another set of giant wooden double doors.

Before even making it through the doors, a deliciously rich scent of food enveloped Heidi. Her stomach growled at the olfactory reminder. Over Margot's shoulder, she saw a large table in the middle of the room, laden with loaves of bread and fruits, all foreign to Heidi. Something was also steaming in a large dish on the table, and Heidi saw several pitchers on the table. Seeing a table set for four, Sylvie noticed Gaëtan already seated.

"Ladies, welcome!" He said enthusiastically, rising from his seat. "Sylvie, I take it you feel better? If you'll permit me to say so, you look stunning."

She felt herself blush deeply and mumbled out a "Thank you."

Just then, Loïc entered the dining hall behind Margot and Heidi.

"Sorry, I'm late. I had...," he started. He raised an eyebrow as his eyes reached Heidi. "I had...well, there was more to pack than I expected," he finished hurriedly. Loïc's reaction made Heidi even more self-conscious than Gaëtan's articulate and polite compliment.

"Can we eat, or are you two simpletons," Margot gestured to Gaëtan and Loïc, "going to be at this for much longer?" she complained.

"You look beautiful too, as always, Margot," Gaëtan mentioned with a smile.

"Oh yes," Loïc added with a smirk, "none can compare." He bowed extravagantly.

"I wasn't jealous," Margot huffed, turning her nose in the air, "I'm hungry, and you're embarrassing yourselves."

"Sure," Loïc replied sarcastically. He walked over to the plate beside Gaëtan and stood behind the seat. "Let's eat then," he said. "Ladies," he added, gesturing to the two empty seats.

Margot took the seat opposite Gaëtan, and Heidi sat opposite Loïc.

The food was exceptional, as everything had been so far. The flavors were rich, and everything was filling and refreshing. Even if the meal hadn't come after weeks of stale food from Hull and scavenged vegetation, Sylvie would have found it delightful.

"You know, Sylvie," Loïc said to Heidi with amusement and admiration, "we can have the cook make more."

Heidi looked around and realized that while everyone else was still working through their first helpings, she had cleaned her plate twice.

"I guess I've missed hot meals," she replied, her eyes on her plate. "Besides, the food is exceptional. I don't think I've tasted anything like it before."

"Loïc's just teasing," Gaëtan answered. "You're free to eat as much as you'd like. You've had a long journey."

After thinking about it briefly, Heidi realized she'd already eaten her fill. "I've had enough, thank you. What I'd like is the chance to have some questions answered."

"I'm sure you would, and you will have answers soon enough," Gaëtan said. "However, I'd wager that you have more questions than we unfortunately have time for now."

"You know," Loïc said after a draught from his goblet, "with Sylvie having no Verdélian learning to speak of, we may as well arrange for her to take all the primary learning, or at least the bulk of it, from the beginning. I'm sure Sir Reynard can accommodate her."

"That's probably not a bad idea," Gaëtan said thoughtfully.

"What's the primary learning?" Heidi asked.

"They teach primary learning to every Verdélian child. Surely the humans have uniform schooling of some kind?" Gaëtan said.

Hull didn't have a formal school. If they learned it at all, children learned to read and write from their parents. Heidi had been lucky since both of her adoptive parents were literate, and her father was well-read, even by the standards of the human nobility. Some bigger human cities and villages had schools, but Heidi had never been.

"My parents—my adoptive parents—schooled me. I can read and write well. I never went to school, though." Heidi admitted.

"Well, then, primary learning will be a great place for you to start," Gaëtan said encouragingly. "I'll talk to Sir Reynard and arrange that."

"With that settled, let's talk accommodations," Loïc said, leaning forward, his elbows on the table. "As I no doubt do not need to remind the two of you," he looked at Gaëtan and Margot, "it would be less than ideal for Sylvie's status to be revealed at this point, especially given the fact that she's not ready to assume that status and likely won't be for some time." He turned to Sylvie, "Again, it's not your fault; it just is what it is."

"With that said," he continued, "it will not take a genius to put two and two together if we have her take up the fourth suite in the palace. We need to find an alternative for now, and I recommend housing her in a cottage on Amber Lane."

"That is probably best," Gaëtan agreed. He looked at Heidi. "Sylvie, we will assign you a palace staff member to help you with anything you need. We would ask, however, that for the time being, you refrain from revealing your identity as a Firstborn and that, if asked, you answer that you are my cousin. I am coming to visit."

"Alright, I will," Heidi answered dutifully.

"You'll like Amber Lane," Gaëtan added with a smile. "It's just behind the palace, but it is quite beautiful, and you'll have a good deal of privacy."

"If you'd like, we can accompany you there now," Loïc offered. "It's getting late, and I'm sure you're tired. It's been quite the day for everyone, and we've not been thrust into a new life." That was quite an understatement.

"That would be nice. I wouldn't mind getting to bed a little early." Heidi said in response.

"Right," Loïc said, standing from his seat. The others stood as well. At that, half a dozen palace staff suddenly entered the room and began clearing the table.

"Hey, you there," Loïc said to one man clearing the dishes, "what's the name of that girl who's been in the palace for a little while, working primarily in the library?"

"A few girls are working the library, sir, I'm afraid..." the staff member began.

"You know the one," Loïc replied, putting his fingers to his forehead, hoping to boost his memory, "longer hair, superb with the books..."

"You're thinking of Nadine," Margot stated.

"I think that's right," Gaëtan interjected. "She'll be a good fit."

"Yes, Nadine." Loïc said, turning his attention back to the palace staff, "Have her report to the vacant cottage on Amber Lane immediately. I believe it's number three. Have her bring all of her things. She's being assigned to our guest here, Sylvie, who will stay at Amber Lane for the foreseeable future."

"Right away, sir," the man bowed and hurried out of the dining hall.

"Hey!" Margot called out after him. He stopped dead in his tracks. "One of the staff has already taken Sylvie's measurements. See that Nadine brings a proper wardrobe for Sylvie with her."

The man nodded, swiveled, and disappeared around the corner.

# VIII

## *3 Amber Lane*

Heidi walked quietly with the other Firstborn outside of the palace. The sun had gone down, and outside, the soft firelight of suspended lanterns battled the creeping dark of night.

Heidi had followed Gaëtan and Loïc around the side of the palace, with Margot walking alongside her. They had taken a cobblestone road from the fountain courtyard in front of the palace and followed it right, past a trellis covered in a climbing rose bush flush with flowers that perfumed the air with an intoxicating aroma. The road ran along the side of the palace, and from it, several small streets ran out to their left. They passed a Jade Lane. Peeking down the way, Heidi noticed beautiful homes, each with a small front yard plentifully garnished with colorful flowers. No two houses were the same, although none seemed out of place.

Ahead, Loïc and Gaëtan turned left at Amber Lane. Following, Heidi noticed the same lanterns that had illuminated their nighttime walk, strung in the air above the street. In front of each home, a lantern hung on the post beside the front yard gate. Below the light, a simple banner hung with a number. Immediately to Heidi's right was number one. Looking on, Heidi saw number three. Loïc and Gaëtan had already reached the front gate, stopped, and turned around.

"Here you are," Gaëtan said, resting his hand on the front gate.

"Nadine shouldn't be far behind with the key," Loïc added.

Heidi looked at her new home. The front fence was simple, carved out of a beautiful grey stone, and about waist high. A hedge of flowering plants fronted it. Bound with beautiful wrought ironwork, the wooden gate looked at once sturdy and attractive. An archway reached over the gateway, covered in a rosebush like the one they had passed on their way out of the palace courtyard. It released the same hypnotic scent.

Behind the wall was a handsome two-story home. By Heidi's standards, this was certainly no "cottage," as Loïc had referred to it. Built out of cut stone and framed with giant beams of dark wood, the windows were stained glass and depicted scenes of nature. The lantern light lit the pictures in a magical glow. The builders had shingled the roof in a colored pattern.

Heidi turned at the sound of feet on the stony lane behind her. She saw a short and thin woman with long, dark hair carrying two large canvas bags rapidly approaching her. *Oh!* Heidi heard the woman think, *she's quite beautiful. And all three of the Firstborn are here. This must be someone important.* Behind her, two women were working together to carry what looked like a portable closet.

"Ah, Nadine, great timing," Gaëtan walked to meet the newcomer. "Here, let me take one of those bags," he offered.

He turned to Heidi, "Nadine, meet Sylvie, our palace guest. She will stay in three Amber Lane for the foreseeable future."

Nadine curtsied politely and smiled at Heidi. "Nice to meet you, miss," she said. Her voice was not much more than a whisper.

"Nice to meet you too," Heidi replied. Heidi noticed Nadine's eyes were a deep golden yellow, much like Margot's.

"If you wouldn't mind, Nadine, could you unlock the door?" Gaëtan asked.

"Of course," Nadine replied, reaching into her dress pocket and pulling out a sturdy metal key.

"Miss Sylvie, I have a copy for you as well," Nadine said as she turned the key in the heavy iron lock on the front gate.

Heidi followed Nadine through the gate and up to the door. Loïc, Gaëtan, and Margot followed, with the other two palace staff close behind.

Nadine used the same key to open the front door and let Heidi inside. The door opened onto a large room, although there was no light to see by. However, Nadine was already tending to what Heidi could barely make out as the silhouette of a hearth, and soon, a small fire was crackling, sending smoke up the chimney. Nadine toured the room, lighting another dozen candles perched in different locations. Within a handful of seconds, the room was well-lit, and Heidi could see the contours of the space. The fireplace on the wall to their left faced a sofa and two plush chairs. On the right, Heidi saw an opening into what looked like a kitchen or dining area, though that room was still dark. In the back corner, a staircase led up to the second story.

"Miss Sylvie," Nadine said, approaching Heidi after having tended to the room, "here is your key." She handed Heidi a duplicate of the heavy metal key she had used to open the gate and door. "If you wouldn't mind following us upstairs and picking your bedroom, we'll arrange everything."

"This is where we'll say goodnight," Gaëtan interjected. "Sleep well, and we'll pick things up in the morning."

He bowed politely to excuse himself and turned to go. Margot made a barely perceptible nod and turned to leave, her posture as perfect as ever. Loïc addressed Nadine.

"Nadine, a word, please?" He said.

Nadine nodded respectfully and followed Loïc onto the front porch.

Curiosity took hold of Heidi, but she could not hear the exchange between Loïc and Nadine. Then, a thought reached her.

*Oh, my! Morwenna!*

Nadine stepped back into the cottage. She looked at Heidi with a new sense of awe.

"If you'll follow me, miss, we'll have you pick your room," Nadine said quietly as she walked towards the rear of the cottage. Heidi turned and walked up the stairs to the second story without a word. From what she could see, there were two bedrooms and a bathroom at the top of the stairs. Heidi chose the room at the far end of the house, which shared the chimney with the living room downstairs and stretched the width of the house, with two windows facing the street and two facing a small backyard—a small bathroom suite connected to the bedroom on the rear side of the home.

Nadine spoke as Heidi watched the darkness of the sky out of her upstairs window. "I will return in the morning to help you with your breakfast and preparations. If you need anything, you can call on me."

"Thank you," Heidi replied, watching her descend the stairs before she heard her bidding farewell to someone downstairs. Curious, Heidi also descended the stairs, only to find Nadine stepping out into the night and Loïc standing near the door.

"Oh, I thought you'd left," Heidi said, almost under her breath, "Is there something you need from me?"

"No," he replied as she walked closer, "But there is something you need from me. I must apologize."

Heidi's eyebrows furrowed. "For what?"

He smiled. "I've been very curt with you today. Rude, even. I leave tomorrow for the Mistralle Peninsula to speak with the Undines. Between preparations for my trip, ensuring the city and palace guard were prepared for my absence, and welcoming you into the city, I was overwhelmed. I suppose some of that came out on you, and that wasn't fair to you."

Heidi was taken aback. Loïc had certainly been abrasive so far, but his apology was genuine, at least as far as she could tell without being able to read his thoughts.

"It's all right." Heidi hesitated, unsure of how to respond. "Do you leave Verdélys often? How long will you be gone?"

"Often enough. Gaëtan is more familiar with local affairs, and Margot...well, you'll come to learn all of this soon enough."

"And you'll return...?" Heidi leaned herself against the back of an armchair.

"In a moon. Quicker if things go well, Solaidi willing. But I want you to know that I wish you luck in learning the ropes around here. I hope you're comfortable."

"I appreciate that," Heidi smiled.

"Of course. I'll bid you goodnight then," Loïc said. With a curt nod towards Heidi, he whispered hastily, "Lunardé," and turned to walk out into the night.

"Sorry," Heidi rushed towards the door to clarify, "what was that?"

"Good night, in the ancient tongue. Lunardé," he repeated.

"Lunardé," she mimicked, smiling and glancing towards the cobblestones.

"Yes, we meet again in a moon," he said and walked away.

Heidi locked the door before letting out a long sigh.

The cottage suddenly seemed much homier without the added guests. She circled the room, blowing out candles, and quickly went upstairs in the dark.

Heidi collapsed on the bed, which was thick with layers of down covers and pillows. She drifted into her dreams, a final thought to herself drifting through her mind: *tomorrow, I wake up as Sylvie.*

# IX

## *First Lessons*

T he morning sunlight through the front windows caressed Sylvie's face and stirred her from sleep. Her emerging consciousness caught the scent of something delicious, which roused her definitively from her rest.

Sylvie propped herself on her elbows, her tousled hair cascading over her face and shoulders. As she squinted against the sunbeams filtering into her room, she briefly debated whether she had dreamt about the previous day's events. Looking around, she recognized the new dress and shoes she was wearing and the beautiful bed she hardly remembered falling asleep on. It had been real.

Sylvie got out of bed and used her hands to straighten the wrinkles in her dress as best as possible. She ran her fingers through her hair like a makeshift brush a handful of times and turned her attention to the subject her nose wouldn't let her forget: breakfast.

Walking into the little kitchen on the first floor, Sylvie returned Nadine's greeting and watched Nadine finish the preparations of a single place setting on the small table in the room's corner.

"Are you well rested?" Nadine asked.

"Yes, very much so," Sylvie responded. She had never once slept in a bed so comfortable, and she hadn't slept in any bed in over a moon now.

"I've made you up some breakfast," Nadine said, turning her attention back to the food and the place setting. "You have a little less than an hour before you'll be expected in the library."

"Alright, where is the library?" Sylvie asked, keenly aware that she knew nothing about her new home.

"The library is inside the palace. It shouldn't take over five minutes to get there."

Sylvie sat and began eating. Like dinner the night before, the food was delicious, combining flavors new to Sylvie. She took the time to savor a thin, flaky cake wrapped around a mixture of thickened cream with a rich floral flavor mixed with berries. In between mouthfuls of food, Sylvie asked Nadine, "Who is expecting me in the library?"

"Sir Reynard is expecting you. I don't know why. They didn't share that information with me."

"He's a scholar of some kind?"

"Sir Reynard is, well…" Nadine looked like she was struggling for the words.

*How do I put this? I'm not cut out for this,* Sylvie heard in her mind.

"You're doing fine," Sylvie said instinctively.

Nadine blushed deeply, her eyes widening in surprise and apprehension as she stared at Sylvie.

*Did she… she must have,* Sylvie heard Nadine think to herself. Sylvie kept her eyes on her plate, embarrassed that Nadine had caught her snooping, and took another bite of her breakfast.

"I…uh…thank you, Miss," Nadine finally managed. "About Sir Reynard, well, he's a bit of a historian, I suppose. You'll have to meet him for yourself. He's one of a kind."

Sylvie finished her breakfast, after which she and Nadine went upstairs, where Nadine helped her with her hair, using a gilded brush to undo what a deep night's sleep had done to Sylvie's golden locks. At Nadine's suggestion, Sylvie changed out of her dress into a sapphire blue gown, letting Nadine select jewelry and hair accessories to prepare for the day. Nadine wrapped her hair with a scarf that matched her dress. Sylvie felt the primping was unnecessary; she had never needed to worry about her appearance back home in Hull. However, Nadine assured her that as a palace guest, others would scrutinize and examine her, and how she portrayed herself mattered.

"You'll get used to it, I imagine," Nadine reassured her as she finished styling Sylvie's hair.

*I suppose I'll need to,* Sylvie thought to herself.

Sylvie followed Nadine through the front garden and out the gate onto the street on their way to the palace. It was a little before midmorning, and the autumn air was warming up, though it wasn't cold. The sky was blue and clear, with a few wisps of cloud meandering about.

The walk back to the palace was quick, returning the way they'd come the night before. Sylvie noticed a few palace staff walking about purposefully on unknown errands, but otherwise, the cobblestone streets were barren.

Upon entering the palace doors, Nadine led the way down a few lavish corridors until Sylvie found herself in front of a set of windowed double doors. Thick drapes hung on the other side of the door, obscuring any view.

"Well, here you are," Nadine said. "This is the palace library. Sir Reynard is waiting inside. I'll be back to get you for lunch." Nadine spun on her heels and hurried down the hall, out of sight.

Sylvie hesitated, her shoulders bunched up in anxious anticipation. She gingerly opened one of the library doors, which glided effortlessly on its hinges. She stepped inside and closed the door cautiously behind her, keeping her eyes on the room before her.

The room was full to the rafters with books. Covered in books, aisle upon aisle of ornate wooden bookcases filled the room. Here and there, glass cases contained what appeared to be ancient texts or artifacts. Sylvie spotted desks tucked away in remote corners of the room and a couple of sitting spaces with upholstered chairs or couches, complete with end tables covered in yet more books. Despite the large windows on the opposite side of the room and panes of multi-colored glass in the ceiling, the number of bookcases dimmed the room significantly. A host of lamps did their best to compensate for the blocked daylight.

"I will be with you in a moment!" Sylvie heard a powerful, gravelly voice boom from behind some bookshelves away to her right. Sylvie heard a chorus of heavy footsteps approaching, and it sounded like at least two individuals were making their way towards her. Ultimately, a single, towering figure emerged from the shadows between two rows of ancient tomes. He was several heads taller than even Gaëtan, who had seemed quite tall to Sylvie. Wisps of white hair draped themselves around a strong but weathered face.

After the initial shock of the sheer size of who Sylvie could only guess was Sir Reynard had worn off, she realized that by focusing so much on his height she had completely missed something even more surprising: his horse-like body. Sir Reynard was a centaur.

Sir Reynard caught the dazed look in her eyes. "Have you never met a centaur before?"

"No," Sylvie began. She was surprised not only by Sir Reynard's appearance but also because his mind reflected precisely what was coming out of his mouth.

"No?" Sir Reynard replied with a chuckle. "Don't worry, we'll get you caught up in no time." Sir Reynard had several massive leather-bound volumes in his sinewy arms, which he placed on a table close to where they were standing. He gently patted the book at the top of the stack. "We'll start with some foundational courses and then get you on an accelerated track."

Sylvie stared at the mountain of books on the table before her. "I'm sorry," she stuttered, "I didn't realize I would do any formal schooling. Am I going to read all of that?"

Sir Reynard smiled empathetically. "The answer is yes," he said, "but do not let that discourage you. There is a lot of knowledge to be gained here, and I will be your guide. I am confident you will learn quickly. That said," he continued, "there's no hiding that you are quite behind, so we can't afford much further delay."

"How behind?" Sylvie asked. She didn't know if she wanted the answer, but part of her had to know.

"Well," Sir Reynard replied, "the standard curriculum is six years, although most Verdélia only need to learn the lessons of their birth season. As a Firstborn, you must cover all seasons and some additional classes unique to your position."

Sylvie groaned. It was hopeless. "I'll never catch that up," she breathed.

"Not with an attitude like that!" Sir Reynard said kindly but forcefully. "I have taught more difficult pupils than you, I assure you. Do as I say, and you'll learn what's necessary before you know it."

Sylvie felt better. Still, the task ahead was daunting.

"After learning from you, will I know what Gaëtan, Loïc, and Margot know? I mean...," she paused. She wasn't sure how to explain herself. After taking a breath, she continued, "Will I understand the things they're talking about around me?" So far, Sylvie had felt like an infant spectator surrounded by educated foreigners when she was around the other Firstborn. She was sure she was nothing more than an ignorant hassle for the others.

Sir Reynard seemed to perceive Sylvie's unease. "I taught Gaëtan myself, seeing as he was raised in the palace after losing his parents. I also taught Loïc, though his education was not so intensive since he lived outside the palace with his family. I will teach you everything I taught them, only on an accelerated schedule. Besides," he added, his solemn gaze locked on Sylvie's face, "as the fourth of the Firstborn, there are things you will know and learn that the others never will. Likewise, they have, or will have, knowledge and skills that you never will. It is simply the nature of your roles. You are as essential as any of the other three."

Sylvie took heart in Sir Reynard's words. She would give her training her best. It was all she could do.

"Didn't you teach Margot too?" Sylvie asked. She found it odd that Sir Reynard had mentioned the other two by name but not Margot.

"Yes, in part." Sir Reynard answered. "As an imp, Margot received the core curriculum lessons at the university. Being unable to use éthéra, she only partially accepted my offer for further education."

"Is that why she's so...cold?" Sylvie asked, "Being an imp? Whatever that is..."

"Margot's very existence is a paradox," Sir Reynard mused, his eyes lost in thought. "As a Firstborn, she is among the most powerful Verdélia ever to exist. As an imp, she cannot harness or manipulate éthéra. Thus, although she is both Firstborn and imp, she is neither. She does not feel as though she belongs either among the four of you as a Firstborn or among the imps. I do not envy her struggle."

"Coming from a human upbringing, I can understand that—at least a little. I still don't feel like I belong among the Verdélia." Sylvie said somberly. "What makes her an imp?"

"An imp," Sir Reynard paused, "Is a fallen Verdélia. They are Verdélian children born in unfortunate circumstances through no fault of their own. But because of that tragedy, they live without the ability to harness the powers that you so easily can adopt. They have no éthéra. You will recognize them by the yellow hue of their eyes. It is a universal mark on those of Verdélian heritage who lack the harnessing ability: Imps."

"No magic, you mean?" Sylvie clarified.

"Yes. The proper name in the ancient tongue was èthèra. Now, to continue, the fact remains that you are Verdélian and, as such, have the innate abilities that you are expected to have as a Firstborn. Margot is not so lucky."

"She sure seems confident for such a conflicted person," Sylvie stated.

Sir Reynard nodded, "Although I believe that is partially a facade, Margot has certain abilities inherent in her role as Firstborn, separate from éthéra. With that said, only your abilities will ultimately be able to confirm my suspicions about Margot's role, as hers have not been made clear yet."

"What do I have to do with Margot's role?" Sylvie asked, head cocked to the side and one eyebrow raised.

"I suppose this is as good a setting as any for a first lesson on the Firstborn," Sir Reynard said. "At the dawn of creation, the Maker planted five seeds in the earth. Those seeds sprouted and grew to become the first generation of Firstborn, the first Verdélia to walk this world."

"Hold on," Sylvie interrupted. "Everyone has been saying that I am the last of the *four* Firstborn to be found. There were originally five. Where is the fifth?"

"We'll get to that," Sir Reynard said matter-of-factly, "Be patient and let me finish."

"Yes, sir," Sylvie said.

"As I was saying," Sir Reynard continued, "the first generation of Firstborn grew and sprouted. Four of those Firstborn, the four that we will concern ourselves with for this lesson, were given control over the elements that comprise this world: air, fire, earth, and water."

"Sephora was the Firstborn given control of the air." Sir Reynard opened an ancient volume to a page inscribed with a beautiful golden bird flying through a thundercloud. "Sephora is represented by the thunderbird and created creatures of the sky. Sylphs and pixies, magical peoples who inhabit this world, owe their existence to Sephora. She is represented by gold and diamond."

"What does 'litel parchon' mean?" Sylvie asked, noting the text on a crest on the page with the thunderbird.

"'Litel parchon' is a phrase in the old language that means 'like lightning,'" Sir Reynard replied. "Sephora's role was to preside, but not rule, over the Verdélia in goodness and wisdom. The role requires a bold, bright presence. Gaëtan fills that role today. His primary responsibility is to work hand in hand with councilors and judges to establish the law of the land."

"I can see that," Sylvie said, glancing towards Sir Reynard.

"Loïc fills the role of Josias, who was given control over the element of fire." Sir Reynard turned to a page darkened by the color of black metal, highlighted in deep scarlet red. "Josias gave life to perhaps the most mythical of all creatures, the dragon, though their continued existence may be only a legend these days. He is represented by the black metal ténébril and rubies. The inscription, 'im haritelle pou tilent,' means 'all things for the good' and references Josias's role as one of service to, and protection of, the people. His role includes the assurance of order and service to others, encouraging others to look outside of themselves for the good of their fellow beings."

Sylvie grimaced, "Alright."

"You disagree?"

"No, he seems willing to help. He's helping Margot presently, correct?"

"Yes, but you don't seem convinced."

"He seems so...irritated by it all. It seemed like a chore, but I suppose we all have our moments."

"Don't let an abrasive exterior fool you," Sir Reynard replied. "Although he certainly has much to learn—as do you all, I might add—Loïc has a sense of duty for which you would be hard-pressed to find an equal."

The following page was primarily emerald, with silver accents.

"This is the crest of Demetrius," Sir Reynard explained. "His symbol is that of the chamigua, a large magical lizard noted for its brilliant appearance, but even more so for its intelligence and wisdom, which it would bestow upon select individuals—represented by silver and emeralds. Fittingly, the crest reads 'pés kiren rhati jet,' or, in other words, 'by reason, not force,' implying a power to compel through reason, logic, and persuasion. Demetrius would do this in his relation to other creatures and cultures. He had the power of prophecy."

"And who falls into that role? Me or Margot?" Sylvie asked.

"As I mentioned, I have my suspicions," Sir Reynard said, "but I believe you will know for certain in a moment." He turned the page, revealing deep blues and metallic accents of copper.

"Morwenna and her mermaid," Sir Reynard said. "Morwenna's motto, 'sébelle pou fecil haritelle' means 'hope for better things,' and embodies Morwenna's deeply empathetic nature and concern for all things living. Part of this unique concern for others stemmed from an ability unique to Morwenna: the ability to know the innermost thoughts of others." Sir Reynard looked at Sylvie for confirmation. Her face told him everything he needed to know.

"And that confirms it," he stated. "You are Morwenna. Which means Margot is the spiritual successor of Demetrius, which I have suspected all along as well."

"But how will I know how to fulfill my particular role?" Sylvie asked. How was she to be the spiritual descendant of some semi-divine Verdélian royalty?

"You will know because the spirit of Morwenna is within you." Sir Reynard replied. "It is an integral part of who you are."

Sylvie sat silently, staring at the crest of the mermaid on the page in front of her. The weight of the responsibility seemed to grow ever larger, something Sylvie didn't think possible.

"Come, let's begin your first *official* lesson now." Sir Reynard said.

"Very well," Sylvie said gloomily.

Not for the first time, Sylvie thought leaving Hull might have been a mistake.

# X

## *Leeks*

Sylvie let her armful of books drop onto the low table in the front room of her cottage with a dull, heavy thud, then plopped herself down into the cushioned armchair near the fireplace.

Sylvie had spent several hours with Sir Reynard, who had given her a heavy load of coursework and expected quick progress in a short amount of time. Sylvie certainly felt out of her depth, but an undeniable excitement was linked to all the new things she would be learning. Leaning forward, she turned her head to the side to re-read the titles on the spines of the textbooks in front of her.

Sir Reynard had assigned her five main courses, all tied to the titles in front of her: History and Lore: The 1ˢᵗ Millennium, Éthéra and the Elements: Air, Creatures of the Air, which Sir Reynard had explained, were foundational topics. Botanical Basics: Crops, and Life: Introductory Properties, were the autumn seasonal topics Sir Reynard had assigned her. He had explained that since they were in the autumn season; he had assigned her reading specific to the season which she could observe in the world around her as she studied, to appreciate better the applications of what she was learning. It excited Sylvie to try it.

There was a knock at the door, and Nadine, accompanied by another palace staff member, entered Sylvie's cottage.

"Good afternoon, Miss Sylvie," she said over a stack of six books high, which she was carrying in front of her with both arms.

"Sir Reynard sent me to deliver these which you are to, in his own words, 'study more casually than your foundational coursework, time permitting.'"

Sylvie felt her excitement dwindle rapidly in the face of the added workload.

"Thanks, Nadine," she managed anyway.

"I've brought you some lunch as well," Nadine continued. The palace staff who had accompanied Nadine uncovered a dish and placed it on the table in front of Sylvie. It revealed a salad neatly dressed with deep, vibrant greens and what appeared to be an assortment of nuts, all topped with crumbly cheese. Sylvie's stomach just about roared. Her lesson with Sir Reynard had gone well past lunchtime.

"Thank you," Sylvie said. "You can leave those books here as well."

"Very well," Nadine said, gently placing the books in the last space on the table in front of Sylvie.

"Unless you need anything else, I'll leave you to your lunch and your studies and will plan to come fetch you for supper," Nadine added.

Sylvie swallowed a mouthful of food before responding.

"That'll work just fine, thank you, Nadine," she said.

"You're welcome, Miss," Nadine said with a brief bow before turning on her heels and heading out the door.

Nadine had just exited the cottage's front door when a thought broke through Sylvie's consciousness: *Oops, clumsy me, get out of the way.* Sylvie recognized Nadine's "voice." Sylvie heard Nadine speak aloud, "I'm so sorry."

Next, Sylvie heard Gaëtan's voice: "No worries, Nadine. Thank you for all of your help with Sylvie. Have a nice day."

Gaëtan strode into the cottage and gave Sylvie a smile and a quick bow.

"Good afternoon, Sylvie!" He said enthusiastically.

Sylvie tried to choke down her mouthful of salad while standing instinctively.

"Oh, no need for that. I'm sorry to have interrupted your lunch," Gaëtan said, approaching the fireplace. "Please, sit, enjoy your meal," he said.

Sylvie sat back in her seat and returned to her salad, a little more conscientious of the size of her mouthfuls. Meanwhile, Gaëtan picked up the book on top of the large stack on the table in the middle of the room.

"I see Sir Reynard has got your studies well underway," he said, flipping through the book's pages randomly. "Everyone remembers the foundational courses," he said with a nostalgic grin.

"With all the basics you're catching up on, is Sir Reynard having you do seasonal study as well?" Gaëtan asked.

Sylvie nodded. "I'm studying autumn. Sir Reynard thought it would be a good idea since I could observe what I'm learning in the real world, seeing as we're in autumn now." She hesitated. "Although, to be fair, I'm not sure what I'm looking for."

Gaëtan smiled, "Well, you could start in the garden," he proposed.

"What garden?" Sylvie asked, perplexed.

"Yours, of course." Gaëtan chuckled. "It looks like you've just about finished your lunch. Follow me, and I'll show you."

Gaëtan led her towards the back of the cottage, where a door led out. Sylvie hadn't noticed it until now.

After passing through the door, Sylvie had to squint against the strong afternoon sunlight. Once her eyes adjusted to the brightness, she noticed that behind the cottage was a little fenced-in yard, filled chiefly with well-kept grass, shrubs, and flowers. A path leading from the cottage went straight towards the back of the yard, where a slightly raised bed of dark earth sat empty.

"Every cottage has its own yard," Gaëtan explained, "and each comes with its own garden. The idea is for the Verdélia to be self-sufficient where possible. Besides," he added, walking to the plot of earth and sinking his hand into the ground, "it's fun."

Sylvie smiled. Amidst all the new, it was nice to find something familiar.

"I had a meeting unexpectedly canceled, which means I have nothing planned this afternoon," Gaëtan said, "so why don't I help you with some of your coursework? We can do some practical application. Plus, I have a field trip of sorts in mind."

Sylvie hesitated, "Well, honestly, I haven't even had time to tackle any of my seasonal reading. You might be putting the cart before the horse with your practical applications." She paused. "But I do like gardening," Sylvie confessed. "What kind of field trip are we talking about?"

Gaëtan's eyebrows furrowed at the expression. Sylvie remembered that there were no carts meant for horses amongst the Verdélia. She set the expression aside in her mind to avoid future confusion. "I think you could use a visit to the city!" Gaëtan grinned. "Come with me!"

⚘

Gaëtan strode confidently down the streets of Verdélys, maintaining a pace that had Sylvie struggling to keep up.

"So," Gaëtan said, "how are you adjusting to Verdélys?"

Sylvie thought for a moment before answering. "Well," she said, "I've been so busy, honestly, that I have thought little about it. The comforts are certainly nice, though. I've never seen, let alone stayed in, any home as nice as what you're calling a cottage. The food is delicious. Almost nauseating sometimes because it's so... overwhelming. And there's plenty to read." She chuckled at her joke.

Gaëtan laughed, "That there is! And then some!"

Sylvie smiled. She hadn't had a casual conversation in over a month. Ever since Ancelin had shown up in Hull, the only topic of discussion had been the Verdélia, the Firstborn, and her role in the lot. It was nice to get back to normal, or as close as she could, in this new life.

Sylvie asked, "What does everyone do in Verdélys when not buried under a mountain of books?"

"Now that's a proper question!" Gaëtan answered excitedly. "Honestly, Verdélys has something to offer for everyone. If you asked Loïc or Margot, I'm sure they'd each have their own answers to tell you."

"I'll keep that in mind," Sylvie said. "What about for you?"

"I'm a bit of an amateur patron of the arts if you will," Gaëtan responded.

"Like painting?" Sylvie asked, a bit confused. There wasn't much art in Hull other than the occasional rough-hewn wooden sculpture or home-spun tapestry. The bigger human cities produced the occasional painter or sculptor, but those were limited to the nobility or wealthy.

"Well, yes, among other things," Gaëtan explained. "Although, if I'm to be honest, my genuine passion is for the theater."

Sylvie gave Gaëtan a puzzled look. "The what?"

"You know," Gaëtan replied, perplexed, "the theater?"

Sylvie shrugged, "No, I don't know. What is that?"

"Humans don't have theater?" Gaëtan asked incredulously. "Poor lot."

"Well," he continued, "the theater is the best way to tell a story if you ask me. There are plays where people act out certain stories. Then there are ballets, which are like plays but put to dance. Then there are concerts, which are musical performances. They're all quite splendid. You'll have to attend some time."

"Sounds fancy," Sylvie replied, "I don't know that I'd fit in."

"Nonsense," Gaëtan answered. "All you have to do is attend and enjoy the show. I'm sure we can organize something for you if you'd like. It would be a great way to familiarize yourself with Verdélian culture."

"Perhaps," Sylvie said. "It sounds fun."

Looking around, Sylvie realized they were reaching the gate that separated the palace and the inner city from the rest of Verdélys. A dozen guards in gleaming armor were posted around the gate and inside of the guardhouse built into the thick stone wall.

One guard gestured towards the guardhouse as Gaëtan and Sylvie approached. Seemingly on its own, the gate parted silently, revealing the bustle of the outer city.

As Gaëtan and Sylvie passed through the open gate, Sylvie recognized Alfric standing watch outside the gate again.

"Good afternoon, Alfric," Gaëtan called out. "How are you today?"

"Well, Master Gaëtan," Alfric replied with a curt bow.

"Have you volunteered yourself to the front gate permanently?" Gaëtan joked.

"Given the current situation, I like to be on the first line of the palace defense whenever possible." Alfric's face was dead serious, as if chiseled out of stone.

"I hope the men don't take your service for granted. We sure don't." With that, Gaëtan gave Alfric a brisk bow of his head.

The gesture seemed to throw off Alfric's stony facade for a moment. Sylvie blinked, and Alfric returned to his sober self, standing stoically at the gate.

"How does the bowing work here?" Sylvie asked. "Are we supposed to bow to Alfric?"

"Not according to traditional societal norms," Gaëtan admitted. "Greeting with a bow is only expected from the seasonal Verdélia to the Firstborn. That said, I find many of the seasonal Verdélia deserve the recognition and respect associated with the gesture, where appropriate."

"What should I be doing then? For example, Loïc doesn't even seem to recognize the people who bow to him. In fact," Sylvie grimaced, "Loïc doesn't seem to recognize most people at all."

"I suspect you will come to do the same eventually," Gaëtan replied. "When it's what is done day in and day out, you stop noticing it. That said," Gaëtan added, "don't let Loïc's demeanor fool you. He is dedicated to the Verdélia, and much of what appears to be a lack of patience or empathy is the weight of the many responsibilities he feels obligated to take on personally."

Sylvie was quiet for a moment. "Sir Reynard said something similar."

"Don't worry about it," Gaëtan reassured her. "You just barely got here. You'll have plenty of time to get to know everyone, especially the three of us other Firstborn. Besides," he added, "it's taken me some time to get used to being around Margot. Now, though, I can honestly say I think of Margot as a friend. It's part of life learning to work with people who aren't quite like us."

"You're right, of course," Sylvie said. "Still, easy for you to say. You seem genuinely happy to see and talk to anyone. I'm not so naturally gifted with being pleasantly outgoing."

Gaëtan laughed, "Well, it's partially personality, but it's been a learned skill, too. Anyway, everyone brings their strengths to the table. I'm sure you have talents that would escape me."

"Maybe," Sylvie mumbled, "but I feel like it will take me forever to figure out just what those are. Look at you; how long have you known you were a Firstborn?"

"My whole life," Gaëtan said matter-of-factly. "I was raised in the palace from hours after my birth. I lost my parents in the struggles that came up during the imp uprising the year of our birth."

"Oh," Sylvie said quietly. "I'm sorry. I didn't mean to broach such a sensitive subject."

"That's alright," Gaëtan replied. "I've made peace with that part of my past, or as much as I can for now."

"This war," Sylvie asked, "is it the same one that chased my mother halfway across the world and landed me in Hull? What caused it?"

Gaëtan's face was serious. "It is the same. Although the details of the war are too complex to get into right now, the short of it is that the Verdélia have been in social turmoil and decline for decades, at least. As a result, the imp population has grown to unprecedented heights over the last hundred years. A faction arose among the imps, inciting violence against the Verdélia. This faction believed that the imps' inability to harness and manipulate éthéra was somehow an injustice perpetrated by the Verdélia, specifically the Firstborn. On the year when the new generation of Firstborn was to be born, the year of our," Gaëtan gestured to Sylvie and himself, "birth, the imps rose up and tried to destroy or steal any seedling that could have yielded a Firstborn birth.

"Luckily, they were unsuccessful. The four Firstborn were brought into the world, as you know. That said, three out of the four of us lost our parents, and Margot, the least fortunate of us all, lost her parents before blooming. As a result, she was born an imp, yet still a Firstborn, something no one thought possible."

"Margot never met her parents? So, of the four of us, only Loïc has a family?" Sylvie asked incredulously.

"That's right," Gaëtan said. "Margot was born an imp because her seed was abandoned or lost, likely because her parents fell victim to the war, although no one really knows what happened to them for sure. A Verdélian seed that goes uncared for doesn't yield a Verdélian child; it yields an imp."

"Her seed?" Sylvie asked timidly, but the question went unheard.

"As for Loïc, he is the only Firstborn with any known living family. They live in the summer district. They're a wonderful family. I'm sure you'll meet them sooner rather than later."

Sylvie was trying to keep all the new information straight in her mind. Between this conversation with Gaëtan and her studies, she felt like she was drowning in new knowledge.

As the conversation subsided, Sylvie looked around her and noticed they were walking among autumn-colored cottages. The roofs were thatched all in hues ranging from light champagne or gold to deep ambers and reds. Although the homes were primarily close together, Sylvie noticed the occasional field full of grains or other crops swaying in the afternoon breeze.

Gaëtan led Sylvie down a few streets and finally onto an open square. There were fields on every side, and in the square itself, there were no buildings, only a couple dozen handcarts of different shapes and sizes, each loaded with bags and crates of indistinguishable wares. Sylvie could only guess this was some sort of Verdélian market.

"Here we are," Gaëtan said, "we'll be able to get you everything you need for your first practical lesson on crops in one trip."

Gaëtan walked straight towards a cart prominently placed closer to the middle of the square, which was being tended to by an elderly woman. As he passed, merchants and shoppers alike turned towards Gaëtan and respectfully bowed their heads before returning to their tasks. Everyone eyed Sylvie curiously. She hurried to keep pace with Gaëtan, hoping to use him as a shield from the strangers' gazes.

"Madam Therese," Gaëtan said cheerfully, "How are you this afternoon?"

The old woman perked up, her eyes recognizing a familiar voice.

"Gaëtan, is that you?" She called out with a smile. "It is! My, my, what a pleasant surprise. It's been quite some time since I've seen you around here. I was thinking you'd forgotten about me!"

"Forget about you?" Gaëtan feigned offense. "How could I? Why, when my friend here realized she needed some gardening supplies, you were the first person to come to mind!"

"Oh, ho!" Madam Therese said, eyeing Sylvie, "Who is this Gaëtan? She's quite a beauty, isn't she?"

Sylvie blushed awkwardly. She hoped Gaëtan would correct the old woman because she didn't dare.

"Sylvie's my cousin, Madam Therese," Gaëtan said with a chuckle.

"Is that so?" Madam Therese answered, slightly deflated. "Still, a pretty cousin at that, and a friend is better than none."

"Agreed," Gaëtan said. "Now, what do you have in terms of autumn seeds?"

"You should know better than to ask such a question, boy!" she answered in friendly indignation. "I wouldn't be the finest merchant of gardening goods in these parts if I didn't carry the largest selection of seeds for any season. Take your pick. I'm sure I've got any seed you could ask for."

Gaëtan turned to Sylvie, "Any favorites? Now's your chance."

Sylvie thought of Hull and the vegetables she had grown on her parents' farm.

"Do you have any leeks?" She asked.

The old lady's eyes shone briefly with a curious look. Gaëtan seemed suddenly nervous.

"Leeks, eh?" Madame Therese said. "That's not one I get a lot of requests for. Hasn't been commonly grown among the Verdélia for quite some time, has it Gaëtan?"

"Uh, no, indeed not." Gaëtan chuckled awkwardly, his beaming confidence shaken. "Sylvie is a guest. She's visiting Verdélys for a time."

Madame Therese smiled, unconvinced. She drew a small canvas bag out of the back of her cart.

"Here we are," she said, "leek seeds. You're not likely to find any of these around these parts." She went to hand the bag to Sylvie, but as Sylvie went to take the seeds, Madame Therese grabbed her wrists firmly. In a calm tone, Madame Therese added, "In fact, you're not likely to find these anywhere west of the mountains, are you now?"

Sylvie looked at Gaëtan with wide eyes.

Madame Therese released Sylvie and looked closely at Sylvie, then to Gaëtan, then back to Sylvie. Finally, she spoke again.

"I may not know exactly who you are, young lady, or what business you have with Gaëtan, but I've been around the block one time too many to be fooled that easily. Visiting, ha! But don't worry, your secret is safe with me."

"Much appreciated, Madame Therese," Gaëtan said with a sigh. "Now, might we get a few more seeds and supplies and be on our way?"

"But of course," Madame Therese smiled, "and this time, perhaps a bit more discretion in your choices?" She winked at Sylvie.

🏃

Sylvie and Gaëtan returned to the palace, the setting sun casting long shadows on the cobblestones. Gaëtan had paid for their supplies, and they were heading back to the palace with arms full. Gaëtan carried heavy bags full of garden soil and fertilizing supplements. Sylvie had her arms full of various seeds and a variety of gardening tools.

"Sorry about the leeks," Sylvie said. "Was that a mistake?"

Gaëtan chuckled, "Leeks aren't a common Verdélian crop. The few you can find around Verdélys are almost all imported indirectly from the other side of the mountains, through the southern cities, which still have limited dealings with the humans. Long story short, it's known as a human crop around here."

"I'm sorry." Sylvie felt foolish. "I didn't know."

"I guess we couldn't have expected you to," Gaëtan shrugged. "Still, let's hope Madame Therese keeps her word and keeps her suspicions to herself."

🏃

Back in Sylvie's cottage garden, Gaëtan was setting out their newly acquired supplies while Sylvie reviewed the introductory basics to crop care found in the texts Sir Reynard had loaned her. It all seemed intimidating to her, with intricate diagrams and charts explaining the various moon phases and other elements that governed and influenced optimal plant growth and yield.

"Gardening was never this complicated in Hull," she groaned.

Gaëtan looked up. "So, you have some experience, at least? Any experience using éthéra in your gardening?"

"Sure, plenty. I taught myself, and, well, compared to your average human, I'd say I was quite the witch." Sylvie giggled at her joke.

"Witch? Yes, I'm sure you were!" He said through a broad grin. "Ok, let's see what you've got!"

Sylvie grabbed some of the seeds that were most familiar to her, beets and turnips, and began placing them in the dirt. Gaëtan watched quietly as she demonstrated her skills. He pulled something from his pocket and popped it in his mouth, offering her one.

"What is it?" She asked.

"A sweet. Lavender. Great, if you're stressed." He held a small transparent candy out to her, pressed into an imperfect disc. Sylvie could see the lavender buds within the candy and thanked him as she popped the candy into her mouth. The disc was soft and chewy, but as her teeth hit the lavender within, it let out a small *crack* as she bit down. She felt an almost immediate relaxing sensation emanate from her mouth and down her arms. Her eyes grew wide.

Glancing toward Gaëtan, he smiled, popping another candy in his mouth. "There's a lot for you to discover here, and if I can be of any use, it will be in the sweets department. Never mind that, anyway. Moving on."

Sylvie smiled as she swallowed her candy and returned to the task at hand. She began with the beets. She worked with them as she had back in Hull, feeling an uncomfortable longing for her garden beyond the mountains. She pushed that feeling as far from her mind as she could manage and consciously tried to incorporate the instructions from her textbooks into her gardening. Her hand spread over the seeds as she lifted slowly from the earth, and tiny sprouts began coming up. She turned her hand over until her fingers pointed towards the sky. She continued raising her arm slowly, and as she did, the green of the beet extended taller and taller. A couple of tiny leaves unfurled themselves from the little growing *sprouts*.

"You taught yourself that?" Gaëtan asked, popping another candy into his mouth. She nodded. "It's superb. You're a natural. That's great. There are a few things, though. No, don't be disappointed," he shook his head at Sylvie's drop in countenance, "Here. I'll show you with the turnips."

He grabbed her hand to hold it over the buried turnip seeds. "Similar plant, nearly identical process." He put his hand atop hers, outstretched. "Do the same by raising your hand from the ground slowly, but fan your fingers and wiggle them a bit. Yeah, you'll feel ridiculous," he laughed. Sprouts began coming up, "The movement encourages the sprouts to weasel their way through the dirt better, and you'll get a better yield. The next step is normally called 'fingertip to sky.' You did that perfectly, no correction from me. Fantastic." He turned her hand over, his still cradling hers from the outside as they raised their hands towards the clouds. He let go, getting down on his stomach next to her. She obliged. And they put their hands near the base of the plant together, his hand wrapped around hers.

"Now, instead of just expanding your hand, you must expand one finger at a time. This allows each ring of the turnip to expand to the largest state it can while retaining flavor." He pulled back his pointer finger, making room for hers. Then the next, and the next. When they finished, Sylvie pulled her hand from his and pulled the turnip from the ground. It was healthier. Larger.

"Should we taste it?" he asked by her side.

"What, just bite into it?" She glanced at him.

"Well, you'll have to awaken it first." He pointed towards it.

"I've never done that before," Sylvie shook her head.

"Ahh, well, awakening, or the breath of life, as it is otherwise referred to. Well, square up to it," Sylvie was still lying on her stomach. She gripped the bulb of the turnip with both hands. "Right, then you just blow on it."

"Hot or cold air?" She asked awkwardly.

"Pucker and blow." Sylvie made a face and smiled, listening to the further instruction: "The éthéra that you use with your hands to grow your plants. Just concentrate that through your breath."

Sylvie nodded and blew towards the turnip. She immediately felt the uneasy and nauseating effect of the turnip in her hands and turned her face away.

"It takes getting used to," Gaëtan acknowledged. "Every detail of the plant is enhanced—the scent, the flavor, the color." Sylvie glanced back at the turnip. It seemed more vibrant. "I imagine," he continued, "that's the reason you enjoy the food so well here."

"It is likely," Sylvie acknowledged. The nausea had subsided, and she took a bite out of the turnip—*awakened.*

# XI

*An Unexpected Bud*

S ylvie had spent many evenings and nights working in the garden under
Gaëtan's tutelage. Overall, she felt she had done pretty well, and Gaëtan
seemed impressed with her abilities as a self-taught learner. Gaëtan helped her
learn things she was vaguely familiar with in practice but had never fully
considered. Primarily, he had explained that the core of Verdélian "magic" was
the harnessing and guiding of the éthéra that already existed in the world rather
than creating éthéra supernaturally. When she thought about it, this made
sense to Sylvie, as this was always what she had implicitly done in practice.

Over the weeks, Sylvie's abilities had improved significantly. Her leek crop
(Gaëtan had recommended they be planted between two rows of tall corn for
discretion) was already sprouting heartily and, by human standards, several
months along. Her corn was already reaching her knees, and her other crops
were all faring similarly well. Gaëtan suggested that at this rate, she would
finish her gardening courses well ahead of schedule.

🦎

Sylvie woke with a throbbing pain in her right temple. Clutching her head,
she rolled over with a moan, oblivious to the fact she had fallen asleep on the
edge of the bed the night before. She hit the wooden floor with a thump.

A few moments later, there was a knock at the door, and Nadine's voice came
through: "Miss Sylvie, are you alright in there?"

Sylvie had to think for a minute, then replied groggily, "For the most part."

"May I come in?" Nadine asked.

"One moment," Sylvie said in a daze, gathering herself up off the floor and
heaving her heavy down blanket back onto the bed. "All right, come on in," she
called.

Nadine came into the bedroom and bowed courteously. She noticed Sylvie holding the side of her head and asked again, "Are you sure you're all right?"

"It's just a headache, I suppose," Sylvie said. "I'm sure it'll disappear after a good breakfast and some water."

Nadine moved Sylvie's hand and swept Sylvie's blonde hair behind her ear. Gold dust fluttered through the morning sunlight around them and drifted slowly to the floor. *Sure enough*, Sylvie heard Nadine think to herself.

"I wouldn't be so sure about that," Nadine said aloud.

"Huh? What's wrong?" Sylvie asked, poking the side of her head curiously. With her hair out of the way, she could indeed feel a lump above and a bit in front of her ear. She made a face and asked Nadine, "What on earth is that? It wasn't there yesterday."

"You're blooming, Miss Sylvie. It's quite natural. For the time being, we'll keep it covered with a headscarf."

"Blooming? Am I supposed to know what that means?"

Nadine looked away and stuttered, "I...well, that's what the dust is for. It fertilizes the flower so that it can bloom. That's why the headscarves. I'm sorry, I'm botching this explanation. You should ask someone more eloquent."

"Ok, well, who would you suggest?" Sylvie rubbed at her temple, and more gold dust drifted lazily from her head, glowing in the shafts of morning sun beaming through the windows.

"I would ask Sir Reynard. He can give you an answer or get you to a book that can," Nadine said. "Now, if you don't mind, let's get you ready. Master Gaëtan has asked that I have you at the palace for breakfast with the Firstborn this morning."

"I'm guessing he didn't tell you why?" Sylvie asked.

Nadine shook her head and gestured for Sylvie to sit at the vanity so that Nadine could help her with her hair.

※

Less than a half hour later, Sylvie and Nadine were on their way to the palace. Upon inspection in the mirror, Sylvie had noticed that there was indeed an odd bump protruding ever so slightly from the side of her head. It reminded Sylvie of a plant bud, where recent growth, such as a branch or flower, would form on the primary plant stem. Nadine had reassured her it was nothing to worry about, all while providing nearly nothing regarding answers. Nadine had carefully swept Sylvie's hair back over the sides of her head, covering her ears, and pinned the lot under a silky lavender scarf with a pearl-studded clasp.

As Sylvie and Nadine entered the dining hall, Gaëtan sat reviewing a pile of important-looking documents while munching on a scone. A man stood behind him, referencing the documents and making comments.

"Are you sure that is what you would like done in this case? There are better ways." *Beyern will not be pleased.* Sylvie recognized the man as she got closer; he was the man who had been discussing things with Gaëtan outside of their office the day she had arrived. Thibault.

"No, I'm sure," Gaëtan insisted. "The imps need more help, not less. We can't continue to push them away."

"It is ultimately your decision," Thibault responded.

Reaching the table, Gaëtan looked up, stood, and gave a bow.

"Welcome, ladies," he said with a smile, "and good morning. Sylvie, please sit. Thibault, this is my cousin, Sylvie. Sylvie, this is Thibault, my advisor. He has held this position since my childhood."

Sylvie came and sat opposite Gaëtan, and Nadine scurried off. "It's nice to meet you." Sylvie smiled.

"A pleasure," Thibault nodded, though no smile crossed his face, just a repeated thought: *Beyern will not be pleased.*

"Good," Gaëtan nodded, "Thibault, you are excused. I will call for you after my meal."

Thibault nodded and exited the room swiftly.

"How did you sleep after an evening of intense gardening?" Gaëtan asked.

"Rather well," Sylvie said, "though I've woken up with a terrible headache, I'm afraid, along with a lump on the side of my head that Nadine can't seem to explain to me in simple terms."

Gaëtan chuckled, "Sir Reynard will fill you in."

Sylvie huffed. Before she could protest, Margot walked in, regal as ever, with her signature look of general boredom for the world on her face.

"What a horrible hour to be awake," Margot said as she slowly made her way to the table.

"Margot, good morning to you too," Gaëtan said without missing a beat.

"Breakfast had better be exceptionally good," Margot replied. Sylvie noticed that Margot also had her hair pinned over the side of her head like she did. Sylvie thought she saw what appeared to be a few flecks of an ashen, soot-like substance mingled in Margot's strands of copper-red hair.

"It's always good," Gaëtan chided, gesturing to a palace staff member attending the door. The doors swung open, and breakfast made its way out to the three Firstborn. The smell hit Sylvie before she could see what was for breakfast, and her mouth watered. Once on her plate, Sylvie went right at it, enjoying a piping hot, flaky roll with a sweet butter-like spread with a nutty flavor she couldn't quite place but devoured all the same. There was a delightfully tangy, deep purple juice and some helpings of cheese and candied fruits. Before she knew it, Sylvie had emptied her plate. Looking up, she noticed Margot staring at her in disgust.

"There's more, you know." Margot scoffed, "You're not in Hull anymore."

Sylvie wiped gingerly at the corners of her mouth with a napkin, trying to conceal her embarrassment. She took courage when she noticed that Gaëtan hardly looked up from his pile of papers.

Margot turned her contempt towards Gaëtan. "Alright, noble Master Gaëtan, why are we here?" she said sarcastically.

Gaëtan picked up his papers and tapped them against the table, shuffling them into a neat stack.

"As you know, Margot," Gaëtan stated, "and as you're about to learn, Sylvie, the winter district has been petitioning for some time to have us fill the vacant Firstborn position with a steward."

Margot rolled her eyes. "Uh, this again," she said with disgust.

"Yes, this again," Gaëtan agreed, "except this time, they've made a formal request under Verdélian law."

"Oh," Margot sat up a bit, her face just barely betraying a sense of concerned surprise.

Lost, Sylvie remained silent as the conversation seemed too crucial to interrupt.

Gaëtan continued, "They just so happened to perfectly time their request with Loïc's departure as well," he sighed, "although whether that's a coincidence, I can only guess."

"Wait a minute," Margot said, her eyes turning to Sylvie, "we can nip this in the bud right now! We've got Firstborn number four right here," she said, gesturing to Sylvie.

Sylvie shrunk back, uneasy with the realization she was the topic of conversation.

"I..." she mumbled, "what's this got to do with me?"

"Well," Gaëtan started, "as you now know, for all of Verdélian history, the Verdélia have been governed by four Firstborn."

"For *most* of Verdélian history, Gaëtan," Margot chided.

"Yes, well, technically that's true, Margot, but if it's alright with you, I don't think we need to get into the minutia of Verdélian history right now," Gaëtan responded.

"Whatever," Margot huffed.

"Anyway," Gaëtan started again, "for our present purposes, there have always been four Firstborn. The entire structure of Verdélian society revolves around it."

Gaëtan took a sip from his glass before continuing.

"Although it's rarely been used, there is a process under Verdélian law to appoint a Verdélian steward in the event of a vacancy among the four Firstborn. Any one or more of the Verdélian districts can lodge a formal petition to appoint a steward. Once the petition has been submitted, each district has fifteen days to present a nominee for the stewardship. The Firstborn then have until the next moon after the filing of the petition to select from among the nominees who will serve as steward."

"Or," Margot interjected, "fill the vacancy with an actual Firstborn." She looked at Sylvie with wide eyes, emphasizing her point. "This is ridiculous. There is no vacancy among the Firstborn. Publicly present her, and problem solved!"

"It is not just that, though, Margot. They want to replace you as well." Gaëtan's face looked solemn.

"Excuse me?" Margot was indignant.

"The petition names two positions that they claim we failed to fill: the daughters of Demetrius and Morwenna. One is an imp with no reigning power, and one is absent. It's unprecedented, as is our situation."

"How dare they!" Margot fumed.

"I understand your frustration," Gaëtan said, placing his hand over Margot's on the table. "I will rule your petition as moot since your position is filled. It would be ideal if Loïc were here to confirm, but we must make do. For you, though, Sylvie, we will need to present you formally before the next moon to avoid a council member taking your place."

Gaëtan paused, then started again.

"I know you're getting a good start on your studies. Has Sir Reynard given you an estimated deadline for the completion of your basic introduction to Verdélian history and culture?"

"He suggested that based on his accelerated curriculum, I could finish the basics by the first winter moon," Sylvie answered.

"Hmmm...." Gaëtan sat back in his chair; his eyes turned towards the ceiling in thought. "Any chance you can do it before the winter moons? I wonder because you will immediately take on judicial responsibilities that have been waiting for Morwenna for nearly twenty years. You should know, at minimum, the basics before taking on the responsibility."

"I...," Sylvie stammered, "I don't know. I can try." She didn't even know what she didn't know, let alone whether she could speed up her already sped-up course schedule.

"I'll talk to Sir Reynard about working with you to prioritize the basics for now. Some of the other classes might have to wait for the time being," Gaëtan said. He sat lost in thought for another moment.

"We'll introduce you at the Festival of Flowers in just seventeen days' time," Gaëtan said.

"*Sooo* perfect," Margot drawled out with a sigh.

"What's the Festival of Flowers?" Sylvie asked.

"A pathetic social gathering for the pompous extrovert." Margot mocked.

Gaëtan shot Margot a look of disappointment, his eyebrows furrowed. He turned to Sylvie, his face regaining its jovial demeanor.

"The Festival of Flowers is one of the traditional Verdélian holidays, celebrating the end of the blooming season. Everyone dresses in their best, and it is typically celebrated with excellent food, dancing, and other games and entertainment. There's a party hosted at the palace every year for the occasion where we dress up the gardens extraordinarily, and many honorary guests attend. It's quite the affair."

"If you're into that sort of snobbery," Margot retorted.

"Come now, Margot," Gaëtan scolded, "it's fun. Please don't listen to her, Sylvie. The timing will be perfect. Your bloom will be an unmistakable proof of your Firstborn status."

"My bloom?" Sylvie questioned.

Margot snickered, "Oh, please tell me this is a joke. No one has talked to her about this?"

Gaëtan gave Margot another disapproving look, but underneath his stern exterior, Sylvie could see that he was blushing slightly.

"Margot, honestly, she was raised in Hull. When do you think the topic was going to come up there?" Gaëtan scolded.

"Well, inevitably, it would come up at some point," Margot chuckled. "Look," Margot turned to Sylvie, "I'm guessing you've noticed a headache coming on recently, probably within the past day or so?"

"OK, Margot, thank you, but I'm not sure now's the best time," Gaëtan interjected.

"Someone's got to tell the poor girl, and I'm not afraid of doing it." Margot shot back, crossing her arms in defiance.

"I'm sure you're not," Gaëtan answered, "but it isn't exactly a topic of conversation for the breakfast table. It's better left for her studies with Sir Reynard."

"Oh sure, let it come from some stuffy old male centaur. That sounds phenomenally not dreadful." Margot scoffed, rolling her eyes. She turned to Sylvie, "Good luck!"

Sylvie swallowed hard over the massive knot in her throat.

泉

Gaëtan walked with Sylvie to the library. Entering through the double doors, he greeted Sir Reynard with a sweeping hand gesture.

"Sir Reynard, it's excellent to see you! I've brought you your pupil, and if you don't mind, I'd like to discuss amending her study schedule with you."

"At your service, Master Gaëtan. How can I help?" the greying centaur asked gruffly.

"We plan to introduce Sylvie publicly at the Festival of Flowers," Gaëtan said.

"An excellent idea," Sir Reynard agreed. "Though," he added pensively, "there's much for her to learn between now and then."

"That was our thought as well," Gaëtan answered. "We'd like you to rearrange her curriculum to focus primarily on Verdélian history and culture, including judicial study, to help Sylvie grasp those basics to prepare for her stepping into her official place as a Firstborn."

"Hmm." Sir Reynard said, his hand stroking his beard. "Yes, we'll see what I can do. However, I would caution against postponing Sylvie's practical education in the elements and éthéra manipulation. The Verdélia will expect her to not only know what a Firstborn should know but also be able to act like one."

Gaëtan furrowed his brow. "Fair point. We hadn't discussed that over breakfast."

He sat thinking briefly, then turned back to Sir Reynard. "Ultimately, we'll leave the matter in your hands. You have failed none of the rest of us three Firstborn; I don't expect you will fail Sylvie. You know the timeline; I entrust her preparation to you."

"I take the responsibility with all due recognition of its significance," Sir Reynard said with a bow.

"Thank you, Sir Reynard," Gaëtan said as he turned to go. "Oh!" He said, spinning back around, "There is one more matter." With that, he approached Sir Reynard and stretched up towards the side of his head to whisper something in his ear. If Sir Reynard were hearing something of interest, Sylvie would have never guessed; his face was as legible as a slab of rough-hewn granite.

"Very well, Master Gaëtan." Sir Reynard said after Gaëtan had stepped back a pace.

"Again, thank you," Gaëtan said to Sir Reynard. He turned to Sylvie and said, "Enjoy your lessons today!" With that, Gaëtan strode out of the library.

Sir Reynard turned his attention to Sylvie. "I hear your lessons in practical éthéra are advancing considerably after only one day. Congratulations."

Sylvie blushed slightly. "Thank you," she replied politely.

"Now," Sir Reynard continued, collecting a handful of select books from a section off to one side of the library, "we will shuffle your course schedule slightly to accommodate your public introduction. That said," he came back to where Sylvie was standing and placed three books on the desk beside her. "There's another matter to be discussed with you."

"Let's get this over with," Sylvie said. Based on everyone else's comments, she was sure that whatever was coming would not be pleasant.

Sir Reynard gave her a puzzled look but handed her the book at the top of the pile.

"What we'll be discussing briefly has to do with the growth you've undoubtedly noticed on the side of your head," Sir Reynard explained. "These three books will provide a little more detail, but I'll do my best to give you a brief introduction this morning.

"The first thing you need to understand for this to make sense is that in many unique ways, the Verdélia are unlike other creatures. Some things about the Verdélia make them more akin to plant life than animal life."

Sylvie raised her eyebrow in disbelief. "How is that possible?" She asked.

Sir Reynard replied, "It is how the Verdélia were created. They are much more connected to this world than the other creatures that inhabit it. One way in which the Verdélia demonstrate plant-like characteristics is how Verdélian children are brought into the world."

Sylvie looked abruptly up from her book. "I'm not sure I'm ready for this lesson," she said, her feet fidgeting awkwardly on the intricate library carpet.

"Ready or not, you have little choice," Sir Reynard said, pointing to Sylvie's temple. Sylvie instinctively grabbed at the side of her head.

"As I was saying," Sir Reynard continued, "Verdélia are born much the same way as saplings. Once per year, Verdélian women bloom. You're beginning to experience that yourself. Although you're only in the beginning stages now, that bump on your head will continue to grow until the Festival of Flowers."

Sylvie touched the budding growth on her temple gingerly beneath her scarf. Gold dust fluttered from her head down onto the carpet.

"That," Sir Reynard said, "is another effect of the blooming. Your bloom will emit dust until it is pollinated. Each Verdélia's bud is unique and comes in various colors, shapes, and textures."

4020 | *Autumn* | *4th Moon* | 8

"Mine seems to be gold," Sylvie said matter-of-factly. "What does that mean?"

"It means you are a Firstborn," Sir Reynard explained. "Only the Firstborn produce golden blooms. Thus why your staff have been careful to cover your bloom with a scarf daily."

"Blooms? Are you saying this...thing on my head is a flower?" Sylvie asked.

"Precisely," Sir Reynard confirmed. "Come the end of the month, at the time of the Festival of Flowers, that growth will be a mature bloom."

"So...as a Verdélian, am I a plant?" Sylvie asked, perplexed.

Sir Reynard threw back his head and let out a hearty laugh.

"Hahahaha! No, I daresay you are not. Although, as I mentioned, you are more connected to the earth than what you might consider 'normal' animal life."

Sylvie stared through the books on the table before her, lost in thought for a moment.

"So, what happens with the flower?" She asked.

"Right," Sir Reynard continued. "After the age of twenty, during the last moons of autumn, every Verdélian woman emits a dust from the pores on their head, over their flower that acts as a pollen or fertilizer. Once a year then, Verdélian women bloom. The Festival of Flowers marks the event in Verdélian culture. On that night, the éthéra of the natural world and that of the Verdélia exist in harmony, such that the éthéra of Verdélian men may turn earth into dust that allows for a Verdélian bloom to produce a seed."

As he spoke, Sir Reynard turned through the book before Sylvie. An illustration depicted a Verdélian woman's bloom in various stages, from bud to bloom. At the final stage, the petals shed, and it produced a seed. It also represented a man's hand holding dirt that shimmered at his touch.

"The seed," Sir Reynard continued, "is planted as any other. Over time, and with care, the seed will sprout and bloom, producing a Verdélian child."

Sylvie scanned the tome's artwork with fascination as the illustrations depicted a seed sprouting and blooming, the petals finally parting to reveal what might easily be mistaken for a newborn human child.

She turned to Sir Reynard, "So Verdélia are grown from the earth?"

"Yes and no," Sir Reynard replied. "Verdélian children result from the joint life force of Verdélian parents and the earth. It is what gives Verdélia their unique abilities."

Sylvie sat pensively for a moment. "So what about imps?" She asked.

"What about them?" Sir Reynard asked back.

"Well," Sylvie explained, "imps have no magical abilities, right? So, presumably, they can't be born in the same way. Where do they come from then?"

"Very perceptive of you," Sir Reynard said. "As you said, imps have no magical ability, meaning that they indeed cannot reproduce in the manner of the Verdélia. Yes, they are born in the way a Verdélia is born; however, in the growth stage of their plant, they are mistreated, malnourished, or abandoned. In those conditions, they do not receive the éthéra required to inherit all the gifts that the Verdélia are blessed with."

Sir Reynard thumbed through the pages of the book in front of Sylvie and stopped on one that depicted a seed amid what appeared to be a weed-ridden garden. On the opposite page was a sketch of an imp's face, the bright golden eyes a dead giveaway.

"Imps are a societal tragedy, living proof of imperfection among the Verdélia," Sir Reynard said somberly. "At conception, all Verdélian seeds have the same potential: to grow into a Verdélian child. However, a Verdélian seed requires significant care to reach its full potential. A Verdélian seed that is not properly nurtured will produce a child without the capacity for éthéra."

"An imp," Sylvie stated matter-of-factly.

Sir Reynard nodded, "An imp. In all respects but one, Verdélia and Imp are the same. The difference resides in the ability to manipulate éthéra, which hinges on one crucial factor: proper upbringing of the seed. For obvious reasons, the Verdélia have strict laws concerning the creation of Verdélian seeds and their nurture and care."

"So, can imps not have children?" Sylvie asked.

"Imps can have children," Sir Reynard replied. "They reproduce like any other species of animal and give birth to another kind of being altogether: humans."

Sylvie looked up in surprise. "Humans are related to the Verdélia?"

Sir Reynard raised an eyebrow and, after a moment, replied, "Yes, though few would consider them related in the traditional sense. Surely, the notion would offend most Verdélia."

"But a Verdélian couple could have a human grandchild, in theory." Sylvie insisted.

"In theory, yes," Sir Reynard said, "though any Verdélian couple who was responsible for the birth of an imp child would be severely punished under Verdélian law and would likely never admit they had an imp child, let alone a human grandchild."

"That sounds tragic," Sylvie whispered.

"It sounds tragic because it is." Sir Reynard affirmed. "The severing of the connection between the Verdélia and the magical éthéra of this world, through the creation of an imp child, is one of the greatest tragedies known to the Verdélia."

"I suppose," Sylvie said reluctantly. "Still," she continued, "the idea that imps, humans, and Verdélia are completely estranged from each other when they are not so different just doesn't seem right. They are family, even if somewhat distant." Sylvie thought of her adoptive parents in Hull, nearly a world away, it seemed and was suddenly swept with a wave of homesickness.

Her thoughts returned to her childless mother. "Sir Reynard," she began awkwardly, "Does this mean I can have children? I always grew up wondering." She paused. He was listening intently, thinking nothing. "My mother, adoptive human mother, had suffered through childbirth, and I never...became a woman, in the human sense. She would worry about it regularly. I would hear conversations between her and my father..." Her voice trailed off. She had always loved children, just as her mother did, but she had never allowed herself to believe it possible.

"I am not broken?" She finally asked.

"You are whole, Miss Sylvie," Sir Reynard placed a hand on her shoulder.

# XII

## *The Theatre*

Through the glass of the library windows, leaves drifted stiffly in the slow autumn breeze. The shadows of the day were getting longer. Sylvie watched mindlessly as a large leaf blew this way and that in the courtyard. Although she was a dedicated student, even she could only handle so much of the leathery tomes Sir Reynard had assigned her. Sylvie had been studying dutifully for days, and after about six hours of continuous study on this day, the words on the pages of her textbooks were turning into a visual soup. Sylvie had turned her attention to the little things that were going on outside. Even a leaf in the wind was more interesting than obscure Verdélian customs.

"Ahem," a timid noise brought Sylvie back to reality. Nadine stood next to Sylvie's study table in the library.

"Oh, Nadine, hello," Sylvie said hazily. "I'm afraid you've caught me in a daze..."

"I'm to bring you to the theater, miss," Nadine said, "To meet Master Gaëtan."

"Oh, right! Time for that already?" Sylvie sat up at the reminder. Gaëtan had proposed to give her a tour of the Aritené, the city's theater. Of the three Firstborn, only Gaëtan had shown anything more than basic politeness to Sylvie, and he had done so enthusiastically. He was the only person Sylvie could consider a friend among the Verdélia, and she looked forward to their time together.

Nadine accompanied Sylvie to the theater, some twenty minutes on foot from the palace. The front of the theater was an intricate, multi-columned masterpiece in stone, covered in towering, arched windows and a dome-shaped roof tiled in gorgeous hues of gold and green. Nadine guided Sylvie to a narrow alleyway that buried itself between the side of the theater and the adjacent building. Slipping into the shade of the little street, Sylvie readjusted the sash on her head and breathed a sigh of relief.

"Right this way," Nadine said, gesturing towards a solitary door underneath an archway and an intricate metal lamp in the theater's side wall. Nadine cracked the door open and beckoned Sylvie inside.

"This is where I leave you, Miss," Nadine said, "If you need anything, have Master Gaëtan send me his familiar."

"His what?" Sylvie asked.

Nadine dipped her head in a shallow bow. "Master Gaëtan can show you himself." With that, she slipped back up the alleyway and turned out of Sylvie's sight.

Sylvie opened the door a little further and sunk into the darkness of the room opposite. After letting the door close behind her, Sylvie had to stand still for a minute, letting her eyes adjust to the darkness. All she could see was a dim light emerging from a doorway ahead of her on her right. She approached the doorway and poked her head tentatively around the corner.

The doorway led into another hallway. Down to the left, Sylvie looked onto a stage milling with people, all dressed in extravagant costumes. Lights danced over the stage from various locations above and around the stage.

"Twenty-minute break, dancers!" a loud voice hollered over the din of moving bodies. "Get some water and meet back on stage!"

Several of the dancers on stage turned and started rushing right towards Sylvie. Just as Sylvie was going to duck back into her hallway, a familiar face popped up above the rushing crowd.

"Sylvie!" Gaëtan called out, "You made it!"

Dancers continued to scramble down the hallway and past Sylvie as they made their way to backstage rooms to make the most of their break. Gaëtan turned into Sylvie's dimly lit corridor.

"I'm so glad you could come!" Gaëtan said with a smile. "Come on, let's show you around!"

Gaëtan stuck out his elbow, inviting Sylvie to take his arm. She barely had time to do so before Gaëtan whisked her out of her hallway and directly towards the stage.

Sylvie's eyes widened, and she gasped as the theater came into proper view. Hundreds and hundreds of velvet cushioned seats lined the enormous hall facing the front of the stage, each edged with golden fringe and tassels and supported by carefully and ornately carved wooden frames, all gilded in yet more golden hues. Above and around the seats on the ground floor, beautiful balconies inlaid with carvings of Verdélia and various scenes of nature hosted still more seats, even more intricate than those on the ground. Heavy tapestries draped across the boxes, tied back with heavy golden ropes. The scene was surreal to Sylvie, like something out of a dream. Immediately in front of the stage, an orchestra of astonishing instruments was assembled in a pit sitting below stage level.

A few rows into what would have otherwise been the audience, a taller man leaned over a mess of papers spread atop a table, shifting his attention rapidly between different scrolls in what appeared to be a great intellectual struggle.

"Mr. Moreau!" Gaëtan shouted. The man looked up, trying to identify the caller. His eyes settled on Gaëtan and widened in recognition.

"Master Gaëtan! How long have you been here?" He asked incredulously.

"Hardly a half hour, sir," Gaëtan responded. "The production is looking wonderful—not that I would expect anything less from you, of course."

Mr. Moreau dipped his head in a grateful bow. "We've been blessed with quite the batch of recruits this season," he said in answer to Gaëtan's compliment. His eyes turned to Sylvie with a look of curious amusement.

"Now, Master Gaëtan, who is your lovely companion?" Mr. Moreau asked.

"Heavens, where are my manners?" Gaëtan chuckled, "Mr. Moreau, please meet Sylvie."

Gaëtan made a sweeping gesture with his arm to introduce Sylvie. Sylvie curtsied politely, trying to imitate what Nadine had shown for a proper Verdélian greeting.

"It is a pleasure to meet you, miss. Any friend of Gaëtan's is naturally a welcome guest of the theater." Mr. Moreau bowed deeply as he spoke.

Gaëtan turned to Sylvie, "And as you may have guessed by now, this is Mr. Moreau, the dance master and choreographer for the Frimédia Dance Company, the premier Verdélian theater group."

"Flattery," Mr. Moreau chided, "but true." He added with a shrug. "Miss Sylvie, have you ever attended one of our ballets?" He asked.

"I'm afraid not," Sylvie said apologetically. "I haven't been to any ballet before." Saying so out loud in such a gorgeous theater made her feel embarrassed and unrefined.

"Oh!" Mr. Moreau exclaimed in surprise. "But it's just as well, I suppose. You're in for a treat for your first ballet ever. This year's performance is shaping up to be stunning in every respect." He turned to Gaëtan, "She is coming, I presume?"

"She'll have a seat in my box this year," Gaëtan confirmed with a smile. Sylvie shot Gaëtan a surprised look, raising one eyebrow questioningly. Gaëtan just grinned back.

"Splendid," Mr. Moreau replied. "Yes, quite the performance this year, and for your first ballet. Oh, how wonderful."

Sylvie smiled nervously, "I'm quite looking forward to it."

"Mr. Moreau," Gaëtan said, "would it be all right if I gave our guest a tour of the theater?"

"Of course, Master Gaëtan," Mr. Moreau replied, "just mind the dancers; they'll be back on stage in a few minutes."

"Of course," Gaëtan assured him. Gaëtan offered Sylvie his arm, "Come, let's look around."

Sylvie took Gaëtan's arm, and he led her off the stage into a dimly lit hallway and up a winding set of stairs.

"I didn't realize this is what you meant when you said you were a patron of the arts," Sylvie said. "You're really in your element here."

"Yes, well..." Gaëtan said casually, "not so much anymore. Here we are."

They had reached the second level of seats in the theater audience and were standing in a small alcove draped in velvet and ornate carvings. Sylvie could see the stage over the golden balcony in front of them.

"Not anymore? What does that mean?" Sylvie asked.

"When I was younger, Mr. Moreau selected me to study under him at the theater. It's always been a very competitive program." Gaëtan explained.

"Oh!" Sylvie exclaimed, "So you've been in the theater before?"

"Not quite." Gaëtan said somberly.

"But you just said you studied under Mr. Moreau," Sylvie said, confused.

"I was selected to study." Gaëtan corrected. "Mr. Moreau trained Margot, Loïc, and me in our formal dances. He requested that I study underneath him after that event. The program is rigorous—only the most dedicated students are admitted, and the demands on a student's time are immense. Between that and all of my other obligations...well...it wasn't possible."

Sylvie looked at Gaëtan empathetically. He didn't need to explain his disappointment; it was written plainly on his face. True to character, however, a charming grin soon replaced Gaëtan's dejected expression.

"No matter," he said with a smile. "I can still enjoy the arts as a spectator."

"I'd venture to say it's not the same," Sylvie said.

"You're right," Gaëtan answered, "but it's second best. Come," he continued, "let's take you backstage."

As they walked through the maze of hallways weaving behind the stage and auditorium, Sylvie glimpsed a dancer, his posture straight and tall, twirling about more swiftly and surely than she would have thought possible.

"That's Basile," Gaëtan mentioned. "He's playing Josias in the upcoming play. He's a good man and an extremely talented dancer."

The two continued behind the stage and reached a hallway with several doors.

"Here are the dressing rooms," Gaëtan explained. "Let's see if we can catch any of the dancers."

Gaëtan knocked on a door labeled "Principals." There was a soft shuffle behind the door, and it slipped open. A young woman stood behind it, dressed in a simple leotard. She had tucked her hair up and out of the way, but wisps of curly brown hair bounced here and there around her face. "Master Gaëtan," she said with a delicate curtsy, "welcome!"

"Maya," Gaëtan replied, "it's great to see you. Let me introduce you to my cousin, Sylvie. I'm giving her a tour of the theater."

"Sylvie, it's lovely to meet you. Any friend of Gaëtan's is a friend of mine." Maya replied with a gentle smile.

"It's nice to meet you too," Sylvie replied timidly.

"Maya is playing the role of Morwenna," Gaëtan explained. Maya nodded proudly.

"Congratulations," Sylvie said.

From behind the half-opened door, another female voice sounded silky and smooth.

"Maya, who's at the door?" A young woman with shining blonde hair and a shimmering robe entered their view just behind Maya.

"Emelia, you know Gaëtan," Maya replied, "this is Sylvie, a friend."

*A friend? A tramp, more like.* Emelia's nasty thought caught Sylvie off guard, mainly because what came out of her smiling mouth was: "So wonderful to see you both!" She turned with a playful smile to Gaëtan.

"We weren't expecting company."

"I'm just giving Sylvie here a tour of the theater," Gaëtan said.

Although Gaëtan remained his usual self, Sylvie couldn't help but notice his enthusiasm had cooled ever so slightly when Emelia came into view.

Gaëtan continued, "Emelia will play the role of Sephora," he explained.

"Congratulations," Sylvie said politely, "I'm very much looking forward to your performance. You must be very talented."

"You're too kind," Maya said with a kind smile.

More talented than you, that's certain, escaped from Emelia's mind.

"Thank you very much," Emelia said with a short curtsy.

Emelia addressed Gaëtan again, her tone quickly becoming more charming. "Will we be seeing you at the afterparty, Master Gaëtan?"

"I'm afraid not," Gaëtan replied, "There's much to attend to in preparation for the following night's festival."

"What a shame," Emelia huffed, a look of angry disappointment barely contained behind her carefully manicured facade.

A young man with hair streaked in shades of blonde and chestnut bounded behind Gaëtan and Sylvie down the hallway, nearly bowling Sylvie over.

"Fredrich, you madman!" Gaëtan called out after him with a laugh.

Fredrich screeched to a halt and turned around, his eyes wide.

"Gaëtan, is that you?" He asked.

"In the flesh," Gaëtan answered with a grin. "Meet Sylvie, a new friend."

Fredrich strutted back down the hall, his chest out and shoulders back, arms swinging exaggeratedly. He reached Sylvie and, with a theatrical wave of his hand and a deep bow, took her hand and kissed it.

"Miss, it is my greatest honor to make your acquaintance," he said somberly. His eyes, however, ultimately betrayed his sense of amusement.

Gaëtan gave him a shove. "Behave yourself, you scoundrel," he said with a chuckle.

Fredrich stared at Gaëtan, mouth agape in feigned offense. "Scoundrel? Me?! Sir, you do me a great injustice!"

Gaëtan waved Fredrich's theatrics off with a hand and turned to Sylvie.

"You've now met the last of our four Firstborns, as Fredrich will play the part of Demetrius."

"You're a natural acting talent," Sylvie said with a grin.

"Finally, someone with a genuine appreciation for the arts!" Fredrich exclaimed. "As much as I would love to stay and chat with a lady of such impeccable taste, I'm urgently needed on stage. Til we meet again!" And with that, Fredrich dashed off towards the stage.

Returning from the theater, Sylvie found herself again with her nose to her books. It wasn't long before she had completed her autumn studies and passed Sir Reynard's impromptu exams with flying colors. The material, which centered on plant growth and care, had felt like an academic version of what had come naturally to her in Hull. The Verdélian textbooks had filled some rather glaring holes in her knowledge, but Sylvie had been pleasantly surprised to find that the basic principles had all been familiar.

The rest of the material, covering basic magical creatures, required more studying. In Hull, the mere mention of magic was taboo. If any of the villagers had ever seen a magical creature—which was unlikely—they certainly wouldn't have shared the fact with anyone for fear of being branded an outsider or a down-right lunatic. All of this material was new to Sylvie, and she found it fascinating.

Sir Reynard had given her an overview of what Verdélians considered intelligent magical creatures: centaurs, mermaids, undines, sylphs, dwarves, and dragons. These creatures shared a unique bond with a specific Firstborn and were regarded as "civilized." The rest (and bulk) of Sylvie's Autumn curriculum focused on creatures resembling the ordinary creatures Sylvie was familiar with from her exploration of the world near Hull. Souresigne, for example, resembled an ordinary swan in most respects, but its eggs possessed specific magical healing properties. The libeau was another magical creature, like a dragonfly in appearance, but whose wings one could crush to create a solution that would allow someone to breathe underwater.

Other creatures Sylvie learned about bore no resemblance to anything remotely familiar to her. Malumen, for example, were simply floating flames notorious for enticing unsuspecting travelers to follow them. They led gullible followers to their demise.

As the Firstborn had discussed, Sir Reynard also gave Sylvie a crash course in Verdélian culture, history, and politics. She had learned about the Verdélian districts (there were four, one for each season) and their basic governance structures, as well as how the districts worked together under the direction of the Firstborn. Sir Reynard had tried to simplify elaborate legal and political procedures, but the details of those concepts had mostly escaped Sylvie, she was embarrassed to say. Sir Reynard had reassured her that a basic knowledge of the underlying principles would be fine for the time being. Sylvie hoped he was right.

Sitting in her cottage, Sylvie smiled ever so slightly at her success in her Autumn courses. After all, if she could complete those successfully, perhaps she could handle her Firstborn responsibilities.

Sylvie refocused herself on the task at hand. Having finished her autumn studies, Sir Reynard put her on her summer curriculum. Her current course of study covered material that was more foreign to her: natural materials and their properties, as well as Verdélian geography. Sylvie had just started and couldn't believe how many ways one could classify what seemed to be just rocks.

In terms of geography, the scope of Sylvie's world had blown her away. On the largest of Verdélian maps, she had found Hull, a tiny pinprick in the far east beyond the mountains. Hull was so small that the mapmaker did not independently identify it on the map—Sylvie had located it based on her familiarity with the area. Most people reading the map wouldn't even know it was there.

A sharp and heavy double knock sounded at Sylvie's front door. Sylvie walked to the door and opened it, expecting Nadine or maybe Gaëtan.

Instead, Loïc stood in the doorway. The sun was setting behind him, bathing the sky in hues of lavender and pink, amber clouds hanging lazily in the distance. There was just enough light in the sky to outline Loïc's frame, which was streaked with the signs of extended travel.

"Sovrène, Sylvie," he said curtly, with a quick bow.

Sylvie stood staring for a moment, a little taken aback.

"Another word from the ancient tongue, Loïc?" she said after a moment of uncertainty. "You should know better. I'm ignorant of almost every phrase."

He smiled at her, "Good evening, Sylvie."

"Good evening, Loïc." She gathered her thoughts and asked, "Did you just get back from your trip?"

"I returned this afternoon," Loïc answered.

"Welcome back," Sylvie said, more as a formality than anything else. "How was the journey?"

"It went about as well as expected. Luckily, we traveled quickly enough to cut a day off from our travel." Loïc said. Sylvie had no clue why Loïc was paying her a visit.

"Yes, we didn't expect you until tomorrow." Sylvie hesitated.

"Listen, I'll cut the awkward formalities and get right to it," Loïc said authoritatively. "I spoke to Margot, and it seems you two have seen little of each other this past moon."

"That's true. I don't have free rein of the palace yet, so... Besides, she's hard to come by," Sylvie mumbled, feeling suddenly accused by Loïc's remarks but not knowing why.

"I understand that. Are you aware of her predicament?" Loïc pried.

Sylvie was still not used to the emptiness of the Firstborns' heads. "Could you clarify?"

"She is considering the possibility of being replaced. Even if she is not, several people are so unconvinced by her abilities that they will seek to overthrow her. Do you have any feelings about that?"

Sylvie stiffened her back and straightened her shoulders. She set her face defiantly against Loïc's. "Yes. But I'm not sure what I can do about it. I've been busy with my studies. I have my own responsibilities to worry about right now!" she shot back.

"No need to get fiery with me," Loïc said, unfazed by Sylvie's strengthened demeanor. "I'm here with advice for your benefit. I assume you've spent most—or more like all—of your time with Gaëtan, then?"

Sylvie tried to think of a way to respond that wouldn't betray her roiling emotions. Her few seconds of silence were all Loïc needed.

"Right," he said, continuing without waiting for an answer. "Here's that advice, then: we need to be a unified front. Margot needs all the companionship she can get. I think she would especially appreciate it from you because you're the only other woman in our party."

"She hasn't even attempted to reach out to me. How has this become my responsibility?"

"We are *all* responsible for making this work."

Sylvie stared at Loïc with a raised eyebrow, inviting him to elaborate.

Loïc sighed. "Having spent all of your time with Gaëtan, you surely didn't notice or discover that Margot has been struggling with her role as Firstborn. What with the potential stewardship I'm hearing about. Gaëtan, of course, is too occupied with a litany of other admittedly important but less crucial matters to give the issue the attention it requires. If you spend all of your time with Gaëtan, going about as if you don't have the time of day for Margot, things will not end well for us."

Sylvie was flabbergasted.

"What on earth are you talking about? Me not having the time of day for Margot? Margot can only ever be bothered to acknowledge I exist if Gaëtan is there, forcing her to interact with me. Perhaps I'm just not reading her right, but it's not too hard to see she doesn't much care for me." Sylvie said, her voice noticeably raised.

"Don't mistake disdain for jealousy," Loïc cautioned, his voice level despite her outburst.

Sylvie again stared at Loïc, not grasping where he was going with this.

Loïc obliged with an explanation. "Surely you've learned by now that, as an imp, Margot cannot manipulate éthéra. Traditionally, the Firstborns' roles have centered on this ability. As the first imp Firstborn, Margot is a mystery and understandably feels ill-suited to the task before her. Many Verdélia legitimately believe she is unfit to lead. I can understand why she might lash out at others who, without work or study, have been gifted abilities Margot could only dream of despite all her efforts."

"It's not my fault she's an imp, and I'm not," Sylvie said.

"It's not hers either," Loïc replied.

After a pause, Loïc started again.

"Look, I didn't come here to point fingers or lay blame. But our particular generation of Firstborn has more than its share of struggles. A working relationship between you and Margot is the bare minimum required if we hope to see this through. Can I trust you to make an effort in that regard?"

Although she didn't appreciate Loïc's to-the-point manner, Sylvie knew the substance of his message had merit.

"I'll try," she huffed, swallowing her pride.

"Thank you," Loïc answered. He paused for a moment, then continued. "Gaëtan told me he has arranged for your inheritance ceremony. The day after the festival, am I correct?"

"Yes," she said.

"Are you prepared?" He asked.

"No. Not at all. I know nothing of it except that it means more responsibilities are being poured out on me. Is there something I should know?"

"Ordinarily, you would have gone through the Inheritance Day ceremony with Gaëtan and I last year," Loïc continued. "For obvious reasons, that didn't happen. The event is important in the life of every Verdélia. It's a symbolic event. Nadine and Margot can help you get ready since it is formal. You'll need to pick four people—Verdélia—to act as proxies for the four elements. As proxies for the elements, each will symbolically bestow on you the gifts of the respective Firstborn associated with each element."

"Four? I don't even know four Verdélia."

"Well, you seem to know Gaëtan well enough. He can be your first. Air. Then it's just fire, earth, and water."

"Just?" Sylvie asked, "You seem to think I've made many friends."

"Have you not?" He asked.

"No. I read books. And sometimes Gaëtan drags me from the cottage. Social events give me anxiety."

"Is it the mind reading?" He questioned.

"Largely, yes. Though without it, I'm just as anxious."

"Do I make you anxious?"

Sylvie pondered the question for a moment: "You seem to speak your mind, but not being able to know that for certain is stressful—like I'm at a disadvantage."

"Interesting," Loïc mused, "though I'd say you're not at a disadvantage; you're simply doing without the advantage you're accustomed to when interacting with everybody else."

"All the same, it feels like a disadvantage to me," Sylvie replied.

"Look at it this way instead—I get to go through the process of getting to know you, learning and understanding who you are, without any tricks or gimmicks. No pulling back the curtain to see your innermost thoughts—until and unless you're ready to share them with me. In a way, it's the best kind of adventure there is. Somewhere along the way, I may make a wrong turn—make an assumption about you that isn't right. But if I keep at it, someday I might come to know you just as well as if I could peer into your mind and see your thoughts and feelings. You get to go through that same journey with the three of us Firstborn."

Sylvie smiled. Inside of her, she felt something she had only ever felt from inside her mother, a kind of gust that lifted her heart and unsettled her stomach, but in an exciting sort of way. She tried to mute her smile as she looked up at Loïc, "I guess I could try that."

It was quiet for a moment, then he spoke. "I should go. I would still encourage you to reach out to Margot. I think she needs it."

"I'll do what I can," Sylvie nodded.

"Lunardé, Sylvie," and with a bow, he receded down the dimly lit cottage path, through Sylvie's gate, along the road, and out of sight.

*Lunardé*, she whispered under her breath. She closed the door, then tried her mother's trick and hummed the butterflies away.

# XIII

*A Royal Outing*

S ylvie woke as usual the following day, with the sun tickling her face.
Sitting up in bed, she had to straighten her neck consciously. Although
her bloom was relatively small, it made the side of Sylvie's head feel unnaturally
heavy. This morning was tough, and Sylvie reached up to caress the scarf that
concealed the flower. Sylvie was grateful that the Verdélia expected one to keep
the bloom hidden with a scarf or other covering. Although she knew it was a
normal part of her Verdélian heritage, the novelty of the whole situation was
off-putting, and Sylvie liked to think about the bloom as little as possible. This
included seeing it as rarely as she could manage. With Nadine handling her hair
and general appearance, it had been several days since she had seen the bud.

This morning, though, a sense of morbid curiosity was grasping at Sylvie.
She felt drawn towards the mirror, and without realizing what she was doing,
she untied her scarf. Her blonde hair fell ramshackle over her shoulders, wispy
tendrils floating in the air and catching the sun's morning rays. There, though,
at the center of attention, directly above her right ear, was a rose of bold yellow,
the petals trimmed in gold. Gold dust shimmered around the bloom,
powdering her hair, shoulders, and nightgown. For the first time, Sylvie
admitted to herself that, despite its strangeness, the flower was undeniably
beautiful.

Standing there staring at her reflection, Sylvie considered Loïc's visit from
the night before and his request: reach out to Margot. Sylvie groaned audibly
at the thought. Since Sylvie had arrived in Verdélys, Margot had only ever been
sarcastically polite toward Sylvie, and then only in situations where it was
obvious that Gaëtan had pressured Margot into it by appealing to Margot's
sense of duty as a Firstborn. Although Margot was admittedly very skilled at
maintaining a regal outward appearance, Sylvie hadn't missed an underlying
turmoil which, until Loïc's observation from the night before, had struck
Sylvie as disdain. Sylvie had thought long on Loïc's words before falling asleep,
though. She could only imagine the daunting task of being a Firstborn without
the abilities that all Firstborn were assumed to be born with. Sylvie had not

been raised Verdélian, but she was born Verdélian—she had the ability but lacked some knowledge and polish. Both would come with study and time. The ability, though, could not be learned, as Loïc had pointed out. When Sylvie thought about it, she pitied Margot. But Margot was Margot, and the idea of trying to converse with her did not appeal to Sylvie in the slightest.

A familiar, soft knock shook Sylvie from her thoughts.

"Come in, Nadine," Sylvie hummed. Sylvie heard an unfamiliar tune trilling in Nadine's mind as she fumbled with the doorknob.

*The flower of spring, a morning dew*
*Will drip drop all the morning through*

The door swung open quietly, and Nadine stepped into the room.

"Good morning, Miss," she said.

Nadine noticed Sylvie standing in front of the mirror and the discarded scarf on the floor.

"It's quite beautiful, isn't it?" She said with a smile.

"Yes," Sylvie nodded, "it is."

Sylvie turned to Nadine with a sense of curiosity in mind.

"May I see yours?" She asked. Sylvie realized that Nadine's black scarf had so perfectly matched her hair and the black servants' attire she wore every day that she had barely noticed that Nadine was wearing a scarf of her own. She had learned that all imps still grow a flower, but without the harnessing of éthéra, it was simply form without function.

Nadine walked towards the vanity in the room and picked up Sylvie's hairbrush, ready to start the morning routine.

"It's not much to look at," she stated matter-of-factly. "Come, sit so I can get started on your hair."

"I'm sure that's not true," Sylvie said, sitting down with her face to the mirror for the first time in a while.

"You'll be able to see it tomorrow night at the festival," Nadine promised.

"Very well, I won't insist."

Nadine made quick work of Sylvie's hair and arrayed her in a beautiful dress and jewelry. Although Sylvie liked to keep her attire as modest as Nadine considered still Verdélia-appropriate, Sylvie had asked Nadine to do more today. That evening, she was Gaëtan's guest at the ballet. Gaëtan had told Sylvie that the occasion was formal, and Sylvie didn't want to feel out of place or to disappoint. Sylvie would be lying to herself if she didn't admit that she was also more than a little excited to attend a Verdélian ballet and with Gaëtan, too.

Nadine was finishing Sylvie's makeup when a knock sounded at the front door downstairs.

"I wonder who that could be," Sylvie muttered aloud. "I'm not expecting company."

Sylvie watched Nadine shrug in the mirror. If someone had been sent from the palace, Nadine didn't know about it.

Making her way down from her room, Sylvie called out, "Who's there?"

"An important guest," a confident female voice called out.

Sylvie didn't recognize the voice, but then, she wasn't sure she would have recognized anyone's voice here besides Nadine's, Gaëtan's, and Sir Reynard's. Sylvie thought about stealing a peep through the front window to identify her guest, but she didn't want to get caught staring, so she decided to just open the door.

To Sylvie's surprise, there stood Margot.

Margot stood on the doorstep in her signature regal posture, head held high as usual. She said nothing. The morning sun glinted off of a flowing satin gown in an exquisite deep green, which accentuated Margot's tall, slender frame.

"Margot," Sylvie mumbled, "Good morning. To what do I owe the pleasure?"

"Invite me in, and I just might tell you," Margot replied with a smile.

"Oh...of course," Sylvie said, shuffling backward. "Please, come in."

"Thank you," Margot mused as she glided past Sylvie.

"Make yourself at home," Sylvie said, following Margot into the living area.

"Hm. I think not." Margot scoffed, surveying her surroundings. "But I will take a seat if it's all the same to you."

Without waiting for an answer, Margot seated herself in front of the cottage hearth.

"Yes...I...make yourself comfortable." Sylvie stuttered. Margot was maybe the last person Sylvie was expecting to see at her cottage this morning, and the timing of it, just after Loïc's visit the night before, seemed surreal.

Sylvie took a breath and composed herself.

"So, Margot, what brings you to Amber Lane this morning?" Sylvie asked her impromptu guest.

"Can't a girl just want some female company?" Margot asked with an exaggerated look of innocence.

"Well—" Sylvie started.

Margot let out a burst of lilting laughter.

"Oh please, darling," she said, wiping a tear from her eye, "I'm kidding. Not that I don't like you, but we're not that close if we're being candid."

Margot was right, but the comment still hurt Sylvie more than she would have expected.

"No, no, I'm here because our mutual acquaintance and dear friend, Loïc, insisted that I reach out to you. Mind you, I'm not in the habit of obliging most people's requests," Margot mused, "but Loïc can be so adorable with his overly inflated sense of duty. We wouldn't want to hurt his oh-so-tender feelings now, would we, Sylvie?"

"I guess not," Sylvie said with a smile.

"Wonderful!" Margot interrupted. "Have a seat, and let's be friends!"

Sylvie dutifully took a seat near Margot.

"I don't understand," Sylvie started. "First, why would you come here at Loïc's request? And why take the time? I mean, you've never exactly..." Sylvie faded out, realizing she didn't know how to politely accuse Margot of not showing an interest in her.

"I've never exactly shown an interest in you?" Margot said, completing Sylvie's thought for her.

"I...that's not what I...well, more or less." Sylvie finally admitted.

"Hm, yes, well..." Margot said. "We can't all be Gaëtan, now can we? So exceptionally extroverted that we'd make friends with a rabid dog if it crossed our path."

Sylvie chuckled a bit. Although the description was perhaps unflattering, it captured Gaëtan's over-the-top exuberance rather well.

"And, I might add," Margot continued, "it's not as if I've received an invitation for a visit from you since you arrived."

"I'm sorry," Sylvie managed through the tension in the room, "I've had little time. Sir Reynard has kept me very busy. I'm not even sure how I could have reached you for an invitation if I had tried. This is all new to me. If it makes you feel any better, I haven't invited anyone over here, ever."

"Fair enough, I suppose," Margot said pensively.

"So...Loïc asked you to come by?" Sylvie asked again, curious to see if she could determine whether that had been before or after he had made a similar request to her the night before.

"Hm?" Margot hummed as if snapped from a daydream. "Oh yes, Loïc, the poor dear," she said, prompted back on topic by Sylvie's question. "Well, he can be a bit...stuffy, can't he?" she said, leaning towards Sylvie.

"I guess I wouldn't know, really," Sylvie answered. "It's not like he's been around since I arrived in Verdélys."

"Fair," Margot noted, straightening herself in her seat. "I suppose you'll find out for yourself soon enough. He just so wants us all to get along," she said mockingly, crossing her hands over her heart in a false embrace. "But not like

Gaëtan. Gaëtan wants everyone to be friends just for the sake of it because, well, Gaëtan is Gaëtan. Loïc wants unity because he thinks it's the right thing. After all, he thinks it's part of our duty as Firstborn. He's very pious in that regard. It's all a bit much for me."

"You know him better than I do," Sylvie said, "but he strikes me as a bit...how should I put it...mechanical?"

"Oooh, good word!" Margot said with a little clap. "Let's face it. He's a bore; that is what he is."

Sylvie giggled. It was silly, but the meaningless gossip with Margot had completely distracted her from the weightier matters that seemed to occupy all of her time and energy.

"Yes, quite a bore," Margot carried on. Then, with an amused smirk, she said, "Not like Gaëtan, though, am I right, Sylvie?"

Sylvie could feel herself blush, but she tried to play it off. "I don't know what you mean," she blurted.

Margot laughed again, "Is that so? So it's not true that you're Gaëtan's special guest at the ballet tonight? You look quite splendid for a boring night in."

Sylvie was reddening fast. "Gaëtan invited me to the ballet," she admitted. "I've never been, and I'm going as his guest, that's all. He told me it was a formal event, so I wanted to look the part."

"Hmmm, yes," Margot hummed, "you certainly look the part. Still, you and Gaëtan up there alone in his box. It'll be quite the evening."

"Gaëtan's my friend. He's helping me ease into this whole Verdélia thing. The ballet is part of that." Sylvie replied. "Are you going?" She asked, desperate to change the topic of conversation.

"Oh no, not me," Margot replied. "A crowded venue, bustling socialites...quite the opposite of my idea of a good time."

"You should come!" Sylvie trilled. "Although I guess I'm not sure whether I am in a position to invite you," she mused.

"Thank you, but no," Margot replied. "And technically," she added, "Gaëtan's box isn't Gaëtan's; it's the Firstborn box. So you could invite me, but I wouldn't need the invitation to attend."

"That makes sense," Sylvie said, feeling a little foolish. "Well, wait a minute, think about this: what if you came to the ballet, and we both invited Loïc to come? There's no way he could say no, what with him asking you and me both to reach out to each other. If we told him we were going to the ballet together on the condition that he come too—how could he refuse? Loïc doesn't strike me as the ballet type, and you can find satisfaction in having forced him into it."

Sylvie was pretty proud of the plan she had just cooked up, although she found the prank a little out of character for her. Plus, for all she knew, Loïc did enjoy the ballet. However, she was sure the idea would appeal to Margot and thought it would be an excellent way to get the four Firstborn together.

Margot sat back in her chair, contemplating the idea. A smile slowly crept onto her face. She turned to Sylvie.

"You know," she said slyly, "you're not half bad. Loïc *hates* the ballet. He makes a point of it in front of Gaëtan every chance he gets. But you're right—if we invited him, he'd have to come. I may not enjoy a stuffy social event, but I'd suffer through more than the ballet to see Loïc squirm. We're doing it."

Sylvie beamed. "Fantastic!" She exclaimed.

Margot stood. "I'd better get appropriately dressed for an evening out, I suppose," she said. "Come on, you can help me. We'll need to invite Loïc together to convince him to come. We should do that sooner rather than later, so he has time to wash a moon's worth of travel off his filthy self and make himself presentable."

"Lead the way," Sylvie said with a smile. Her outings with Gaëtan had been fun but had felt so on-script like he had been accompanying her through everything she was supposed to do. This was different. Margot had a rogue personality, utterly opposite of Sylvie's own. There was a thrill in getting up to some innocent mischief, which Sylvie rarely did.

Margot floated over the cobblestones back to the palace. She seemed to put no effort into her long, flowing strides. They chatted about Sylvie's coursework on the way, Margot recalling all the things she had hated about her time in university and the mischief she had gotten into as a student. Some of Margot's stories caused Sylvie to laugh as she imagined a younger Margot terrorizing teachers and fellow students.

When they reached the palace, Margot led Sylvie upstairs and down a few hallways before they reached Margot's suite. After walking into a massive closet, Margot turned and gave Sylvie (or rather, her outfit) a good look.

"Hm...," she said contemplatively as she turned and disappeared into a maze of dresses and fancy gowns. A few moments later, she reappeared with a gorgeous black dress in her arms.

"This should do," she said with an air of false modesty.

A short while later, Sylvie and Margot approached Loïc's suite. Margot, who, in Sylvie's opinion, had already been dressed elegantly, had opted to change into an even more formal black dress embellished with intricate lace. With the help of some palace staff, she added lavish diamond jewelry and hair accessories to finish her look. Margot had told Sylvie it was to match Sylvie's wardrobe, but Sylvie couldn't help but think that Margot wouldn't be caught dead in public looking second best to anyone, especially not the new human-raised farm girl. It seemed a very Margot thing to do, and Sylvie shrugged it off.

After a brief walk through the palace, the girls reached an enormous set of wooden doors. With her fist, Margot hammered away on the door and immediately yelled, "Loïc, be a dear and open up, will you?"

There was no answer, and Sylvie couldn't make out any movement behind the door. Margot beat on the door again, clearly unbothered by any formalities of etiquette that might have suggested she be a little more restrained in her efforts.

"Hmph," Margot scowled, "I suppose I should have known better than to think he wouldn't be off tending to some oh-so-urgent duty. You!" she said firmly, addressing the member of the palace staff that was dusting a sculpture carefully set in the hallway opposite Loïc's suite, "where's Loïc?"

The servant curtsied deeply as she answered, "I believe he was last seen at the guardhouse near the palace gates."

Margot rolled her eyes. "Of course he was." She turned to Sylvie, "Come on, let's go fetch him."

A few minutes later, Sylvie and Margot were reaching the palace gate. Sylvie could make out several guards milling around the guardhouse built into the wall immediately adjacent to the gate.

"Hello boys!" Margot called out as they drew a little nearer. The guards stood stiffly, as if taken by surprise, and turned with wide eyes to find the source of the greeting. Upon seeing Margot, they quickly turned to face her and bowed respectfully.

"Miss Margot," they said in unison.

"Yes, yes, hello," Margot replied with a wave of her hand. "You boys haven't seen Loïc hereabouts, have you?" She asked.

"Master Loïc is inside the guardhouse with Commander Alfric. They're discussing matters of palace—and city—security." One guard answered.

"How dreadfully boring," Margot said with a frown. "Come on, Sylvie," she added, entering the guardhouse.

Sylvie followed dutifully, awkwardly cutting her way through the guards.

Inside the dimly lit guardhouse, Sylvie could make out Alfric in an adjoining room, hunched over a table sprawled with several parchments and a few weapons. Shields, spears, swords, and helms lined the walls, and other more elaborate-looking devices were neatly arranged throughout the guardhouse. Margot was already making her way into the next room.

"Hello, gentlemen," Margot called out as she entered the room. Following behind, Sylvie could see Loïc standing opposite Alfric at the table; his hands stretched out over a map, several sets of blueprints, and other plans.

"Margot," Loïc said, a look of surprise on his face. "And...Sylvie?" he added in a puzzled tone. "What brings the two of you down to the guardhouse today?"

"Don't be daft. We're looking for you," Margot replied.

"I'm in the middle of something rather important with Alfric here," Loïc replied, gesturing to Alfric and the contents of the table.

"Yes, I'm sure you are," Margot answered without so much as a glance towards Alfric or what Loïc had been studying. "However, that appears quite tiresome—no offense, Alfric—and if you don't come with us now, you'll be late for a rather important event, Loïc."

Loïc face showed bewilderment. "I'm sorry, you'll have to explain. What event is that?" He asked.

"The ballet, of course," Margot said with a devilish grin, unable to contain herself any longer.

Loïc sighed and rolled his eyes. "You've hunted me down for that?" He said incredulously, "Margot, you know I don't attend the ballet. That's Gaëtan's scene." He paused. "And since when do *you* attend the ballet, anyway?"

"Since today," Margot said nonchalantly, "now come along. All four of us are going to the ballet."

Loïc shook his head. "I can't. Palace and city security have been needing attention for far too long. I can't put this off any longer. As fun as the ballet may be," he said sarcastically, "it's going to have to be for another day."

"So you're not a practice what you preach sort, then?" Margot asked with a stunningly believable tone of sincerity, eyes wide in pretend innocence. "Because I seem to recall a recent request from a certain someone about taking time to reach out and show unity and all those squeamishly sappy things."

Loïc looked wedged between a rock and a hard place. Sylvie chimed in.

"Come on, Loïc. You did want us to spend more time together, didn't you?" As she uttered the word '*us,*' she couldn't tell if she meant the Firstborn or just the two of them.

"I..." Loïc said, visibly trying to find a justification to stick to his current task.

Instead, all he could manage was, "You two are making me regret I ever encouraged you to make nice." He turned to Alfric. "I'm sorry, but that must be all from me for today. Let's implement what we discussed, and know you have my full trust and backing in your command."

Alfric bowed deeply. "Of course, Master Loïc. The guard thanks you for your devoted leadership."

"How noble," Margot said with a mocking clap, "now come, with all the effort that's going to be needed to make Loïc presentable in public, at this rate, we're going to be late."

"Hilarious," Loïc said, gathering a few things. "After you," he said, gesturing to the door.

꘎

"This is fantastic. I'm so glad you thought of this," Margot said with a smug grin.

Sylvie and Margot sat on a velvet-cushioned bench in the hallway just outside Loïc's suite, waiting for him to get ready.

"Did you see Loïc's face?" Margot went on, "Priceless."

Sylvie giggled. Loïc had seemed surprised, and Margot's use of Loïc's advice and request against him had been rather funny to see.

"He didn't seem to enjoy taking his own medicine so much as giving it, that's for sure," Sylvie replied.

"Classic Loïc," Margot chuckled, "serves him right."

The doors to Loïc's suite opened, and out stepped Loïc, his hair still wet and face clean-shaven and finally free of grime. He dressed in a dark suit that looked to Sylvie to be some sort of uniform, though she wasn't familiar enough with Verdélian attire yet to know for sure. To Sylvie's surprise, she had to admit that he looked dashing.

Margot stood with her habitual air of disinterest on her face.

"Great, you're no longer an animal," she huffed to Loïc, "Let's go then, shall we, before we're all late and Gaëtan wonders where Sylvie dear has run off to."

"We wouldn't want that," Loïc said with a smirk.

"Guys," Sylvie groaned, "cut it out."

"You know, I would," Margot replied, "if it weren't so fun. Now let's go see your date!"

Sylvie groaned again, rolled her eyes, and followed Margot towards the palace entrance.

꘎

Before they had reached the theater entrance, Gaëtan noticed them and, with a look of surprise, called out.

"Sylvie! And Margot and Loïc? Are you attending the ballet with us?"

"Yes, we are," Margot stated regally.

"But I thought you hated the ballet. I thought you hated all social events." Gaëtan answered, perplexed.

"I do. Now, let's get to our seats." Margot replied without stopping on her way up the theater steps.

"I...," Gaëtan stuttered, "I mean, of course, but...well, and Loïc, you've always refused invitations to the ballet. What's going on?"

"It's a long story," Loïc said. "If I didn't know better, I'd think you were disappointed we showed." He turned and gave Sylvie a wink. Sylvie wished she could disappear.

"Not at all; I'm excited you all came," Gaëtan said quickly, "I'm just a little surprised, is all." He turned to Sylvie, "And to my only official guest, welcome," he said. "You look wonderful!"

"Thank you," Sylvie said with a quick curtsy of her head, "you look quite the part yourself."

Gaëtan was wearing a light-colored outfit overlaid in gold. It seemed the opposite pairing to Loïc's somber and structured wardrobe, although just as formal.

"Let's not keep Margot waiting," Gaëtan said as he escorted Sylvie inside. Loïc had already followed Margot into the theater.

The four of them made their way towards the Firstborn box upstairs. As they walked, Sylvie noticed the theater staff, patrons, and others were staring and beginning to whisper amongst themselves.

Once in the box and the heavy curtains behind them drawn, Loïc turned to Gaëtan and said, "That was subtle."

"Very," Margot chimed in from her seat at the edge of the box.

"Keep in mind I only formally invited Sylvie," Gaëtan said with an uncomfortable smile.

"What are you talking about?" Sylvie asked.

"Remember that as of now, you're only publicly known as a palace guest, a cousin, and even then only by a select few," Gaëtan explained. "However, seeing you here with the three of us and attending the ballet in our box." Gaëtan paused, "Well, people are clever enough to draw their conclusions. Not to mention even just the three of us," he gestured to himself, Loïc, and Margot, "haven't been seen in public together at a non-religious or political event in who knows how long."

"I suppose you didn't think about that before coming here?" He said in a tone of mock reproach to Loïc and Margot.

"Don't look at me. It was their idea," Loïc answered, pointing to Sylvie and Margot.

"Oh, relax," Margot scoffed, "the Festival is tomorrow. Everyone's going to be fine."

Gaëtan shrugged. "I suppose you're right. In that case, let's enjoy the ballet!"

"Oh yes," Margot said, her voice dripping with sarcasm, "let's."

The comment drew a chuckle from Loïc, now sunk deep into his chair, arms folded over his chest.

"Ignore them," Gaëtan told Sylvie, "this will be great!"

"I am looking forward to it," Sylvie said. She sat between Gaëtan and Loïc and turned her attention to the program.

※

Performed on the stage this evening, you will witness the recreation of the earliest of Verdélian tales. The birth of our people is a story of growth, creativity, love, betrayal, and power. Our starring leads for the performance are as follows:

Sephora: Emelia
Josias: Basile
Demetrius: Fredrich
Morwenna: Maya
Rhys: Dumas

Our story begins with five seeds planted, each blooming into glorious Firstborns. Act 1 will reminisce on the births and divine creations of the early Firstborns. Sephora and her creatures of the air danced to the "Whirlwind Suite." Josias and his creatures of the fire danced to "Variations of a Flame." Demetrius and his creatures of the earth danced to "Earthen Tembré." Morwenna and her creatures of the water danced to the "Ripple Waltz." Act 1 will close with a greeting and farewell from the Fallen Firstborn, Rhys. Who will be born in the walled garden, share a table with the Firstborn, climb the wall, and forfeit his place? This will be performed to the award-winning piece, "He Who Walks."

Intermission

Act 2 will resume the walled garden and explore the budding romances taking place there. We will begin with Josias and Morwenna, their act of falling in love, and the culmination of that love through Solaidi's gift of Ancelin of the Awakening, where summer and spring will begin on the earth. This will be performed

*144*

to "The Warmth." Following will be the romance of Demetrius and Sephora and the gift of Ancelin of Rest, where autumn and winter will complete the cycle of creation and be performed to "The Chill."

Intermission

Act 3, the closing act, will begin with Rhys returning, attempting to awaken the others' creatures, and failing, then birthing chaos through creatures of darkness. Darkness and misery will reign through a depiction of fallen days when all Firstborn leave the walled garden to enter his waiting world beyond the wall. This will be performed to the piece "The Tale of the Fallen." In the end, Rhys' capture is accomplished by the four whom we hail to this day. Peace and prosperity then reign. His imprisonment and the ensuing peace is performed to "Acts of the Ancient."

⁂

A few seconds later, the lights in the theater dimmed. There was a moment of silence in the dark. Then, the light notes of a flute could be heard. The heavy curtains covering the stage receded slowly, revealing a small, quivering light flittering about on the stage. The glow swayed in time with the music, and as the melody came to a rest, the fire sank to the ground. With a muted flash, four buds appeared on the stage. The music picked up again, and as it grew, so did the buds, culminating in four golden flowers.

With a burst of sound, the first flower bloomed, and out of the bloom bounded a graceful dancer, which Sylvie recognized as Emelia. She was arrayed in white and gold to represent Sephora and danced gracefully across the stage and out of sight. She returned to the stage, a conglomeration of dancers in textured costumes representing birds and dragonflies in her wake. The other flowers bloomed in their turn, and the Firstborn Demetrius, Josias, and Morwenna were all represented, the stage illuminated in their respective colors during each number. Each of the Firstborn were displayed vaulting about on stage, ribbons and other embellishments in hand as beautifully crafted props appeared on stage amidst flashes of light representing various magical creatures. At one point, mermaids swam out of the stage and seemed to venture into the audience. Sylvie couldn't tell if it was simply an impressive stage lighting trick or if the mermaids were authentic creations. Regardless, she was stunned by the skill of the performers.

"This act represents the creation of the contents of our world as we know it," Gaëtan whispered to Sylvie as a dragon glided about on stage.

145

"It's wonderful," Sylvie answered, her eyes fixed on the stage.

As the first act came to a close, the creatures of the world left the stage, the stage dimming to bring the focus of the story back to the Firstborn. Josias and Morwenna stepped forward and engaged in a duet. The two dancers spent the opening moments apart, occasionally touching, only to leap away from each other again. As the performance progressed, the artists danced nearer and nearer, such that towards the end, Sylvie could hardly differentiate them as they spun and leaped across the stage in impressive unison. The scene culminated in a kiss.

Sylvie watched. Morwenna and Josias. Sylvie and Loïc. Her breath quickened involuntarily as she felt her chest tighten. She glanced towards Loïc's hand resting on the arm of his chair. He balled his hand into a fist and relaxed it again, unaware of her gaze.

After a moment of silence on the stage, the music erupted again, and spring and summer colors flooded the stage. Eventually, Demetrius and Sephora made their way to the stage, danced a duet, and ended with a kiss.

Gaëtan leaned into Sylvie, "Fredrich never failed to remind me he wasn't looking forward to that," Gaëtan said with a chuckle. Sylvie giggled softly. From the other side of the box, Sylvie could hear a groan. Margot was rolling her eyes.

"Spare us," she moaned.

"Now, now Margot," Loïc said softly, speaking for the first time in over an hour, "you assured me you're a patron of the arts now. Enjoy the show."

Sylvie giggled again at the two of them and at the thought that Margot's prank on Loïc seemed to have backfired on her.

Down below, the four dancing Firstborn gathered at the center of the stage, Sephora and Morwenna now sporting large golden blooms. After a last dance, with the music softly building, each couple came together and proudly displayed a golden seed for the audience to see. The music lilted as the seeds grew into beautiful buds and then fully formed flowers. The Firstborn couples raised their hands higher and higher as they danced, proudly showcasing the blooms. Reaching its climax, the dancers' arms were fully outstretched. Suddenly, the music resolved and ended, and the dancers stopped. The light focused on the Firstborn, but even more so on their precious flowers. It didn't end. Soon, a shadow crossed the stage, and sleeping creatures were brought to the front of the stage, where Rhys attempted to awaken them. Suddenly, the stage was swimming with shadows and monsters.

The stage darkened as the second intermission began. "I'll be right back. There is someone I'd like to speak with in the lobby," Gaëtan said.

"Where does a girl get something to drink?" Margot pressured.

"I'll accompany you," Gaëtan offered, extending his arm to her, "Would either of you like to join us? Sylvie, Loic?"

"No," Loïc stated bluntly.

"No, thank you," Sylvie smiled. And just like that, they were left alone. Sylvie glanced back at Loïc's hand. He turned to face her, and Sylvie awkwardly turned her attention to her folded hands in her lap.

"Enjoying yourself?" He asked.

"Quite," she nodded.

"What was your favorite scene?"

Sylvie hesitated, thinking back to the kiss, "Well... the duets were impressive. To have that type of control and fluidity in movement with two people. It's... what was your favorite?"

"The dragons, obviously," Loïc laughed.

Gaëtan and Margot returned to the box, and it wasn't long before the third act began and ended. It was a blur for Sylvie, who found herself glancing at Loïc's hand every few minutes. Eventually, she awoke from her trance as the stage went dark again, and the curtains dropped to hide the dancers.

Gaëtan and Sylvie joined the audience in applause. Loïc clapped stiffly. Margot stretched and let out a yawn.

"Well, what did you think?" Gaëtan asked Sylvie amid the noise.

"Far too whimsical for my taste. Thank you for asking," Margot replied sarcastically.

Sylvie made a face at Margot and turned to Gaëtan, "It was wonderful! The dancers were graceful, and the lights, costumes, and stage were magical."

"I agree," Gaëtan beamed. "Come on, let's catch some dancers backstage," he added.

Sylvie heard Loïc sigh at the suggestion as she stood to follow Gaëtan. Loïc and Margot followed suit.

In the corridors of the theater, all eyes were again on Sylvie, the mystery girl accompanying Verdélian royalty. She knew that starting tomorrow, she would have to get used to the attention, but for now, she wished she could sink into the shadows and disappear back to her cottage.

Once backstage, the four friends could barely hear one another over the bustle and noise of the dancers congratulating each other on a successful performance. Sylvie recognized Fredrich bouncing from room to room, loudly praising individual performances.

"Fredrich!" Gaëtan called out. Fredrich smiled and marched over to the Firstborn. On second glance, he realized that the three Firstborn and Sylvie were all present. With a look of surprise, he bowed quickly.

"It's an honor to have you all here!" He said.

"No need to be so formal, old friend," Gaëtan chuckled.

"It's not every day we get all the Firstborn together at one of our performances," Fredrich reminded Gaëtan. "In fact, I believe this would be the first time."

"And probably the last," Sylvie heard Margot mumble under her breath.

"Shhhh," Loïc hissed quietly to Margot, unable to suppress a chuckle.

Fredrich, who seemed to have missed Margot's remark, turned to Sylvie.

"Sylvie, our special guest! How did you enjoy the performance?" He asked.

"It was splendid. You're very talented. All of you are," Sylvie said.

"You flatter me!" Fredrich replied with a brief bow.

"Nonsense," Gaëtan said, "You were remarkable."

"Thank you," Fredrich said. "Oh!" He added as an afterthought, "Sylvie, Maya was looking for you. She's two doors down on your right."

"Oh?" Sylvie asked, puzzled. Clearly, Fredrich expected her to find Maya, so she hesitantly separated herself from the group and ventured down the hall. She found Maya's door open. Maya smiled when she saw Sylvie.

"Sylvie," she said with a deep curtsy, "Fredrich must have found you. Please, come in."

Sylvie stepped inside, still unsure what Maya could be wanting.

Maya approached an intricate vanity against the wall and picked up a dark blue box.

"I was so honored to have you present for this performance," Maya said as she approached Sylvie, box in hand. "Especially with my being cast as Morwenna. I couldn't have asked for a better opportunity. I wanted you to have this as a souvenir of your first ballet."

Maya opened the box. Inside, a beautiful copper tiara sat on a velvet cushion. The craftsmanship was flawless, and the metal was wrought carefully to resemble flowing water. In the center, a large blue gem grabbed Sylvie's eye. Sylvie drew in a sharp breath in surprise.

"It's gorgeous," she breathed.

"It suits you," Maya said kindly. "If you permit me to say so, even if you'll be wearing the real thing soon enough, I hope a simple theater prop will help you remember tonight."

Sylvie stared at Maya with wide eyes.

"But..." she stammered, "How did you...I mean, what do you mean?"

Maya giggled, "Oh, come now," she answered, "not everyone gets a personal tour of the theater from Gaëtan. But the real giveaway was the four of you attending the performance tonight. I don't think anyone expected that, but the message was clear enough."

Sylvie grimaced. "I was told nothing was being said until tomorrow."

"Yes, well, we're close enough now, I think," Maya reassured her.

Maya placed the open box with the tiara in Sylvie's hands.

"It was my honor to portray Morwenna," Maya said. "Now it's your turn, and not just for show. You'll be magnificent." Maya curtsied deeply again.

Sylvie quickly remembered the need to find four people to represent the elements for her inheritance ceremony. "Can I ask you one other favor?" Sylvie asked Maya.

Maya looked at Sylvie with an air of curious excitement.

"Of course, anything."

"I'm sorry, you absolutely can say no if you feel uncomfortable with this, but my inheritance ceremony is soon, and I've no one to stand in for the water... person—"

*Is she asking me?*

"Yes. I want to ask you if you would do that for me. I haven't many friends, and if anyone represents water well, you did it tonight on stage. I could see myself in you, and I hope to carry the position with as much grace as you carry your role on stage."

"I'm honored." Maya's mouth gaped open for a moment before she remembered her manners. "May I invite Fredrich to accompany me?"

"Yes, of course. You'll have to get the details from Gaëtan, I'm afraid. He knows the ins and outs of what's happening. I'm just doing what I'm told."

"I will," Maya said with a smile.

Sylvie stared at the tiara in her hands. To her, it symbolized the weight of her new calling.

# XIV

## *Festival of Flowers*

S ylvie sat staring at her several reflections shown in the many facets of the large blue gem set in the crown she was to wear to the Festival that night. The beautiful copper crown perfectly portrayed the formality and nobility of her new life. She felt entirely inadequate to be revealed publicly as Verdélian royalty, but the time for preparation had passed, and she had little choice now.

Sylvie sighed and sat up. She looked around at the beautiful room around her. That morning, Nadine and some other palace staff members had moved her belongings from 3 Amber Lane into her new suite in the palace. The suite was probably barely smaller than her entire cottage had been on Amber Lane. In the center of the far wall was an enormous poster bed covered in deep blue bedding embroidered with copper thread. Sheer drapes hung from the bed frame. The colors of the Firstborn Morwenna, deep watery blues and copper, arrayed the room.

Sylvie stood and began pacing the floor as she ran the schedule of events over in her mind. Gaëtan had spent hours reciting the events of that evening with Sylvie to help her feel a little more comfortable with the whole thing. Still, she knew that the Festival would mean hundreds of guests, all staring at her and judging her worthiness as the long-awaited Morwenna. Sylvie felt the knot in her stomach tighten.

She had also experienced sudden worry when discussing the festival with Sir Reynard. She questioned if the women showing off their flowers and the men being present were inviting a litany of seeds to be born. Was she going to be a mother after this weekend? He had laughed.

No dear. All male attendees are expected—or rather required—to wear gloves for the event. In any event, the misuse of the power that blooms on the night of the Festival of Flowers is a capital crime. The ceremony celebrates the beauty of Verdélian women and their blooms, and all in attendance will treat it accordingly.

A soft knock at the door shook Sylvie from her thoughts.

"Come in," Sylvie said nervously.

Nadine entered the room. Sylvie noticed she had set her hair sash aside for the Festival, and there above Nadine's ear was a fully formed chrysanthemum, the petals tinged in a perfectly black soot. It was a strangely beautiful thing.

Nadine smiled at Sylvie and bowed quickly.

"You look your part, Miss Sylvie," she said, "none will doubt your identity tonight."

Sylvie instinctively glanced in the mirror nearby. Over the locks of blonde hair, she displayed the rose that had been growing beneath her sash these past few weeks. As golden as her hair was, the rose eclipsed it unequivocally.

"They may not doubt my identity," Sylvie muttered, "but most will doubt my ability."

"Perhaps," Nadine said, "but you'll just have to prove them wrong."

*Easier said than done*, Sylvie thought, though she appreciated Nadine's reassurance.

"In fact," Nadine continued, "you can start right now. I was coming to bring you down to join the others."

"Very well," Sylvie said somberly. There was no getting away from it now.

Sylvie followed Nadine down to the ground level and through several hallways towards the palace's rear gardens, where hundreds of guests gathered to celebrate the Festival. As they approached a set of large doors that opened onto a sprawling stone balcony that led down into the gardens, Sylvie could make out Gaëtan, Loïc, and Margot. All three dressed elegantly in their respective colors and bore elaborate crowns on their heads, matching Sylvie's. Sylvie blinked hard to ensure she was awake; the scene seemed like an outlandish dream.

Loïc noticed her first and bowed politely. She noticed his black gloves, mainly because they were out of character.

"Welcome, Sylvie. Come, take your place with us," he said.

His invitation took her off guard but bolstered her fledgling confidence.

"Sylvie! This is so exciting!" Gaëtan said in true Gaëtan fashion. "Sweet for the nerves?"

"Yes, please," Sylvie said, putting out her hand. Gaëtan dropped a hard candy into it.

"Chamomile," he whispered, "It's hard, don't bite it. Just let it dissolve on your tongue."

"You're finally here. The sooner we get you out there, the sooner we can send everyone home." Margot added with a sigh. Gaëtan rolled his eyes with a smile.

"Nice to see you joined us," Sylvie said, opting for humor in response to Margot's characteristically moody comment. She rolled the candy over in her mouth awkwardly.

"They did not inform me this was an optional commitment," Margot said with a smirk. Sylvie shrugged, sharing Margot's sentiment.

"Ready?" Loïc asked the group.

Before anyone could answer, the doors swung open, and Loïc began making his way outside. The four Firstborn walked side by side to greet their guests. Sylvie had to quicken her pace to take her place between Loïc and Gaëtan.

As rehearsed, the four of them made their way out across the stone plaza and stopped in front of the balcony, looking down into the gardens. Bright torches and lanterns illuminated the venue. Sylvie tried not to show her alarm as she gazed down at hundreds and hundreds of regal Verdélia, now turning their attention to the balcony on which she stood.

"Good evening!" Gaëtan announced in a compelling tone. Sylvie barely recognized Gaëtan's voice, which seemed far more formal and measured.

Gaëtan continued, his voice a mesmerizing echo on the refreshing night breeze.

"Good evening and welcome, fellow Verdélia! Thank you for joining us tonight as we celebrate the Festival of Flowers!"

There was a brief round of polite applause. Sylvie looked out at the women. Flowers upon flowers floated about on the heads of every woman present. True to Sir Reynard's word, the men all wore gloves carefully designed to compliment their formal ensembles.

"Tonight, we are honored to celebrate doubly with you. We, the Firstborn, present Sylvie, our long-awaited Morwenna." Gaëtan gestured to Sylvie. Loïc and Margot turned to Sylvie so that all eyes were on her. If she didn't feel nervous before, she did now. A burst of barely restrained whispering chatter emerged quickly from the crowd, almost drowning the applause that followed Gaëtan's announcement.

Loïc stepped forward slightly and took his turn to address their guests.

"The ranks of Verdélian royalty are now filled. We stand ready to serve our people more fully and perfectly than ever before. We thank you for your support." Another round of polite applause followed.

"Now, please, enjoy your evening," Loïc continued.

The four Firstborn descended the steps into the gardens. All eyes were on Sylvie, and as they stepped onto the lush grass, guests bowed reverently as Sylvie passed. Soft voices whispered, "Welcome, Morwenna," one after another as the Firstborn continued into the garden.

Finally, they made it to the center of the yard, surrounded by beautiful hanging lanterns strung from the immaculate trees and plants growing in the perfectly manicured grounds. The Firstborn turned and stood in a circle; their backs turned towards each other, and they waved, welcoming their guests. Almost immediately, Sylvie saw a dark figure approaching purposefully, the silhouettes of two women in tow. Loïc also seemed to notice and inched ever closer to Sylvie.

"High Councilman Beyern," Loïc called, more for Sylvie's benefit than anything else. "We're so glad you could join us."

*Beyern. Where have I his name before?* Sylvie wondered.

Councilman Beyern bowed as he reached them. "Rumors were spreading of a special announcement tonight. I wouldn't have missed it." His voice was rugged and low. As he spoke, his deep-set eyes scoured Sylvie, a mixture of curiosity, doubt, and disdain set in his weathered and bearded face. "Morwenna, welcome," he said with another bow, this time directed squarely at Sylvie. *Children to lead this people in such a time.* Sylvie made a concerted effort to prevent her features from betraying the fact that she was privy to Beyern's internal criticism.

*That's right*, she thought. *Gaëtan's advisor was worried about what he would think.*

"Perhaps," Beyern continued, straightening his frame, "we will finally be witness to true leadership from the Firstborn now that your ranks are complete. Your announcement comes not a moment too soon, considering our petition to appoint a steward." Sylvie didn't have to access Beyern's mind to see that he disapproved of Sylvie and was bitterly disappointed he could not have a steward appointed in her place.

"Indeed," Loïc said. "It would have been a substantial loss for the Verdélia to have a steward appointed when the rightful fourth Firstborn was out there, after all."

Sylvie could feel the tension of the political stakes in what appeared to be a simple conversation, but she was not well-versed enough or confident enough to engage. She was grateful for Loïc's help. *This exchange would be a disaster without him*, she thought.

"A great loss indeed," Beyern agreed, at least verbally. *Shield her while you can, boy. She'll have to face reality eventually*, Sylvie heard Beyern think as he turned to Sylvie, "I have someone to introduce you to, Madam..." he gestured to receive her name.

"Sylvie," she smiled, taking his outstretched hand in greeting.

He gestured to the woman over his left shoulder. "This is Lysandra. I had the pleasure of voting for her appointment as advisor to Morwenna nearly nineteen years ago. Unfortunately, she has been set on the sideline all this time, as your position was unknown. I will be glad to see her finally put to use."

4020 | Autumn | 4th Moon | 25

"Oh," Sylvie glanced at the woman. Her skin and hair were both dark, her eyes almond-shaped, and her cheekbones high. Sylvie thought this woman looked far more regal than she did. "Lysandra," she repeated.

"Yes," she bowed, "It will be a pleasure to serve under you finally. I wish I could've known of you directly when you arrived. I thought I might've known, considering Margot's advisor—Seraphine—and I are quite fast friends. Though it seems the secret was kept carefully within the bonds of the Firstborn."

"A testament to our caution, I suppose," Sylvie replied politely.

*Or your lies*, she heard Beyern think.

"Tell me," Sylvie continued, "What do you hope to accomplish as my advisor?"

Lysandra's mind stuttered before she spoke. "Only to offer my advice and serve you in the best capacity I can, ma'am."

Sylvie nodded, "And if you don't mind me asking, what is it about you that earned Councilman Beyern's vote of confidence to be Morwenna's advisor?"

Lysandra hesitated a moment before jumping into a response that sounded like it had been rehearsed hundreds of times, "I've served for many years under the tutelage of various council members in positions of service—secretary, researcher, and similar. I know the ins and outs of government processes as I've studied them extensively both within the university and afterward. I am sure I will offer you guidance and direction in times of uncertainty, though I plan to allow you to make most of the decisions without me if that pleases you."

Loïc's eyes were on Sylvie now, questioning her boldness. Sylvie nodded in response to Lysandra's answer and expressed joy at having someone new to work with. Loïc stepped back into the conversation.

"Beyern, will you be present tomorrow? We have planned for Sylvie's inheritance ceremony. Although we scheduled your time for another purpose, I hope you are still planning to attend as a witness." Loïc posed the question, knowing the answer.

"I am in your service, Master Loïc." He bowed again before walking away. Lysandra and the other woman, whom he had not introduced, followed him.

Sylvie paused a moment, "There's something up with him."

"What do you mean?" Loïc whispered without looking at her.

"I don't know yet. He's just off," she shrugged.

"You would know better than the rest of us," Loïc admitted.

Sylvie touched Loïc's arm softly. "I have a question for you. I still have chosen no one to represent fire, and I would be honored if you would accept my... invitation to perform that part of the ceremony for me."

Loïc smiled at her. "The honor would be mine."

He began turning to lead her in another direction, "Careful with him, by the way," Loïc whispered to Sylvie. "Councilman Beyern wields tremendous influence on the Council."

Sylvie nodded quietly. And over their advisors, too, it seemed.

The night went on, and Sylvie met the High Councilmen from each district, along with a handful of other Council members who had attended the celebrations at the palace. Although each High Councilman was intensely wary of Sylvie, none had been so overtly condescending as Beyern. Gaëtan had taken over for Loïc at Sylvie's side and had helped stoke some lively conversation between Sylvie and a few of their guests. Later, Sylvie found herself without a companion and noticed Emelia in the distance.

She turned to Nadine, who was hovering nearby.

"Did Gaëtan invite Emilia?" She asked.

"Not quite," Nadine answered. "Emilia is the daughter of Councilman Philippe, the other Winter Councilman. Beyern is the first. All Council members, along with their families, are invited."

"Ah," Sylvie said with a nod of her head. "Do you know Emilia? I think she doesn't like me."

*More than I'd care to, and she doesn't like anyone much other than herself*, Sylvie heard Nadine think to herself.

"Not well. I'm sure she'll take to you." Nadine said out loud.

"I guess I should go say hello," Sylvie said, feeling a sense of responsibility. Her mouth puckered at the thought of what seemed to be an inevitably unpleasant interaction. She took a breath and started across the lawn.

"Emelia," Sylvie sang brightly as she approached Emelia, "how are you? I never got the chance to congratulate you on your performance at the ballet. You were splendid!"

Emelia turned to see who was addressing her.

*Ah, the new Verdélian "celebrity,"* Sylvie heard from Emelia's mind. *Of course, I was splendid.*

"Sylvie," Emelia said with a short curtsy, "how kind of you to mention the ballet."

"Of course!" Sylvie replied with a smile, ignoring Emelia's mental dialogue. "I'm happy to see you at the palace."

Emelia smiled politely.

"I'd love to meet your family," Sylvie continued, forcing her way through the one-sided conversation. "I assume you're here with them?"

"I am," Emelia answered. She turned to an older man with an average build and a woman by his side.

"Mother, Father," she said, "please meet our host, Sylvie."

"It's an honor," Sylvie said.

"Please, the honor is all ours," Emelia's father said as he and his spouse greeted Sylvie with dignified bows.

"I am Phillipe," Emelia's father said, "and this is my wife, Ruth. We're so glad to meet the long-awaited fourth Firstborn. Welcome to Verdélys."

"Thank you very much. That means a lot to me," Sylvie said with a smile.

Emelia chimed in. "My father is councilman of the Winter district. I assume you'll be working closely with him from now on."

Phillipe seemed slightly embarrassed by the comment but said nothing.

"I suppose I will be," Sylvie agreed.

Phillipe was a quiet man, both inside and out. Sylvie had gotten a read on Councilman Beyern through his thoughts. She wasn't getting anything from Phillipe. His wife, Ruth, was a non-stop stream of negativity. Some aimed at Sylvie, but most at Nadine, who had followed close behind Sylvie. Ruth considered herself significantly above Nadine on the social hierarchy. Sylvie worked hard to keep her face from betraying her disgust at Ruth's ugly thoughts. Over her ear, her lavender flower was nearly covered by a gaudy, golden earpiece.

Sylvie excused herself from Emelia and her family, curtsied to her guests, and walked away, beckoning Nadine closer. "The earpieces," she whispered, "What are they?"

"The marriage tokens?" Nadine asked, "The women wear the earpiece to show they are wed. Men have the armbands." Sylvie nodded, happy to get an answer to a question that had been lingering since her first day in Verdélys.

Eventually, the Firstborn made their way back up onto the rear plaza. The festivities died down as eyes turned upwards towards them. Gaëtan welcomed their guests for coming and declared an end to the festivities. A few minutes later, the last invitees were ushered out by palace staff. Once the gardens were empty, the Firstborn turned and retreated into the palace. Overall, the evening seemed to have been a success, and Sylvie had enjoyed meeting several of the Verdélian politicians and socialites, many of whom were fascinating individuals.

The Firstborn all made their way up the stairs. Once at the top, Loïc turned to the others and addressed Sylvie.

"Congratulations, Sylvie, you just survived your first official public event as a Firstborn."

Sylvie smiled bashfully. "Thank you," she replied.

"Only a lifetime more to go," Loïc added with a hint of a grin.

"Yes, yes, great job." Margot interrupted with a yawn. "Now, good night." She turned and strode quickly down the hall towards her suite.

"Good night, Margot," the three remaining Firstborn called out after her. Margot lifted her arm in acknowledgment but did not turn around and disappeared beyond the corner.

"I will follow Margot's lead," Loïc said. "Good night." He, in turn, made his way towards his room.

"Good night Loïc," Sylvie and Gaëtan said.

Gaëtan turned to Sylvie with a smile.

"You did wonderfully tonight! I'm sure you're going to do great things as a Firstborn."

Sylvie couldn't keep a big smile from creeping across her face.

"I sure hope you're right," she said.

"Of course I am," Gaëtan replied.

Gaëtan stuck out an arm. "May I escort you to your room?"

Sylvie tucked a stray piece of hair behind her ear as she gingerly placed her arm around Gaëtan's.

"Yes, please," she said.

The two friends crept towards Sylvie's new suite in the palace. When they reached her door, Gaëtan stopped and turned to Sylvie.

"Good night, Sylvie," he said with a bow.

"Good night, Gaëtan," Sylvie replied.

Gaëtan bowed to go, and as he did, he took Sylvie's hand and gently kissed it. Sylvie blushed as she watched Gaëtan recede down the hall and out of sight. Her cheeks may have turned red, but she waited for a stirring of the heart that never came. In the quiet of the palace, she retired to her suite for the night.

# XV

*Inheritance*

S ylvie felt the velvet tickle of a petal between her fingers. She was lying on
her stomach in bed, waiting to open her eyes, still exhausted from the
previous night's events. Something tickled her nose, and she jerked her head
back, opening her eyes. On the pillow, she noticed the fallen golden petals from
her bloom. She sat up on her knees and pulled her blanket around her to keep
out the chill.

The petals glowed, laying on the pillow, but they were all too soon losing
their luster. Sylvie touched her temple where the flower used to reside. It felt as
natural as it had before her Verdélian days. A smile crossed her face as she
gathered the petals and set them aside on her desk for Nadine to preserve or
discard as she saw fit.

Before long, she sat comfortably around the breakfast table with the other
Firstborn. Gaëtan was reading, which Sylvie recognized as a breakfast habit for
him. Loïc ate purposefully, focusing on a city map he occasionally scribbled on
with red ink. Meredith had hardly touched her food, preferring to fidget with
a large emerald ring on her right forefinger. Sylvie had made it through most of
her breakfast but was gazing vacantly through a window now, her mind
wandering. Rousing herself from her daydream, Sylvie excused herself, ready
to return to her studies.

"Sylvie, before you go," Loïc said as Sylvie stood.

Sylvie turned to face Loïc. Gaëtan and Margot also glanced up as if part of
whatever announcement Loïc had planned.

"Yes?" Sylvie asked curiously.

"Being that your inheritance ceremony is tonight, I don't suppose you have
questions," Loïc explained.

Sylvie had learned a little about Inheritance Day as part of her Verdélian
culture and customs courses with Sir Reynard. Each Verdélia, to prepare for
their twentieth year, received an inheritance to see them successfully begin

their lives as independent members of Verdélian society. There was a ceremony associated with it, though at the moment, the details had slipped Sylvie's mind.

"Just that I needed four people to represent each Firstborn and their element."

"Yes, four people you know that best represent those things. And you've found them all?"

Sylvie nodded erratically. "Yes, you and Gaëtan, understandably. Maya, from the ballet. I asked if she could represent Morwenna—water. And Alfric, I asked him yesterday if he would take Demetrius' place—earth. I would've asked you, Margot," turning to face a stern gaze, "Only I was under the impression that the council wouldn't allow it, otherwise—"

Margot interrupted, "Yes, you're quite right. No need to apologize." She waved it off quickly.

"I could use some clarification on a few points, though," Sylvie said. "Last time we spoke of it, Loïc, you had mentioned that each person will symbolically bestow on me the gifts of the Firstborn. What are their gifts?"

"You'll at least know yours," Loïc replied, tapping the side of his head with a finger as a hint.

"The mind reading for me, I suppose," Sylvie replied, rubbing the side and nape of her neck to keep her hands busy.

"That, and theoretically, the whole world's history may be available to you through the water supply," he smiled.

"But the gifts aren't literally bestowed on all Verdélia, surely?" Sylvie questioned.

"No, it's symbolic."

Gaëtan leaned back, folded his leg over his knee, and got back into his book.

"Right," she nodded.

Loïc's hand flashed up near his ear as a small fly seemed to take an interest in him. "Mine is related to fire: physical strength and agility, as well as endurance," he slapped at the air again. A realization dawned on him, and he glared in Gaëtan's direction.

Sylvie followed Loïc's gaze and, to her surprise, saw Gaëtan smiling from ear to ear behind his book. Margot was chuckling. Loïc spoke up, "You know, for a patron of the arts, you're a horrible actor."

"Well, what? We had to put that physical agility of yours to the test," Gaëtan said with a sly smile. "Me fire! Me so strong!" Gaëtan mimicked as he beat his chest with one hand.

Margot crowed with laughter.

Loïc rolled his eyes. "Good heavens."

Sylvie was smiling but still lost. "What is going on?"

"Gaëtan's gift is more subtle," Loïc said, turning to face her. "He can manipulate light to create illusions."

"Oh, the fly!" Sylvie recognized quickly, and suddenly, a butterfly fluttered around her head.

"Yes," Gaëtan replied, "I've never found much use for it except for ridiculous pranks."

Margot had calmed down and sat back in her chair, far more relaxed.

Sylvie turned to her, "And Margot, yours?"

"Prophecy," she replied stoically, "But alas, I'm an imp."

"But isn't that just a winter ability?" Sylvie asked honestly.

Margot shook her head, "Not exactly. Prophecy flows through them from another source, and it's very visual. Historically, the Firstborn descended from Demetrius—me—could say something, and it was certain to be realized at some later time. I don't know all the rules exactly. I've never been able to do it," she shrugged.

"Oh," Sylvie began, "that sounds incredible."

Margot just shrugged.

※

Sylvie stood nervously on the steps of the beautiful little chapel in the rear gardens of the palace. At Sylvie's request, Margot stood nearby, her vibrant red locks swaying in the winter breeze. Margot wore an elegant green dress, though it was not as sophisticated as Sylvie's.

Sylvie dressed formally. Margot and Nadine—neither of which had had their own Inheritance Day ceremony—had reminded Sylvie that the event was one of deep cultural and spiritual significance and was treated with deep reverence. Sylvie's dress reflected this as she stood in a white silk dress overlaid with highly sophisticated lace all over the bodice, which, like so many things in Verdélys, was woven into scenes of nature. Sylvie's long skirt cinched at her waist with the help of beautiful pearl buttons and flowed elegantly down, draping along the floor. Her sleeves were long and made of lace, clasped at her wrists with more pearl buttons. A large crown of white flowers sat on her head, pinned into place by a beautiful golden tiara adorned with yet more pearls, some hanging from delicate golden chains that draped around Sylvie's head. She wore earrings and a lavish necklace to match her crown.

The chapel itself was quaint by palace standards but perfect in its craftsmanship and exquisite. The ceiling donned many panes of multicolored glass, and the masonry was smooth and clear, embellished with sculptures and engravings of trees and flowers.

The heavy wooden doors of the chapel, carved to match the landscapes engraved in the chapel's stone walls, swung open, creaking deeply as two guards opened them.

"You're up," Margot whispered beside Sylvie.

The little chapel hosted a very humble gathering. As Sylvie walked up the aisle down a beautiful velvet carpet, she saw Sir Reynard and Nadine seated in the ornate wooden pews lining the aisle. Fredrich was there, too.

Loïc, Gaëtan, Alfric, and Maya stood up a short flight of steps at the end of the little chapel. All attendees were dressed formally: Loïc and Gaëtan in uniforms she had seen before, Alfric in armor too beautiful to take into battle, and Maya in a gorgeous blue dress with an oversized chiffon skirt. Maya smiled big as Sylvie entered the chapel. She made her way towards her four friends. A fifth Verdélia, a Winter Verdélia who Margot explained would officiate the ceremony, was dressed in a long white robe with a large hood embroidered in gold. Her raven hair fell out of her hood in perfectly straight lines, in beautiful contrast to the immaculate white of her attire.

Sylvie reached the bottom of the stairs and stopped. There was silence, and Sylvie could feel the attention of all in attendance on her.

"Children of Solaidi, welcome," the officiator stated.

"We gather today to witness Sylvie's passage through the elements of this world, that she may emerge blessed thereby and equipped to walk the path marked for her by Solaidi. Let us begin."

The black-haired woman turned to Maya.

"Maya, you stand as proxy for the element of water, which soothes, cleanses, and brings life. As water nourishes and quenches, so too may this inheritance nurture Sylvie's spirit."

Maya stepped down to meet Sylvie, a beautiful tiny porcelain cup in her hand.

"In this sacred water, Solaidi blesses you Sylvie with the power to bring comfort and life where it is wanting. May it connect your soul to others and weave you into the tapestry of our shared history."

Sylvie put her hands out, forming a bowl. Maya poured the contents of her receptacle into Sylvie's hands, the water brisk on Sylvie's skin. As instructed, Sylvie let the water run through her fingers and onto the ground. Maya turned and walked back up the steps.

The officiator spoke again.

"Loïc, you stand as proxy for the element of fire, which purifies, refines, and consumes. May this inheritance remove the dross from Sylvie's being that would prevent her from reaching her fullest potential."

Loïc approached Sylvie. He extended his hand, palm upwards. Before Sylvie's eyes, a flame burst to life from Loïc's hand.

"Through this living flame, Solaidi blesses you, Sylvie, with the determination and fervor needed to see your destiny to its righteous ends. May it be a strength to body and soul and a remedy for all ills."

As instructed, Sylvie ran her hand in a swift horizontal motion through the fire. The warmth was welcome on her frigid fingers. She gazed up at Loïc as he offered her a quick nod.

Loïc regained his place at the front of the chapel.

The officiator addressed Alfric.

"Alfric, you stand as a proxy for the element of earth, which grounds and stabilizes all living things and is the foundation of all wisdom. May this inheritance grant Sylvie knowledge of things otherwise unknowable."

Alfric stepped solemnly down towards Sylvie. Sylvie extended her hands, palms down.

"In this holy ground, Solaidi blesses you with the opening of your inner eye. May it reveal to you truths concealed to ordinary observers and the ability to transcend barriers."

Alfric marked the back of Sylvie's hands with a dark, moist clay. Then he turned and walked back up beside Loïc.

"Gaëtan," the woman said, turning to the last of the four at the head of the chapel, "you stand as proxy for the element of air, which is fleeting yet forceful. May this inheritance grant Sylvie the ability to manifest her pure desires."

Gaëtan approached. Sylvie held up her hands, her palms towards Gaëtan, and her fingers spread apart.

"In this all-encompassing air, Solaidi blesses you so that you may weave your dreams into the fabric of reality and that by so doing, you may knit bonds as strong as the sky is wide."

Gaëtan held out his hands, forming a stage in front of his chest. He exhaled deeply through his nose, and a miniature gale formed in his hands. He pushed the little windstorm towards Sylvie, and she felt it flurry between her fingers before dissipating. Gaëtan walked back up the stairs and stood beside Alfric.

The officiator continued.

"Sylvie, you have received your inheritance from Solaidi. By so doing, you have bound yourself to this world and its fate. In return, the elements bind themselves to you and grant you power to become a force for good, to benefit all things, living or otherwise, that are part of this beautiful world. May you live your life conscious of this charge."

The officiator gave a short bow of her head and smiled.

Sylvie looked around. All about her, her friends beamed, their eyes and attention turned to her. Sylvie suddenly felt a wave of emotion take over her as tears of joy bubbled in her eyes. Then her eyes rested on Beyern seated amongst the attending council members, and the smirk of a smile on his face gave Sylvie a feeling of dread. Behind the council sat the Firstborn's advisors, Lysandra's eyes burrowing into the back of Beyern's head.

*I will become a force for good*, Sylvie thought in answer to the admonition.

# XVI

## *The Trial of Belthégor*

"Sylvie!" A knock at the door sounded. Another knock, louder this time, sounded before Sylvie could respond as she waited for Nadine to finish buttoning up her dress.

"Yes?" she called out. The door opened, and Gaëtan walked in, a look of worry plastered on his face. He turned his head sideways when he realized she was amidst dressing, and once Sylvie realized why he averted his eyes, she said, "It's alright. I'm finished dressing." She could feel Nadine fastening the top button.

Gaëtan nodded and continued, "You will need to redress, regardless."

"Why is that?" The imp servants quickly made their way out of the room to afford Sylvie and Gaëtan privacy. Sylvie placed her hand on Nadine's forearm, momentarily motioning for her to stand nearby.

"It seems that the council has decided to... well, let's just call it a baptism by fire."

"That sounds like something more suited to Loïc."

Gaëtan hardly smiled. "Your first hearing as High Arbiter has been scheduled for this afternoon."

"Scheduled by whom?"

"The Council. Beyern, most likely. It wouldn't worry me so much, except that the case in question is high profile. The highest profile case in Verdélys." Gaëtan was pacing now.

"Well, reschedule it," Sylvie hoped.

"I would. Really, I would. However, a proclamation was published throughout all of Verdélys yesterday evening announcing a historical judicial process where we will finally see the acquittal or execution of one 'Belthégor.'" Gaëtan's voice was getting more firm with every word.

"Who is he?" Sylvie questioned.

Gaëtan stopped pacing and glanced back at Sylvie. "Solaidi, save us. Sylvie." His facial expression hinted that she should know this name. "The war of our birth. He's the imp who was arrested and charged with treason. He was the mastermind behind the disappearing children and dead Verdélia across the city. Twenty years he's sat in prison awaiting his trial at your hand since only Morwenna can try a capital case. I figured it would come up. It just seems that someone intends you to make a fool of yourself at your first trial in front of the whole of the city."

He paused, then continued, "Everyone knows. The court will be full. You will preside over the case—"

"Gaëtan. I only know the basics—nothing of the practice. I can't make such a dire decision in one afternoon, and I can't run the procedure," Sylvie choked out.

"We have to find a way," Gaëtan shrugged nervously. "If you're a cynic, then you might think that this was planned to make us look incompetent to the public. Perhaps it is, but I need you to pull through for us as best you can." His eyes lit up as an idea came to him. "I will find your advisor. She will help you. In the meantime, decide what preparation will be best for you and pour yourself into it. I trust you." He hurriedly dashed out of the bedroom, and without glancing at Nadine, Sylvie leaned in towards her.

"I don't trust my advisor... Will you inquire as to what I am supposed to wear for this... event? I have something I need to do."

"Yes, Miss Sylvie," Nadine curtsied and rushed from the room. Sylvie's bare feet felt sticky as she fled down the marble staircase, spun around a few corners, and found herself in the library.

"Sir Reynard!" She called out upon entering. She explained the situation as they stood before the glass door entrance. "What I need," she explained, "Is for you to come and think in your head what I should do to help direct me. I'll be able to read your thoughts—"

"I cannot do that for you, young one," he explained, "As you may have noticed, not a thought comes into a centaur's mind that we do not directly voice. Very young, we learn not to think things we wouldn't want heard. If I were to think my thoughts, they would come out in the same fashion. I cannot hide my thoughts from the crowd and conceal them in a package for you. You will need to find an alternative."

Sylvie's heart sank, and her shoulders drooped.

"How frightfully inconvenient. I have no time, Sir Reynard. Who do I go to for help?"

He spoke immediately, "Alfric. If he cannot help you, he has many men at his disposal whose abilities and gifts he knows. Unfortunately, I am somewhat more familiar with books than people and cannot help you more than that."

Sylvie rushed towards the gate where Alfric was usually found. She bowed to the guards as she approached the gatehouse and walked inside. "Alfric!" she called out.

A calm and collected face glanced up from his desk of papers towards his visitor. She could see her face through his eyes. *Miss Sylvie,* he thought and stood quickly.

"There is no need for pleasantries," she began. "I need someone who knows judicial practice. My first trial has been scheduled for this afternoon without notice, and I need guidance. Is that something you are capable of, or do you know someone? Someone I can trust."

His eyes looked up as he thought, and a few names and men crossed his mind before he settled on one face. "I have a captain of one of my guards. Captain Durand. He studied judicial practice before settling in the military. He is knowledgeable, but more than just that, I can attest to his character. I know he will guide you in the best way he knows how."

"May I meet him?"

"I will call for him presently."

Before long, a man stood before her with dark flowing hair tinged with red, hiding his forehead and falling to just below his ears. His eyes were deep blue-grey, and he nodded to Sylvie as he entered the room.

"Captain Durand?" She asked.

"At your service, miss," he bowed.

"I understand you are familiar with judicial practice. I find myself unexpectedly scheduled for my first judicial hearing today. I'm looking for someone who would feel comfortable sitting near the stand... or on the stand, potentially, with me. I want someone who can think through the process as it unfolds and guide me through the procedure and decisions in their mind. You will need to be comfortable with having your mind open to me so that I may access any information on the judicial process I might need. I will also need your knowledge given up clearly so that I may make informed decisions at different stages in the process. You do not need to decide the outcome for me. I simply need your wisdom as to the process and my options."

"Yes, miss. I am willing." He looked Sylvie in the eyes, sure, and decided.

"Alfric speaks to your character, and if I only had his opinion to guide me, I would trust you very much; however, I must know you have the knowledge I will need."

"I have a perfect memory, miss. Every book I have read, every case and procedure I have studied, I can recall at will. I can walk you through everything I know as needed. I am no lawyer, mind you, but the theoretical knowledge will be available to you." Sylvie watched in his mind as he cycled through visions of books and parchments before him.

Sylvie nodded, "Very well. What are the first words I will speak during the trial?"

"You will call the trial to order by stating, 'This trial is hereby called to order. May Solaidi guide us to justice.'"

"Thank you, Captain. You will share this plan with no one. There are those who would... well. Just keep it secret. Alfric, you as well please."

"We are bound by your command, miss," both soldiers stated with a bow.

※

After a whirlwind of preparations that morning, Sylvie was dressed in a white dress and robe trimmed with navy lace and embroidered with copper thread. She met Alfric, Captain Durand, and twenty other guards at the gates, who walked her through the streets towards the courthouse in a regal procession. As they walked, Durand whispered procedural information into Sylvie's ear.

"You'll be presiding over the proceeding," Durand explained. "You'll be expected to call the matter to order. You call in the accused, and then you give the Sword the first audience."

Sylvie recalled from her lessons with Sir Reynard that the Sword was the Verdélia responsible for bringing the case against anyone charged with a crime.

"The Sword will call witnesses against the accused. The Sword will question the witnesses audibly, but of course, you will be free to conduct your own investigation into the minds of the witnesses and others."

"Can I question the witness?" Sylvie asked.

"You may," Captain Durand nodded.

"The Shield may also question any witnesses called by the Sword."

Sir Reynard explained to Sylvie that the Shield would defend the accused. It was the Shield's duty to examine and expose flaws in the Sword's case against the accused.

"When the Sword's witnesses have all been examined, the Shield is granted their audience. Like the Sword, the Shield may call its witnesses to support the defense. Once all witnesses have testified, you will be expected to make your ruling."

Sylvie swallowed nervously. Not one person with whom she had conversed that morning had failed to impress upon her the gravity of the crimes Belthégor stood accused of. The list of offenses was enough to justify death multiple times over under Verdelian law. Sylvie would be the final judge of this man's guilt—and whether or not he would live or die.

Sylvie and her escorts reached the courthouse, a beautiful and intimidating structure. Large stone pillars carved into trees soared overhead. On the facade of the building, Sylvie saw an intricately carved mural centered around the image of a fire. On the one side of the flames, individuals were throwing weeds and other chaff into the flames to be consumed. On the other side, a smith was purifying metal for his forge.

An enormous crowd had gathered below the stairs leading up to the courthouse entrance. Over a dozen guards barred access to the courthouse steps, shields and spears in hand. The members of the crowd were visibly agitated, voicing their opinions and concerns raucously as they milled about. Sylvie couldn't make out anything coherent from the noise.

When the crowd recognized Sylvie's procession, it turned its collective back on the courthouse and swarmed towards Sylvie. Before she could feel any apprehension at the approaching mob, her guards instinctively formed a defensive barrier between her and the crowd, shields raised and spears forward.

"Step back!" Alfric cried in a voice so powerful Sylvie had to remind herself the command was not directed at her.

The crowd slowed and halted a pace away from the glinting tips of the soldiers' spears.

"Give us justice!" a man yelled towards Sylvie over the noise of the mob. "Justice for my beautiful wife and baby!" The man's voice broke, and he fell into sobs as the crowd followed Sylvie towards the side of the courthouse.

Instead of heading up the main steps and into the courthouse, Sylvie followed her guides along the side of the courthouse and through doors built into the structure. The doors were heavily guarded both inside and out, and the procession passed through several inspection points before gaining access to the main court offices.

Durand pointed to a prominent door atop a short staircase a little ways ahead of them.

"That door leads to your place in the courtroom," the Captain explained. "From your place in the courtroom, you will face the Sword, Shield, the accused, and the audience. Based on what we saw outside, I expect quite a crowd."

"You'll be next to me, right, Captain?" Sylvie asked for reassurance.

"Of course."

Alfric spoke next.

"Four other guards will accompany you on the stand. Another four will guard the base of the stand. The rest will be positioned at various points in the courtroom."

Sylvie nodded.

"You should take your place on the stand," Durand advised.

Sylvie nodded again, somewhat less enthusiastically this time. She made her way towards the three stone steps leading up to the door that would let her into the courtroom. With a heavy push, she made her way through the door.

The door gave way to a short, dark alcove that obscured the central part of the courtroom. She went directly to her right and around a corner into the light.

She found herself in a large room with particularly imposing ceilings. The glass roof was several stories above her and filtered in the sunlight in many different colors, as Sylvie had become accustomed to in Verdelian structures. As she took her place on the stand to her left, she looked out in front of her. Immediately in front of her stand was a large empty area with a single stone seat in its center, surrounded by a short stone wall. This central area was separated from a gallery with row upon row of upholstered pews behind a wooden banister. A balcony with similar benches hung over the lower seating. All seats were full. In the center of the balcony seating, three individual seats featured prominently. There, Sylvie saw Margot, Gaetan, and Loic. Margot looked as bored as ever. Gaetan was nervously cheerful. Loic's brow was deeply furrowed, and Sylvie could tell he was deep in thought. His eyes were fixed on her, and she thought she detected a fleeting look of concern behind his dark eyes.

The onlookers, who had been loudly murmuring only a moment ago, fell silent as Sylvie took her place. At Durand's mental suggestion, Sylvie seated herself and drew a deep breath.

"The trial of Belthégor is called to order. May Solaidi guide us to justice," Sylvie said in a voice as firm as she could manage. She was grateful for Durand's concise, unspoken guidance.

"Present the accused!" Sylvie ordered.

At her command, a door on the side of the courtroom that opened directly onto the empty stone dais in front of Sylvie swung open. Four heavily armed guards dragged a shackled and disheveled man into sight, bringing him squarely before Sylvie.

"Let the Sword present the charges," Sylvie said.

Sylvie could see Councilman Beyern seated just beside the Firstborn on the balcony. He focused entirely on Sylvie; she could tell his intent was not benign.

A Verdélian man, appearing about middle-aged and with sharp dark eyes, stood forward at this instruction. He wore an elaborate robe with the symbol of Verdelys—a sun-shaped flower on a four-leafed stem—embroidered onto its chest.

"Belthégor stands accused of capital crimes against Verdélys and its people," the Sword called out in a sure and compelling voice. "The charges are as follows: unlawful capture of a person, conspiracy to commit the unlawful capture of a person..."

The crowd began to murmur again as the charges were read.

*Demand order in the court,* Durand nudged Sylvie.

"Order in my court," Sylvie called out over the Sword's charges and the crowd's whisperings.

Sylvie turned to the Sword.

"Please, continue."

The Sword nodded respectfully before turning back to the charges. From his spot on the balcony, Beyern seemed annoyed. Loic showed just the faintest bit of a smile. Was he proud of Sylvie?

"...murder, conspiracy to commit murder," the Sword continued, "defiling Verdélian blooms, conspiracy to defile Verdélian blooms..."

At this, a man stood in the gallery.

"Rot in eternal torment!" the man yelled contemptuously towards the accused. Through the rage, tears flowed freely down the man's face.

*Order him removed,* Durand instructed.

"Remove that man from the court," Sylvie ordered.

"Solaidi, curse you to the end of your days and beyond!" the man screamed as two guards lifted him off of his feet and carried him from the courthouse.

"Continue," Sylvie instructed the Sword.

Again, the Sword nodded and continued to read the charges.

"...insurrection, conspiracy to cause insurrection, and treason."

Sylvie turned to the accused.

"If you are guilty as charged, do you wish to confess now to clear your conscience before Solaidi?"

The man stared coldly back at Sylvie, his face haggard.

"No," he replied.

Though she could not tell if the accused was guilty; however, what stirred in the prisoner's mind was foreboding.

"The audience is to the Sword," Sylvie proclaimed.

The Sword nodded respectfully.

"Lieutenant Matthias is called to the Stone Seat," the Sword said in a clear, commanding tone.

A soldier in a uniform fit for the occasion and embellished with several medals made his way forward from the gallery past the wooden banister and towards the seat in the center of the audience.

Following Durand's instruction, Sylvie addressed Lieutenant Matthias.

"Lieutenant Matthias, you are called now to the Stone Seat to witness before this court and Solaidi, to whom you will account if your testimony is not true this day. Are you prepared to proceed?"

"I am," the Lieutenant replied solemnly.

Sylvie nodded towards the Stone Seat, and the Lieutenant was seated.

The Sword began his questioning.

"Lieutenant, please introduce yourself to the court."

"I am Lieutenant Matthias with the Fourth Regimental City Guard. I have been with the City Guard for over forty years."

Sylvie saw memories of the Lieutenant's time in the City Guard flash through his mind. Most memories were well-aged and centered on a dark night and the figure shackled before the court.

"Lieutenant, do you recognize the accused?" The Sword asked.

"I do," the Lieutenant replied with a nod.

"Have you personally met this man before today?"

"I have."

"Please explain to this court your history with the accused."

Lieutenant Matthias began his tale. Sylvie followed primarily in the Lieutenant's mind, where the story and related images and feelings were more vivid and true. So far, his testimony was consistent with his memory.

Lieutenant Matthias relayed a story going back twenty years. In his memories, Sylvie saw a younger and enthusiastic sergeant.

"We had just received intelligence from our superiors regarding a group of conspirators within the city," Lieutenant Matthias explained. "Someone had provided an address where they were known to gather. Our squad was assigned to investigate. My men and I arrived at the location in the dead of night."

Sylvie saw the guardsmen, about twenty strong, walking swiftly and quietly through the streets of Verdélys. Anger and a terrible sadness swam together through the witness's consciousness. Something was coming that the Lieutenant did not want to remember.

The Sword insisted.

"What happened next, Lieutenant?"

Reluctantly, the Lieutenant replayed the rest of the story in his mind as he continued his testimony.

Upon reaching a dark house in the Autumn District, the guards surrounded the house. Sylvie saw Lieutenant—or rather sergeant—Matthias gesture quietly to a handful of men, indicating they were to follow him inside. The men drew swords. Sylvie barely heard Lieutenant Matthias telling the story as she watched it unfold in his mind.

"We breached the door, and all hell broke loose," Lieutenant Matthias explained.

Through the Lieutenant's eyes, Sylvie saw a startled man jump to his feet as Matthias broke down the house's front door.

Lieutenant Matthias could see into the home's parlor through the ill-kept entryway. Several men stood watch over women huddled in a group on the floor, their dresses and hair in tatters, the residue of many tears etched onto their faces.

Through his shock, Lieutenant Matthias saw the surprised sentry reaching for his sword. The Lieutenant lunged at him and sent him limply to the floor.

"What's this—" Sylvie heard the memory of a sinister voice in the Lieutenant's mind. A darkly dressed figure with a sword at his hip came down the stairs. The top half of the person's face was concealed behind a grotesque mask.

From the edge of her consciousness, Sylvie noticed something: the story in Lieutenant Matthias's mind was being shared with someone else in the room—but from a different perspective.

"Men, seize these animals!" Matthias cried out in the story of his past.

The masked man smirked.

Sylvie turned her attention from the Lieutenant's mind and towards the individual reliving this same story. In this version, Sylvie was staring directly at the young lieutenant. Malice and contempt swirled around Sylvie in this new take on the tale.

"Kill the prisoners," Sylvie heard. The order came from the very person whose mind Sylvie found herself in.

Realization dawned on Sylvie. She turned her attention to the accused.

Though his face would not betray it, Belthégor watched in his mind's eye the events of Lieutenant Matthias's story unfold in his own memory.

Lieutenant Matthias's voice was trembling in the Stone Seat.

Sylvie watched in the Lieutenant's memories now as the men under Belthégor's command turned on the women in an instant, slaying them where they sat in that dark, dismal room. One woman cried out in despair as she watched her fellow prisoners cut down without mercy before she, too, was silenced forever. In Belthégor's mind, there was a satisfaction that made Sylvie ill.

The Lieutenant's memory became a haze, obscured by grief and rage. Sylvie watched as he threw himself after Belthégor, cutting down two of the criminal's followers in an instant as they tried to block his access to the stairs. The noise of battle was all around him, but his focus was singular: to reach Belthégor.

In Belthégor's mind, Sylvie watched as he bounded up the stairs in a flash, the young soldier Matthias pounding up the stairs behind him.

Keeping her thoughts on the story that the Lieutenant was reciting, Sylvie drew a quill from the affairs in front of her on her imposing bench and scratched out a quick note to Captain Durand:

*When can I make my ruling?*

Sylvie waited for Durand to read the note, then listed internally for his response.

*At any time. Typically, you would wait until the conclusion of all testimony, but it is not required.*

In the Lieutenant's story, Matthias cornered Belthégor in an upstairs window. Belthégor's back was to the window. In Belthégor's mind, the events of that night were vivid, and a sense of pride accompanied the memories.

"Pathetic fool, do you truly believe you can prevent the things that the great Rhys has set in motion?" Belthégor spat at Matthias.

"Perhaps not," Matthias answered through gritted teeth, "but I can certainly stop murderers and traitors like you."

"Such arrogance," Belthégor sneered. In a flash, he grabbed a vase on the window sill and hurled it at the Lieutenant's face. As he did so, Belthégor whirled about and crashed through the window, careening down to the ground below. He hit the ground hard and rolled with a thud.

Without hesitating, Lieutenant Matthias followed, but by the time he reached the ground, Belthégor was already a rapidly receding figure in the alleyway that backed the house. To Matthias's horror, two guards posted to the rear of the house were prone on the ground. A pool of blood was growing quickly beneath one of them. Only moments earlier, Sylvie had watched in Belthégor's mind as he dispatched the two soldiers as he fled.

Sylvie scratched out another note to Durand.

*Can I interrupt the questioning if I'm ready to make my decision?*

*Yes*, came Durand's reply a few seconds later.

*How?* Sylvie scribbled.

*Raise your hand*, Durand instructed.

Lieutenant Matthias immediately stopped his testimony. There was a whispered exchange among the members of the gallery. Loic raised an eyebrow, and Beyern's gaze on Sylvie intensified. The Sword turned his attention to Sylvie as well.

"I have reached a decision," Sylvie announced.

The whispering in the gallery intensified.

"I object!" Cried the Shield, who had been silent up to this point. He, too, was arrayed in a formal robe akin to that worn by the Sword, except that it was not adorned with the symbol of the city.

"I have not been allowed to counter-examine even this witness, let alone present any exculpatory evidence!"

*None of that is necessary for you to make a ruling,* Durand prompted silently before the Shield even finished his thought. *You can entertain his request, however, if you would like to do so.*

"That will not be necessary," Sylvie said aloud. "I have seen more than enough. Do you doubt my judgment?"

The Shield wavered.

"I...no, of course not, Miss," he said with a nod.

"Well, I, for one, certainly do!"

The voice belonged to Belthégor, who up until then had been silent.

"Who are you to pass judgment on me?" His eyes shone defiantly as he stared at Sylvie.

Sylvie tried to measure her response.

"You have not yet heard my ruling. Why do you protest? Is it that a guilty conscience drives you?"

Belthégor's boldness wavered for a moment.

"I am innocent," he growled as he gathered himself upright, his face upturned haughtily. Inside the mind of the accused, a storm was raging between the truth in his memories and the lie of proclaimed innocence.

"We will hear no more of your lies," Sylvie answered forcefully.

Her words ignited a barely restrained commotion in the gallery.

"Order in my court!" Sylvie called out. Silence returned to the court.

"On the charge of unlawful capture of a person, you are guilty," Sylvie proclaimed. Muted whispers were heard in the gallery. Belthégor's eyes narrowed with a burning malice as he stared at Sylvie. From within his mind, Sylvie watched as he and hooded figures under his command stole away Verdélian women and brought them tied in rope and chain to hidden places, like the house in Lieutenant Matthias's dreadful tale. That had been one such tragedy. There had been many more.

"On the charge of conspiracy to commit the unlawful capture of a person, you are guilty," Sylvie continued. "On the charge of murder, you are guilty."

Some in the gallery cried. "On the charge of conspiracy to commit murder, you are guilty."

As she pronounced her ruling, a flood of memories surged in Belthégor's foul mind. Though she had not seen enough to confirm guilt on all charges in Lieutenant Matthias's story, Belthégor was now confessing to her his guilt on all counts.

"On the charge of defiling Verdélian blooms, you are guilty."

Belthégor's mouth was now upturned ever so slightly. The gallery was visibly ready to erupt, but for now, it remained relatively quiet.

"On the charge of conspiracy to defile Verdélian blooms, you are guilty. On the charge of insurrection, you are guilty. On the charge of conspiracy to commit insurrection, you are guilty. On the charge of treason, you are guilty."

At this last pronouncement, Sylvie caught a fleeting glance of an exchange between Belthégor and another figure. It passed almost unnoticed in Sylvie's mind, except that, at that moment, she looked up at the gallery and recognized the same face reflected in Belthégor's mind. There, on the row behind Beyern, was a councilman Sylvie did not recognize. She tried to access his thoughts, but the jumble of emotional and mental turmoil from the gallery was too great. In the chaos, however, she felt a surge of guilt, though she could not pin the source.

The atmosphere in the courthouse was tense and heavy. Sylvie knew everyone was waiting for her to continue her pronouncement and issue a sentence. But she had to be sure.

She drew her quill again and wrote to Durand.

*I believe one of Belthégor's conspirators is in the gallery. Can he be apprehended and questioned now?*
Sylvie felt Durand's shock as he read her message.
*Yes*, Durand replied dutifully. *Who is the person?*
*Behind Beyern and two to the right*, Sylvie wrote out.

An image of the man appeared in Durand's mind.

*Councilman Victor?* Durand asked in shock.
That was the man, though Sylvie was just now learning his name.
*What do I do to get him down, arrested, and questioned?* Sylvie scribbled on her notes to Durand.
*Call him to the Stone Seat*, Durand said.

When Sylvie turned her attention back to the gallery, she saw that all eyes were on her, questions in everyone's eyes.

"Before I pronounce the sentence of the accused, I call Councilman Victor to the Stone Seat," Sylvie ordered.

Councilman Victor's complexion changed to match the white marble tiles at Sylvie's pronouncement, and he began to shake visibly. Still, he protested.

"This is highly irregular," he managed shrilly. "I've done nothing wrong and have no personal knowledge of this affair."

Captain Durand spoke audibly for the first time.

"Councilman Victor, you have been called to the Stone Seat. Come of your own volition, or my men will enforce the court's order."

The Councilman continued his protest.

"I am a law-abiding Verdélian citizen! I know my rights!"

Captain Durand gestured to the guards standing post at the rear of the gallery balcony. Two stepped forward at his command and stood on either end of the pew where Councilman Victor sat. The one closest to the Councilman reached over, forcibly took Councilman Victor by the arm, and hoisted him to his feet and out of his row.

"Get off of me!" Councilman Victor yelled. The guard did not reply but did not release his grip as he moved to the back of the gallery and down a set of stairs with the Councilman in tow.

"Unhand me!" Victor continued as his escorts pulled him through the lower gallery and towards the Stone Seat. A few moments later, Councilman Victor was forced into the seat, a guard on either side of him.

Sylvie addressed the Councilman.

"Councilman Victor, you are called now to the Stone Seat to witness before this court and Solaidi, to whom you will account if your testimony is not true this day. Are you prepared to proceed?"

"I am not!" The Councilman argued. "What is this about?" He tried to stand but was pushed back into his seat by the attending guards.

Sylvie was stuck. She was keenly aware of Beyern's disapproving gaze upon her.

Durand provided a prompt.

> *Refusal to testify is contempt of the court, and in this case, the Firstborn. It is a serious offense punishable by imprisonment. Remind him.*

"Councilman Victor," Sylvie said, "if you refuse to testify, you will be held in contempt of this court, and I will have you imprisoned."

At this, Victor settled somewhat.

"Are you ready to proceed?" Sylvie asked again.

Councilman Victor said nothing, then nodded.

"Yes," he replied in a shaking voice.

"Have you met the accused before today?" Sylvie asked.

In the Councilman's mind and Belthégor's, Sylvie saw the two men meeting.

"No," Councilman Victor answered loudly but without conviction.

Sylvie scoured the memories of the two men.

"Are you certain you did not meet this man at the Amber Oak?" Sylvie asked, using a detail from Victor's mind to sharpen her questioning.

The Councilman looked like he was going to be sick.

"I..." he stuttered, "am certain."

Sylvie watched the truth unfold in the Councilman's mind. At a dark table in a corner of the Amber Oak, a tavern in the Autumn District, Victor and Belthégor sat and conspired.

"Twenty pieces per woman," Belthégor said, "plus half again if they are brought already growing a seed."

"Thirty," Victor replied. "Do you realize what I'm risking?"

Belthégor scoffed. "Do I look like I care? You'll get twenty and not a bit more. Don't push your luck with me, Councilman."

The Councilman stood with a huff, draped his cloak about himself, and walked out.

In the joint memory of the Councilman and the accused, Sylvie witnessed the Councilman upholding his end of the sinister bargain struck with twisted Belthégor, facilitating the capture of many Verdélian women and their seeds.

Sylvie exited the darkness of these two sickly minds and realized that the courtroom was eerily silent. It had been longer than she had realized.

Sylvie wrote to Durand.

> *He is guilty. He helped Belthégor kidnap Verdélian women.*
>
> He responded: *The charge is unlawful capture of a person if he did it himself. If he was a conspirator, it is conspiracy to commit the unlawful capture of a person. If those captured died, he can be charged with conspiracy to commit murder as well. If he was a Councilman at the time, he can be charged with treason.*

Sylvie could tell Durand was trying to get her as much information as possible while still keeping it manageable.

She turned to address Councilman Victor.

"Councilman Victor, I charge you with conspiracy to commit the unlawful capture of a person..."

"What?!" The Councilman protested, trying to stand. He was again forcefully pushed back into the Stone Seat.

"...conspiracy to defile Verdélian blooms, and treason. You are guilty on all counts."

Councilman Victor sank in despair and let out a groan. Belthégor was grinning from ear to ear.

"Belthégor, for your crimes, I sentence you to die," Sylvie said. "Councilman Victor, for your crimes, I pronounce the same sentence."

The weight of her declaration hung over Sylvie. But she had seen the inner workings of these men. If they felt any remorse for their heinous acts, it was only because they now faced the consequences of those actions. From what Sir Reynard had taught her, capital punishment was not only an appropriate choice—it was the only appropriate choice.

Councilman Victor wailed in his seat.

"Nooooo!" He cried. "Have mercy!"

"I am appointed to do justice. May Solaidi have mercy on you," Sylvie replied.

In desperation, the Councilman tried again to escape the Stone Seat. He did not make a single stride before being grabbed forcefully by the two guards watching over him, who slammed him forcefully back into the Stone Seat.

"Restrain him," Captain Durand ordered.

A guard emerged from one of the corners of the room with a set of shackles, which the guards fastened on the Councilman's wrists.

"The execution will take place immediately," Sylvie ordered. "Take the prisoners to the Tarnished Grounds."

"Clear the gallery!" Captain Durand ordered.

At his command, the onlookers filed out of the courthouse under the guards' direction. Loic, Gaetan, and Margot were the last to exit.

Captain Durand gestured to the guards watching over Belthégor and Councilman Victor. The guards took hold of the shackles, restraining the prisoners, and dragged them towards the courthouse doors. Sylvie stood and followed Captain Durand down and into the space where the Stone Seat sat. Sylvie looked at that imposing monument before following Durand out of the courthouse.

Sylvie squinted as they exited the building, her eyes adjusting to the light. The other Firstborn were nearby at the top of the courthouse steps.

"You were magnificent," Gaetan said, approaching Sylvie. "Your gifts...incredible. Only you could have implicated Councilman Victor. I cannot believe he was a traitor to Verdélys."

Margot said nothing but approached nonetheless in anticipation of descending the court steps with the other Firstborn.

Loic approached last.

"Very well done," he said quietly. "You have brought much-needed justice to Verdélys and revealed a sickness in the very heart of Verdélys that can hopefully now begin to be treated."

In Loic's eyes, Sylvie saw genuine admiration. She beamed as she blushed, her heart soaring with pride.

"We should follow," Loic suggested, pointing to the procession of guards escorting the condemned to their place of execution.

Sylvie walked in silence with the other Firstborn as Alfric, Durand, and other guards escorted them towards the Tarnished Grounds, the historic site of Verdélian executions. Her thoughts were deep as she walked alongside Loic, Gaetan, and Margot. Many Verdélia who had come to witness the trial followed the somber procession.

Sylvie was jarred out of her thoughts by Loic's arm, which he suddenly thrust protectively in front of her. By the time Sylvie could look up and see what was happening, several loud bangs, like the sound of breaking glass, sounded in the street ahead of them, and a dense but fluid smoke rose from the cobblestones, obscuring the prisoners ahead of them.

"Protect the Firstborn!" Alfric commanded forcefully. He, Durand, and several other guards immediately formed a protective barrier around Sylvie and the others. Loic was close to Sylvie now, close enough for her to feel how tense he was, his sword in hand.

"Secure the prisoners!" Alfric shouted at the guards ahead of them, now completely hidden from view.

"Captain, go see that the prisoners do not escape!" Alfric ordered Durand.

"Right away, sir!" Durand replied as he rushed through the haze to where the prisoners had last been seen.

Sylvie could hear shouting and the ringing of steel on steel from above in the fog. Occasionally, she could make out the silhouettes of combatants she could not identify before they sank back into the mist. Through it all, Sylvie began to recognize a name in the thoughts of their assailants.

*Follow Silas!*
*Protect Silas!*

Who was this Silas? Before Sylvie could ponder the question more, Durand came sprinting back through the haze.

"Belthégor has escaped," Durand reported to Alfric through heavy breaths. His sword was unsheathed and stained with blood.

"The assailants were imps and scattered after Belthégor was freed. I dispatched what guards were available to follow the prisoner and the attackers, but we need to organize a city-wide search as soon as possible if we want the best chance of catching Belthégor."

Alfric nodded, his mouth pulled into a taught grimace.

"Thank you, Captain. Please see that the Firstborn are escorted safely to the palace and organize the palace guard into search parties—but leave an increased guard at the palace gate and walls and increase security at the palace itself. I'll stay here and get the rest of the guard on the hunt for our runaway."

"Right away, sir," Captain Durand nodded.

"What of Councilman Victor?" Sylvie interjected.

"He is still in custody," Durand explained. "Under the circumstances, I believe his execution will have to wait."

"Agreed," Loic confirmed. "Secure him in the dungeons. As Belthégor's accomplice, he may be able to help us locate him."

"Leave it to me," Alfric replied. "Captain Durand, get to the palace in haste."

Captain Durand nodded. "Follow me, please," Captain Durand said, turning to the Firstborn.

Escorted by their guards, Sylvie and the others turned away from the mayhem and made their way under heavy guard back to the palace.

# XVII
## *Council Meeting*

A stew of internal and external voices flooded Sylvie's mind as she sat at the front of the throne room with the other Firstborn. Urgency and concern filled the air as the Verdélian council exchanged heated debate regarding the events of the day prior.

The Firstborn had reached the palace safely, and the palace guard had been mustered and dispatched throughout the city in search of Belthégor. They had searched all the rest of that day and into the night, and as far as Sylvie knew, they were still searching, but there had been no sign of the criminal. Now, Sylvie sat with the other Firstborn in an emergency assembly of the Council to discuss Belthégor's escape.

Looking out at the semi-circle of seats in front of her, Sylvie saw Emelia's father, Phillipe, enter with High Councilman Beyern. They quietly took their seats. High Councilman Francis of the Autumn District spoke boisterously and frantically with his fellow Autumn District Councilmembers, the long brown waves of his hair bouncing as he emphasized his rhetoric with sweeping arms and hands. Seated among the Councilmembers of the Summer District, High Councilman Oliver sat quietly, staring at the Firstborn as a fellow Councilmember whispered something into his ear. His blonde hair was pulled back into an immaculate bun, revealing the pensive concern etched onto his face. The only High Councilwoman, Eve, stood at her seat in the Spring District section conversing calmly with several Councilmembers. She seemed to be taking notes. Her piercing pink eyes were bent on taking in as much information as possible that couldn't be communicated through speech.

"Thank you all for coming!" Loïc said curtly and loudly. "We're going to begin. Please take your seats."

The noise abated as Councilmembers took their seats. Hushed whispers continued here and there.

Gaëtan began. "As you know, our order of business today pertains to the escape of Belthégor yesterday evening. Commander Alfric has been organizing the search for the criminal, but he has not yet been recaptured. For those of you who were not present yesterday, Belthégor was freed by ambush on the way to the Tarnished Grounds."

"Taken by ambush? Where were the guards? How did they know Belthégor's whereabouts?" A Councilman asked.

Loïc scoffed.

"Perhaps because this esteemed Council deemed it wise to publish Belthégor's trial to the whole city?" Scorn was etched clearly on Loïc's face as he spoke. The Councilman shrunk down in his seat at the reproach.

"Respectfully," High Councilman Beyern cut in, "the people had a right to know. Belthégor's trial had been postponed for far too long. The victims of his crimes needed to see justice."

"Respectfully?" Loïc asked the High Councilman. "You hide your disdain for the Firstborn poorly, Beyern. I don't need to ask Sylvie to confirm that you were behind this ill-advised maneuver to try and catch her unawares. Rest assured, there will be consequences if something similar happens again."

The High Councilman scowled.

"Like what? Will you have another member of the Council arrested on trumped-up charges?"

Sylvie felt her blood pulsing as the blame came to lay at her feet.

Loïc was raging.

"That kind of talk is treason! Retract it now, or I will have you arrested!"

Beyern smirked in satisfaction. He had made his point. He bowed with exaggerated respect.

"Of course. My apologies. I withdraw my statement."

Loïc wasn't done.

"Perhaps Sylvie's ruling is complicated for you to digest since I seem to recall that you and Councilman Victor were close. Given your relationship and devotion to Verdélys, it's surprising you couldn't detect Victor's treason yourself. Or perhaps..."

Gaëtan took Loïc by the arm.

"That's enough," he said.

Beyern's eyes were burning with hatred under his dark brow.

"We're here to jointly work towards a solution for Verdélys. Accusations will get us nowhere," Gaëtan said.

Loïc sat back in silence but continued defying Beyern's gaze.

"The attackers used alchemy—or something worse—in their ambush," High Councilman Oliver noted, "the list of individuals with that kind of knowledge and skill should narrow our search, no? Do we know the identity of their leader?"

"You were present," Gaëtan replied. "The band was difficult enough to see, let alone identify. Even if we had identified any of the assailants, we can't know who their leader was or if he was even there personally."

Oliver looked down in disappointment.

"One name was divulged," Sylvie said.

All eyes turned to her in surprised anticipation.

"A common name was in the minds of our assailants: Silas."

Anxious whispers raced around the room as the Council processed this new information and Sylvie's demonstration of her ability. A Spring District Councilwoman spoke, "Do we know the number of followers joined to Silas's cause? Do we assume there are more than those who were present yesterday?" She asked.

"We do not," Gaëtan admitted. "The palace guard is investigating that as part of their search for Belthégor."

"Are they involved with dark éthéra?" Beyern called out, retaking the floor.

The room grew eerily still as the Council waited for the answer to the question they had been too timid to ask.

"As far as we know, they are not," Gaëtan answered firmly. "Their tactics appear to be purely alchemical in nature."

"Surely I don't need to remind you how crucial it is that we be sure of this?" Beyern insisted.

"Of course," Gaëtan said firmly, "if we had any indication of dark éthéra use, we would immediately take the appropriate measures and inform the Council."

"We would expect as much and, to be quite clear can tolerate nothing less," Beyern replied firmly. "With the utmost respect, let me make our situation abundantly clear: you are an exceedingly young governing body. We are now faced with a threat to the security of the palace and possibly all of Verdélys, the likes of which we have not seen since the end of the last Imp Rebellion. Lack of experience in times like these is a weakness we cannot afford." Beyern's piercing gaze ran along the four Firstborn. "We," he gestured to the Council as a whole, "will expect immediate updates on all developments relating to these imp intruders." The Council nodded its assent.

"You will be notified of all such developments," Gaëtan said.

"Very good," Beyern answered. "Now, let's discuss emergency security measures."

# XVIII

## *Menagerie*

I n her luxurious suite, Sylvie tried to focus on her studies. Sir Reynard had insisted that she continue with her coursework despite all the upheaval. The other Firstborn had agreed, but Sylvie found it hard to slog through a textbook while her friends bore the brunt of what struck Sylvie as much more real responsibilities handling government affairs.

The sun was high in the sky, shimmering through the sheer drapes adorning her windows. The events of the past two days whirled about in her mind. A heavy knock at her door roused her from her thoughts. Sylvie got up and cracked the door open. Loïc stood straight and square in front of her.

"Hello, Sylvie," he said.

"Hello, Loïc," she answered, opening the door a bit wider.

"How are your studies coming along?" He asked.

"Well enough, I suppose," Sylvie replied with a sigh.

"That's quite the mess of books you've got in there," Loïc mused as he looked over Sylvie's shoulder. Her bed was strewn with thick books and journals, pictures of wild and magical creatures interspersed among them.

"There's a lot to learn," Sylvie admitted. "And the writing in some of those books can get pretty dense."

"It looks like you're studying magical creatures and wildlife?" Loïc asked, a sudden glint of interest in his eye.

"Yeah," Sylvie confirmed. "It's not my favorite."

"That's because you're studying it wrong," Loïc said. A smirk crept onto his face. "Let's take a walk." Loïc turned to make his way away down the hall. "Come on, let's go," he called.

"I'm supposed to be studying!" Sylvie reminded him.

"This counts!" Loïc hollered over his shoulder without stopping.

Sylvie looked back at her bed and the mound of books on top of it. With a sigh, she closed her door and chased after Loïc.

⁂

The winter air whipped about Sylvie's legs as she hurried to keep pace with Loïc. Despite the sun, Sylvie shivered, and she found herself wrapping her arms about herself to keep warm. She had forgotten her cloak in her hurry, and a spike of pride had pushed her to turn down Loïc's suggestion that she take his. *Silly me*, she thought, but she couldn't bring herself to ask for the cloak now.

At the gate, Sylvie and Loïc had been stopped by the palace guard, who were now doing thorough checks on all ingress and egress to and from the palace. Commander Alfric had wanted to send a guard member with them, but Loïc had insisted that he could be responsible for their security on his own. On proving that Loïc was wearing a sword, Alfric had begrudgingly permitted them into the city without an escort.

"What a hassle," Loïc huffed as they entered Verdélys.

"I mean, Alfric's worry isn't exactly unjustified given recent events," Sylvie countered.

"No, and I know he's just doing his job. But still." Loïc insisted.

After a few minutes of walking in silence, Sylvie figured she'd try to strike up some conversation. "How is it that you've got time for a trip through the city with me? Given what's happening, I figured you'd have a thousand things more important to attend to," Sylvie asked through chattering teeth.

"Well, I spent the better part of yesterday and today meeting with Alfric and the garrison commanders for the four districts," Loïc answered. "Why do you ask? Are you afraid I'm shirking my responsibilities?"

"No, not at all!" Sylvie replied, embarrassed, "It's just that I figured...I guess I don't know what I figured," she admitted.

"It's alright," Loïc said, "but I thought it important to check in with you and keep you involved. You have much to learn, but you're still a Firstborn."

Sylvie was grateful but didn't say anything.

"Have you learned anything about the imps?" she asked, curious to see what discoveries she was missing while holed up in her room.

"Not much, unfortunately," Loïc answered. "We still don't know anything about their group, where they come from, or where they might be found within the city. And Belthégor is still missing."

The two Firstborn had made it deep into the Autumn District. Sylvie couldn't tell if this part of the city had been built into and around a forest that

*193*

had been there long before or if the homes had been built and a forest of trees planted around them afterward. Either way, the beautiful homes, built mainly of a soft brown stone and heavy wooden carpentry, looked inviting and mysterious under the shady clutches of the overhanging branches, only a few of which still bore the last of the unfallen leaves. Vegetation of all kinds and domestic animals of every sort were everywhere—many of which Sylvie did not recognize. Loïc and Sylvie's boots crunched through a carpet of leaves as they walked.

After a few more moments, they saw an impossibly large building with a glass dome ceiling in front of them. A heavy growth of trees, vines, and other creeping vegetation obscured much of the building. Sylvie could make out a large glass greenhouse attached to the east side of the building.

"Time for the rest of your wildlife lesson," Loïc said with a smile.

Upon entering the building, Sylvie noticed they were in a clean lobby with three separate hallways, one going left, one going right, and the third leading straight ahead. A Verdélian was standing behind a stone desk in the entryway and was shuffling through a large bookshelf tucked against the wall. Loïc made straight for the left hallway. Sylvie followed suit.

The dark hallway turned into a sort of tunnel, and in the darkness, Sylvie was afraid she would trip right into Loïc. After a short walk, they made it out into what appeared to be a barren desert wasteland.

"Are we...outside?" Sylvie asked Loïc.

"No," Loïc chuckled, "we're still in the menagerie."

Sylvie couldn't believe her eyes. She could see now that there was a roof above them, but it was built and decorated so that without careful inspection, it could easily have been mistaken for the open sky. From where she stood, Sylvie couldn't make out any walls.

As she scanned her surroundings, Sylvie spotted a small fox. Its ears stood on end, and its eyes gazed curiously back at her.

"Look!" Sylvie called excitedly to Loïc as she pointed. The sudden move startled the fox, who took off into the desert. As it did, its tail blazed to light. Sylvie watched as the lively flame whisked this way and that behind the fox as it fled.

"A vulpinis," Loïc said calmly.

"I read about those today!" Sylvie said. This was significantly more exciting than her books.

"I'm sure you read that their tails can ward off predators, but did you know they also keep evil spirits at bay?" Loïc asked.

"Evil spirits?" Sylvie questioned.

"The spirits of the damned. Followers of Rhys and others like him. Those cursed to wander this land like strangers forever." Loïc explained.

Sylvie smirked. "That's just a ghost story. You're trying to scare me. Well, I'm not falling for it." Sylvie hoped she was right.

"I guess you'll have to find out for yourself," Loïc whispered.

He walked a few paces down the path and pointed into the undergrowth.

"Look here," he said.

Sylvie looked but saw only brush and some charred rocks.

"What am I supposed to be seeing?" She asked.

"Look closely," Loïc insisted.

Sylvie looked again. On closer inspection, she saw what appeared to be a leg protruding from what she had considered a blackened stone.

"Is that...a toad?" She puzzled.

"Humans might call it that," Loïc said with a chuckle, "it's a charâme. They nest on live embers, and as the ember transfers its heat to the creature, éthéra is transferred from the charâme to the coal. After the charâme leaves it, the coal will absorb the spiritual essence of the next living thing to touch it. A popular custom among the Verdélia is to have these coals imbued with the spiritual essence of loved ones, to preserve their memory after they pass on."

Sylvie's interest in these creatures was multiplying. These abilities and characteristics were surreal to her. Learning about the wildlife of the Verdélia seemed to open up endless possibilities. She turned to make her way down the path, and in her excitement, she soon overtook and passed Loïc.

Suddenly, she froze. Just to the left of the path was a giant cat, its black fur showing through the undergrowth, glowing eyes focused intently on Sylvie.

"Loïc!" Sylvie hissed under her breath.

"Hmm?" Loïc hummed, strolling up to her side in a state of apparent obliviousness.

"Can't you see? What do we do?" Sylvie muttered urgently.

"About what? About him?" Loïc said, nodding towards the ferocious-looking predator crouched not four paces from where they stood.

"Obviously," Sylvie said, slightly relaxing as she realized that Loïc wasn't concerned about their safety in the slightest despite being well aware of the wild beast right in front of them.

"He won't hurt you," Loïc said with a smile, "although under a different set of circumstances, he just might."

Loïc leaned out sideways towards the creature as if letting himself fall to the ground. Right where Sylvie expected him to fall on his face, Loïc stopped midair as if leaning his shoulder against a wall.

"See?" Loïc said, "courtesy of some winter enchantments. It allows for encounters you couldn't safely recreate in the wild."

Sylvie reached out her hand. Sure enough, she felt a formidable, soft barrier about where the path ended. Her eyes saw nothing in front of her.

"I do have a lot to learn..." she whispered.

"Yes, you do," Loïc said, "but so do we all. Come on, there's much more to see."

Loïc guided Sylvie about the menagerie for several hours. Sylvie had never seen Loïc so genuinely excited about anything as he shared intricate details about the different animals and plants with her. He was adept at locating even the most well-hidden beasts and creatures. The knowledge that had seemed so dull in the dusty pages of her textbooks was alive in front of her and full of wonder, thanks to Loïc's help.

As they made their way out of the menagerie, Loïc looked at Sylvie.

"Not such a boring subject after all, are they?" He said with a smile.

"No," Sylvie admitted, "not when you learn it that way. Thank you."

"You're welcome," Loïc replied as they made their way out the front doors of the menagerie. The clear night sky was swallowing up the last rays of the sun.

"Too proud to take the cloak on the way back?" Loïc teased.

Sylvie thought about it momentarily, and a sudden gust of cold winter air helped her quickly decide.

"No, hand it over," Sylvie said with a smile.

Loïc didn't answer. He unclasped his cloak and draped it over Sylvie's shoulders. It was several sizes too large for Sylvie, but that suited her just fine, as it easily covered the full length of her legs.

"Thank you," she said.

"Of course," Loïc replied.

Sylvie and Loïc made their way to the palace gates in good spirits. The adventure and fresh air had allowed Sylvie to temporarily forget the storm of events that had rocked the last few days. Sylvie and Loïc waited as the guards asked them a few questions about their business in the city and asked Sylvie to open up her cloak. Loïc gave Alfric a smug look when they had finished and joked, "Made it home in one piece."

Alfric nodded dutifully. "No one is more pleased about that than me, Master Loïc. Still, you might consider taking an escort into the city until we're sure Silas and his band are no longer a threat."

"As far as Sylvie and Margot are concerned, that's an excellent idea. I'm quite capable of handling myself, however," Loïc insisted.

Alfric sighed, "Very well, Master Loïc," he conceded with a bow.

Sylvie thought Alfric's proposal more than reasonable, but ultimately if Loïc was unwilling, what choice did Alfric have? She shrugged in Alfric's direction and followed Loïc towards the palace.

Loïc and Sylvie hadn't been in the palace one full minute before seeing Gaëtan approach quickly, a look of questioning disapproval on his face.

"Where have you two been?" Gaëtan demanded swiftly.

# XIX

## *Sylph Delegation*

Gaëtan's tone caught Sylvie off guard. She'd never seen him be anything other than jovial.

"We were at the menagerie. Sylvie's studying magical creatures and wildlife." Loïc answered, unfazed by Gaëtan's accusatory tone.

Gaëtan's eyes looked like they might jump from their sockets.

"We're in the middle of a security crisis and you thought it was an appropriate time for a jaunt through town?" Gaëtan asked incredulously.

Loïc's countenance darkened at Gaëtan's insistence.

"There's been no harm done here, Gaëtan. I know we're all under the stress of recent events, but if you're going to accuse me of not pulling my weight, come out and say it. I can assure you I have been, though." Loïc said, a calm overtone masking his frustration.

Gaëtan took a moment to take stock of the situation. His temper seemed to cool, and he breathed deeply.

"You're right," he said after a short pause. "My apologies. However, the situation has suddenly become a bit more complicated. We've just received an unannounced visit from a Sylph delegation."

Loïc raised an eyebrow, "The Sylphs?"

"Yes," Gaëtan said. "Margot and I have been hosting her for over an hour. Hurry, make yourselves presentable."

"We'll meet you in the throne room in fifteen minutes," Loïc said. Sylvie and Loïc each made their way to their suites. Sylvie's mind was swimming in questions.

A short while later, Sylvie made her way into the throne room. Loïc had beat her there and was sitting in his seat next to Margot, now wearing more formal attire appropriate for the occasion. Sylvie made her way to the empty seat between Loïc and Gaëtan. As she approached her place, Gaëtan noticed her.

"Ah, Sylvie, welcome," he said with his usual smile. He turned to the large stone expanse at the base of the steps that led up to the four Firstborn thrones that dominated the room. There, Sylvie noticed who she could only assume was their guest.

Sylvie thought she was looking at a ghost or a wisp of cloud. The Sylph's contours were made up of gusts of wind, her entire body devoid of color or any apparent substance. Only her eyes, a piercing sky blue, contained any natural color. Her hair flowed about her as if floating in water.

"Princess Cyndriel, please meet Sylvie, our long-lost Morwenna," Gaëtan said.

"Alondra, Morwenna," the Sylph said with a bow. Her eyes were locked on Sylvie's.

"Alondra, Princess," Sylvie replied, mirroring the Sylph's use of the ancient Verdélian greeting.

"Now that we're all here, we may begin," Gaëtan said, sitting beside Sylvie. "Please, Princess, what brings you to Verdélys?"

"Thank you, Master Gaëtan," the Princess said, her voice echoing in the air. To Sylvie, it sounded as if the words came not from the Sylph, but the wind itself.

"I am aware that your time is valuable, and I appreciate your entertainment of my unexpected delegation. I will try to keep the matter brief. I come seeking diplomatic assistance," the Princess continued.

"On what matter specifically? We have not been made aware of any diplomatic issues involving the Sylphs," Gaëtan asked.

"The development is recent but urgent enough that I felt it prudent to involve you immediately." Princess Cyndriel replied. "We have reason to believe that the City of Grisdon is sanctioning the violation of long-standing treaties. We fear that the dwarves are emboldened by their confidence that Verdélys will align with them in the event conflict intensifies."

"You allege violations of which treaties, specifically?" Loïc asked.

"As I'm sure you are aware," the Princess replied, impatience winding its way into her voice, "the Sylphs have been granted exclusive use and stewardship over the Orpap trees of the northern mountains for several millennia, as the trees form an integral part of Sylph cultural and religious rituals. Recently, however, the Orpap trees are being felled and harvested by those not of our kind. We believe this to be the work of the dwarves, who have long coveted the timber of the trees for use in their mines."

"The accusation is quite serious," Loïc pressed Cyndriel. "Do you have any proof to support your claim?"

"The evidence is circumstantial only at this point," the Sylph replied boldly, "but paired with a sense of Sylph intuition, we are confident in our claim."

"Hmmm...." Loïc mused, sitting back in his seat as he considered the Princess's answer.

Gaëtan spoke. "Thank you for presenting your quandary to us, Princess Cyndriel. What relief are you hoping to receive from Verdélys in support of the Sylphs?"

The Sylph looked at Loïc, then Gaëtan, with a disapproving smirk. "I had hoped that the esteemed Firstborn would have a solution for us, their humble subjects," she replied with disdain.

"You say you decided to bring this issue directly before us," Gaëtan answered, ignoring the Princess's snide remark. "Have you inquired of the dwarves about this matter?"

"We have not," Cyndriel said dismissively. "We can expect only denials from them. An inquiry would have been fruitless."

"Have you undertaken any independent investigation of the matter?" Loïc asked the Sylph. "You seem to have been quite quick to seek the help of Verdélys on this issue."

Princess Cyndriel's blue eyes flashed with anger. "I bring before you a significant diplomatic issue!" She said, her voice a shrill note on the air. "The Sylphs consider these actions aggression on Sylph culture and civilization, worthy of armed retaliation if necessary! If you cannot take the steps necessary to protect the integrity of the Sylph people, we will be left with little choice but to govern ourselves accordingly!"

Loïc sat up in his seat, his shoulders square and his face stony, "Princess, I would be wary of coming into this chamber to threaten war. You have come to us unannounced with unsubstantiated allegations against another free people. We will not take action against the City of Grisdon based on your accusations alone, and we strongly dissuade you from doing so. Now, if you would be so kind as to give us a moment to deliberate, we will have a proposal for you shortly."

Loïc's response drew silence from Sylph, but her demeanor remained defiant as she bowed and exited the throne room.

"What an absolute treat she is," Margot sighed.

"She's Sylph royalty," Gaëtan said flatly, "and we must treat her accordingly. Now, let's put our heads together on this. How do we approach a potential treaty violation?"

"There's been no treaty violation," Loïc cut in. "She has no proof whatsoever. We won't accuse the dwarves of what amounts to military aggression on the word of one Sylph. That's a recipe for disaster. I'll remind us all that Verdélys relies heavily on trade with Grisdon for stone and ore."

"Well, who else would be cutting Orpap trees up there?" Gaëtan replied. "It's not like there are other timber-cutting peoples in that region."

"I don't know. But without some evidence that the City of Grisdon is sanctioning the harvesting of the trees, we can't make a direct inquiry that the dwarves might well take as an accusation." Loïc said.

"So what do we propose to Cyndriel?" Gaëtan asked.

"We can dispatch a small number of Verdélian soldiers to investigate," Loïc proposed. "The gesture is more symbolic than useful since even with the whole army; it would be impossible to monitor the entirety of the northern forests. The Sylphs will have to take it as a gesture of goodwill and assume the majority of the investigative work themselves—which is what they should have done before coming down here to point fingers at the dwarves anyway."

"Given current events, that's not going to go over too well with the Council or with Alfric," Gaëtan said.

"We can spare a company of men," Loïc insisted.

"Besides," Margot added, "it would be worse to do nothing and essentially admit that recent aggression against the Firstborn has crippled the Verdélias' ability to maintain peace and diplomatic relations among neighboring peoples."

Gaëtan nodded, "Fair point. I doubt Princess Cyndriel will be too impressed with a couple hundred Verdélian soldiers to take care of what they consider foreign aggression."

"I doubt Princess Cyndriel will be impressed by anything," Margot scoffed.

"Too right," Loïc grunted. Gaëtan didn't say anything, but it didn't look like he disagreed.

"Very well," Gaëtan said, "are we all in agreement then? Sylvie, we haven't heard from you."

"Couldn't we assist in regrowing the Orpap trees?" Sylvie asked.

Sylvie thought she heard Margot stifle a snicker.

"No one has ever been able to cultivate an Orpap tree," Gaetan explained. "The trees don't produce seeds, so they can't be planted and grown like other trees—at least not as far as we know. In some ways, they're more like certain minerals than plants."

"Oh," Sylvie mumbled, feeling foolish. "I didn't know."

"It's alright," Gaetan assured her, "it was a good idea."

Gaetan looked at each of the Firstborn in turn.

"We're agreed then; we'll send a company north?"

Loic and Margot nodded.

"Yes," Sylvie whispered.

Gaetan turned to the guards standing at the ready at the doors of the throne room.

"Please see the Princess in."

The guards nodded obediently and opened the doors in unison, motioning for the Sylph to enter. She floated back in, her eyes still piercing and defiant.

"Princess Cyndriel," Gaëtan announced, "we have agreed to send a company of Verdélian soldiers to the northern forests to assist in your investigation of the matter regarding the Orpap trees and assist in their protection where necessary. Our troops will be ready to depart before the week is out."

"A single company of soldiers to protect our sacred Orpap trees? Has Verdélys fallen so far that that is all the aid that can be spared in times of need?" Princess Cyndriel sneered.

"Perhaps the Sylphs would prefer to resolve this problem on their own?" Margot proposed.

Princess Cyndriel stared at Margot contemptuously but did not respond.

"We expect the Sylphs to assume primary responsibility in investigating this matter. If evidence is discovered that warrants further intervention on the part of Verdélys, it is to be reported through the military command of the soldiers who will be dispatched north according to your request." Gaëtan informed the Princess. "Now, is there any additional business that needs to be attended to tonight?"

"None." The Princess said coldly.

"Good. In that case, this audience is adjourned. We bid you good night, Princess."

The Sylph glared at the Firstborn for a moment, then finally turned and exited the throne room.

# XX

### *People & Pastries*

S ylvie walked purposefully down the cobblestone lane leading away from the palace walls. The winter air was particularly brisk this morning, and she nuzzled her face into a thick wool scarf wound tightly about her neck and face. Her heavy cloak brushed up small flurries of snowflakes behind her as she walked.

Sir Reynard had taken a few days of absence with strict instructions on what Sylvie would study while he was away. Sylvie had begun the reading, but an idea had formed in her mind and taken hold of her. She had been in Verdélys several moons now and had read countless books. Still, despite all that, she felt she knew far too little about the Verdélia, their culture, and their lives. Other than the other Firstborn and the occasional palace guest, Sylvie had interacted only with a select few Verdélia and then only briefly in very formal capacities. How was she to lead a people she didn't know?

This idea had prevented any productive study and had led to the hatching of a plan Sylvie knew Sir Reynard and the other Firstborn would not much appreciate. But then, they didn't have to know. Sir Reynard was gone, and the other Firstborn were fully occupied with government affairs, especially now that a small military force was dispatched north on a diplomatic mission.

With Nadine's help, Sylvie had dressed in common Verdélian attire in preparation for a trip into the city. Knowing she would inevitably be discovered at the palace gate, she took the initiative to approach Alfric in advance and share her plan with him. He had begrudgingly agreed to allow her into the city without informing the other Firstborn on the condition that she allow him to accompany her personally. Sylvie and Alfric had negotiated an agreement that he would forego his flashy armament and wear ordinary clothing while accompanying Sylvie.

As she walked, she felt proud of her initiative. She still wasn't sure exactly what she would do, but she felt confident that she needed to get out into the city among the Verdélia if she was ever going to learn about them. She peeked over her shoulder at Alfric, who followed closely behind. He was doing a surprisingly good job of looking inconspicuous, and if Sylvie hadn't known that he was following her, she would have taken him for just another passerby.

Sylvie made her way toward the Spring District. She had decided to go through the Districts in order: Spring, Summer, Autumn, then Winter. Sir Reynard would be gone for five days, giving her just enough time to visit all four and make a laughable attempt at gaining a rudimentary knowledge of the topics Sir Reynard had assigned her during his absence. She knew it wouldn't come close to satisfying Sir Reynard, but it would hopefully be enough to convince him that she hadn't abandoned her studies altogether.

As Sylvie walked along, she kept her mind open to the thoughts of the Verdélia about her. One man was deep in thought about a floral arrangement he was working on, wondering if there was a better pairing for the yellow roses he was using as a centerpiece. Another reminisced on the kiss he had received from his wife as he left his home that morning. Yet another was enthralled with the smell of baked goods being carried on the frigid breeze.

All around her, Sylvie noticed the flowers. Although snow covered the ground and it was well into the first moon of winter, blooms could be seen sheltering beneath archways and inside windows of every home and shop in the district. Most Verdélia that Sylvie could see were working with flowers in one way or another. Some were arranging fanciful bouquets. One shop was full of individuals weaving magnificent crowns from flowers of every kind. Over there, Sylvie saw pressed and dried flowers being fashioned and incorporated into jewelry and other glassware.

Suddenly, a smell hit her. As sweet as the flowers had been, this was fuller, richer. Almost instinctively, she followed it to the door of a homely shop built of light grey stone and adorned with intricate woodwork. She peered through the window at the cakes and breads decorated with small floral bouquets and colorful fruits. The pastries steamed up the cold glass and made Sylvie's mouth water.

"Miss Sylvie?" She heard suddenly. She turned quickly and recognized Fredrich.

"Fredrich? What a surprise." Sylvie said, embarrassed that her supposedly undercover venture into Verdélys had been thwarted immediately.

"A surprise? I think the surprise is seeing you out here, out and about among us *ordinary* folk. And all on your own at that!" Fredrich replied, looking this way and that to confirm that none of the other Firstborn, or maybe some palace staff or guards, were accompanying Sylvie.

"Not so loud," Sylvie shushed.

Fredrich raised an eyebrow, "Oh? On a secret mission, are we?" He whispered.

"Something like that," Sylvie said with a smile. "If anyone asks, you didn't run into me today."

"I did not run into you today," Fredrich replied with a large grin.

"Thank you," Sylvie said, relieved.

"Admiring the delicacies, I see," Fredrich said, turning his attention to the bakery window. "I'd hate to sound pretentious, but I'd wager Warren's offerings rival even what you get at the...at your home."

"They *look* amazing," Sylvie admitted.

"They taste even better," Fredrich added. "Come on, I'll show you." He walked to the door and opened it for her, inviting her inside. Sylvie timidly entered, the rich smell multiplying ten-fold as she entered. The bakery's warmth enveloped her as she left the cold behind.

"Alondra, Fredrich, and friend," said a burly man behind the counter as he tended to a large brick oven built into the bakery wall. "Let me know when you've found something you like, and I'll be right with you."

Sylvie gazed in amazement at the incredible sights before her. Combined with the otherworldly scents, the scene drew her in with an irresistible embrace. She spotted more traditional-looking breads and cakes next to intricate pastries that had been fashioned to resemble flowers, animals, and more. Some were embellished simply with a powdered topping or a frosting. In contrast, others wore beautiful floral crowns and immaculate glazes, some even carefully laid out to depict landscapes and other images and scenes. Several creations caught Sylvie's eye as they seemed to float on clouds of colored vapor.

"Pick one that speaks to you," Fredrich encouraged.

"How could I choose? They all look amazing." Sylvie gasped.

"I know the dilemma," Fredrich sighed in a tone of playful consternation, "I come here most days, and I still haven't made my way through all of Warren's creations."

Sylvie spent a few more moments hunched over, carefully surveying the food before her. Finally, she settled on a small cake sprinkled with small white flowers.

"Elderflower," noted the baker, "For protection. It seems to be reaching out to you."

"Does it?" Sylvie asked. The baker nodded.

"I'll take it then," Sylvie said, standing up straight.

"Anything for you, Fredrich?" Warren asked as he lifted the pastry gingerly from its place.

"How about this one today?" Fredrich said, pointing to a braided bun that appeared to be caught under a minuscule snow flurry.

"A snow bun, a great choice. It's new, and I'm rather proud of how it turned out." Warren scooped his hand underneath it and lifted it out from behind the glass. The snowstorm followed. Sylvie stared, mesmerized.

"It's quite the work of art," Fredrich congratulated the baker.

Warren handed the pastries to their new owners, seeming almost sad to part with them.

"Enjoy," he said as Sylvie and Fredrich each handed him a coin in exchange.

"We will," Fredrich said with a smile.

"Thank you," Sylvie added as she began to make her way out of the shop. She turned. "Actually, could I get one more?"

"Certainly," Warren said. Sylvie selected a smooth bun with a deep red stuffing that showed around the rim of the pasty. Warren bagged it gently and handed it to Sylvie, and Sylvie followed Fredrich back out into the winter air.

Sylvie stood in the cold, holding her treat in one hand, inches from her face, and the bag with her other pasty in her other hand. The warmth of the flowery bun escaped in steamy breaths that caressed Sylvie's frigid lips.

"So," Fredrich said, "what can you tell me about this secret mission of yours?"

"I'm just exploring Verdélys," Sylvie said, keeping her eyes on her cake to avoid betraying her true motives.

"Alone?" Fredrich asked, one eyebrow raised in skepticism.

"Sort of," Sylvie said, nodding toward Alfric, standing a few strides away down the street.

"Huh?" Fredrich asked, confused.

"I have an undercover escort. They wouldn't let me leave the palace without it." Sylvie explained.

"Ah," Fredrich said. "With everything going on, it probably is for the best."

"Probably. Still, a bit overbearing." Sylvie replied.

"You're right, I suppose," Fredrich agreed. He paused for a moment, and they stood there in silence. Then he spoke again.

"So what are you really doing out and about in Verdélys?"

"I just told you I'm exploring," Sylvie answered defensively.

Fredrich smiled. "Sylvie, Firstborn don't just *explore* the city."

"Well, I am," Sylvie insisted, "Verdélys is still new to me."

"Right," Fredrich said, still clearly skeptical. "If you'd like, you can explore your way with me to the theater. I'm due for a rehearsal there shortly."

"I'd be happy to," Sylvie said.

As the two friends made their way towards the theater, Fredrich asked.

"Is it true that you can read peoples' thoughts?"

"Yes," Sylvie answered.

*Fascinating*, Fredrich thought.

"How does it work?" He continued.

"It depends on the thought I'm reading—or seeing, or hearing, as the case may be," Sylvie explained.

"Ok, tell me what I'm thinking then," he proposed.

The words *thirty-seven dancers* floated through Sylvie's mind.

"Thirty-seven dancers," Sylvie said.

*Incredible*. Fredrich grinned, his eyes wide with surprise.

"How about now?" He asked again.

Sylvie saw a picture in her mind's eye of a pair of bright red birds flitting about in the breeze through the snow.

"It's two bright red birds flying through the snow," Sylvie explained.

"Wow," Fredrich whispered in amazement.

"Do you live in the Spring District, then?" Sylvie asked, hoping to change the topic of conversation and shift the focus away from herself.

"I do," Fredrich said.

"With your family?" Sylvie questioned.

"Oh no. They live in the Summer District. I moved out here after getting my inheritance to be closer to the theater." Fredrich explained.

"I see. Do you have your own home out here then?" Sylvie asked.

"No, not yet. I figured that could wait until I settled down and got married. For now, a humble bachelor pad is more than enough." Fredrich said with a grin. An image of a smiling Maya danced across Fredrich's mind as he mentioned marriage.

"Does Maya live in the Spring District, too, then?" Sylvie asked, hoping the question wasn't too on the nose.

"Uh..." Fredrich said, evidently taken aback by the sudden change of topic, "Yes, she does."

Sylvie bit her lip. "Sorry, I guess it's rather rude to pry into your private affairs like that," she said sheepishly. "It's just that, well, you said marriage and thought of Maya...I shouldn't have asked."

Fredrich shrugged it off. "There are no secrets around Morwenna," he said. "That's well known among the Verdélia. I've just never experienced it firsthand. Besides, I'm not embarrassed about how I feel for Maya."

Sylvie smiled at Fredrich.

"Still," he added, "I would greatly appreciate it if you would keep the marriage bit to yourself for the time being."

"Of course," Sylvie said solemnly. "My lips are sealed."

"Thank you," Fredrich said, a look of relief washing over his face.

The snow continued to flurry about their feet as they kept walking down the cobblestone streets. Sylvie shuddered under her cloak as a particularly virulent gust of wind made its way into the crevices of her clothing and bit at her skin.

"So, does Maya live here alone, or is her family living in the District?" Sylvie asked Fredrich.

"She lives here in the District in an apartment of her own. Her family doesn't even live in Verdélys." Fredrich said.

"Oh really? Do they live nearby? I thought Verdélys was the only Verdélian city." Sylvie said with curiosity.

Fredrich shook his head, "No, they're not nearby. Her family lives in Lumivale."

Sylvie's raised an eyebrow. "Really? I thought that was primarily an imp city." She said. She had read about Lumivale in her studies of Verdélian history. Although her textbook had been relatively light on details, from what she had understood, Lumivale had been founded far to the south as a community of imps, either societal outcasts or individuals disenchanted with life in Verdélys.

"It used to be that way," Fredrich said. "And that's the way it's still taught here in Verdélys. Most Verdélia think the same as you. But there's a growing number of Verdélia living in Lumivale together with the imps that have been down there for generations. I learned most of what I know about it from Maya. It's pretty fascinating."

"I had no idea," Sylvie said, intrigued. "What else has Maya told you?"

"Lots, I suppose," Fredrich said with a shrug. "She loves it down there. Maya's always talking about how different it is from Verdélys —less...formal, I guess. It took Maya some time to adjust to the culture of Verdélys even though she's Verdélian, what with all the structure and tradition built into everything we do here."

"I know all about that," Sylvie said with a sigh. She thought momentarily, then asked, "Has Maya ever mentioned to you how the Verdélia interact with the imps in Lumivale?"

Fredrich thought for a moment. "Some," he answered. "For example, she did mention that she found it odd that the imps have their own district here in Verdélys. Keep in mind that one of the primary reasons behind the existence of Lumivale was for the imps to create a Verdélys of their own, minus all of the limitations imposed on them here. For example, imps cannot have children among the Verdélia—it's forbidden. So many of them decided that rather than stay alone among the Verdélia, they would leave. When Verdélia began leaving as well—either because they were romantically involved with an imp or just because they became disenchanted with life in Verdélys—those in Lumivale decided they would not create the social and cultural divisions that they saw as being responsible for their 'exile,' so to speak."

Fredrich's words weighed on Sylvie's mind.

"That certainly makes sense in that context," she said, as much to herself as to Fredrich.

"I think so, too," Fredrich agreed.

They walked a bit longer in silence, both contemplating their exchange. Soon, they were reaching a part of Verdélys Sylvie was familiar with.

"We've reached my destination," Fredrich said, breaking the silence. "This is where I must leave you, my friend. Say hello to Gaëtan for me when you see him."

"I will," Sylvie promised. With an elegant bow, Fredrich turned and entered the theater, leaving Sylvie alone with her thoughts on the frosty stone steps.

Sylvie turned to face Alfric and motioned to him to come nearer to her. She opened her bagged good and handed it to him. The package was still warm, and steam had escaped from the opening.

Alfric bowed his head as he accepted the gift.

"Thank you, Sylvie," he said.

"Thank you, Alfric," Sylvie replied. "For entertaining this nonsensical quest."

"Unorthodox, perhaps," Alfric countered, "but nobly motivated. The people need you—and the other Firstborn—perhaps now more than ever. Your desire to know them honors you."

Sylvie felt Alfric was sincere, and this comforted her.

"Why do you say the people need the Firstborn, especially now?"

Alfric sighed.

"I have been under oath to protect Verdélys nearly all my life. In that time, and in that role, I have seen many things that most Verdélia have not—or will not. I suppose it is a soldier's burden to confront the darkness that hides in the recesses of the world. That darkness is growing. It is growing within Verdélys itself. Many are ignorant of this. Some are complicit."

Sylvie thought of Councilman Victor.

"Do you mean Councilman Victor?" She asked.

"Him and his kind. Traitors. Though most are more cunning in their craft and subtle in their execution."

"What do you mean?" Sylvie asked. She had suspicions of her own, but if Alfric knew something, she wanted to hear it from him. In the Commander's mind, members of the political elite of Verdélys mingled with common criminals. One face she recognized.

"Do you suspect Councilman Beyern?" Sylvie asked in hushed incredulity.

Alfric stiffened.

"I am afraid I have spoken out of turn," Alfric said.

"Alfric, if you suspect something, you must tell me," Sylvie insisted. "I have my suspicions about the High Councilman."

"There is no evidence, only intuition," Alfric responded. "As I said, there are many more cunning and subtle than Councilman Victor, and even he went unpunished for his atrocities for twenty years."

Sylvie stood pensively in the snow. She was beginning to believe what Ancelin had told her from the beginning: she had a part to play in Verdélys.

Sylvie turned her attention back to Alfric.

"Verdélys is truly blessed to have you, Alfric. In times like these, loyal friends are priceless."

Alfric bowed deeply.

"You honor me," he said.

"I speak true," Sylvie said, placing her hand on his arm to pull him from his bow. "Now, let's see what else the Spring District has to offer."

# XXI

## *A Forgotten Lullaby*

For the remainder of the day, Sylvie had familiarized herself with the Spring District, but nothing major had come of her time in the city. As far as she could tell, she had made it back in time to avoid any suspicions and had been rather content with what she considered a successful excursion.

Today was a new day and adventure in the Summer District. The air was cold again, and light snow sprinkled down from a thick blanket of grey clouds that hung lazily in the sky. Sylvie recognized a few sights from her arrival at Verdélys, which had taken her through the Summer District. Trees and flowers were less prominent in this part of the city, though they were still plentiful. Instead, the emphasis here was on the workmanship of the stone, wood, metal, and glass that comprised the buildings, trellises, lampposts, and other structures built in the district. Everything appeared utterly flawless. The other districts were undoubtedly charming and neat, certainly by human standards. The level of sophistication in the homes and other built things here was almost unbelievable.

Today, Captain Durand and another palace guard took Alfric's place. Loïc had summoned Alfric to dispatch troops to aid the Sylphs, and to avoid suspicion, Alfric assigned Captain Durand over Sylvie's expedition. Captain Durand, looking average as ever, laughed with his companion behind her. They were both cautious to never seem focused on or pay her any special attention, but Sylvie felt safe under their watch.

As Sylvie walked, she tried to sift through the cacophony of mental voices that jostled through her mind. Sylvie reached an open plaza and sat on a simple bench tucked slightly out of the street she had been traveling on. From her new vantage point, she admired Verdélia from all walks of life who went about their day. As she sat, the mind of one Verdélian in particular seemed to take a pre-eminent role in the tumult of her thoughts. As she tuned into the consciousness, Sylvie heard a beautiful, melodic tune. The music was simple but moving. It was also strangely familiar, though Sylvie couldn't explain why. Sylvie began scanning her surroundings to locate the Verdélian responsible for the song. Sylvie got a mental image of a woman, her face framed in thick, silky, chestnut-colored hair. She stood to get a better view and tried to match the image in her mind to the scene before her eyes.

Suddenly, Sylvie could feel the song receding. Without knowing why, Sylvie began moving, desperate to find the melody and the woman associated with it. Just as she thought she would lose her mental grasp on the music, she noticed thick chestnut locks walking away from her off to her right. Sylvie took off briskly without thinking twice, determined to catch up to this stranger.

As she followed, the tune grew stronger and stronger. It was repeated over and over, without words, but full of emotion. It enveloped Sylvie in an unexpected sense of homesickness and nostalgia, yet she still could not place the song.

Sylvie was gaining on the woman, and with a few more emphatic strides, she was walking right behind her. Drawing up her courage, Sylvie tapped the woman on the shoulder. The music did not stop nor even waver.

"Excuse me," Sylvie said. "Could you please point me in the direction of the Museum of History?"

"Yes, I could," the woman said warmly, "In fact, I'm heading in that direction now if you'd like to join me?"

The fates were aligned. "Yes," Sylvie said, "that would be wonderful. I'm...Nadine." Sylvie squirmed internally at the subterfuge, but keeping her identity concealed was integral to her plan.

"Alondra, Nadine." The woman said. "I am Adelais. And this," she said, using her head to gesture at a bundle carefully tied to her chest, "is Felicity, my daughter."

Sylvie looked down in awe at the beautiful Verdélian baby tucked snuggly against Adelais' body. She was clearly very content, and from that tiny person's mind came the tune that Sylvie had been following. It flittered through her thoughts like a bird through the spring sky, repeating a sense of comfort for the child to hold onto and associate with her mother's smiling face. Had her father sung her the same song long ago, Sylvie wondered?

"She's beautiful," Sylvie gasped. "How old is she?"

"She's nearly one year old now," Adelais said proudly. "She bloomed last Winter."

"Congratulations," Sylvie replied.

"Thank you," Adelais beamed. "Now, let's get you to the Museum, shall we?"

"Yes, thank you," Sylvie said, following Adelais' lead through the snow.

"Do you live in the District with your daughter then?" Sylvie asked, trying to strike up a conversation.

"No, not anymore," Adelais replied. "I live in the Spring District with my husband. He's an apprentice at the hospital there."

"So, is he originally from the Summer District as well?" Sylvie continued. As a hospital apprentice, Adelais' husband would work with healing éthéra, which, although not a strictly Summer Verdélian ability, was far more common among the Summer Verdélia than any other seasonal Verdélia.

Adelais nodded, "Yes, he is. We met in the Summer District growing up."

"Very cute," Sylvie noted with a smile.

"Thank you, I think so too," Adelais chuckled.

"What about you," Adelais continued, turning the conversation on Sylvie, "Where are you from? I take it not the Summer District?"

"No," Sylvie hesitated, "I'm...I work in the palace."

Adelais looked surprised at Sylvie. "The palace, huh? We don't get many palace workers out and about in the city. I hear they keep you pretty busy up there."

Sylvie hoped she hadn't blown her cover, "Yes, they certainly do. I don't get out much. I guess it shows?"

Adelais laughed, "Just a bit. It must be especially hectic now, what with the new Firstborn at the palace and all?"

Sylvie felt like what should have been a simple conversation was turning into a balancing act taking place on the edge of a knife.

"It sure is," she said. "I can't say much about it, though. What have you heard?"

"Not much," Adelais admitted. "I know a man who works in the palace, though, and he tells me good things about the new Morwenna. I hear she's inexperienced and nervous but eager and determined. He thinks she'll be a blessing for the Verdélia, as hoped. I trust him."

Sylvie didn't know who Adelais was talking about, but the anonymous vote of confidence warmed her heart.

"We're coming to my parents' house," Adelais cut in, "which is where I'll leave you. You'll only need to follow the road a little before reaching the museum."

"Thank you very much," Sylvie said gratefully.

Sylvie and Adelais crossed a bridge overpassing a small stream and came upon a stone fence with a beautifully carved gate. Behind the gate, a stone path led through a beautiful, overgrown garden to a stone house brimming with the glow of a warm fire.

"Adelais!" A young girl called from the front yard as she noticed the two women approaching. Another little girl looked up and smiled in recognition.

"If you have the time, I'd love to introduce you to my family before you go," Adelais invited.

"It would be my pleasure," Sylvie said.

"Hello, girls," Adelais said, unwrapping Felicity from her pouch. "Meet my new friend, Nadine."

"Nice to meet you," Sylvie smiled.

"These girls are Liesel and Poppy," Adelais said, pointing to the two girls. "They're my sisters. Liesel is the older of the two and a Summer Verdélia. Poppy is the youngest and a Spring Verdélia."

"Adelais, is that you?" A voice called out from the inside of the home.

"Yes, mother," Adelais called back. "Come meet my new friend!"

An older woman opened the front door and came to meet her guests as she wiped her hands on an embroidered apron.

"A new friend, you say?" She said as she walked down the stone path. "Let's get a look at you, then."

"I'm Nadine," Sylvie said with a smile. "It's lovely to meet you."

"The pleasure is mine," Adelais' mother said. "My name is Bergita."

"You have a lovely family," Sylvie said.

"Thank you," Bergita said, "Of course, you say that because you haven't seen my boys. My husband and oldest son are away working. My younger sons are off fetching and splitting wood for the stove. You might think otherwise if you saw the likes of them around."

Sylvie giggled with her new friends. "I'm sure they're lovely as well," she replied.

"Would you care to join us for lunch?" Bergita proposed to Sylvie.

"Oh no, I need to carry on," Sylvie said, afraid to get too deep into a conversation with Adelais, who apparently had an inside source at the palace.

"Very well," Bergita said, "but do stop by sometime; we're always happy to have pleasant company by for a visit."

"I'll try to do that," Sylvie said. Bergita smiled, then turned and rounded up her two younger daughters. The three of them made their way back into the house. Adelais lingered at the fence for a few moments longer.

"It was very nice meeting you, Nadine," Adelais said. "We should keep in touch, your schedule at the palace permitting."

"I would like that," Sylvie replied. "Have a great day!"

Sylvie shuffled on through the deepening snow. She turned to steal a look back at Adelais, her unexpected friend, just in time to see her retreat into the house. The glow of the fire from within looked ever more inviting as the snow continued to fall.

Darkness fell over the city as Sylvie hurried back to the palace. The guards abandoned at the gate behind her; she hurried past the keystone pool but stopped when she heard whispers. She recognized the call of the water, but this was different, warped somehow. Sylvie stopped and glanced back at the pool. There was a second voice coming from the pool.

The beat of her heart quickened, and her hands suddenly felt clammy. She took a step towards the pool, the whispers getting louder. Intertwined with the familiar call of the water was an individual consciousness. But whose?

Another step and she could see into the reflective pond's surface, the stars gleaming behind the silhouette of her frame. The water, typically so still, was troubled.

As if moved by some force, she extended her hand and reached into the water. In one moment, she wondered what memories the pool would share. Before she could finish her thought, liquid tendrils grabbed her wrist, and she felt herself pulled forcefully toward the water's surface.

She screamed. This was no longer the inviting pull of water she was used to. As she cried out, the mysterious consciousness drew back and Sylvie fell forcefully backwards into the snow. She shook the water off her hand, noting her hair standing on edge down her arm and shaking herself free of the panic that had set in.

Sylvie groaned as her tailbone shot a bolt of pain up her back in protest of her fall. Inside the pool, Sylvie felt the second presence recede deep beneath the waters, a single word occupying its thoughts: *Morwenna*.

# XXII

## *The Prophet*

It was morning again, and Sylvie sat with the other Firstborn around breakfast. She had all but finished her meal and pondered the previous night's living nightmare. Gaëtan flipped through the pages of a small, well-worn journal. Loïc was on his second—or was it third—plate of food, and Margot was staring out the window, watching the snow drift heavily to the ground. Things seemed to be mostly normal, which was all good news as far as Sylvie was concerned. She wouldn't disturb the peace until she could figure out how to put what had happened at the fountain into words.

"What are you reading?" Loïc asked Gaëtan, wiping up the last bits of food from his plate.

Gaëtan looked up as if he had forgotten he was sharing the room with anyone else.

"Huh? Oh...I've found a curious book about theories on element manipulation. The author presents some interesting ideas based on extensive research and experiments," Gaëtan explained.

"Anything worth sharing?" Loïc pressed.

"Well," Gaëtan continued, "there are some notes here about some theories specific to the Firstborn. It's pretty well accepted that the Firstborn have a certain proclivity for manipulating their given element. The author discusses a connection that follows those specific elements as they are found in certain living creatures created from those elements."

"What does that mean?" Sylvie asked.

"Theoretically, each Firstborn has an éthéra-based connection with creatures formed from their given element—for example, Loïc would benefit from this bond with any of the fire-based wildlife," Gaëtan explained.

"Sounds interesting, actually," Loïc admitted.

"Very," Gaëtan said enthusiastically. "There's been a lull in obligations with the council today, and I plan to test the theory myself at the menagerie."

"You're going to the menagerie today?" Sylvie asked, suddenly very much concerned with Gaëtan's plans. The menagerie was in the Autumn District, Sylvie's planned destination for the day.

"I was planning on it, yes," Gaëtan said. "Would you care to join me?"

"I..." Sylvie stuttered, "I would, but I have a lot to get through before Sir Reynard returns."

As soon as the words had escaped her mouth, Sylvie wished she could recall them. She wasn't sure why she had turned down the invitation. If she went to the Autumn District now and ran into Gaëtan, he would know she had lied at breakfast, and she would have to explain herself. She clenched her jaw in frustration at her oversight.

Gaëtan nodded, "Fair enough, I'm sure you've got plenty on your plate."

Sylvie noticed Loïc staring, his eyes digesting her exchange with Gaëtan.

"So," Loïc said finally, addressing Gaëtan, "what are these tests you plan on running at the menagerie?"

"The idea is that a Firstborn can share éthéra with a creation of their element. To put it another way, when the common elemental éthéra of the Firstborn and the creature are joined, the souls touch, creating a sort of surge of éthéra in both participants." Gaëtan said.

"I've heard kissing can elicit a similar response," Margot said with a snicker.

Sylvie thought she might send her drink out her nose.

Loïc leaned in, not wanting to miss out on the fun.

"I'm curious," he said, a devious grin on his face, "which creature are you planning on 'joining' with today?"

Gaëtan rolled his eyes. "You are all children," he said with a sigh.

"Do send us an invite when you've found your soulmate," Margot continued, leaning back in her seat. Sylvie and Loïc chuckled as Gaëtan shook his head.

"Go ahead and laugh," Gaëtan said with a smile, "but I might just prove these theories right, and then we'll see if you still think it's all a joke."

Sylvie continued to chuckle with the others, but inside, she made improvised changes to her plans to avoid running into Gaëtan in the Autumn District. She would visit Winter today.

೫

Sky blue and lavender streamers lined the streets. The snow fell heavier than yesterday, and Sylvie kept herself concealed beneath the hood of her cloak. Combined with the heavy snowfall, the narrower streets of the Winter District gave Sylvie's outing a somber, intimate feel.

The Winter District was the smallest and least populated district in Verdélys. The Winter Verdélia were also a particular sort, a fact that was reflected in the architecture. The buildings were tall and narrow, with unusually high, peaked roofs adorning most buildings. Windows were also typically tall and slim and intricately trimmed. The structures seemed built from materials different from those Sylvie had seen in the other districts, with an exotic white stone's prominent role in the construction. Where the other districts exhibited a heavy use of wood in their construction, metal was the norm here. Sylvie felt like she had left Verdélys behind.

Sylvie drifted along, a wisp in the ever-intensifying snow. The only other Verdélia around was Alfric; if Sylvie hadn't known better, she would have thought she was totally alone. After some time, a voice broke its way through the snow flurry, a distant cry on the wind. Sylvie couldn't make out anything intelligible but picked up her pace.

The voice grew louder as Sylvie spied an opening in the narrow street before her onto what appeared to be a courtyard of some kind.

"Heed my warning!" she heard. The voice cut in and out beneath the snow. "The slumbering darkness . . . "

Sylvie left the shadows of the narrow street behind her and came out onto the square. The brightness of the snow-covered courtyard temporarily blinded her, even with the sun concealed behind heavy snow clouds. When her eyes adjusted to the light, she immediately noticed the owner of the voice she had heard.

Standing firmly on an empty planter, a short, disheveled man stood upright and called out to any and all within the sound of his voice. His gray hair had been tied back at some point, but a good portion of it had since escaped, following the winter wind this way and that. His clothes showed years of wear.

Sylvie also noticed other Verdélia in the square for the first time since entering the Winter District. Most seemed not to notice the stranger clamoring for their attention. A few turned to face him as they walked by, but none stopped to listen.

"There is no more time to delay," the man was crying, "the darkness is upon us, already within the walls of our city! Too long have we allowed chaos to take the place of order, contrary to the wishes of Solaidi!"

Sylvie reached out with her mind. She saw only smoke and shadow from the man's thoughts and a sense of determination spurred by dread.

"See for yourselves!" The man continued, "Go to the Plentiful Hills if you wish to witness the destruction at hand! The creatures and wildlife of that place are dying—they are dying because Rhys is returning!"

*Rhys?* Sylvie thought.

The old man carried on. "As I speak to you now, he is gaining strength! Every moment, he draws more towards his cause! Soon, he will be ready to execute his vengeance upon the Verdélia and submit all to his will!"

Sylvie inched forward, still careful to stay on the perimeter of the square so as not to draw attention to herself. Unsuccessfully.

"You, Miss!" The man shouted.

Sylvie looked around. She was the only one in the square.

"Why do you linger? Why don't you pass by—or flee—like the others?" He asked, making his way towards her.

Sylvie put her hand out behind her to stay Alfric from intervening.

"I find your message intriguing," Sylvie replied.

"Intriguing," the man said pensively, "Or perhaps credible?"

"That is not what I said," Sylvie answered.

"And yet..." the man said as he studied his single-member audience.

After a moment, he pointed to Sylvie.

"Come with me if you would like to learn more," he said quickly. With that, he turned and started walking at a brisk pace.

Sylvie weighed her options briefly, then decided to follow. She was hard-pressed to keep up with the older man, who was quicker than Sylvie thought he had any right to be. In the time Sylvie had needed to make up her mind to follow him, he had gained a considerable head start, and the heavy snow reduced Sylvie's mysterious guide to an obscure shadow. They drifted quietly through alleyways and streets, making their way away and across to the far side of the District.

After some time, they made their way down a dead-end road. The buildings here were neglected. Only the house at the end of the street showed any indication that it was inhabited, and then only just. The old man made his way up to the imposing ironwork gate that led into the front garden and opened it with a rusty key. Without turning to confirm that Sylvie was following, he went through the gate and up to the house, a decrepit and sinister ghost of a house that would have been quite beautiful in a previous time.

Sylvie paused at the gate as she surveyed the scene before her. She turned to look over her shoulder and noticed that Alfric was just a few short strides behind her, his hand reaching inside his cloak, probably on his sword. Now that she had considered her situation, he was right to be on edge. Still, something about this man and the turmoil within him told her she needed to find out more.

She walked over to Alfric.

"I'm going in the house," she said, "please wait here."

He looked at her with grave concern, torn between his duty to Sylvie's commands as a Firstborn and his obligation to protect her.

"Miss," Alfric said politely, "with all due respect, we don't know anything about that man or what could be in that house. For all we know, he's in league with the imps, and this is a trap."

Sylvie nodded, "I understand, but I am going into the house, and I don't want him to suspect who I am. I don't sense any other minds in the house. I think he's alone."

"Maybe so, Miss, but appearances can be deceiving." Alfric insisted. "This man could be dangerous."

"That's a risk I suppose I must take today." Sylvie shrugged. "There's something here I need to learn."

*If something happens to her*, he thought, *I will never forgive myself.*

"If something happens to me, it will be my fault, as you are following orders," Sylvie offered.

"That will not absolve me should something happen to you," Alfric answered. He sighed. "If you're resigned to go yourself, it is my duty to oblige you. Still, take this." He reached inside his cloak and pulled a long, sheathed dagger from his belt. He helped Sylvie fasten it to her belt.

"Thank you," Sylvie said. "I'll be alright."

With that, she made her way up to the house. She knocked twice, then walked inside.

The inside of the house was dark and cold. What looked like decades of dust was accumulating on every surface of what appeared to be a once well-decorated home. Books were stacked and strewn everywhere, with sheaves of papers containing notes, diagrams, and drawings littered about the entryway.

"In here," the man's voice called off from within the house. "What took you so long?"

"I...I fell behind," Sylvie said as she followed the voice deeper within the house. She saw evidence of many years of obsessive study everywhere she looked: books of every shape and size, pages and pages of notes crammed in every crevice, and strange instruments whose purpose Sylvie couldn't fathom.

As she made her way into a study, she found the man rummaging through some items in the corner of the room as he mumbled to himself.

"I once was the palace's top advisor on all things darkness and chaos," he muttered.

"You worked at the palace?" Sylvie asked incredulously.

"What's that?" The man asked as he turned to look at Sylvie. "Oh, yes." He confirmed. "I advised the Firstborn on all such matters. Then, when the last set of Firstborn passed some twenty years ago now, I was dismissed by the

Council. They called me crazy." He scoffed. "I'm not crazy. If anything, those arrogant buffoons are the crazy ones. I warned them the imp uprising was the work of dark forces beyond their comprehension. But did they listen? No, they wanted to keep the Verdélia—and themselves—coddled in a false sense of security. So they labeled me a madman and sent me on my way." He resumed his digging through his dusty affairs.

"I didn't know. What is your name?" Sylvie asked.

"Thaddeus," he said. "Ah, finally, here we are," he continued, holding up a small wooden box. "Come, we haven't time for any more pleasantries. Look here." He walked to a mirror nestled into a shallow bowl hanging on the wall. Sylvie followed.

Thaddeus opened the box and revealed several hexagonal compartments within. Each held some trinket or token. He selected a small, dried flower from the box. *Enclave*, Sylvie heard him think—the name of the flower. Thaddeus took the bloom and threw it against the mirror on the wall. To Sylvie's complete surprise, the flower stuck to the surface of the mirror and let out a ripple across its surface. The flower sat there for a few moments, then sank into the mirror.

"How..." Sylvie protested, "How did that happen?"

"Whatever do you mean?" Thaddeus asked as if nothing strange had occurred.

"The flower. It fell through the mirror." Sylvie explained, eyes wide in confusion.

"Well, of course. What else would you expect to happen when you drop something in water?" Thaddeus replied, puzzled.

"Water?" Sylvie asked. "How is water hanging on the wall like that?"

Thaddeus looked at her, intrigued. "It's just a gravitational enchantment. This old back can't spend too much time hunched over a bowl of water nowadays."

Sylvie stared at the water's surface, which had returned to its still, glassy state.

"Now look carefully," Thaddeus instructed, "watch the water."

As Sylvie observed the water, a scene came into view, blurry and translucent at first, then sharper and more vivid. She seemed to be standing near a copse of trees, staring at a beautiful summer meadow. The tall grasses swayed in the wind. Insects buzzed about the flowers lazily. The bright sun glittered through the overhanging leaves of the trees.

Then, from the edge of the meadow, Sylvie noticed a subtle but growing change. The grass, which was green and tall and firm, was beginning to droop and lose its color. The disease spread throughout the meadow as living things turned to dried-out husks of their former selves. Insects stopped mid-flight and

4020 | *Winter* | *2nd Moon* | *19*

fell to the earth. Eventually, even the trees withered and died, skeletal limbs bare in the darkened sky.

"What is this?" Sylvie asked.

"It is a vision of things to come, things quite literally on the doorstep of our civilization," Thaddeus explained.

"How can you be sure?" Sylvie pressed. "How do you know it's not just an illusion conjured by the flower?"

"You could go to the Mistralle Peninsula, where I picked this flower, and confirm for yourself," Thaddeus proposed, "but there's no need. You can be sure that what you're seeing is exactly what is happening in that part of the world now."

"If what you say is true, what's causing this?" Sylvie asked worriedly.

"Rhys," Thaddeus said matter-of-factly.

"That's impossible," Sylvie said, shaking her head. "Rhys has been imprisoned since nigh on the beginning of our world."

"Rhys has been imprisoned for many, many millennia," Thaddeus confirmed, "but that does not make what I say impossible."

"If Rhys is imprisoned, how could he be causing such destruction?" Sylvie countered.

"It's quite simple, really," Thaddeus replied, his hands animating each point he made. "Although the illustrious Firstborn Sephora, Josias, Demetrius, and Morwenna did exceptionally well to learn how to imprison Rhys, they were unable to imprison his spirit—his essence, if you will. If my research is correct, it's quite impossible to do so anyway."

"You see," he continued, "although Rhys has been prevented from retaining a physical form and acting upon this world personally, his spirit has been very much free to manipulate the world to the extent possible. And that spirit—the spirit of Rhys—is the spirit of death. Solaidi created him to act as the sentinel overseeing the bridge over which all must pass twice—once when they enter this life and once again when they leave it." He bustled through books and pictures as if trying to find proof to hand over to Sylvie, but he was always coming up short. "However, through pride and rebellion, Rhys left the garden. Losing his ability to give life and turning to the darker éthéra of the world to serve his purpose, he eventually became a tyrant, not a sentinel, over that bridge, sending some over before their time and refusing others their rightful passage. His éthéra—what we call dark éthéra--is a perversion of the kind manipulated by the Firstborn and the Verdélia, and he used it to further goals contrary to the instructions of Solaidi."

"So Rhys is a ghost?" Sylvie asked.

"No, no," Thaddeus said, shaking his head. "Remember, Rhys cannot take physical form—not even the ethereal form of a spirit or wraith. Rhys can only exist in what we perceive in our world as a spirit. You might think of this as an idea."

"But if that's the case, how could he cause the destruction you claim is happening in the world now?" Sylvie questioned.

Thaddeus paused.

"I...am not entirely sure," he admitted. "However, my theory is that Rhys has found a disciple—a pupil who is being guided, perhaps even unwittingly, by the whisperings of Rhys." He glanced at a painting on his wall. A younger version of him stood beside a young woman with raven hair falling in ringlets over her shoulder. She sat in an armchair gazing towards the painter, and he gazed at her. They were both dressed in shades of indigo.

"Who is she?" Sylvie asked.

"My deceased wife," in his mind, a vision of his wife erupted. She was screaming, her eyes unable to understand her surroundings. She tossed herself about, and he pleaded with her.

"What happened to her?" Sylvie asked.

He looked at his hands. "She experimented with the dark éthéra. It broke her. In retrospect, it was my fault. In my ambition to destroy it, I gave her the tools to practice it. She gave in to the whispers. She went mad. I tried to free her from its influence but ran out of time. Now, I seek to cleanse her beyond the grave. You must think me mad." He wouldn't look Sylvie in the eyes, but she could feel his heart as if it was breaking again.

"Do you know the identity of Rhys' pupil?" She asked after a moment.

"No," Thaddeus said, hanging his head, "but the extent of the decay that we just witnessed makes me think it is someone who has been involved with the dark éthéra for some time and has found followers of his own."

*Belthégor*, Sylvie thought to herself.

Thaddeus scrutinized Sylvie's face.

"You know something of what I speak," he said.

"I..." Sylvie began, "I can't say for certain."

"There is no time for doubt now, Miss," Thaddeus warned, "whatever you know, I urge you to take action, for tomorrow may be too late. You must find a way to tell the Firstborn. The council will not allow me near them."

Sylvie took a deep breath. The stakes seemed too high. She looked out the window and realized it was beginning to grow dark.

"I must go," Sylvie told Thaddeus. "Do you live here?"

"I do," Thaddeus replied.

"I may visit again," Sylvie said. "I may have questions about Rhys."

"Very well," Thaddeus said with a short bow.

Sylvie left the house and covered her head with her heavy hood. Relief swept over her when she saw Alfric standing dutifully under the overhanging roof of a nearby house. As she drew nearer, she saw the relief on his face.

"Thank Solaidi," he said softly, "a few minutes more, and I was going in after you."

"Sorry to keep you," Sylvie said, "let's get back to the palace. Do not tell anyone of this visit—or this man."

"Very well, but you should confide in someone," Alfric said.

With that, they started through the deep snow back towards the palace.

⚘

Sylvie nervously returned to her suite and slipped out of her cloak and into something more comfortable. She was sure, having been out so late, that the other Firstborn would be suspicious.

"Where have you been?" Nadine said in a mix of a whisper and an anxious cry as she hurried into Sylvie's suite, careful to close the door behind her.

Sylvie jumped at Nadine's sudden appearance.

"You almost gave me a heart attack," Sylvie said, taking a breath and placing a hand over her heart.

"You're so late!" Nadine continued. "I covered for you as best as I could, but you missing dinner has got everyone on edge."

"I'm sorry," Sylvie said, "but I got carried away. I found something."

A knock at the door interrupted their conversation. Nadine and Sylvie looked at each other with big eyes. Sylvie gestured her head towards the door, instructing Nadine to check who was there.

"Yes?" Nadine said, opening the door just a sliver.

"Hello, Nadine," Sylvie heard Loïc say, "Is Sylvie back yet?"

"She..." Nadine said, flustered. They agreed to the story that Sylvie had been in her suite the entire day.

"She..." Nadine continued, "She's...she's been in all day. Can I relay a message, perhaps?"

"Perhaps," Loïc answered. "Perhaps you could relay the message that, for the time being, I'm the only one who knows that Sylvie has not, in fact, been in the palace all day, nor yesterday, nor the day before. Perhaps relay that if she'd like to keep it that way, she can let me in for a chat."

"I..." Nadine said, trembling, "I will let her know."

"Wonderful," Loïc replied calmly. "I'll wait here."

230

Nadine quickly shut the door and looked back at Sylvie.

"What do I tell him?" Nadine asked desperately.

Sylvie sat without speaking, running her options through her mind.

"Let him in," she said finally. "You can be dismissed for the night," she added.

Nadine nodded in assent and slowly made her way back to the door.

"Miss Sylvie will see you now," Nadine said as she opened the door.

Loïc walked in, his shoulders square and straight as usual. Nadine curtsied and shut the door behind her as she left the room. Sylvie swallowed nervously.

"So..." Loïc said casually, glancing around the room, "where have you been? Did you decide to skip the Autumn District today?"

"I..." Sylvie began. She wasn't sure if she should double down on her story, make up something new, or tell the truth. How much did Loïc know?

"First of all, what makes you so sure I haven't been in the palace?" Sylvie retorted. Maybe Loïc was bluffing after all.

Loïc smiled.

"Sylvie, please," he said, "I meet regularly with Alfric. There's not anything that happens involving the palace guard that I don't know about. Within the past few days, Commander Alfric and Captain Durand have been on 'special assignment' in the city that no one, not even Alfric, wants to give me the details on. On those very same days, you're suddenly nowhere to be found. Seems a bit odd, doesn't it?"

"That doesn't mean anything," Sylvie answered, trying to keep her voice from wavering. "There are some serious security concerns in Verdélys right now. They could have been on any number of 'special assignments.'"

Loïc raised an eyebrow in amusement. He knew more, and cornering Sylvie was becoming a game for him.

"You expect me to believe that Alfric and his most trusted Captain were up to something that I was not only not aware of but that they refused to inform me of?" Loïc countered with a smug, subtle smile. "You see," he continued, making his way around Sylvie's room as he spoke, "there are exactly three individuals who could swear Alfric to secrecy against me: Gaëtan, Margot, or you. Gaëtan hasn't spoken to Alfric since last week. Margot never speaks to Alfric. So that leaves you."

He stared at Sylvie. She held his gaze out of principle but knew that her secret was out.

"You'll be glad to know," Loïc went on as he went back to circling the room, "that Alfric did not betray you—Alfric is far too loyal for that. Captain Durand's integrity was also unimpeachable. However, the rest of the guards weren't quite so tight-lipped when pressed."

"Okay, fine," Sylvie blurted out. "I've been out in the city. What do you care?"

"Plenty, actually," Loïc said, a look of triumph on his face. "What have you been up to out there? Sir Reynard will be livid when he returns, and you haven't got the faintest grasp of the material he assigned you, so it had better be worth it."

Sylvie sank in her seat. Her little adventure had been worth it, but she was not looking forward to Sir Reynard's impending disapproval.

"Well...it has been worth it so far, if you must know," Sylvie said out loud.

"I'm glad to hear it," Loïc said, pulling a chair close to Sylvie and taking a seat. "Is it worth it, not just in the 'I didn't have to stay in a stuffy room and study' sense?"

"Yes," Sylvie nodded. "I decided to take a few days to get familiar with the Verdélia—ordinary Verdélia, not just Councilmembers and the like."

Loïc didn't say anything, but his demeanor reflected approval.

"Anyway," Sylvie continued, "I met some wonderful people in the Spring and Summer Districts. I was going to visit the Autumn District today, but I skipped that because...well, you know why. So I decided on the Winter District instead, and I think I stumbled onto something there."

When Sylvie didn't immediately continue, Loïc spoke up.

"Well, out with it then," Loïc urged.

Sylvie recounted her encounter with Thaddeus and his warnings. She also explained the strange things she had seen in the old man's thoughts.

"It was odd," Sylvie said. "It was like seeing something by looking at its shadow only...a similitude of the real thing, but two-dimensional and distorted. I don't know how to explain it."

Loïc was listening intently, evidently expecting her to continue.

"Actually," Sylvie continued, "now that I think about it, I can remember the same sensation once before—at Belthégor's trial and during his escape."

Loïc leaned in as the story stoked his interest.

"Do you think Thaddeus and Belthégor are working together then?" He asked.

"I...am not sure," Sylvie admitted. "But I don't think so. Thaddeus seemed familiar with the darkness, but not by choice."

Loïc sat back, his hand to his chin in thought.

"You were able to recognize something different in the minds of Belthégor and Silas' followers, which you then recognized in the mind of a man who claimed he was the Firstborn's foremost expert on dark éthéra twenty years ago," Loïc said. "It sounds like we should find out if Thaddeus is indeed who he says he is. If so..." he faded off, an idea forming behind his dark eyes.

"If Thaddeus is right, and he was the advisor he says he was, and dismissed by the Council..." Sylvie began. "Well, isn't it possible that whoever dismissed him was involved with Rhys? We know the Council isn't immune to his influence—look at Councilman Victor."

"That is a serious claim, if true," Loïc said.

"I don't want to condemn anyone. There have just been whisperings that hint at it, and I've been sensitive to the advisors' antics. I wouldn't say or do anything until I was certain. But I am suspicious of our advisors all the same—and Alfric suspects Beyern."

At this, Loïc raised an eyebrow in surprise.

"Alfric told you this?" He asked.

"Well...not out loud. And he did say he wasn't certain, just suspicious," Sylvie replied.

Loïc sat pondering the new information for a moment before speaking.

"As High Councilman, Beyern appointed all of the advisors. In all honesty, I keep my advisor at arm's length. His motives never really seemed aligned with the good of Verdélys itself. Maybe I'll keep him around more so you can get a sense of him, too. His name is Romain. I'll introduce you."

Sylvie nodded and, without anything more to say, just gazed at Loïc's hands, now clasped in his lap. Even relaxed, the strength in Loïc's hands was betrayed by the veins and sinews visible beneath his skin.

"I assume you were planning on visiting the Autumn District tomorrow?" Loïc asked Sylvie. The apparent change in subject caught her off guard.

"I...hadn't thought it through completely, to be honest." She stuttered. "It was either that or the Imp District."

"Great," Loïc replied excitedly. "Given the circumstances, I think we can skip the Autumn District. If you were to sense this feeling that you found in the minds of Belthégor and Thaddeus, do you think you would recognize it again?"

Sylvie thought for a moment, catching on to Loïc's plan.

"I think so," she answered. "You want me to try and find Belthégor and Silas in the Imp District?" She asked.

Loïc chuckled, "Oh no," he answered, "I wouldn't want you alone in the Imp District with those two under any circumstances. I want *us* to try to find them in the Imp District. I'm coming with you."

❧

Sylvie and Loïc had been up late into the night in preparation for their quest into the Imp District. First, Loïc had taken them to review palace historical records, which had confirmed that Thaddeus had indeed served in a counseling capacity to the Firstborn several years prior. With that information, they had moved on to the logistics of their outing.

"The Imp District is quite particular," Loïc explained. "Verdélia only rarely enter the District, and the imps mostly keep to themselves. Anyone involved with Belthégor and Silas will be suspicious of any Verdélia in the District. To fix that problem, it's time for a crash course in practical winter éthéra craft—specifically, shape-shifting."

As a Firstborn, Sylvie could harness the skills of all the seasonal Verdélia, Loïc taught. Shapeshifting was an ability otherwise unique to the Winter Verdélia. Skilled Winter Verdélia could shift into completely different creatures or objects. Feats of that kind were complex and extremely taxing on the caster.

"For now, we can limit the change in your appearance to the yellow irises of an imp and darken your hair," Loïc suggested. "Watch," he added.

Before Sylvie's eyes, Loïc's typically dark eyes began to change. His irises began to ripple as if made of some liquid that had suddenly been disturbed. The color went from nearly black to amber and finally to a deep gold.

"I'll keep my hair but change a few of my features to avoid being recognized," Loïc added. A few moments later, his nose was shifting, moving slightly up and shrinking. His mouth widened, and his lips narrowed. Soon, Loïc was unrecognizable.

"Incredible," Sylvie gasped.

Loïc guided her through the process, explaining how she could manipulate the éthéra within her to alter her physical self.

It took her several hours to grasp the enchantment. The task significantly differed from the relatively straightforward magic she had practiced involving plants. The complexities of her own éthéra and the challenge of bending it to her will were elusive. She practiced at length in front of a mirror as Loïc coached her firmly.

Finally, she saw a small ripple in her eye, like in Loïc's. She felt a channel open, and éthéra spilled through like a flow of water that was suddenly unstopped. Soon enough, her eyes were bright green, like summer foliage.

"That's a good start," Loïc said, "but you've only amplified an existing feature. You need to control the éthéra and dictate your appearance."

Now, the exercise was more like what Sylvie was used to. With the éthéra flowing, she could guide it and rein it in as necessary. Soon, she had replaced her typically green eyes with light straw-colored ones, and her hair had gone from gold to jet black.

"Well done," Loïc complimented. "You'll want to make some minor adjustments to some of your other features, but the change in your hair color is significant enough that you shouldn't need anything major."

"Thank you. I suppose when Sir Reynard returns, I'll have this to show for all of the material I didn't get around to studying, which is something." Sylvie said. She felt pretty proud of herself. Loïc had said shapeshifting was one of the more difficult arcane practices, and even though what she had accomplished was relatively minor in the realm of self-alteration, the result would allow them to investigate the Imp District as planned.

"Let's get some rest. You'll need as much éthéra as you can get if you're going to stay shifted all day tomorrow," Loïc instructed. "I'll see you in the morning."

Once in bed, Sylvie lay buried in her blankets, contemplating her day in the Winter District and the adventure that awaited her on the morrow. A mixture of excitement and anxiety bounced around in her head, but even that couldn't stop the day's weariness from dragging her down into a deep sleep.

# XXIII

## *Among the Shadows*

S ylvie followed the morning routine she had discussed with Loïc the night
prior. As usual, the Firstborn had shared their breakfast in the palace.
From there, Sylvie had excused herself and made her way towards 3 Amber
Lane, her old home. Loïc had suggested the cottage as a place to meet, shift into
their imp disguises, and make their way into the city. Things had been arranged
with Alfric in advance—otherwise, two unknown imps making their way out
of the palace would have raised suspicion.

She sat in her old living room, waiting for Loïc. He didn't take long.

"Hello again," Loïc said as he entered the cottage. "I have the rest of our
disguises. You can change upstairs; I'll stay down here." Loïc set a large bag on
the table in front of Sylvie. He opened it and placed a neatly folded set of black
clothes beside the sack on the table. Sylvie and Loïc would be using palace staff
uniforms to complete their disguises.

A few moments later, Sylvie had changed into her somber ensemble. She
took a last look in her old vanity mirror to confirm that even she couldn't
recognize herself. She looked the part. Sylvie made her way down the stairs and
had to remind herself that it was indeed Loïc waiting for her in front of the
door.

"Come on then, let's get right to it," Loïc said.

※

Sylvie and Loïc were stopped only momentarily at the palace gate, and Alfric
personally saw them through. They set out through the city towards the Imp
District.

"So, what's the plan once we get to the Imp District?" Loïc asked Sylvie.

"I suppose we'll just need to cover as much ground as we can to allow me to
listen in to as many minds as possible," Sylvie replied.

Loïc made a face. "I guess it's a bit of a long shot when you put it that way."

Sylvie didn't reply. He wasn't wrong.

As they neared their destination, their surroundings began to change noticeably. The profusion of trees and other plant growth prevalent in the other districts was nowhere to be found. The architecture and construction were still skillfully executed but less intricate and detailed. Sylvie guessed it had something to do with the imps' inability to manipulate éthéra. She made a mental note to ask Sir Reynard about it later.

Sylvie cast her mind out like a net, hoping to find any sign of the darkness she had felt in Belthégor and through Thaddeus.

*Good grief, I forgot to refill the family's soumais serum again*, thought an older imp.

*Dinner at Gresham's tonight,* thought a younger woman excitedly.

*I'd fancy a mielaluer tea right about now*, another woman groaned inwardly.

Sylvie noticed a difficulty getting a clear read on any one mind. The hundreds of minds she had crossed in the days prior seemed to be blending within her, and for every one of them, a small piece of her mind seemed to float out of place to make room for the new thoughts. She shook herself in an attempt to refocus.

Sylvie and Loïc walked for hours through the district. Occasionally, they would sit just out of the foot traffic and let the imps do the walking as Sylvie scanned for the familiar, unsettling aura. However, it was already afternoon, and even though they had skipped lunch, the search had come up empty. Sylvie could feel her enchanted mask draining her. She wouldn't be able to keep this up forever.

"We're going to have to think about making it back to the palace at some point soon," Loïc reminded Sylvie. "Have you found anything?"

"Nothing yet," Sylvie said. "Give me a little longer."

"Very well," Loïc replied, "but we're running out of time for today."

Sylvie was all too aware of that. She raced through as many minds as she could reach.

There was one thinking about a meal.

There was another thinking about a list of chores to be completed.

A melody ran through the thoughts of another.

Sylvie swam doggedly through a lake of different thoughts and feelings. None drew her any closer to her goal.

Then, at last, there it was.

*...Belthégor himself could attend? What a thought.*

"There," Sylvie breathed to Loïc.

"Where?" Loïc asked.

*It's a new time for us imps. I'll be there, no doubt.*

Sylvie tracked the thought, trying hard to pin it on someone in her line of sight.

"Come on," she whispered to Loïc as they set out down the street.

After a few moments, Sylvie and Loïc settled in behind a lone imp. He looked sickly—his posture was poor, and he was clearly underfed. His hair was unkempt and thinning. His mind was volatile but circled around Belthégor and an event that evening.

"Where are we going?" Loïc asked quietly.

"I'm not sure where," Sylvie said, "but that man is thinking about an event he suspects Belthégor may attend tonight."

"Our lucky day," Loïc replied. "Are you holding out alright with your disguise?"

"I'll be fine," Sylvie answered, though she knew it would only be a matter of time before they had to head back.

Twilight began to set in as Sylvie and Loïc followed their wandering quarry through narrow streets and alleyways. Finally, the man stopped before a worn but occupied inn. He looked around and then made his way inside.

"Come on," Loïc said, "let's get closer."

The building was set back from the street. It had a good-sized courtyard behind a mid-height stone wall, and a stable was adjacent.

"In here," Loïc said, grabbing Sylvie's hand and pulling them into the stable. It was empty. From where they were, they could look out between cracks in the wooden boards that formed the stable walls and into the courtyard in front of the inn. They had a great view of the front door but couldn't see inside.

"I can't hear anything," Loïc said quietly. "Can you make out what's going on?"

"I can make out someone behind the counter, but he's alone for now," Sylvie answered.

Just then, a woman walked into the courtyard and up the steps into the inn. A muffled conversation ensued.

*...the meeting...*

Sylvie could just make out the woman's thoughts.

"She told the bartender she's here for the meeting," Sylvie explained to Loïc.

"Is that it?" He asked. "Seems like there'd be more to it."

Sylvie shook her head, "There's something else. An action of some kind. I couldn't tell what it was."

Sylvie reached out to the innkeeper. He was putting something silver in a leather pouch.

"It's a coin. Silver." Sylvie explained.

"Does it look like this?" Loïc asked as he pulled a large coin out of his purse. The coin had an intricate bloom embossed on one side.

"Yes!" Sylvie exclaimed quietly.

"One met," Loïc whispered. "That's a handsome sum for most imps in Verdélys."

He returned his hand to his purse and pulled out a second coin.

"Here," he said, handing it to Sylvie. "I'll go first. Wait a few minutes, and then you come in after me."

Loïc stood, brushed the straw from his clothes, exited the stable, and marched towards the inn. Sylvie watched from her spot in the stable as he made his way inside. She heard an indecipherable exchange and Donovans' footsteps as he receded further into the building.

*Must be one of Eglantine's recruits*, she heard the innkeeper think as he put Loïc's coin in his pouch.

She sat, waiting for what seemed an eternity. Finally, she stood and made her way to the inn.

The inn was poorly lit. She squinted, trying to make out the details of the room as she walked in. She made her way to the counter on her left.

"I'm here for the meeting," she said to the innkeeper.

*Another one from the palace?* She heard the man think.

"Who invited you?" The man asked.

Sylvie hesitated for a moment.

"Eglantine," she replied.

The man grunted. Sylvie placed her coin on the counter.

"Go to the end of the room, through the door, and down the stairs on your right," the innkeeper said, retrieving Sylvie's coin. "The meeting is starting; best get going."

"Right," Sylvie said, making her way to the back of the room. Once through the door, she noticed a stairway winding down to her right into what seemed an abyss. She made her way down carefully, keeping her hand on the wall. As she wound down the narrow, unswept stairs, she finally could make out the edges of a door that let in the tiniest sliver of torchlight. She opened the door.

Inside was a large cellar full of imps. Sylvie tried her best not to gasp. As with the rest of the inn, there was little light to see, but from what she could make out, individuals were stuffed into corners, on and around large crates, and anywhere else that could accommodate a body. Everyone was facing a wall opposite the door, where a makeshift stage had been cobbled together using boxes, barrels, and other furniture. The room was heavy with the presence of so many imps. More than that, Sylvie could feel it—the same depressing essence that had permeated Belthégor's mind and Thaddeus's. It was all around her.

"Nice to see you made it," Loïc said suddenly from beside her. Sylvie jumped.

"It's just me," Loïc whispered.

Sylvie breathed a sigh of relief.

They waited a few minutes, standing there with the rest of these rogue imps, not knowing quite what they were waiting for. Then, from across the room, Sylvie could make out movement on the makeshift stage.

"Welcome!" Shouted a large, cloaked man from atop the stage. Two equally formidable men backed him. The chatter that had hung about the room grew still.

"Welcome, one and all!" The man continued. "My, it is wonderful to see so many gathered tonight. What a sight this is."

There was some cheering from the crowd.

"We encourage you to continue your efforts to bring as many as possible to join us in our struggle for justice, for equality," the man went on. "As you know, the Verdélia will not willingly relinquish their grasp on the power and dominion they exercise over us day and night."

The crowd jeered at the mention of the Verdélia. After a moment, the man raised his hands to calm the imps.

"Yes, we know we have a fight before us," the man called out, "but we are prepared! As most of you have heard, we have succeeded in freeing our brother Belthégor, one of the fathers of our fight!"

There was more cheering. The man continued, speaking ever louder to carry over the crowd.

"We now have the kind of leadership that can guide us to victory and freedom! Belthégor is a true disciple of Rhys, ready to teach us to wield powers that will bring the Verdélia to their knees! Behold!"

Suddenly, the man drew from his cloak a small lizard-like creature struggling to escape his grip. Sylvie watched in horror as the man began an inaudible incantation. The creature in his grasp started to move more and more slowly. More disturbing still, its tail began to disintegrate into a black ash. The decay moved its way up the body. Soon, the entire creature was nothing but an ashen husk. The man finished his spell and crushed what was left of the beast in his hand. Black dust flitted about.

With a yell, the man cast his hands forward, and a bolt of light shot from his hands and struck a barrel nearby, splintering under the impact.

The imps gathered in the cellar went wild, shouting and cheering at the man's demonstration.

"Yes!" He yelled, "Soon, all will be prepared for us to force the Verdélia to recognize us as equals!"

Sylvie felt ill. The man's consciousness was empty. She couldn't explain it, but from within the cloudy void of his mind, Sylvie thought she could sense a second being, one much more powerful and cunning—the puppeteer commandeering his servant.

Sylvie felt her disguise slip. She gritted her teeth and forced it back into place.

She looked around desperately for Loïc. He was still nearby.

"We need to go," she whispered to Loïc urgently.

The cellar had become a madhouse. The imps were fanatical.

Loïc looked down at Sylvie. He seemed to recognize the situation and nodded.

"Right, let's go then," he said, ushering Sylvie back to the stairs.

They struggled through the press of frenetic strangers, through the door, and up the black stairway.

"Leaving early?" The innkeeper said, looking surprised to see them.

"We can't be away from the palace too long," Loïc replied curtly. "Wouldn't want to raise suspicions."

"Fair enough," the innkeeper said.

Loïc and Sylvie made their way out into the frigid night.

"Hold onto that disguise a bit longer," Loïc whispered.

Sylvie was struggling. Loïc's strides were swift, and Sylvie's focus was torn between keeping up her pace and maintaining her shifted face.

In the haze of her mind, Sylvie made out another presence just behind them on the dark cobblestone streets. Under the circumstances, had it been any other presence, she might have ignored it. This one, however, was focused intently on Loïc and Sylvie. Sylvie rushed a few steps to catch up to Loïc. She grabbed his arm, partially to get his attention and partially to help her keep up.

"We're being followed," she whispered.

Loïc kept walking, giving no visible indication he had heard her.

"Are you sure?" He asked.

"I..." Sylvie focused. The presence was still behind them, still focused on them.

"I'm pretty sure," she said.

"Let's keep walking," Loïc instructed, "if they don't try something between here and the palace, we'll lose them at the gate."

Sylvie and Loïc continued through the cold. Sylvie did her best to stay aware of their follower, but fatigue kept her from staying focused.

Just as they were about to make their way onto the main thoroughfare leading out of the Imp District, three cloaked figures appeared before them, blocking their path.

"Halt," one of them called out.

Sylvie could still feel the presence behind them but realized too late that it had been many followers, not just one. The consciousness was familiar—the puppeteer from the cellar was here. She looked over her shoulder to see another three cloaked individuals blocking the narrow road behind them.

"Friends of Eglantine's, right?" One of the dark figures said as all six drew nearer to Sylvie and Loïc.

"That's right," Loïc answered. "We need to make it back before our absence is noticed."

"Ah," replied the stranger as he continued to draw closer. Sylvie could feel his mind focused intently on Loïc. It was dripping with malice. Then, she saw it— in his mind, the stranger saw himself swiftly drawing a blade and running Loïc through.

She squeezed Loïc's arm as tightly as she could.

"Némor," she said, using ancient language in the hope that the imps would not immediately understand.

Loïc didn't hesitate. With a quick motion, he drew the blade hidden at his back and beneath his cloak just in time to parry the thrust from the first cloaked assailant. Loïc's stroke was forceful and visibly unexpected. The man lost his grip on his sword, which went spinning through the air and clattered against the stone building to their left. Loïc held the tip of his sword to the man's breast.

"We'll be on our way now," Loïc said.

Sylvie saw a foul smirk on the man's face beneath his cloak.

"We think not," he said.

Sylvie saw again the thoughts of another assailant, this time one that had come from behind. As she felt his mind send his blade plunging toward Loïc, she lashed out, her only focus deflecting the strike. She felt her mind push against her foe's. His mind gave way, and the intent directed at Loïc shifted— to the assailant's companion beside him. The man with the sword jerked violently to his left and forced his sword into his accomplice. The victim fell without a sound. Sylvie recoiled as she witnessed the result of her action and felt the consciousness of the man abruptly end. The other imp standing behind Sylvie and Loïc let out a cry of dismay.

*Morwenna!* Sylvie heard the imps think to themselves in alarm. From the corner of her eye, she could see that her hair had retaken its natural hue. Her effort to save Loïc had drained her to the point that she could no longer maintain her magical facade.

The imp Loïc was holding at sword point made a move for Loïc's weapon. Loïc's reaction was instantaneous. He buried his sword in the man's chest with a swift, smooth lunge. The two other imps blocking the Firstborns' path drew their swords simultaneously and charged Loïc. Amidst a flurry of blades, Loïc parried their blows before retaliating. He struck a heavy blow to one assailant's arm, drawing a howl of pain from the man as Loïc shoved him forcefully into his companion. The two imps struggled to separate themselves, with the wounded man falling into the snow, his open wound staining the ground a deep crimson color. The other man turned to face Loïc again and raised his weapon, but he was too late. Loïc had taken full advantage of the confusion and was on the imp in a flash, dispatching him with a heavy stroke of his sword across the man's neck.

Loïc turned to face the two assailants behind him, but they were gone. They had given Sylvie a look of terror after she had pushed the one imp to slay his companion and had fled back down the moonlit street.

Loïc turned to the wounded imp, who was groaning in pain and holding his arm, which was still gushing warm blood onto the snow-covered cobblestones.

"Why were you following us?" Loïc barked.

The man didn't answer and continued to writhe in pain in the powdery snow.

Loïc placed a boot on the man's damaged arm and stepped down. The man screamed.

"Why were you following us?!" Loïc asked again.

The man coughed and spat in Loïc's direction. "Verdélia scum," he groaned hoarsely.

Loïc put more of his weight down on the man's damaged arm. The imp screamed again. Sylvie covered her ears and screwed her eyes shut. She hadn't signed up for this.

"Answer my question," Loïc commanded.

"I don't answer to you," the imp said through ragged breaths.

"You will," Loïc said. He kicked the man's sword away, reached down, grabbed the man's cloak, and dragged him to his feet.

"Let's go. We can continue this interrogation in a more appropriate location."

"You fool, I'm not going anywhere with you," the imp scowled. With a twisted grin and a deft motion of his good hand, he shoved something into his mouth, bit down, and swallowed. Almost instantly, he began to convulse and collapsed to the ground. A few moments later, he was dead.

"Curses," Loïc muttered.

Sylvie was beside herself. The snow around her was blood-stained, and four dead imps lay at her feet.

She slowly came to as Loïc was forcefully calling her name.

"Sylvie!" Loïc said. "Come on, we haven't got time. We need to get to the palace and get troops here now." Sylvie stared at Loïc blankly. He dragged the bodies out of the roadway and off to the side of a building, then took Sylvie by the arm and began walking swiftly towards the palace. Sylvie's thoughts were consumed with the violence and death she had just witnessed—and primarily the life that had been taken as a direct result of her actions. The feeling of the man's consciousness ending replayed in her mind repeatedly. Loïc dragged her in a daze through the city to the palace gates.

Once they reached the palace, Loïc began barking orders immediately, and Sylvie barely noticed as the palace guards milled about urgently.

"Get Alfric here right away!" Loïc called out. A member of the guard dashed into the night at Loïc's command.

Loïc called the ranking palace officer and ordered a contingent of men to leave immediately for the inn where the imp gathering had been held. Using a map of the city provided by the guards, Loïc pointed out the inn's location and gave a quick briefing of the night's events. Several of the soldiers tightened their grip on their swords as they realized the severity of the situation. After a few final instructions from Loïc, the soldiers set out at a near run through the snow towards the Imp District.

"When Alfric arrives, send him to the study right away," Loïc ordered one of the gate guards.

"Yes sir," the guard replied firmly.

Loïc turned to Sylvie.

"Come on, let's get you home," Loïc said gently.

"I..." Sylvie said, still in a stupor. "I killed that man..."

Loïc put his arm around her shoulder as he guided her toward the palace.

"Yes, you did. And in doing so, you saved my life." He said.

Loïc's words comforted Sylvie, but a storm of emotions continued to rage within her. She huddled into Loïc.

As the pair entered the palace, Loïc called to one of the palace staff.

"Fetch Nadine right away," he said.

The servant nodded and darted upstairs. A few moments later, Nadine came rushing towards Sylvie.

"Oh my..." she said as she noticed Sylvie's vacant expression. "What happened?"

"There was an incident in the Imp District," is all Loïc provided as an explanation of the night's events. "She'll be alright, physically speaking. See that she gets into something comfortable, and give her a hot bath with valerian. I'll be in the study with Alfric if you need me."

Loïc and Nadine coaxed Sylvie out from under Loïc's arm, and Loïc swiftly approached the study. Sylvie leaned on Nadine as they made their way up to her suite.

"You look like you've been through a lot," Nadine consoled Sylvie. "Let's get you upstairs."

Sylvie sat silently on a chair as Nadine prepared a bath for her. Nadine added some valerian to the steaming water, as Loïc had instructed, for its soothing qualities. Sylvie slipped out of her palace staff uniform and felt as if she was shedding a part of her being—one she thought she'd just as soon forget. She lowered herself gently into the hot water and let herself sink completely beneath the surface.

She sat in the bath for what felt like an eternity. Between the comfort of the water and the crippling weight of the night's events, Sylvie wished she might dissolve into the water itself.

Eventually, Nadine suggested she get some rest.

"I don't assume to know what you've been through," Nadine said timidly, "but it's very late, and some rest could only do you good."

Sylvie knew she wouldn't be sleeping that night. The skirmish in the snow under the moon played again and again in her head. She watched as the imp she had pushed to murder sank his sword into his ally, over and over again. She felt the dying man's mind extinguish. She recoiled at the thought.

Regardless, Sylvie had exited the bath and draped herself in a thick, comfortable towel. Nadine helped her into a smooth silk nightdress and a heavy velvet robe.

"Will you take me to the study, please?" Sylvie asked timidly as Nadine prepared to leave.

"Of course," Nadine said with a nod.

The two made their way down the dimly lit palace stairs. They walked across the vast entryway and towards the study, where Sylvie had first met the Firstborn. Nadine opened the door and walked Sylvie inside.

Loïc was in an animated discussion with Alfric and still wore his palace staff uniform. A map was out on the table, and a hearty fire was crackling in the hearth. Loïc and Alfric looked up as Nadine and Sylvie entered the room. Loïc looked at Sylvie empathetically. She felt an inexplicable urge to run and hide under his arm, the only other person who knew exactly what had happened a few hours ago in the Imp District. Loïc's features conveyed understanding without the need for words.

"Alfric," Loïc said, turning to the Commander, "thank you for coming so late and on such short notice. We will resume this conversation shortly, and I will make myself available as needed by the guard. You are dismissed."

Alfric bowed, gathered a few items on the table in front of them, and made his way towards the door. He bowed deeply as he approached Sylvie.

"Miss Sylvie," he said respectfully. Sylvie nodded, and Alfric made his way out.

"Thank you, Nadine," Sylvie said, turning to Nadine. Nadine took her cue and exited the study, closing the door behind her.

Sylvie stood there at the door. Loïc stood opposite the room from her, looking directly at her.

"I can't sleep," Sylvie said finally. "I can't get it out of my head." She fought back tears.

Loïc made his way towards Sylvie.

"Come," he said softly, guiding her towards the oversized, plush couch facing the fireplace.

Sylvie walked over to the couch. Loïc seated himself against the arm and reached out to Sylvie, inviting her to sit beside him. She sat and let her head fall against his chest. Finally, she stopped fighting and let herself cry.

# XXIV

## *A Mermaid*

S ylvie woke to the sounds of wood snapping in the fireplace. Muted sunlight filtered in through the drapes covering the windows.

"Good morning," Loïc said. His voice sounded incredibly close.

Sylvie took in her surroundings. Her head was lying on Loïc's chest as he sat upright on the couch in the study facing the hearth. She was nestled under a heavy blanket in her nightdress. The previous night's events came flooding back to her. She buried her face into Loïc's shirt and groaned.

"Take your time," Loïc said, his hand on Sylvie's shoulder. "When you're ready, I had breakfast brought in for you. Some warm food and some mielalur tea will do you good."

Sylvie shut her eyes so tightly that she thought she was seeing stars. After a moment, she sat up, keeping the blanket wrapped tightly around her. She looked at the tray on the table before them, covered in delicious-looking berry cakes and an assortment of steaming breakfast sausage. A cup of tea fumed nearby.

She realized Loïc was looking at her. As usual, his expression betrayed little, but he seemed concerned. She tucked a strand of hair behind her ear, hoping to stave off embarrassment by keeping her hands busy.

"Did you sit here all night?" She asked finally.

"Yes," Loïc answered.

"I...I'm sorry," Sylvie replied. "I didn't mean to...it's just I couldn't sleep, and I didn't...I wasn't sure what to do, and you're the only one who was there last night, who knew what happened, and so..." Her voice drifted off.

Loïc shook his head gently. "I don't mind. I know you're going through a lot right now. I'm here to help however I can."

He turned to the breakfast on the table and grabbed a little cake.

"Here," he said, "why don't you start by eating something?"

Sylvie took the cake. It was still hot and smelled unexpectedly like her forest back in Hull. She took a bite and was suddenly aware of how hungry she was. She had skipped dinner in the commotion of the previous night's events. Combined with the stress of her outing in the Imp District, her body demanded she eat more. In a few short moments, she had devoured the berry cake and was making her way through the rest of her breakfast.

At last, she sat sipping her tea, staring at the fire's mesmerizing dance.

Loïc, who had been silent throughout her meal, broke the silence.

"A few items you should be aware of," he said. "The guards made it to the inn last night. It was empty when they arrived, with no trace of any of the imps who participated in yesterday's gathering. Eglantine, our local palace spy, is also nowhere to be found. The bodies of our assailants were also gone by the time the palace guards reached the Imp District."

Sylvie cringed at the mention of the corpses. One had been her doing.

"Finally," Loïc continued, "the whole episode is going to cause quite a stir and no doubt we're going to hear from Gaëtan sooner rather than later."

There was a short knock at the door as if on cue, and Gaëtan entered quickly, shutting the door behind him. His face had a bewildered look mingled with what looked to Sylvie to be anger.

"Are you out of your mind?" Gaëtan blurted out towards Loïc.

Loïc gave Sylvie a look. Without turning to face Gaëtan, he gestured to a chair next to the couch he and Sylvie were sitting on.

"Good morning Gaëtan. Have a seat, and we can talk." Loïc said calmly.

Gaëtan marched over to the couch but did not sit down.

"I don't know what you were playing at or why, but I thought you were smarter than to drag Sylvie out to the Imp District, given the current circumstances. From what Alfric has told me, it sounds like a miracle you two weren't both killed last night!" Gaëtan fumed. Gaëtan's attention was divided between Loïc and Sylvie, in anger at the former and concern at the latter.

Sylvie watched as Loïc bore the brunt of Gaëtan's wrath, all for an idea that had been hers from the start.

"Frankly, Gaëtan, I understand and appreciate your concern," Loïc answered, "but now is not the time for this conversation. I promise you'll get the full report on yesterday's events soon."

Gaëtan glared at Loïc and looked over at Sylvie protectively. He sighed.

After a moment, he said, "I'm glad you're both safe," and walked briskly out of the room.

Sylvie and Loïc sat in silence for a few more moments.

"Why didn't you tell him the whole thing was my idea?" Sylvie asked Loïc.

Loïc chuckled, "And make it look like I'm blaming a brazen, irrational decision on the inexperienced newcomer? I don't think Gaëtan would have taken too kindly to that, even if it was true."

Sylvie nodded in agreement and buried herself a bit deeper in her blanket. What a mess she had caused. The two friends sat in silence, the only sound coming from the crackling flames of the glowing fire.

After a few minutes, Loïc turned to Sylvie.

"Look," he said somberly, "I don't know how to say this delicately, so I'm just going to come out with it. There is no wrong in what you did last night."

Sylvie shuddered as the scene of the imp slaying his companion flashed across her mind.

Loïc continued. "You are a Firstborn, and as such, it is your solemn duty to do everything necessary to protect that which is good—and sometimes, that means destroying that which is evil."

Sylvie sat and stared at her tea. Loïc's words rang true, but she still felt a deep wound in her soul as she faced the reality that she had taken a life. She suspected this wound would not heal quickly.

"How do you deal with it? Taking life, I mean." Sylvie eventually asked, her eyes still on her tea.

Loïc sat and stared at the fire.

"It's like making any other choice," he said. "I consider my options. Yesterday, there were two: defend myself or let us both die. In that light, the choice was easy."

In that context, the choice to return violence on violence seemed simple. Still, Sylvie remained troubled.

"But couldn't there be some way to defend oneself without taking life?" Sylvie asked out loud.

"In certain instances, yes," Loïc answered, "but you know better than anyone that those imps yesterday had in mind to kill us if they could. I allowed them the opportunity to let us pass, which they refused. From there, it was certain that not all of us would make it away from that street alive."

Loïc sighed, then continued.

"Having said that, I understand your point. You're coming at this from a place of empathy, thinking that there must be a way to diffuse conflict between individuals through means other than violence. In a perfect world, that would be so. However, there is a very real evil in this world, and that evil cannot be reasoned with or entreated. It operates from a place of malice and seeks only to control by force and inflict suffering and pain on others. That kind of evil can only be vanquished because it will not repent."

Sylvie was amazed at Loïc's self-assured determination. She was convinced he would give his life and every bit of his strength in the fight to protect the Verdélia and what he thought right. Sylvie aspired to anchor herself to her values similarly—though she still wondered if Loïc's view was entirely correct. She sat and contemplated Loïc's words.

After another several minutes, Loïc spoke again.

"Give it time, and know I'm here if you need to talk about it," he offered. "Now, I'm going to insist that you take the rest of the morning to get outside and get as much sunlight as possible to recharge yourself. I've arranged with Sir Reynard to have you take the morning off. You'll meet with him in the gardens after lunch."

Sir Reynard. What was he going to think about the state of her studies? Sylvie wished she could go back to bed and wake up to realize this had all been a bad dream.

⁂

The morning had passed uneventfully for Sylvie as she rested in the sunlit gardens behind the palace on the edge of a large pond. The freshly fallen snow amplified the silence, which was a welcome escape from the madness of recent days. Lunch had been brought to her outside, and everything cleared away as soon as she was finished. A few minutes later, she saw Sir Reynard approaching her from afar.

"Good afternoon, Miss Sylvie," he said in his gravelly voice as he reached where she was sitting on a finely crafted stone bench.

"Hello, Sir Reynard," Sylvie replied politely.

"I hear you've been involved in quite a series of events lately," Sir Reynard continued.

"That would be an understatement," Sylvie sighed.

"I take it there hasn't been much time to study the material I left behind, then?" Sir Reynard said.

Sylvie winced. "No sir, I'm sorry."

Sir Reynard studied her for a moment, then spoke.

"When all is said and done, I teach with practical application as the end goal. From what Loïc tells me, in my absence, you have taken ambitious action for the benefit of your people, the Verdélia. I would be willing to wager that you learned more than you might have had you only studied the materials I left for you."

Sylvie looked up in surprise. Sir Reynard had an approving smile on his face.

"Now come," he continued. "Loïc asked that I teach you to summon your familiar."

The sun was dipping below the horizon, and still, Sylvie had failed to make her familiar materialize.

"You must calm your mind, young Verdélia," Sir Reynard instructed.

"I'm trying," Sylvie said, taking a deep breath to calm herself. She had been working at this for hours. Sir Reynard had taught her that a Verdélia could summon a familiar, an extension of the self, using éthéra. The familiar carried all of its summoner's knowledge, courage, and spirit and could be called upon for several purposes.

"The familiar is an extension of your physical, mental, or spiritual self. You will feel the connection strongest near the base of your skull," Sir Reynard advised again.

Sylvie focused on the éthéra within her for what felt like the hundredth time. She felt éthéra building within her and directed it slowly towards her neck. She sensed the éthéra begin the merge, strands of it leaving her body. She opened her eyes and saw silver wisps begin to float aimlessly in the air before her. Instinctively, she tightened her jaw as she began to force more and more éthéra into the apparition, willing the familiar into being. She watched as the lazy form began moving more and more quickly. Sylvie felt her body stiffen as she tried to keep a grasp on her enchantment, but it was too late. The éthéra shot off to the right like a thread under tension being suddenly cut in two. Powdery snow went flying through the air.

Sylvie drew a deep breath, trying not to yell in frustration.

"What am I doing wrong?" She asked Sir Reynard.

"You are fighting your own familiar," Sir Reynard replied. "You clench your teeth; you plant yourself like a soldier at the ready. Your familiar is not your enemy but a part of you—a companion and an ally."

"Maybe it's hopeless," Sylvie said with a sigh. "I'm so anxious following what happened last night...I feel like I'm walking on the edge of a blade. How can I summon a familiar now?"

Sir Reynard looked at her through the quickly fading light.

"You are likely to want to be able to summon your familiar most when outside influences are least conducive to it," he warned. "Now is a perfect time for you to learn."

Sylvie breathed deeply again. She cleared her mind and forced her body into a relaxed state. She felt the éthéra inside her well up again, directing it towards the base of her head, as Sir Reynard had instructed her.

Images of her fight with the imps the night before flashed through her mind. She felt the éthéra begin to unravel. Instead of tensing herself, she tried to still her mind: *a companion and an ally.* Sylvie replayed Sir Reynard's words in her mind: *an ally.* The scene from the Imp District continued in her mind, but this time, the primary actor was Loïc, her ally, outnumbered and risking his safety for her sake. Éthéra flowed from her in a smooth, controlled stream.

"Very good!" Sir Reynard exclaimed.

Sylvie opened her eyes.

There, flitting about in the air in front of her, was the animated image of a beautiful miniature mermaid made from what appeared to be a combination of moonlight, smoke, and liquid. It danced about in the air as if swimming through water. The mermaid looked at Sylvie, smiled, and waved.

Sylvie smiled and waved in return as she wiped beads of sweat from her forehead. The air was cold, but her efforts had left her sweating and exhausted.

"Worth the effort, is it not?" Sir Reynard asked Sylvie.

Sylvie just nodded.

"Now, let's complete this lesson. Why don't you have your familiar deliver a message?" Sir Reynard proposed.

Sylvie thought for a moment.

"I'll send Nadine a message letting her know I managed to summon my familiar—although, I think the familiar will carry that message fine without any additional wording from me," Sylvie said with a smile. "Do I give her the instructions verbally?" Sylvie asked.

"As an extension of your mind, a mental note will do just fine," Sir Reynard said.

*Introduce yourself to Nadine as Sylvie's familiar,* Sylvie thought. The little mermaid nodded and took off quickly through the air towards the palace.

"How long will she take?" Sylvie asked Sir Reynard.

"At this distance, not long at all. She'll be substantially faster than you or me," Sir Reynard said. "However, she will take time, and her assistance will be unavailable to you for so long as she is gone. You will need to exercise discernment regarding how you utilize your familiar so as not to find yourself wanting in dire situations."

Sylvie considered Sir Reynard's admonition. "Perhaps sending her to Nadine was a bit frivolous," she said aloud.

"A familiar is not only for use in an emergency," Sir Reynard tempered, "I advise caution, is all. Besides, Nadine will be thrilled to get your message— though you won't know until you see her again."

"Right," Sylvie recalled, "Nadine has no familiar."

Sir Reynard nodded.

"Can I send my familiar to anyone?" Sylvie asked.

"Virtually. As a Firstborn, your stronger éthéra gives you access to essentially anyone with less éthéreal capability. Seasonal Verdélia, imps, and creatures can all be accessed through your familiar, as long as you personally are familiar with the recipient. However, the reverse is not true, as Firstborn can conceal themselves from or reject the receipt of unknown familiars."

"I don't understand," Sylvie said.

"Here is an example: Loïc, for instance, has access to you and you to him because you share éthéreal status. His family are seasonal Verdélia, so although he can freely send his familiar to them, they cannot return the gesture without his acquiescence."

"Why hasn't he found Belthégor then?"

"The previous Firstborns, at the end of their lives, attempted to do what you're suggesting before Belthégor's capture. They were unsuccessful. He was hidden behind a dark shadow. His position was then—and I assume is now still—unclear. Familiars are made up of light and cannot live amidst the darkness."

Sylvie sat thinking for a moment.

"Sir Reynard, has there never been an imp able to manipulate éthéra?" She asked.

Sir Reynard looked at Sylvie intriguingly.

"Not in my lifetime," Sir Reynard said, "and from all my studies, I have never come across any able to do so. The ability is strictly a Verdélian one and is lost when a Verdélian child is born an imp."

"Is that why the imps are turning to dark éthéra?" Sylvie asked.

Sir Reynard's face grew dark. "These are serious matters that should not idly escape your lips, Miss Sylvie." He said. "But I do believe that many imps likely feel that they must resort to forbidden and arcane arts to be considered equal to the Verdélia. The Verdélia bear their part of responsibility in this."

"Why the... enmity?"

"There are many reasons. There is an economic aspect. Because imps cannot harness éthéra in growing their crops, craftsmanship, or any other industry, their abilities for gainful occupation in Verdélian society are limited. Because they are forbidden to marry in Verdélys, they also have no family ties, so a sense of community with Verdélia is lacking. Then there is the treatment of the imps by the Verdélia themselves, many of whom view the imps as a fallen or even tarnished race."

"So it does come down to ability," Sylvie thought out loud. "Wouldn't imps be able to have children after the Verdélian manner if they were capable of harnessing éthéra?"

Sir Reynard looked at Sylvie in astonishment. "Truly, you never cease to catch me off guard, Miss Sylvie." Then added, "I do not know the answer to that question."

"Imps would be, barring perhaps in appearance, every bit Verdélian if they could harness éthéra, wouldn't they?"

Sir Reynard shook his head. "That I cannot say. As I said, however, remember that I am unaware of any instance where what you are hoping for has been realized."

"If it's alright with you," Sylvie said, "I'd like to learn as much as possible on this topic. Could you recommend some resources for me to begin with?"

Sir Reynard smiled, "I most certainly will. I will have Nadine deliver some books to your suite. Consider, however, that your studies may not lead you to an answer you wish to find, and do not neglect your other duties in the search for a miracle cure that may not exist."

"I'll keep that in mind; thank you, Sir Reynard," Sylvie said.

She looked at the stars shining on the pond's glassy surface. Something about the scene was calling to her.

"You've done well today, Sylvie," Sir Reynard said. "We will conclude for the day."

"Thank you Sir Reynard," Sylvie said. "I think I'll stay here just a moment longer and enjoy the garden air. I'll see you tomorrow."

Sir Reynard made his way back towards the palace. Sylvie turned her attention back to the pond, and the night sky reflected on its smooth facade.

As she stared, the stars seemed to sway and dance on the water's surface. She drew nearer as the water seemed to beckon her over. For a moment, Sylvie hesitated as she recalled the incident at the Keystone pool. Tonight, however, the invitation from the water was pure and familiar. She crouched on the bank and dipped her finger in the freezing water. Sylvie thought of her pond in Hull, and a wave of nostalgia and homesickness washed over her.

*I think I'll stay here just a moment longer.* Sylvie heard her voice call out to her, coming from the water's surface. Sylvie's finger lingered in the frigid pond.

Looking back at the palace, Sylvie stood and untied her cloak, draping it over a low-hanging branch nearby. She quickly slipped out of her over-dress and hung it up with her cloak. *Just a moment,* Sylvie heard as she stepped into the water. Her muscles nearly seized as the cold clawed at her skin, but the water seemed to warm inexplicably as it enveloped her, almost pulling her in. Sylvie took a final breath and dropped beneath the water's surface. With her eyes open, she watched in familiar amazement as the water began to share its memories with her.

She watched as Sir Reynard, more accurately, a very recent version of himself, looked on as Sylvie finally summoned her familiar. Sylvie smiled at her success. The water blurred, and the vision faded.

Now Sylvie watched as a new scene came into focus. She was an outsider observing the Festival of Flowers.

"Do you think the rumors are true?" A muffled Verdélian voice asked. "Has Morwenna returned?"

As the scene shifted again, there was another, less noticeable ripple. Sylvie was still seeing the Festival of Flowers.

"It's a disaster. Half of these so-called Firstborn aren't fit to be called by that name, and those that are are woefully underqualified... And I say that having to interact with the best of them." It was a man with greying hair, still young, speaking to Beyern.

The water blurred again, but before it could come back into focus she felt a sudden pull on her waist as she was hoisted from the water.

She coughed and choked as she breached the water's surface unexpectedly. Instinctively, she began to flail to get away from whatever had got hold of her. Whatever had grabbed her wasn't expecting a struggle, and she tumbled to the bank. She spun about and looked up to see Loïc looking down in shock.

"What on earth are you doing?" Sylvie exclaimed.

"What am *I* doing?" Loïc asked incredulously. "Not playing dead in a pond, for one thing!"

Sylvie wanted to argue but held her tongue. Trying to view the scene from Loïc's perspective, she giggled, partially in embarrassment.

"What's so funny?" Loïc asked. "I thought you were dead!"

Sylvie continued to laugh, covering her face with her hands.

"You are truly a mystery, vivillèn," Loïc chuckled, shaking his head. "What were you doing?"

"The water...it was calling me," Sylvie said. "What is vivillèn?"

"The icy water was calling you in the dark of night, and you thought it was time for a swim?" Loïc questioned.

"Well....yes," Sylvie said. "But you didn't answer my question. What is vivillèn?"

Loïc shook his head again in confusion. "Unbelievable," he muttered. "It doesn't translate cleanly; it is a play on the ancient language. Vivillèn essentially means daughter of water. That's what you are."

Sylvie smiled. She liked it.

"What were you doing out here anyway?" Sylvie asked.

"I saw your familiar come through the palace. I wanted to come to congratulate you. Sir Reynard said you had decided to stay in the gardens longer, so I set out to find you," Loïc explained. "Then there you were, laying under the water, eyes open like you were dead. Turns out it was all a ploy to have me make a fool of myself," Loïc gave her a playful shove with his elbow.

"That was not the intention," Sylvie said with a grin, "but a fortunate byproduct nonetheless."

"Yes, I'm sure," Loïc replied. "Come, let's get you inside before you freeze to death. Just throw on your cloak; I'll grab your dress."

Loïc took down her cloak and dress and draped the cloak over her shoulders.

As they entered the palace, Sylvie realized how cold it had been outside. She shivered and noticed her teeth chattering uncontrollably.

Just then, Gaëtan and Margot rounded the corner. Gaëtan sized them up with a look of surprise covering his face. Margot seemed amused.

"What on earth happened?" Gaëtan asked.

"Sylvie opted for a nighttime dip in the garden pond," Loïc stated.

"It's freezing outside," Gaëtan said, dumbfounded.

Sylvie piped up. "The water warms up to me pretty quickly," she said with a smile.

Gaëtan stared on in confusion. Margot suppressed a giggle.

"Actually, it's a good thing we ran into you," Loïc carried on, "Gaëtan, I had a few things I wanted to go over with you before the Prophets' Day ceremony."

Gaëtan raised an eyebrow curiously and followed Loïc towards the study.

"There are easier ways of getting the boys' attention," Margot said with a snicker.

Sylvie felt herself blush. "I wasn't trying to get anyone's attention, thank you very much," she shot back playfully.

"All the same..." Margot replied, her voice drifting off.

"You'd better get yourself dry before you flood the palace," Margot said, glancing at the puddle gathering at Sylvie's feet.

# XXV

## *Zaria's Handmaiden*

I t was the next day, and Sylvie was walking down the sunlit hall to the library. Sir Reynard had had several volumes of books delivered to Sylvie's suite, all concerning the imps. Books covering everything from the particularities of imp culture to imp anatomy and other topics littered Sylvie's desk, bed, and floor. She had been poring over the material for the better part of the morning, searching for anything that might give her a clue as to whether the idea of imp magic had ever been explored or considered. In her reading, she found a reference to a grimoire that had not been included in the texts sent to her room, so she went to the library to retrieve it.

As she reached the library's double doors, she noticed Margot sitting in a little alcove off to the right, bordered on either side by wall-length windows. Margot held her hands draped on her lap over an ancient-looking book and was deep in thought, her gaze fixed on the wall opposite her. She didn't seem to notice Sylvie's approach.

Sylvie followed Margot's gaze and looked at a large painting in an ornate frame. The painting depicted a beautiful woman seated on a throne, raven hair flowing in a loose braid over her shoulder. Beside the throne, another woman was seated, attending to the other woman's dress. Two creatures—a dragon and a bird—were flying in the air above the throne. From their white, wispy portrayal, Sylvie recognized the creatures as familiars.

Sylvie looked back at Margot, whose eyes were still locked on the painting.

"Hello Margot," Sylvie said with a smile.

Margot looked like she was coming out of a trance.

"Huh?" She said softly. "Oh. Hello Sylvie."

Sylvie looked a bit more closely at the book on Margot's lap.

"That book wouldn't happen to be—" Sylvie started.

"The last remaining book in the library that has anything to do with imps?" Margot challenged.

"Uh..." Sylvie replied, taken aback.

"I thought you might come looking for this at some point," Margot said. "Here, have a seat."

Margot shifted on the bench, leaving a spot for Sylvie on the velvet upholstery.

Sylvie strolled over to Margot and sat down. For a moment, neither Margot nor Sylvie said anything.

Finally, Margot spoke.

"Do you want to tell me why you've taken it upon yourself to become the palace's foremost expert on all things imp?" Margot asked.

"I..." Sylvie didn't know how to answer the question. "I have questions about the imps and their relationship with the Verdélia. I'm trying to get some more information."

"A wonderful non-answer. You should be a lawyer." Margot chided.

Sylvie sighed. She supposed there was no real reason to keep Margot in the dark.

"Ok," Sylvie said, "I'm curious about the possibility of imps receiving or recovering the ability to manipulate éthéra. That's what all my research is about."

Margot's eyes reflected a mixture of several emotions. Sylvie thought she could see curiosity and even excitement but also a deep sadness in Margot's gaze.

"It's an interesting idea, but I'd wager yours is a fool's errand," Margot said. "Don't you think if such a thing were possible, we'd know about it?"

"Perhaps," Sylvie admitted, "but I'm going to try to find out for myself one way or another."

Margot studied Sylvie for a moment.

"While you're here, then, take a look at this painting," Margot said as she turned to face the painting of the two women opposite Sylvie and Margot.

Sylvie looked obediently. It was a beautiful painting, but if Margot had a purpose other than artistic appreciation, Sylvie wasn't picking up on it.

After several seconds of silence, Margot turned back to Sylvie.

"Notice anything in the painting?" She asked.

Sylvie looked, trying to decipher Margot's meaning. She saw the woman on the throne, whom she recognized as Zaria, the dragon Firstborn, who had lived many thousands of years ago. She looked at the two familiars floating about the throne playfully. Finally, she looked down at the portrait of the woman seated by the throne, identified in the painting's title only as the "Beloved Handmaiden." Her hair was dark and littered with flowers. Sylvie began to shrug. She was at a loss.

Just then, Sylvie caught a glimmer of color as a sunbeam drifted through the window beside them and reflected off the painting. *Could it be?* Sylvie thought. The lady-in-waiting's eyes were an unmistakable yellow. After recognizing this detail, Sylvie was shocked she hadn't noticed it earlier.

"Her eyes..." Sylvie said softly.

Margot smiled. "Her eyes indeed."

"But Zaria lived before the first record of imps came into being," Sylvie protested.

"Correct. Sir Reynard will be very pleased with your historical mastery," Margot said, grinning sarcastically.

Sylvie waved away the comment with a smile.

"But if that's the case, how...I mean, that woman is clearly an imp." Sylvie insisted.

"That would certainly seem to be the case, which isn't even the strangest thing about the painting." Margot agreed.

Sylvie looked again. Of course. The familiar.

"She had a familiar," Sylvie said, her eyes widening in recognition.

Margot sat back, folding her arms.

"That is certainly how it appears," she said, disappointment underlying her tone.

Sylvie turned to Margot.

"Doesn't this prove that imps have been able to manipulate éthéra in the past? Summoning a familiar is éthéra manipulation," Sylvie stated.

"That is not one of the accepted interpretations of this particular piece of art, no," Margot said.

"Well, why else would the painter have depicted two women and two familiars together in a single painting?" Sylvie asked, genuinely curious to hear the answer.

"Depending on who you ask, you might get a few different answers," Margot replied, sitting back in her seat. "Some say the bird is just an artistic liberty the painter took—that there was no second familiar in reality. Others claim the familiar belongs to another individual—a Verdélia—not shown in the painting. Most think that, because we have no record of imps during Zaria's time, the yellow in the eyes of the handmaiden is either a mistake or an artistic rendition."

Sylvie frowned. None of those answers satisfied her, nor did they seem particularly plausible.

"The fact that the handmaiden was an imp and that the bird is indeed her familiar seems to make the story much simpler and more believable," Sylvie said.

"I suppose we'll never know, will we?" Margot asked in resignation.

Sylvie thought for a moment.

"We might," she said, turning to Margot, an idea forming in her mind.

Margot could see a plan written on Sylvie's face.

"Oh dear. Whatever it is you have planned, leave me out of it," she pleaded.

"Help me find an answer to my question!" Sylvie asked Margot excitedly.

"What if we found a way to allow you to summon a familiar, just like Zaria's handmaid?" Sylvie proposed, pointing at the painting.

Margot stiffened up.

"No," she replied sharply, "absolutely not."

Sylvie was surprised by Margot's sudden change in demeanor.

"But..." Sylvie said, leaning back in surprise, "why not? What if the painter was right? What if an imp can harness éthéra?"

"And what if not?" Margot shot back. "Then how do I look?"

Sylvie was confused.

"Weak, that's how," Margot continued. "I look like the pathetic imp Firstborn who's desperately resorting to hopeless fantasies in an attempt to live up to the expectations placed on me."

Margot shook her head, "That won't be me. I won't do it."

Sylvie sat quietly, taking in Margot's objection and the unenviable position Margot found herself in as the first imp Firstborn. Sylvie felt a yearning to help Margot.

"Or perhaps," Sylvie suggested, "you appear strong enough to pursue knowledge others have long since abandoned. Think about the revolutionary good this could do for relations between Verdélia and imps!"

Margot thought for several moments. She took a deep breath.

"If you were to be right on this, it would indeed be revolutionary," Margot admitted. "But I cannot participate, not actively."

Sylvie's shoulders drooped in disappointment.

"Ask your servant girl," Margot suggested. "No one will think twice if you two are holed up somewhere in the palace together."

Sylvie had to admit Margot had a point.

"And Sylvie?" Margot asked.

"Yes?" Sylvie replied.

"Keep me informed in the event you do discover anything, will you?" Margot asked. Her face was again a storm of emotions, but hope swelled to the forefront.

Sylvie nodded, "I will, I promise."

The two friends sat staring at each other for a second, the light dancing on their faces.

"I suppose you'll want this, then?" Margot said, lifting the hefty, dusty tome on her lap.

With Margot's arms out of the way, Sylvie recognized precisely the book she had come looking for.

"Yes, please," Sylvie said with a smile.

Margot carefully handed the book to Sylvie.

"I've read every book you've taken claim on today. Hopefully, you find something that I missed. Good luck," Margot whispered as Sylvie stood to head back to her suite.

# XXVI

## *Futures Foretold*

Sylvie stood silently in the palace entryway with Gaëtan, Loïc, and Margot. She was wearing a ceremonial dress adorned with an elegant copper belt and intricately embroidered with glistening blue thread. She wore a matching cloak, also adorned with elaborate Verdélian art in threads of copper and blue. The cloak was fastened at her neck with an enormous brooch fashioned into the shape of a flower. On her head was Morwenna's crown.

Gaëtan, Loïc, and Margot were similarly attired. The men wore ceremonial uniforms whose beautiful metal buttons reflected the torchlight, complete with formal boots, gloves, and heavy cloaks. The swords were so lovely that they seemed more like art pieces than weapons hung at their waists. Margot wore a dress similar to Sylvie's but in her customary green hues with silver embellishments. All wore the crowns that made clear their royal status.

It was Prophets' Day. This night, the Firstborn would honor tradition and make their way to the cathedral in the Winter District, where four Winter Verdélia, selected for their gifts of clairvoyance, would deliver prophetic instruction to each Firstborn. The event was highly revered among the Verdélia and was treated with the utmost respect. Gaëtan had explained that it was customary for the Verdélia to line the road between the Palace and the cathedral to watch the Firstborn procession pass and wish that year's prophecy to carry omens of good fortune and grace for the Firstborn and the Verdélia.

Sylvie shuffled her feet beneath the train of her dress. This would be an important public event for her, and she was anxious about what impression she might make on the Verdélia. She closed her eyes and took a deep breath.

The palace doors opened, and Alfric walked in amidst a gust of snow-laden wind.

"We're ready for you, your majesties," he said with a bow. Alfric, too, was dressed for the occasion, his ceremonial armor glistening in the firelight. He approached Sylvie and the other Firstborn.

"Sir, if I may," he said, primarily addressing Loïc, "it's not too late to reroute you tonight. We can escort the prophets to the palace and hold the ceremony in the chapel."

Loïc lifted his hand as if to stop Alfric.

"Thank you, Alfric, but no," he said, "the people need to see us honoring the traditions of our ancestors, especially those carrying such spiritual and cultural significance as Prophets' Day."

"Loïc's right," Gaëtan confirmed, "although we appreciate your concern."

Alfric nodded, "Very well."

He turned to face the palace door as he prepared to lead the Firstborn towards the city.

Sylvie and the other Firstborn walked towards the palace gate. They walked four abreast, following behind Alfric. The night was dark, and the heavy snowfall dampened the light of the moon. Sylvie's boots sank without a sound into the powdery snow that buried the cobblestone street.

At the palace gate, a contingent of fifty soldiers stood at attention, arrayed in their formal uniforms and armor. Four soldiers stood slightly apart from their comrades, each holding a lantern. As the Firstborn drew near, each soldier extended his lantern. Sylvie took hers, as did the other Firstborn. At Alfric's command, twenty soldiers broke away from the group and headed for the city.

"These men will lead the way," Alfric explained. "We will follow, with a close guard of ten soldiers and myself. Twenty more will follow close behind. As a precaution, I have posted squads at various intervals along our route and another two hundred men around the cathedral."

"We are fortunate to have you, Alfric. Thank you," Loïc said with a nod.

Alfric's instructions sobered Sylvie to the precarious situation in Verdélys. She gained a renewed appreciation for Loïc's insistence that the Firstborn show their determination to continue Verdélian tradition in the face of this current conflict.

With that, Alfric led them out of the palace gates and onto the main road to the Winter District. Already, Sylvie could make out the dancing lights of lanterns held by the Verdélia, who had come out to brave the falling snow to honor the procession.

The Firstborn walked gracefully through the snow—four regal pilgrims in the storm guided by the light of their lanterns. As they walked, Sylvie noticed more and more Verdélia lining the streets and others looking on from candlelit windows overlooking the road. With each step through the deepening snow, Sylvie could hear the salutations of the Verdélia and the audible prayers issued on their behalf.

"Alondra, royal ones," said an old woman as she leaned on a wooden cane.

"Peace and plenty on you and Verdélys," said a man with two small children huddled about his legs.

Sylvie saw a look of hope and a look of pleading for good things to come on the faces of all the Verdélia who had come to see the Firstborn make their way to where they would receive their omens. With each hopeful face, Sylvie felt the weight of the expectations placed on her grow. Tonight, however, she also felt a growing strength and determination to live up to that hope and help these Verdélia—her people.

The procession continued solemnly through the streets of Verdélys between the lights of thousands of flickering candles and lanterns. After a long walk, Sylvie looked on in amazement as they approached the cathedral hosting their sacred ceremony.

The building was built out of the same stone common throughout the Winter District, a beautiful white stone reflecting the yellow glow of the many flames that lit the night. Scenes carved in stone on the face of the structure seemed to come to life as the firelight danced across them. Massive vaulting buttresses were seen on all sides, flying up towards a pair of imposing bell towers, the tops lost in the falling snow and dark night sky. The Firstborn followed Alfric up the broad stone steps towards the enormous metal doors of the cathedral.

Upon entering the cathedral, Sylvie was engulfed in the ethereal sound of voices in song. A choir of Verdélia stood on the very far side of the cathedral, all attired in pristine white hooded robes. The music felt like a water current, carrying Sylvie away to a place full of magic and wonder. She stopped with the other Firstborn behind Alfric as they reached another short, broad staircase leading up toward an altar engraved with a depiction of the firmament. Behind the altar stood four Winter Verdélia, each wearing a long white hooded robe, similar to those worn by the choir, but embellished at the hems and overlaid with a blue outer robe.

The choir reached its climax as the Firstborn approached and suddenly went quiet.

"Alondra, Firstborn," the four prophets said in unison.

"Alondra, oracles," the Firstborn replied together.

One of the prophets stepped forward.

"On this hallowed day, we welcome you, rightful rulers of the Verdélia, to this night on which the Maker will endow you with a gift of foreknowledge, with the intent that it be used to bless those who look to you for guidance."

"May it be so," Sylvie responded with Gaëtan, Loïc, and Margot.

"Master Gaëtan, please approach," one prophet said.

Gaëtan stepped forward, up the stairs, and approached the altar opposite the prophet, a tall, slender woman with straight silver hair that spilled out of her hood. Sylvie noticed the cathedral had filled behind her with Verdélia reverently awaiting the seer's proclamation.

Gaëtan knelt at the altar before the prophet. She stretched out her hands before her and closed her eyes. For a moment, all was still. Then, the prophet opened her eyes, which now glowed with the light of the evening stars.

> *But one winter you will wait*
> *For seed to plant into your fate*
> *Protection over two unnamed*
> *Until the beast shall then be tamed*
>
> *The golden leaves that fall by force*
> *Will stir up fury in due course*
> *Man and merfolk enter in*
> *One as beggar, one as kin*

The prophet's eyes fluttered as they regained their usual appearance. She who had been so tall and straight suddenly seemed aged, as if having overcome an arduous task. She retreated among the other three prophets. Gaëtan stood and reclaimed his place with the Firstborn at the base of the stairs.

"Miss Margot, please approach," said the second prophet, a younger woman with auburn hair and a soft, pale face.

Margot stepped forward obediently, kneeling at the altar like Gaëtan before her. The fair-skinned prophet stretched out her hands like her predecessor and closed her eyes. Once again, the prophet's eyes took on a celestial glow upon opening.

> *Nature's soul within you lives*
> *A lifelong friend new senses gives*
> *By seeming friends you'll captured be*
> *Until from you flows prophecy*
>
> *Gift of gifts you'll both receive*
> *And give to him who soon shall leave*
> *Hope don't forsake, but trust instead*
> *For life that's new will raise the dead*

The prophet heaved a sigh and trembled visibly as she drew back. Margot descended the stairs back to her place.

The third prophet stepped forward, a bald man with sharp features.

"Master Loïc, please approach," he said in a rasping whisper.

Loïc took his turn at the altar to receive his prophecy. The prophet put out his hands and closed his eyes. With a beam of light, they reopened, and the prophet spoke:

*Thrown from throne to face your fate*
*True friends in peril for you await*
*With flame to guide, you'll travel far*
*Through beauties now by darkness marred*
*A healing touch to leave no scar*

*A father's promise you'll receive*
*If promised without want to leave*
*Back home you'll go, but as a foe*
*And on your path a kinly woe*

Beads of sweat trickled down the prophet's face as he stepped away from the altar. Loïc nodded and left the altar. It was Sylvie's turn now. She swallowed nervously.

The fourth prophet stepped forward. He was an ancient man, his face furrowed with deep wrinkles. His steel-colored hair flowed from under his hood to his shoulders, and a well-kept beard adorned his face.

"Miss Sylvie, please approach," he said softly.

Sylvie walked forward and took the steps up to the altar. The few steps up felt never-ending as Sylvie watched the altar approach. She knelt and placed her hands on the altar as she had watched the Firstborn do before her.

The prophet stood before her and stretched out his hands, almost touching the sides of her forehead. He closed his eyes and opened them again, a pale glow shining on Sylvie.

*A river dammed through you released*
*A true love gone to seek the beast*
*Your road to former home will lead*
*Where you will serve in time of need*

*Shut up in darkness with a queen*
*A trial by fire is foreseen*
*But fire is friend, not foe to you*
*By grace of him who to you flew*

Sylvie began to rise when she noticed the light from the prophet's eyes intensifying. She heard a gasp from the crowd of onlookers.

*As powers of darkness greater grow*
*In strangers' hearts you'll friendship sow*
*A servant gives the ancient oath*
*To lead true friends through ritual growth*

*As rightful ruler your crown you'll bear*
*Through battle's field and war cry's scare*
*To free from malice those since lost*
*But valiant quests bear heavy costs*

The old prophet closed his eyes and collapsed.

Sylvie gasped as she stood to check on the man. The other three prophets rushed forward to their fallen friend.

Loïc and Gaëtan ran up the stairs to assist the fallen man.

"Alfric!" Loïc called, "Get two of your men and have them get this man to a healer right away!"

Alfric gestured to the two nearest soldiers, who dutifully ascended the steps, lifted the old prophet's limp body, and quickly carried him away from the altar and out the back of the cathedral.

"Is he going to be alright?" Sylvie asked. "What happened?"

"Acting as the conduit for these prophecies is a demanding task," Loïc explained. "It takes a significant toll, even on Verdélia who are experienced in éthéra manipulation."

Sylvie felt responsible.

"Will he recover?" Sylvie asked.

Loïc thought for a moment before responding.

"I don't know," he said finally.

As the shock of the prophet's fall wore off, Sylvie and the other Firstborn turned to regain their position at the base of the stairs. Looking back at them, they saw the faces of the numerous Verdélia who had come to witness the prophecies, thousands strong standing, crowded together, candles and lanterns in hand. Their faces all bore a similar look of concern.

The Firstborn lined up, side by side, with lanterns in hand, facing the cathedral's great doors as they prepared to return to the palace. They looked on at the faces of their subjects, which expressively conveyed their disappointment and worry. The hoped-for prophecies of peace and plenty had not come.

Sylvie marched with the other Firstborn back to the palace in silence, the words of their prophecies playing over in her mind. Combined with the dark of night, the swirling snow obscured all details, and Sylvie could barely make out Alfric, who was only a few yards ahead of them. A fitting setting, Sylvie thought, to reflect the mystery of the night's events. Lost in her thoughts, Sylvie continued through the wintery night.

# XXVII

*Rune Casting*

"I don't understand what you want me to do," Nadine said quietly.

"I want you to try to cast the runes," Sylvie explained again.

Sylvie and Nadine were seated around a small table in Sylvie's suite, a soft leather bag full of runes open in front of them.

*You said that already*, thought Nadine internally.

"I don't understand," Nadine said out loud. "I can't cast runes."

Sylvie hadn't explained the details of her experiment to Nadine; just that she wanted Nadine's help with some unexplored trials in éthéra harnessing.

"You can't—or rather, you haven't—cast runes yet. But have you ever tried?" Sylvie asked.

*What's the point? Everyone knows an imp can't manipulate éthéra*, Nadine thought.

"I suppose not," Nadine said.

"Well, that's what I'd like your help with today: having you attempt to cast runes," Sylvie replied.

Sylvie had picked rune-casting because it was a relatively straightforward task as far as éthéra manipulation was concerned and because it was an ability inherent in the Summer Verdélia, and Nadine, had she not been born an imp, would have otherwise been born a Summer Verdélia.

"But rune casting requires éthéra manipulation. I'm an imp. I can't do it," Nadine protested soberly and directly. She wasn't lamenting her lot in life; she was just stating a fact.

"I...," Sylvie started, "I know it doesn't make much sense. But I'm doing some research, and I need your help with this."

Nadine shrugged. "Very well," she said, "what do I do?"

"Wonderful, thank you, Nadine," Sylvie said with a smile. "Alright, runes. You probably know that a runic cast is typically used to reveal insight into the future. That's what we're going to focus on today. We'll start simple, with a single-day read."

Sylvie reached into the leather pouch and took hold of a rune, a small white token made of stone. With a single motion, she released éthéra into the stone and cast it onto the table. The white rune lay on the wooden table, a deep green symbol glowing faintly on its face.

"Gnattire," Sylvie said, "a burrowing plant, and it symbolizes grounding or laying a foundation. So today, I'm going to be doing something foundational."

"But won't it be different if you cast it again?" Nadine asked.

"Not until tomorrow," Sylvie answered. "Watch this."

Sylvie put the rune back into the pouch, shook the bag, and cast a rune again. The gnattire rune fell face-up on the table. To make her point, Sylvie repeated the exercise again. The same thing happened.

"If you cast it correctly, it'll be the same every time," Sylvie instructed. "Now you try."

Nadine obediently pulled the bag to her side of the table.

"I just reach in and pull any rune?" Nadine asked Sylvie.

"Grab the first one you touch and toss it onto the table," Sylvie confirmed.

Nadine put her hand in the pouch, grabbed a stone, and threw it on the table before her.

"Alimout," Sylvie said, looking at the green rune on the table. "Another earth rune. There are ten of each element. This one represents stability."

"I suppose you'll want me to try again to see if I cast the same one?" Nadine asked.

"That's right," Sylvie replied.

*Here goes nothing*, Nadine thought as she put the rune back in the bag and shook the pouch quickly. She reached in, grabbed a rune, and tossed it on the table.

A blue water rune lay on the table before them. Sylvie recognized the rangdèf, symbolizing unity.

*No surprises there*, thought Nadine.

"It's alright," Sylvie said, trying to mask her disappointment. "It was always going to be a bit of a long shot on the first try. Let's try again."

Nadine sighed softly. "Miss, the problem is that they're just stones to me. I'm just grabbing one of many out of the bag. If I'm supposed to feel a connection to any given rune, I wouldn't even know what that would feel like."

Sylvie thought for a moment. How could she explain it to Nadine? She had been born with it—she didn't know what it felt like to be unable to harness the éthéra that permeated her world.

"I suppose the only way I can describe it is like a chill down the neck," Sylvie told Nadine, "although, to be honest, I have no idea if it's the same for other Verdélia. From there, the éthéra just flows in my direction—a bit like water through a channel."

"I'll have to take your word for it," Nadine said with a smile.

"Let's just try again," Sylvie said.

Try they did, for several hours. At first, Nadine tried casting on her own, with Sylvie coaching and instructing her on how to connect to the éthéra and guide it along an intended path. Sylvie had no idea if her explanations made any sense, but Nadine was a good sport about it and listened politely to Sylvie's explanations.

After several more attempts without any indication of success, Sylvie had proposed something new.

"Perhaps you can channel éthéra from me," Sylvie suggested. "Take my hand."

*This is hopeless,* Nadine's mind murmured as she took Sylvie's hand. Sylvie guided éthéra along her arm and down to her hand, trying to will it through Nadine's skin. To Sylvie, it felt like she was trying to pump water through a stone. Nadine's hand was an impenetrable barrier. Maybe something would open up when Nadine tried to cast.

"Ok, try it now," Sylvie requested.

Nadine dutifully put her free hand in the rune pouch and cast a rune. A fire rune this time. She quickly put the rune back in the bag, shook the bag briefly, and cast another rune. Another different fire rune sat on the table.

"Try it again," Sylvie asked.

Nadine did as Sylvie requested. Two different casts and two different runes landed on the table.

Outside, the sun began to touch the horizon, and iridescent beams of honey-colored light flooded Sylvie's suite.

Sylvie sat back in her chair.

"I think you've helped me plenty for today, Nadine. Thank you." Sylvie said.

Nadine nodded. "My pleasure, Miss," she said.

"If it's alright with you, I would like to continue this with your help," Sylvie added.

"As you wish," Nadine replied.

Sylvie felt grateful for Nadine's willingness but also couldn't help but think that Nadine saw it as her obligation to entertain Sylvie's seemingly outlandish whim.

"Perfect. I'll call for you tomorrow, and we'll try again." Sylvie said. "The rest of the evening is yours."

Nadine nodded again, but before leaving, she spoke. "I need to come clean to you about something."

"What is it?" Sylvie asked, worried.

"The other night when you sent for me with your familiar, I came to find you to congratulate you. You didn't see me because I came out at the servant's garden entrance. It's behind the stairs, kind of hidden. Anyway...I came out of the door, and Master Loïc was there with you. I didn't want to interfere."

"Oh, you saw all that?" Sylvie laughed.

"Yes," Nadine seemed to look relieved, "Anyway, I just wanted to let you know that your relationship with Loïc is...well, I'll keep it a secret until you say otherwise."

"Relationship? Secret?" Sylvie asked, "We're friends. What's secret about that?"

"But..." Nadine began, visibly confused and embarrassed, "he called you vivillèn." She said so matter-of-factly as if Sylvie should know what that meant.

"Yes, daughter of water..." Sylvie said.

Nadine shook her head, but a humored expression crossed her face. "That is certainly one very technical way of translating that phrase."

"What do you mean?" Sylvie asked.

"If you were to find the word in a dictionary, you might read that as the translation. The word, as with many other words in the ancient tongue, has taken on a much deeper meaning from which it can't really be separated. Water among the Verdélia is an emotional element. So vivillèn means 'daughter of water,' but it's commonly used to describe someone empathetic and tender-hearted."

"Okay," Sylvie shrugged.

"It's traditionally a term of endearment, Miss Sylvie," Sylvie's eyes widened with realization.

"Oh!" She placed her hands on the side of her neck, leaning back in her chair.

"To be fair," Nadine said quickly, trying to play things down, "it is quite outdated. You would rarely hear the term nowadays. But Master Loïc has always been a traditionalist, so I just assumed if he was calling you that..." her thought trailed off.

"I don't think he meant it like that," Sylvie said, and just like that, Sylvie began giggling, which spurred a smile in Nadine. She could feel that feeling in her heart again: her mother's feeling.

"I'm so sorry," Nadine said, shaking her head with a massive smile. "This is none of my business. I should never have—after all, I'm your servant."

"You're my friend," Sylvie insisted, taking Nadine by the hand.

Nadine bowed reverently.

"I'm honored," she said, "Your secret is safe with me."

"What secret?"

"That you like him." Nadine stood and slipped quietly out of Sylvie's suite.

Sylvie watched Nadine go, then turned her gaze back to the table, where a single rune was bathed in the glow of the setting sunlight.

# XXVIII

## *Countermeasures*

S ylvie looked about her anxiously, realization dawning on her. She was back in the imp district, on the fateful street that led away from the inn. Snow drifted down from a sky laden with ominous clouds. The shadows were deep and foreboding. Movement in her peripheral made her heart skip a beat as she whirled her head to the right. It was just a snow flurry.

Sylvie picked up her pace as she returned to the main road. Every detail seemed drawn out of her memory. She drew towards what she knew was coming next. Dread welled inside her. She braced herself and wanted to yell out.

Three dark, cloaked figures stepped out in front of her. She turned to run, but three other figures blocked her retreat. Sylvie's eyes darted around, seeking an escape. One figure began making its way towards her. It drew aside its cloak to reveal the hilt of a heavy sword. With a metallic ringing, he pulled a sword from its sheath, its blade reflecting the pale moonlight as an omen of death.

Sylvie scanned her side, searching for Loïc. She saw nothing. Turning at the perfect moment, she saw her attacker lifting his blade to deliver a lethal strike. She screamed.

Sylvie's eyes shot open, her breathing heavy and strained, her entire body tense. She looked around in her confusion. Drenched in a cold sweat, she realized it had been another dream. Another terrible dream. Her thin nightgown clung to her skin, and her covers were strewn about her bed as a result of her unconscious struggle. Sylvie tried to get her breathing under control.

She had had the same dream three times since her trip to the Imp District with Loïc. The scene replayed in her mind, but each time, Loïc was absent. Each time, her helplessness consumed her.

Sylvie shook the last tendrils of her nightmare from her mind as she sat up in bed. She looked out the window. The palace courtyard was still dark, the deep navy of the night sky turning a lighter shade of royal near the horizon. She took a deep breath and lay back on her pillow, pulling the covers over her face.

She lay there for what seemed like an hour, contemplating the nightmare and the events of that night in the Imp District. Sleep evaded her. She had had this lengthy internal debate for weeks now. She resolved not to be defenseless should another such scenario present itself.

Sylvie embraced the thought, got out of bed, and wrapped her robe around her nightgown to keep warm. Without bothering to brush her hair, she made her way out of her suite. Even the palace staff were still asleep at this hour.

Sylvie closed her eyes, focusing her éthéra. A moment later, a familiar, ethereal mermaid was floating in the air before her.

"Take me to Loïc," Sylvie whispered.

The mermaid turned and swam through the air down the dark hallway. Sylvie followed, her bare feet brushing the cold stone floor. Shortly, she faced the double doors of Loïc's suite. Her familiar dissipated into the air, its task complete. Sylvie knocked on the door, rushing past the possibility of second-guessing herself. The silence of the palace engulfed her as she waited for a response.

"What is it?" She heard Loïc call out groggily.

"It's—" Sylvie said. Before she could finish, Loïc opened the door. His tousled hair hung in strands around his face, and he was tying a robe over his bare chest. His eyes were sharp despite just waking up. Loïc's surprise was visible.

"It's me," Sylvie finished.

"I can see that," Loïc replied, a grin forming on the edge of his lips. He relaxed, leaning back from the door.

"I had a nightmare—" Sylvie started. The words didn't have the chance to leave her mouth before she screwed her eyes shut, realizing how childish she sounded. Loïc's grin grew into a full-fledged smile.

"That's...not exactly what I meant," Sylvie said. "I mean, I did have a nightmare; it's just—" Sylvie wished she could stop talking, but the words kept flowing as she tried to explain that she had a valid reason for waking Loïc well before dawn. Sylvie sighed.

"Will you teach me how to fight?" Sylvie said, deciding to cut right to the chase, hoping to avoid further verbal blunders.

Loïc raised an eyebrow and continued to smile.

"Fighting, huh? Not a very lady-like activity," he teased. "What sort of fighting did you have in mind?"

"The kind that lets me defend myself," Sylvie replied.

Comprehension kindled behind Loïc's eyes.

"I see," he said. He hesitated briefly by the door, deep in thought. Sylvie held her breath.

"As fate would have it," Loïc said, "I'll be at the barracks today for combat training. How about you join me there after breakfast, and we'll hold your first lesson?"

Sylvie nodded and breathed out a long sigh. "I would like that. Thank you, Loïc," she said.

"That settles that, then," Loïc said. "I'll notify Sir Reynard as well."

Sylvie smiled and nodded again in gratitude. There was a moment of silence as Loïc and Sylvie stood there.

"Was there anything else?" Loïc asked.

Sylvie snapped out of her daydream.

"Oh, no, thank you!" she said.

"Very well then," Loïc said. "If it's all the same to you, I wouldn't mind getting a little more sleep tonight. You might try doing the same." Loïc yawned and tilted his head towards Sylvie's suite to emphasize his point.

Sylvie blushed, "Of course," she said, "sorry to wake you. And thank you again."

"You're welcome, Sylvie," Loïc said with a smile as he shut his door.

Sylvie promptly returned to her suite in higher spirits.

※

It was after breakfast, and the sun shone in the clear winter sky. It was still freezing as Sylvie made her way to the barracks located within the palace walls but away from the street that ran from the palace to the gate. She was not wearing a dress for the first time since she had entered Verdélys. Instead, Loïc had sent her a comfortable pair of pants tapered to her shape but loose enough to allow freedom of movement. The pants were paired with a shirt made from an incredibly smooth yet sturdy fabric that was similarly fitted: tight enough to be out of the way without being restrictive. Her shirt was tucked in snugly to her pants, which cinched at her waist through the use of leather ties on either side of her waist. Supple and snug leather boots covered her feet, and at Loïc's instruction, she had firmly secured her long blonde hair into a bun on top of her head.

Sylvie heard the shouts of soldiers and the sounds of combat before she could even see the training compound. Metal clashed on metal, wood on wood, and heavy footfalls pounded on the stone and dirt as strong voices carried on the brisk air. The barracks were on a large property and comprised several rows of long, narrow buildings where the soldiers were quartered. A large building was set in the center of the several houses. On the cobblestones before her, several sets of soldiers were engaged in spirited duels, swords in hand. An archery range was off to the right, where soldiers were deftly firing arrows at targets that magically floated and moved through the air. Farthest back, Sylvie could make out a group of men running drills in a large open field.

As she approached, a soldier in full uniform, spear in hand, bowed respectfully.

"Miss Sylvie," he said, "Master Loïc is expecting you in the training hall." The soldier pointed to the large building in the center of the compound.

"Thank you," Sylvie said timidly. She felt incredibly out of place. She walked past the fighting soldiers and on to the training hall. She walked through a set of heavy wooden doors and immediately was hit with the smell of sweat and blood, which was strong but not unpleasant. In here, soldiers were engaged in unarmed, hand-to-hand combat. Some were sparring, while others wrestled on the ground, struggling to control their opponents. Sylvie scanned the room and, off to her right, recognized Loïc. He was facing off against three opponents, who circled him carefully. Loïc's eyes darted between his three foes; his fists raised as he bounced lightly on his feet. The three soldiers looked at each other as if looking for a cue. Loïc noticed and used the split-second that his opponents' eyes were off of him to direct a ferocious strike with his leg toward one of them.

The blow connected solidly with the side of the man's leg, and he yelled out in pain as his leg gave way. He fell to the floor. The two remaining soldiers rushed towards Loïc, evidently hoping to overwhelm him.

Loïc ducked and launched himself backward, avoiding the attack. He weaved this way and that as the soldiers held up a consistent assault. After a few moments, Loïc found an opening through one of the soldiers' strikes and landed a heavy blow to the man's ribs. The man retreated, a grimace of pain on his face. By now, the third soldier had regained his footing and had rejoined his comrades. However, Sylvie could tell he wasn't putting his full weight on his damaged leg.

The one soldier who hadn't been hit yet pushed in, trying to use Loïc's attack on his ally as a window to land a strike on Loïc. He threw a heavy punch, but Loïc was too quick. Grabbing the soldier's wrist with one hand and upper arm with the other, Loïc threw his attacker over his shoulder, slamming him to the floor with a heavy thud. The man rolled slowly to his side but did not get up.

Loïc turned quickly to face his other two opponents, but it was too late to avoid a heavy kick to his ribs. Sylvie winced, and saw Loïc flinch ever so slightly. In the split-second the kick connected with Loïc's side, Loïc clamped his arm down in an iron grip on his foe's leg. The assailant, his leg trapped, was left bounding around on one foot to stay upright. Loïc steered the soldier into his comrade, who had been moving in against Loïc. Loïc used the soldier as a shield to keep the other opponent at bay for a few moments.

Eventually, Loïc sent a swift kick to the soldier's supporting leg. As he did so, he forcefully shoved the man's other leg away. The soldier went tumbling backward into his partner.

Loïc used the confusion to attack. He had closed the distance between himself and the soldiers in a flash. With a few fluid movements, Loïc had landed vicious strikes on both soldiers' bodies. As one soldier hunched over and backed up in pain, Loïc kicked him to the floor. Loïc advanced on the other, who was still reeling. The soldier held up his hand in a sign of submission.

Loïc dropped his hands and stood straight. He helped the two grounded soldiers to their feet while the third put his hands on his knees, sweat dripping to the floor. Loïc seemed to be checking on his opponents, ensuring they were alright. One soldier tended to his leg, while the other, who had been thrown to the floor forcefully by Loïc, put his hands on his head, breathing deeply.

Loïc looked towards the door and smiled as he recognized Sylvie. He waved her over.

Sylvie approached timidly.

"Sylvie, welcome to the training compound," Loïc said with a smile. His skin glistened with sweat, and his hair was damp.

The other soldiers bowed respectfully.

"Alondra, Miss Sylvie," they said through ragged breaths.

"That was impressive," Sylvie said with a smile to Loïc.

Loïc continued to smile and shrugged. "It was good enough, I suppose. There's always room for improvement," he replied.

One of the soldiers spoke up. "Master Loïc isn't one to boast of his achievements, but you won't find anyone in Verdélys who will best him in single combat," the man said proudly.

"You should know better than to try flattery in the barracks, Armitage," Loïc chided playfully. "Besides, Alfric gives me a good match," he added.

"He beat you once, over two years ago," Armitage replied.

Loïc shrugged again. "We're getting carried away here," he said. "Gentlemen," he continued, addressing the soldiers, "thank you for being my sparring partners this morning. That will be all for me today."

The soldiers bowed and stepped away to the other side of the training hall.

"Ready to begin?" Loïc asked, turning to Sylvie.

"Here?" Sylvie asked, terrified.

"That was the idea," Loïc said, "is that a problem?"

Sylvie looked around her at the soldiers, skillfully honing their combat skills.

"It's just..." she began, "everyone here is a skilled fighter, and I'm...not. I'm going to make a fool of myself."

Loïc nodded.

"I understand," he said, "follow me then." He walked towards the rear of the hall and slipped through a door to the right. Sylvie followed and found herself in a stable that opened onto the giant field she had seen when she first walked into the compound. The stable was empty, and from where she was, Sylvie could see several soldiers on horseback outside, riding in formation.

"This is the best we're going to be able to do privacy-wise," Loïc said as he walked towards one of the stable stalls. "The rest of the compound isn't exactly organized for discretion."

"Thank you," Sylvie said, following Loïc.

Loïc reached over the stall door to open the latch and ushered Sylvie inside. The door clicked shut behind Loïc as he walked into the stall after her.

Looking around the straw-covered stall, Sylvie suddenly felt quite nervous. Loïc seemed to notice.

"You've got nothing to worry about," he assured her. "We'll cover a few basics today to ease you into this."

Sylvie nodded, but the knot in her throat did not dissipate.

"Now, let's get started," Loïc said.

Sylvie walked to the middle of the stall and turned to face Loïc.

"The first thing to learn in combat is your balance. You're already at a disadvantage if you are caught off balance."

Loïc circled Sylvie as he talked.

"Feet shoulder width apart, knees bent, not locked. Stand on the balls of your feet—planting your heels will make you too slow to react and will get you beat every time. Like this."

Loïc demonstrated.

"You want to be comfortable and ready to move at any moment," Loïc said, "but also capable of staying firmly in place if necessary. Now you try."

Sylvie tried to copy Loïc.

"Let's put your stance to the test."

Loïc stepped towards Sylvie and, using both hands, pushed softly but firmly on her shoulders.

Sylvie took several quick steps backward to avoid falling over into the straw crunching beneath her feet.

"Not bad," Loïc said, "now try to stay put." He pushed her a little harder, and she remained in place.

"Keep in mind, I'm not trying to knock you over now. A true enemy will put all of his energy into bringing you down. With that in mind, I will teach you something additional you can do to keep yourself firmly rooted in a conflict. As a Verdélia, you can quite literally anchor your éthéra to that of the earth," Loïc went on, "you can also look at it as putting down invisible yet powerful roots. The idea is very similar to what you're already used to in plants, except instead of helping a plant put down roots and grow, you're sending your éthéra into the earth. Give it a try."

Sylvie focused and began channeling éthéra like she was used to doing in Hull and as she had honed here in Verdélys. Following Loïc's instructions, she sent the éthéra directly from herself deep into the earth. She felt as if she was physically merging with the soil beneath her. It was a strangely comforting experience.

"Let's see how you did," Loïc said.

Loïc pushed Sylvie's shoulders forcefully. Sylvie swayed slightly but did not move.

"Very good; you're a natural," Loïc said with a smile. "In combat, the trick will be maintaining that connection while staying agile enough to outmaneuver your enemy. It will only come with practice."

"Let's talk basic offense. In a fight, you'll want to incapacitate your enemy before he can incapacitate you. That means you need to know when, where, and how to strike. We'll start with the when because it's the easiest: you want to strike first."

Sylvie raised an eyebrow. "I thought you were teaching me how to defend myself. I don't intend to initiate any fights," she told Loïc.

Loïc chuckled and shook his head, "Sylvie, I don't expect you to go out starting fights. However, if you ever find yourself in a situation where a fight is upon you, you want to take the initiative away from your opponent and strike first. Especially where you are not the instigator, doing so will likely catch your assailant off-guard and give you a crucial advantage at the outset of the fight."

"But doesn't that then make me the attacker? I wouldn't feel comfortable doing that," Sylvie protested.

Loïc looked at Sylvie seriously, "Sylvie," he said, "I don't have to ask if you remember those men who stopped us in the street in the Imp District. You, of all people, knew well before any of them drew their swords what their intentions were. Striking first in a situation like that does not make you the villain. It makes you smart. In situations like those, only one side is coming out alive, and perceived moral superiority isn't going to do you any good if you're dead."

Sylvie wondered if she was ready for this, but Loïc was right. She had to come to learn how to defend herself.

"Ok," Sylvie nodded, "I understand."

"Good," Loïc continued, "So, as I was saying, you want to strike first when you can. Specifically, you want to target one or more of several sensitive areas: the eyes, nose, throat, groin, or knees. These areas are the most susceptible to pain, and if damaged, they can seriously hinder your foe's capacity to retaliate. Let's practice."

Loïc looked around and walked over to a large sack stashed in the corner.

"This sack of oats should do the trick," Loïc said, lifting it swiftly with one arm. He tied the top of the sack over the edge of the stall, leaving the rest of the bag hanging down the stall's wooden wall.

"Right." Loïc said, turning to Sylvie, "Here we have our fearsome enemy."

Sylvie suppressed a giggle.

"We're going to practice striking, both with our hands," Loïc punched the sack of oats playfully, "and with our feet." He kicked the bag gently.

Loïc coached Sylvie on the proper techniques for striking an enemy with the hands. Taking her hands, he helped her form a proper fist, carefully showing her what to avoid to prevent damaging her hands and fingers. Sylvie felt Loïc's powerful hands and fingers as he explained, and she understood how he could quickly confront and subdue an enemy. She wasn't convinced that she would be so capable.

Loïc had her practice on the bag hanging against the stall repeatedly. He watched and gave advice frequently. Occasionally, he would walk over to Sylvie, taking her arm and showing her how to articulate her shoulder and elbow to land her strikes more effectively.

"Your power comes from your stance and core," Loïc explained. "This is why a good stance is the foundation you build on. Build strength in your legs and through your core, and as you twist, you send that energy down your arm and into your target."

Loïc demonstrated, and Sylvie began to notice how what originally had appeared to be a movement of the arm and hand was, in fact, a concerted effort of the entire body. Sylvie watched as Loïc's movement began in his legs, flowed through his core, and flew violently out into a heavy punch.

"Now you try," Loïc said.

Sylvie tried a few times, hitting the target as hard as she could, but not quite to Loïc's liking.

"Here," Loïc said, approaching Sylvie from behind. He put his hands on her waist.

"You're starting too square," he taught. "Your shoulders and hips are directly parallel to your target, so you have no room to twist and generate any power. Try this instead."

Loïc twisted Sylvie's hips slightly to the right. He tapped her right leg, inviting her to bring it back slightly. Taking hold of her shoulders, he shifted her stance so she stood at a bit of an angle to the target.

"Keep your enemy in front of you and try again," Loïc said, stepping back.

Picturing Loïc's technique in her mind, Sylvie built strength up from her legs and punched the bag hard.

"Much better!" Loïc said with a smile.

Loïc continued to coach her on her technique, helping her strike once, then again and again, with both hands.

"That's a good start for hand strikes," Loïc said after a while. Sylvie wiped her forehead with the back of her sleeve. Although the stable's air was fresh, her lesson's physical strain had her sweating steadily. Her chest rose and fell quickly with each breath as her body worked to get air to her laboring muscles.

"Let's run the basics of using your legs, and then we'll incorporate everything against a live opponent—me," Loïc said.

"The foundations of a successful leg strike are the same as when using your arms. You build from your legs and use your core for power." Loïc explained. "Like this."

Loïc kicked the bag of oats, now looking seriously misshapen, with a precise, heavy strike. Sylvie thought the bag would surely burst open under the impact, but it did not.

"Now you try," Loïc commanded, stepping out of the way.

Sylvie stepped up to the bag, squared herself to it, and then shifted her stance slightly, as Loïc had taught her. She tensed the muscles in her leg, and then, using her core, she brought her right leg up and around and kicked the target as hard as she could.

"Not bad," Loïc said, his eyebrows raised.

Loïc gave Sylvie a few additional pointers, demonstrating his own technique slowly so that Sylvie could mimic his movements.

"Great," Loïc said after yet another attempt by Sylvie on the disheveled sack of grain hanging on the stall fence. "Let's put it all together."

Sylvie was excited. The apprehension she had initially felt had melted away under Loïc's expert and careful tutelage. She could feel her blood pulsing through her veins, and a steady adrenaline rush pushed her on.

"Right," Loïc said, taking the oats off the wall and placing them back in the corner. "Meet me in the center of the stall."

Sylvie obediently walked to the middle of the space and turned to face Loïc.

"Let's review before we get started," Loïc instructed. "I will take the role of the assailant. What will you do?"

"I will strike first and target sensitive areas of your body to hopefully incapacitate you," Sylvie replied.

"Good," Loïc said, nodding in approval. "Now let's get started."

Sylvie felt a new adrenaline surge as she entered a fighting stance and anchored herself. Loïc approached.

Sylvie opted for a kick to the side of Loïc's knee. She aimed and fired her blow, but Loïc danced out of the way, closed the distance between them in a flash, and tightly enveloped Sylvie in his arms, restricting her movement completely. She felt the incredible strength of his arms around her, and his chest was tense and solid against her own as he held her captive. She felt a wave of new emotions crest within her that clashed sharply with the disappointment of failing her first attempt at deterring Loïc's attack.

"Not bad," Loïc said encouragingly, "but your move was too easy to anticipate. I saw you stare at my leg for several moments before you struck, and you attacked early while I was barely within your striking distance, which made it easy for me to avoid the blow. Let's try again."

Loïc approached Sylvie again. This time, Sylvie waited for Loïc to get just a bit closer before she engaged him, this time trying a kick to his stomach. Just as her leg was about to connect with Loïc, Sylvie felt his iron grip on her ankle. Loïc's other hand grabbed her thigh just above the knee, stopping Sylvie's attack cold. Sylvie stood awkwardly on one leg for a moment before Loïc released his grip on her leg.

"A good effort, honestly," Loïc said. "Someone with less combat experience would likely have not blocked that. Let's continue."

Sylvie appreciated Loïc's encouragement but was still frustrated she hadn't managed to hit him. She had to remind herself that just earlier, Loïc had handily beaten three trained soldiers simultaneously. She knew it was unlikely she would successfully hit Loïc unless he allowed it, but she was still going to try.

At Loïc's instruction, Sylvie tried repeatedly to prevent Loïc's pretend assaults. She varied her strikes, first striking at Loïc's leg, then his stomach, then his other leg. She tried using kicks as well as punches. Each time, Loïc either evaded the attack or blocked it. Several times, he followed through with a mock attack of his own, taking hold of Sylvie forcefully and preventing her from doing anything. Sylvie was all too aware that this was the equivalent of her being defeated and possibly killed in a scenario involving a real enemy.

After several attempts, Loïc nodded in apparent satisfaction.

"Good," he said. "I have one final lesson for today: to escape a situation where an enemy has overpowered you."

Loïc brought his arms in, mimicking a scenario where an invisible foe was restricting his movements.

"An enemy who breaks through your defenses is likely to either kill you immediately or overpower you and restrain you in such a way that will make it difficult for you to continue to fight back," Loïc explained. "We won't bother with the first possibility since...well...there's not much to be done in that event."

"However, if you find yourself restrained by an enemy, you'll need to be ready to use any parts of your body that are not being controlled to try and escape. Elbows and knees are good options, but your head can also do in a pinch. You'll also need to be prepared to use other parts of your body as leverage or create space between you and your attacker to allow you to move. Examples can include using your back and hips if you are being attacked from behind," Loïc demonstrated by rounding his back out, "as well as your chest, knees, and head if being attacked from the front. Shoulders work, too. You might have to get creative, but you want to open up space that will allow you to move and either get free or strike your enemy. Here, I'll demonstrate a few so you can get an idea. Come grab me around my arms from behind."

Sylvie obediently reached around Loïc's broad chest from behind, grabbing onto his forearms. Sylvie could barely get a workable grip on Loïc, and she felt his muscles rippling under his skin as her fingers closed onto his arms. She knew she couldn't hold him for more than a split-second if he tried to escape.

"Remember that I'm trying to create space between you and me, and I'm assuming I don't have the use of my arms because of your crushing grip."

Sylvie could hear Loïc withholding laughter as he pretended to be at Sylvie's mercy.

As Sylvie held on, Loïc suddenly arched his back, pushing his shoulders back into Sylvie. At the same time, Loïc walked his legs forward. Sylvie reached forward awkwardly, trying to keep her grip on Loïc's arms. Once enough space had been created between them, Loïc twisted his body about to face Sylvie. Sylvie's grip broke, and Loïc slipped out of her grasp.

"Easy for you," Sylvie said with a smirk, "you're twice my size and ten times as strong. You don't need any fancy tricks to get away from me."

"It's just to demonstrate," Loïc said with a smile, "you'll be fearsome enough before you know it."

Sylvie scoffed.

Loïc showed Sylvie several other examples, each time having Sylvie grab his arms or otherwise assume a position as if she had bested Loïc and was now trying to escape. Loïc was gentle but firm in his movements.

"In a real combat situation," Loïc explained as he gently tapped Sylvie's stomach, "you would want to strike as hard as you could with your knee." Loïc stood back and faced Sylvie. Sylvie's shirt was now thoroughly drenched and hung tightly to her skin. Her hair, too, was sticking to her face and neck. For his part, Loïc seemed to be barely breaking a sweat, though Sylvie did spy a few beads of perspiration at Loïc's hairline.

"Alright," Loïc said, "let's have you try."

Loïc grabbed Sylvie from behind, wrapping his arms around her and taking hold of her arms, pressing them tightly against her chest as he pulled her entire body into him. Sylvie felt her breathing become restricted under the force of Loïc's grip, and her thoughts spiraled momentarily as she tried to recall the things Loïc had just taught her.

Collecting herself, she stomped down with all her strength on Loïc's right foot. She felt Loïc step back and used the space to lift her foot again and kick back against Loïc's knee. Loïc released his grip on Sylvie, and she whirled about to face him.

"You let me go, didn't you?" Sylvie scolded.

"Well...yes," Loïc admitted, "but you did well. Good use of your legs; you got my knee pretty good." Loïc rubbed his knee as he spoke. Although Sylvie felt guilty at the thought that Loïc might have been hurt, she also felt a secret sense of pride that she might have landed a real blow against him.

"Let's go again," Loïc said, approaching Sylvie another time.

Loïc and Sylvie practiced several more scenarios, each time Loïc gripping Sylvie firmly from different angles and positions, each time Sylvie using the skills Loïc had taught her to try to extricate herself from Loïc's control.

"Excellent," Loïc said after Sylvie escaped Loïc's grip again by using her head as a club against Loïc's chin to break his grasp on her.

"One last time, and then we'll be finished," Loïc said.

This time, Loïc stepped forward and grabbed Sylvie by the wrists, holding her arms back against her chest, elbows folded up. Sylvie tried to use her legs to get at Loïc's legs and ribs, but Loïc kept her at arm's length, and she was unable to reach him. She tried to twist her arms to break Loïc's grip, but his fingers stayed tightly bound to her. Sylvie could tell Loïc was treating this round more seriously than the others. It was to be her final test of the day.

Sylvie pushed and pulled against Loïc's strong arms without any indication of success. She tried again to kick him to get him off balance, but he deftly avoided her blows. Her efforts grew more frantic.

"Good," Loïc coached, keeping a firm grip on her, "remember, we're simulating a real attack. You shouldn't be giving your opponent time to think or rest."

Taking the advice to heart, Sylvie abandoned all restraint and pushed into Loïc to try to close the distance between them. She ran at him, pressing her chest against his arms and driving powerfully with her legs. Loïc's arms bent slightly as he started to take steps backward. After a few steps, Loïc planted himself and began to push back against Sylvie. Sylvie kept pushing with all of her strength.

Just as Sylvie felt she was about to be overpowered by Loïc and be forced backward, she suddenly stopped resisting Loïc. Loïc came barreling forward, and Sylvie side-stepped swiftly. In a single motion, Loïc put a leg forward to catch himself as he kept Sylvie's arms firmly in hand, and Sylvie seized her opportunity, striking with the heel of her foot heavily on the inside of Loïc's knee.

Loïc's knee buckled, and he went crashing sideways. What Sylvie had not accounted for, however, was the possibility that Loïc might still keep his grip on her arms. As he fell, Loïc brought Sylvie down with him. Loïc fell heavily onto his back on the stall's dirt floor, pulling Sylvie down on top of him in a chaotic heap of intertwined limbs. Sylvie felt Loïc's chest rising and falling beneath her in steady but accelerated breaths. Sylvie's heart was pounding, and her breathing was coming in gasps as her chest pushed back against Loïc's. After a few seconds, Loïc released his grip on Sylvie's arms, but his hands stayed trapped between their bodies.

"Well done, miss," Loïc said softly.

Sylvie pushed her hands against his chest, propping her body up to look at Loïc's face. He was smiling proudly.

"You were supposed to let go!" Sylvie explained, blushing as she assessed her situation.

"Yes," Loïc answered as he looked up at Sylvie. "In hindsight, that would have been ideal. I guess instead, we have a great example to show us that things don't always go according to plan."

Sylvie felt herself grow redder still, but she didn't answer. After a few moments, Loïc spoke again.

"If it's not too inconvenient, could I trouble you to let me up?" He asked Sylvie.

"I suppose so, but only because you asked so nicely," Sylvie replied with a grin.

Loïc chuckled as Sylvie tried awkwardly to untangle herself from him and regain her feet. With one smooth motion, Loïc regained his feet.

"I'd say today was a success," Loïc said, brushing dirt from his pants. "You should continue training, and if you're serious about defending yourself, I would encourage you to learn to use a weapon."

Sylvie nodded, "I would like that. Can you teach me that too?"

Loïc nodded, "Of course."

Sylvie gathered her cloak, which she had removed for her lesson, and prepared to go.

"One last thing," Loïc called out to her.

Sylvie turned quickly to face Loïc, excitement bubbling up inside of her. "Yes?" She asked.

Loïc was fidgeting with his sleeve. Sylvie almost missed it, but she saw something new in Loïc.

*Is he ...nervous?* She thought to herself. It couldn't be. Not Loïc.

"Well," Loïc began, his voice not betraying his anxiety if he was nervous, "since you've joined us in Verdélys, you've been somewhat of a sensation, what with the long-lost Morwenna being found and all."

Sylvie listened carefully but wasn't sure where Loïc was headed.

"My family has naturally heard a lot about you from myself and others. They've met Gaëtan and Margot. I'd like them to meet you and for you to meet them, if that's alright with you."

Loïc looked at Sylvie, a particular vulnerability replacing the ever-present steely confidence that was otherwise a constant in his gaze.

For her part, Sylvie felt as if her stomach was floating inside of her, and her pulse quickened.

"I'd love to meet them, Loïc," she replied.

"Wonderful," Loïc said, a look of relief flashing across his face. "I'm going home tonight for dinner. Would you join me?"

Tonight. Sylvie was excited to see this side of Loïc, away from his duties and the palace, but she was also nervous. What if she didn't live up to expectations? In any event, she figured she would have had more than a single afternoon to prepare. Apparently, she was mistaken.

"Yes, of course," Sylvie said with a nervous smile.

Loïc nodded, "Very well, if you could meet me in the foyer approximately an hour before dinner, we can walk together."

Sylvie nodded excitedly. She couldn't stop smiling. She took her cloak, exited the stall, and returned to the palace.

# XXIX

## *Breaking Bread*

The sun was setting, adorning the sky with a myriad of colors. Sylvie had washed and redone her hair and donned a dress for dinner. She went to the palace entrance, where Loïc was waiting for her.

"Good evening, Sylvie," Loïc said with a short bow. "You look lovely."

Sylvie smiled and curtsied politely. "Thank you, Loïc," she replied.

Loïc had cleaned up nicely himself and was dressed in dark pants tucked into brown leather boots. He wore a white shirt under a green jacket and a cloak over it all. As usual with Loïc, a sword hung at his side.

"Are you ready to go?" Loïc asked.

"I am," Sylvie answered, nodding.

Loïc offered Sylvie his arm, and the two Firstborn made their way out of the palace doors.

"Alfric is insisting we take four guards with us," Loïc sighed as they approached the gate. "He wouldn't even take a no from me. It's a shame that it's come to this in Verdélys."

Sylvie nodded in agreement. The beautiful city seemed overshadowed by the threat of unpredictable violence. As expected, at the gate, Sylvie and Loïc were joined by four palace guards in uniform. With their escort in place, Sylvie and Loïc made their way into the city.

As they walked through the Summer District, Sylvie thought she noticed a lack of color among what had not long ago been vibrant scenes. The sky, though multi-colored, was less vivid. Though still adorned with decorations, the homes were no longer as lively. Sylvie couldn't imagine what might cause such a thing and almost dismissed it.

"You're seeing it too, aren't you?" Loïc asked.

Sylvie looked at Loïc in surprise. "Seeing what?" She asked.

"The decay," Loïc replied somberly.

"I thought I was imagining things," Sylvie said, relieved she wasn't going crazy.

Loïc shook his head, "You're not," he said, "though in many ways I wish you were. In my recent travels, I sensed a change in the land, creatures, and peoples around me. I brushed it off then, but when I returned to Verdélys to see the same phenomenon...well, it became clear that something was wrong."

"This is the first time I've noticed a change," Sylvie admitted, "but compared to my arrival in Verdélys, which was full of color and life, there is something missing in the heart of the city."

Loïc grunted softly, his mouth a grim line on his face.

After a few minutes of walking, Loïc spoke again.

"I suppose I should warn you," he said, "my family is rather large by Verdélian standards. There will be quite a few people to meet. Don't feel bad if you can't keep all the names straight."

Sylvie smiled, "I'm sure it'll be wonderful."

"I certainly hope so," Loïc said. "We're almost there."

Sylvie looked up. Until now, she had followed Loïc's lead without much thought about where they were headed. The area seemed familiar as she observed their surroundings, but Sylvie couldn't remember why.

"Tell me a little about your family before we arrive," Sylvie entreated Loïc.

"My mother and father live at home with my two younger brothers and two younger sisters," Loïc explained. "I have an older sister who lives in the Summer District with her husband and small baby—my niece." Loïc smiled as he spoke of his family, pride radiating from his face at the mention of his niece.

"We're coming to my parents' house now," Loïc continued. "It's just over the bridge and to the right."

*It can't be*, Sylvie thought.

She had walked this road recently with a friend and her baby.

"Loïc, wait," Sylvie said, stopping shy of the bridge.

Loïc turned to look at Sylvie, a puzzled look on his face.

"Is your sister's name Adelais?" Sylvie asked.

Loïc raised an eyebrow. "Uh...yes, it is. How do you know that?" He asked.

Sylvie threw her head back in exasperation.

"What are the odds," she muttered.

"What are the odds of what? When did you meet my sister?" Loïc asked, clearly confused.

"I met her when I was visiting the districts," Sylvie explained. "When I came to the Summer District, I met Adelais by chance and started a conversation. We came here, and I also met your mother and sisters."

"I guess that takes care of the introductions," Loïc said. "Let's go," he continued as he turned to cross the bridge.

"There's...one other thing," Sylvie said, embarrassed.

"What is that?" Loïc said, turning back to Sylvie.

"When I met your family, I...I didn't want anyone to know that I was a Firstborn. I thought it might impact the way they would interact with me. So I may or may not have introduced myself to your family as Nadine." Sylvie made a face and took in a sharp breath.

Loïc chuckled. "Well, that should make this interesting," he said. "Come along now; let's reveal your true identity to my family!"

Loïc and Sylvie stepped up to the door, and Loïc knocked heartily before opening the door and letting himself in with Sylvie in tow.

Adelais was standing in the entryway, speaking to her mother, Bergita.

"Loïc!" Adelais called out excitedly. "And...Nadine?" She added as Sylvie came into view from behind Loïc.

Loïc laughed. "Hello, sister," he said, embracing Adelais. "Meet Sylvie," he said, gesturing to his guest.

Adelais' eyes grew wide, and her mouth dropped open. After a moment, she placed a hand on her head. "Of course, I should have known—you 'work in the palace,' just like Loïc," she said. "I feel foolish."

"Sorry for the ruse," Sylvie said apologetically.

"No harm done," Adelais replied, "I'm glad you're here!"

Bergita approached Sylvie. "Welcome to our humble home, Sylvie. We're all delighted to officially meet you," she said. "Come, make yourself comfortable!" She gave Loïc a hug and a kiss on his cheek. "Welcome home, son. It's been a little while," she said. Sylvie could tell just how proud Bergita was of Loïc. Following Adelais, they made their way into the next room.

The room was centered around a large circular oak table sunk into the floor and surrounded by beautifully plush seating. The couch was covered in cushions bearing handsome embroidered designs, tassels, and other decorative elements. The table itself was laden with a varied assortment of delicious-looking food that steamed visibly under the glow of a humble chandelier centered over the oak table. Several floral arrangements completed the scene.

Loïc's father was already seated. "Over here," Loïc said, guiding Sylvie to the table's far side. They settled in with Loïc sitting just to his father's right. "Father, this is Sylvie," Loïc said, introducing Sylvie.

"So I've heard," Loïc's father replied. "It's a pleasure to meet you, Miss. My name is Lionel."

"Alondra, sir," Sylvie replied courteously. Lionel looked surprised, then quite pleased at Sylvie's formal manners. He sat back in his seat.

"Children, Loïc is here! Let's eat!" Lionel called out.

From within the home, Sylvie could hear Loïc's sisters running towards them.

"Loïc!" They yelled as they saw their brother. "And Nadine!"

"Actually," Loïc said with a big smile as his sisters jumped around his neck, "this is Sylvie."

Liesel and Poppy stood quickly upright, looks of shock on their faces.

"The new Firstborn?!" They said in unison.

"Yes," Loïc said, "our Morwenna."

The girls looked at Sylvie in amazement. As if remembering their manners, they both curtsied politely.

"Alondra, Miss," they said together.

Sylvie blushed. "There's no need for that," she replied. "It's lovely to see you both again."

The girls giggled as they went to their seats opposite Loïc and Sylvie.

Adelais took her place beside Sylvie.

"May I sit next to you?" She asked as she sat.

"Of course! This is your home, after all," Sylvie answered quickly.

A tall, averagely built man sat on the other side of Adelais, the little Felicity on his lap. His thick, unruly hair was tied back in a knot on the back of his head.

"This is my husband, Antoine," Adelais explained. "Antoine, this is Sylvie," she said, pointing to Sylvie.

"It is an honor," Antoine said with a bow of his head.

"It's a pleasure to meet—" Sylvie began before being interrupted by the bang of a door being kicked open.

"Move!" A younger, exuberant male voice exclaimed. Heavy boots stomped on the floor.

"Shut the door!" She heard another voice yell.

Again, there was a heavy slam as the door that had been violently opened a few moments ago banged shut. "Let me through; I was in first!" the first voice yelled. "You were not!" the other voice replied.

Bergita rolled her eyes and started making her way towards the commotion.

Just then, Sylvie heard a loud "Hey!" Followed by a thundering crash. From the hallway, a mountain of neatly cut wood could be seen tumbling into the entryway and dining area.

One of the boys was laughing hysterically. As the laugher approached, a stack of lumber with legs came into view.

"Here you go, Mom!" The walking wood-pile said.

"Thank you, Sigmund," Bergita replied, "please go put that—"

Bergita didn't have time to finish her sentence. The other boy came into view, but as he did so, he tripped on one of the scattered pieces of wood. His momentum carried him right into Sigmund. Sigmund managed to keep his footing, but not without dropping his armful of firewood, some of which bounced off his unfortunate brother on its way to the floor in another rambunctious clatter.

"Nice going, troll," Sigmund said to his brother, who was picking himself up off the floor.

"Serves you right, cheater," his brother grinned.

The two looked like they were about to start a brawl, the younger brother picking up a piece of wood as a weapon when Bergita intervened.

"Ahem!" She called out loudly. The two boys looked up wide-eyed as if realizing for the first time that they weren't the only ones in the room.

"Oh, hi, Mom," the youngest said with a grin.

"Hello, Theo," Bergita said, fists on her hips. "Now, would you two be so kind as to stop acting like savages for just long enough to pick up this enormous mess you've just created and get the wood to the fireplace so we can start dinner?"

"Sure thing, Mom!" The two boys said in unison.

Loïc chuckled and sighed as he got up from his seat and approached his brothers to help.

"Maybe fewer logs this time?" He suggested as he helped Sigmund and Theo load up with a manageable amount of firewood.

"Thanks, brother!" The boys exclaimed as they made their way to the fireplace to deposit their loads, still pushing and shoving each other as they went. They took their seats between Antoine and Polly. Loïc returned to his seat next to Sylvie. He sat close, and Sylvie could feel his leg against hers.

Lionel spoke up.

"Let's get started, everyone." The family quieted down. "Before we do, a special welcome to Sylvie, our royal guest. We're honored to have you tonight." Everyone nodded their assent. Sylvie bowed her head politely in recognition.

"Loïc," Lionel continued, "See that our guest is served first."

"Yes, Father," Loïc said as he took up a hefty serving dish containing a savory-smelling fish recipe. He placed a serving on Sylvie's plate and reached for a loaf of golden bread. The family joined in, and soon, everyone ate amid a hearty conversation. After a while, the discussion turned to Prophets' Day, and the prophecies received that night.

"Certainly not the kind we had hoped for," Lionel said seriously.

Bergita shook her head, sharing in her husband's dismay.

"Agreed," Antoine said between bites. "A beast, capture, foes, peril...even death. I suppose the overall message is not unexpected...only disheartening. Only time will give us the details, of course."

"It was certainly unexpected to me," Bergita replied. "Things may not be the best they've been in Verdélys, but talk of war? That's more than I think we'll see in a year's time. You know, the prophecies are often metaphorical."

Antoine shook his head, "Yes, of course. But I don't believe that is the case this time. The Verdélia have been due for a reckoning since before my birth. You would know, Father, you took your family from the city because of it. The time is coming, and according to the prophets, it is coming soon."

Adelais patted her husband's cheek. "Oh, come now, let's not shower tonight with unnecessary gloom," she said with a smile and a laugh.

"It's not unnecessary," Antoine protested with a grin, "it would be foolish to ignore the benefit of foresight conferred on us. Loïc, what do you think about the prophecies received this year? One was directly addressed to you, after all."

Loïc put down his fork and knife and reclined against the cushioned back of the couch.

"To tell you the truth," he said, "I don't know what to make of them. Mine for example: thrown from throne. Are we staring down a revolution?"

"A certain faction of imps certainly seems to think so," Antoine replied.

"But are they powerful enough to make good on their threat?" Loïc asked.

"You would know best out of any of us," Lionel said to Loïc.

Loïc shrugged but did not reply. Instead, he turned the conversation to the other parts of his prophecy.

"Distant travel isn't anything new," he said. "As for the rest...I can only hope for the best, but it's true that parts of it concern me."

"A kinly woe," Adelais said softly.

Loïc nodded in acknowledgment, and Sylvie could see genuine worry on his face, an uncommon feature.

"And what about you then, Miss Sylvie?" Bergita said, trying to shift the focus of the conversation.

"Yes," Antoine concurred, "the longest prophecy in some time if I'm not mistaken. What do you make of it?"

Sylvie looked around nervously. All eyes were on her.

"I suppose I agree with Loïc," she said, trying to avoid saying anything too inflammatory. "Much of the prophecy is unclear to me, but there is good and evil to be seen in it."

"Loïc's prophecy implied conflict," Lionel said, "yours explicitly addressed war and battle. Certainly, something to think about soberly."

Lionel's words echoed thoughts that had been running through Sylvie's mind since that fateful night. Would there indeed be war among the Verdélia?

"You are all such pessimists," Adelais chimed in. "Let's talk about the fun stuff. A true love, isn't that right, Sylvie?"

Sylvie felt herself blush. She tried to laugh it off.

"I suppose we will see whether that references a man or something else entirely," Sylvie said awkwardly, giggling. Adelais gave her a sly smile, her grin reaching from ear to ear.

"Well, it's not like it's some big mystery, is it?" Sigmund piped up. "Do you like Gaëtan or Loïc, Miss?" He asked brashly.

Antoine swatted the back of Sigmund's head firmly.

"What?!" He protested loudly. "It's a perfectly valid question. I guess we'd need Loïc's input on it, too, though." He turned to Loïc quickly. "Margot or Sylvie?"

Antoine smacked Sigmund again, louder this time.

"Sigmund!" Bergita exclaimed. Theo's eyes were wide open in anticipation of the coming drama, and his face barely contained his glee at what he perceived to be a choice comedic moment. Adelais put a hand to her mouth in surprise. Sylvie thought she was going to die.

"What?!" Sigmund replied again, brazenly defending himself.

"That is extremely inappropriate with Sylvie as our guest, son!" Bergita scolded. "Apologize, and watch your words, please."

Sigmund looked to his father wide-eyed and shrugging, pleading his case without a word.

"If it were up to me, the consequences would be worse. Do as your mother instructed," Lionel said.

Sigmund dropped his shoulders in defeat.

"Sorry," he mumbled to Sylvie and Loïc. "But you didn't answer the question," he added barely audibly.

"How dare you! Go clean the kitchen," Bergita scolded. Sigmund seemed to know better than to protest at this point, so he obediently got up from the table and left the room.

"I am so sorry about Sigmund," Bergita said, turning to Sylvie, "he is completely out of place. I don't know what to do with these boys of mine sometimes."

"That's alright," Sylvie said quietly, trying to conceal her mortification at Sigmund's question.

"We should be going anyway," Loïc added. Sylvie looked at Loïc and noticed that he, too, seemed uncomfortable, as if he was trying to escape the situation. Loïc made his way to his parents.

"Father, Mother, thank you for dinner," he said, leaning down to embrace them.

"Thank you for coming, son," Lionel replied.

"We wish you would come by more often," Bergita said.

Loïc turned to his siblings. "So long, everybody," he said with a wave. On his way out, he kissed his sleeping niece's head.

"Good night, Loïc!" They replied, more or less in unison.

"And good night, Sylvie," Bergita added. "It was truly a pleasure to have you with us. Do come again."

"Thank you so much for having me," Sylvie answered. "I would love to see you all again, circumstances allowing."

Loïc and Sylvie made their way to the front door. Just before leaving, Loïc turned back.

"Oh, Adelais," he said, "I'll be sending something for Felicity this week for her birthday."

"Thanks, Loïc," Adelais said with a smile, the sleeping Felicity resting on her shoulder.

With that, Sylvie and Loïc left the warmth of the family home and made their way out into the dark winter night.

They walked silently through the cold, their armed escort taking up their positions around them on the street. They reached the palace gate, where the guards stayed, and Sylvie and Loïc continued towards the palace alone.

"So...," Sylvie said, a nervous knot in her throat. "Sigmund was right...you never did answer his question."

Loïc shot Sylvie a look of surprise. Sylvie's comment had caught him off guard.

He groaned. "This conversation just doesn't seem to be able to die, does it?" He said in exasperation.

Sylvie chuckled. "Well...," she said as she swished the skirt of her dress side to side over the cobblestones.

Loïc sighed. "You know by now that the Firstborn marry each other. It's more than tradition. Call it fate, destiny, what you will. It's always been that way, and it seems like it always will be."

Sylvie nodded. Loïc carried on.

"Until you arrived in Verdélys, we thought the fourth Firstborn might never present herself. For quite some time, the prevailing theory was that the imp

305

rebels had succeeded in killing Morwenna. This created a conundrum between Gaëtan, Margot, and me."

Sylvie hadn't thought about that.

"Anyway," Loïc continued, "I...well...I guess I had always planned on ending up married to Margot."

The words out of Loïc's mouth were unexpectedly sharp on Sylvie's ears.

"What about Gaëtan then?" Sylvie asked.

Loïc shrugged. "I guess it didn't matter much to me," Loïc said, "whatever he decided, he would at least see his real desire materialize: family."

Sylvie furrowed her brow for a moment; then realization struck her.

"Oh, I see...," Sylvie said softly. "Margot can't bear a Verdélian child, can she?"

Loïc shook his head. "No, she can't. Gaëtan grew up an orphan, and family has always been his dream. I knew he couldn't have that with Margot, so I guess I just sort of accepted that I would marry Margot, and he would marry either Morwenna when she appeared or some other woman—likely a girl from the theater."

"But what about what Margot wants?" Sylvie asked. "It doesn't seem fair to her to make that decision based on Gaëtan's desire for a family."

"I've considered that more times than you know. I realize it probably is not fair to Margot to essentially decide for her, but it's not like she's expressed an interest in Gaëtan—or anyone, for that matter," Loïc said with a sigh. "I suppose the decision is not set in stone anyway. Besides," he said, looking into the clear night sky, "your arrival changed many things."

"But how?" Sylvie asked warily. "The circumstances remain the same. Gaëtan can't have a family of his own by marrying Margot. Whether I came to Verdélys or not wouldn't have changed."

"No, that hasn't changed...," Loïc said quietly, his voice drifting off into the dark.

"Then what has?" Sylvie asked insistently.

Loïc looked into her eyes as they neared the palace. He opened his mouth as if to answer, then closed it again. Sylvie thought she understood some of the meaning behind Loïc's silence, but she wished with everything within her that he would say something and explain himself and remove the doubt from her mind. Loïc did not speak, however, and instead opened the door to the palace and ushered her in. He walked her to her suite, wished her good night with a bow, and went down the hall to his room, leaving Sylvie in the candlelit hall, a tempest of emotions embroiled in her heart.

# XXX

## *A Dance in the Library*

The scent of sawdust and freshly cut wood filled the air. Sylvie fidgeted with a piece of oak as she sat inside a modest wood shop near her old cottage home on Amber Lane. She replayed her conversation with Loïc from the night before over and over again, scrutinizing every word and facial expression, searching for meaning.

Nadine entered the shop, and the sounds of her feet on the wooden floorboards roused Sylvie from her daydream.

"Hello, Miss," Nadine said politely.

"Hello, Nadine," Sylvie replied with a smile.

Nadine closed the door behind her and approached Sylvie, who was seated at a table covered in various woodworking utensils and several neatly cut pieces of wood, ready for use. A book was open on the table, which Sylvie would be referencing throughout their lesson.

"I thought we could try totem carving today," Sylvie said, compulsively straightening the materials on the table before her.

"As you wish," Nadine said obediently.

"I'll make a totem of you, and you can try making one of me," Sylvie continued, handing Nadine a wooden block of her own. Nadine reached for a chisel.

"Actually," Sylvie said, putting her hand on Nadine's, "you won't need that for what we're doing today. The totem isn't carved with tools."

Nadine withdrew her hand. "Oh," she said.

"Totems are carved without tools. Éthéra shapes the wood into the desired likeness," Sylvie explained. "A piece of the subject—typically a hair—is incorporated into the totem to give it useful properties."

*How am I supposed to carve wood with my bare hands?* Nadine questioned internally.

Sylvie ignored the thought.

"If we're successful, the added benefit of this lesson is that I'll have a totem of you, and you'll have a totem of me. The totem can be used as a proxy for the subject it's modeled after—I could put a crown of blue violets on your totem, and it would act on you as a ward against evil, for example."

"That does sound like it could be useful," Nadine admitted, "though couldn't a totem be used for nefarious purposes as well?"

"I suppose so," Sylvie replied, "but I like to think that a totem can be used for much good between friends. Besides, you can only use a hair freely given, so no totem likeness can be made of you without permission given. Let's get started."

"First," Sylvie said, isolating a strand of hair from her head, "you'll need a strand of my hair," she yanked the blonde strand out of her scalp, "and I'll need a strand of yours."

Nadine followed suit, plucking a jet black hair from her head and handing it to Sylvie.

"Now, the carving begins," Sylvie instructed. "Using your small finger, you want to work a valley into the top of your block of wood." Sylvie reviewed the book on the table to remind herself of the correct technique.

"The finger moves in a circular motion," Sylvie said, keeping her eyes on the text, "and the wood's éthéra is manipulated to create a space to place the strand of hair from the subject."

Sylvie's block of wood yielded to her movements, and soon, a valley was formed at the top of the block. Sylvie placed the strand of Nadine's hair into the space and looked up to check on Nadine.

Nadine dutifully mimicked Sylvie's actions, but the results did not follow. To any outside observer, it looked as if Nadine was brushing the top of the block of wood with her finger.

"Let's see if I can help at all," Sylvie said. She had already tried funneling éthéra into Nadine when they had tried casting runes. This time, Sylvie thought she could put the éthéra into the wooden block, and Nadine could take it from there. Sylvie placed her fingers on the side of the block of wood and focused her éthéra into the oak without directing it any further.

Without success, Nadine tried for another minute or so to shape the wood.

"Here, maybe—" Sylvie began.

"I'd like to request leave," Nadine said simultaneously.

Sylvie sat up and looked at Nadine for a moment.

"You...," Sylvie started, "you want to stop?" She asked.

Nadine sighed, "I do," she confessed. "I know your efforts are genuine, and I'm honored that you would go through this trouble for me and those like me," she continued, "but I don't want to waste your time, or mine, when we both have things we could be doing that can be of real service."

"But this could be of service," Sylvie protested, taken aback by Nadine's request. Nadine had never expressed herself like this before.

"This could be maybe the greatest thing to happen to both Verdélia and imps in centuries or more," Sylvie added.

"For your sake, I want to believe that you're right, miss," Nadine answered, "but we are walking in the dark, looking for a door we don't even know exists. From the things we have tried, there's been no indication what you're hoping for is even possible."

Nadine hung her head, and Sylvie could hear from her tone that she was fully resigned to the conclusion that she would never successfully manipulate éthéra.

"But we have only just begun," Sylvie insisted, unwilling to abandon her hope. "There is so much we could still try, so many ways this *could* work."

Nadine looked up at Sylvie. Speaking up made Nadine uncomfortable, but Sylvie could see she truly wanted to end this experiment. Sylvie could hear Nadine struggling internally, caught between her obligations to Sylvie and her discomfort at the task she was asked to fulfill.

"Perhaps," Nadine replied softly, "but all of our failures so far stem from the same thing—that I cannot manipulate, or even channel, éthéra." Nadine smiled ever so slightly. "And I am at peace with that. There are many things I *can* do. I can serve in the palace, and I can serve you, a wonderful Firstborn who cares about all of her people, both Imp and Verdélia. Many Verdélia can't boast as much. I would like to return to my duties, those I know I can fulfill."

Sylvie sat quietly. She was devastated, but Nadine didn't deserve to be treated as an experiment against her will.

"Very well, Nadine," Sylvie said, "you are free to go. I need you to know we are still friends, and I have no grudge against you for backing out. I knew it was a long shot anyway."

"Thank you, miss," Nadine said, relief washing over her facial features. "I am sorry; I know you meant well."

"It's all right, Nadine," Sylvie said, straightening her shoulders and smiling. "And I am very grateful to have you. I don't know what I would have done—or what I would do—in Verdélys without you."

Nadine smiled. "That's very kind of you to say, miss. It's been my pleasure."

"Thank you, Nadine," Sylvie answered softly.

Nadine bowed and made her way out of the shop, wood shavings drifting behind her in the skirts of her dress. The door shut behind her with a wooden thud.

*What was I thinking?* Sylvie thought as she dropped her head into her hands. How could she have been so foolish to believe that she could single-handedly discover a technique that, if it had ever existed, had been lost for thousands of years? It hadn't even been a whole year since she had first learned that Verdélia and imps existed, and here she was thinking she knew better than thousands of years' worth of collective Verdélian knowledge.

*I'm such a fool.* Sylvie despaired. She felt her throat tighten, and tears welled up in her eyes.

Just then, a smoky scorpion fled into the room through the window. *Lysandra*, Sylvie thought.

"What do you want?" She asked.

"Hello, Miss Sylvie. I want to request a private audience to discuss upcoming events. We need to schedule trial in several pending matters—the people need to see you fulfilling your appointed duties. Please contact me so we can schedule a time to discuss this." The scorpion bowed and slipped away.

"Begone, you cursed insect," she muttered, referencing her advisor as much as the familiar. She stood, putting away her tools and materials. She summoned her familiar, and the little mermaid jumped about her head. She glanced towards her, and before she could utter the words, 'Meet me,' she sighed and said, "Never mind. You stay put. I'm not dealing with Lysandra tonight."

"Come along," she hummed, "To the library."

That evening, Sylvie took dinner among the bookshelves. She sat on an emerald green couch. Vines and ivies grew up the window panes and across the arched windows. Nestled in the middle of it all sat Sylvie, buried in her books of imp anatomy, imp activity, imp birth, imp brain function, scientific journals, psychological papers, and more, still with no answers. None.

The door at the other end of the library opened, and Sylvie noticed Loïc walking in, attended by someone else. She shuffled her books around quickly, laying some supplemental school material atop the other more curious studies she'd adopted. Their voices grew closer.

Sylvie glanced up, and Loïc, acting as if he'd just noticed her, said, "Sylvie, you must meet my advisor. I don't think I've introduced you yet. This is Romain."

"Oh, good day." Sylvie stood and shook his hand. "Or rather good evening, I suppose." She glanced towards the dimness outside of the window and smiled.

"Morwenna," he bowed, "we meet at last." Sylvie realized she recognized his voice. This was the man in the garden pool who had been talking to Beyern about their uselessness on the night of the Festival of Flowers. He was another friend of Beyern's. Another plant, she was sure of it.

"And how is it working with Master Loïc? He is difficult, is he not?" Sylvie joked.

Loïc scowled at her, and she smirked at him.

"He certainly has a mind of his own," Romain said.

"Yes, he does. Do you find yourself disagreeing often?" She asked.

"More and more of late." His curt reply could not mask his mind's focus on each breath. She could hear his inhales and exhales as if in her ear.

"Well, hopefully you will resolve your differences soon," she said.

"Yes," Loïc interjected, "Anyway, Romain, you are excused. I have some catching up to do with Sylvie. Go be with your family; it's late."

"Master," he bowed to Loïc, gave a quick nod to Sylvie, and left.

"Dinner in the library?" Loïc asked as he sat in an armchair across from her.

"Yes. Some of my studies aren't turning out the way I'd hoped, so I'm putting in a little extra time," she said.

He leaned back more comfortably in his chair, "Get a read on Romain?"

Sylvie shrugged. "Not really. He was intently focused on his breathing—I haven't met anyone like that before. But I did recognize his voice. I heard it while I was in the pond the other night. He spoke with Beyern—he has no faith in the Firstborn."

"That's not news." Loïc leaned forward to inspect the books Sylvie was studying.

Before he could move the top books aside, she pressed him for further conversation: "So, what have you been busy with today?"

"This and that. Nothing exciting. I sent Felicity her birthday gift today."

"Oh really, what was it?"

"A travel pack for her to travel in. They like to get out of the city occasionally, so it's more for my sister than Felicity. A coat. A doll. Some sweets," he said.

Sylvie sat back and gazed at Loïc. "You know, Felicity is the reason I met your sister."

"Why's that?"

"She was humming a tune. I recognized it. I couldn't place it, but it was familiar. Just a tune, no words, but I was intrigued, so I started searching for the mind that was singing. And then there was a baby."

"So babies have perceivable thoughts?"

"Yes, but it's much more in emotions, images, colors, that sort of thing. Not words. And the tune, for example, she can't speak yet, so the words aren't clear enough for her to put them together in her mind. Just the tune. You probably know what song it is."

"Probably," he admitted.

"If I hummed it right now, would you tell me?"

"You sing?"

"I hum. To myself. Sometimes."

"You don't sing?"

"I do. Just in private."

He was nodding and smiling, "Hum away, miss."

She glared at him and cleared her throat. She began humming the familiar tune before she could finish the first line he spoke.

"Of course I know that. It's a popular lullaby, which explains Felicity knowing it. Légetoil's Cradle. Lovely humming voice, by the way."

Sylvie's cheeks warmed, and she looked down, embarrassed.

"How did you come across that lullaby?" He asked.

"My father must've sung it to me. He... lived among the Verdélia for a long time. Must've picked it up and continued it with me."

"Lived amongst the Verdélia?" Loïc seemed genuinely interested.

"Yes. Before I was born. Long before. He used to hum me tunes but usually didn't sing the words. I could hear him thinking the words sometimes, though. So he had to stop after a while because the strange tunes and words would raise suspicion in the village. If I just started singing, you know. Something happened to him out there; he walks with a limp now. It's just gotten worse and worse as I've grown older..." memories were now pouring from Sylvie's heart, "When I was finally able to learn the local dances that I would be expected to participate in in Hull, my father couldn't teach me so my mother learned the male parts and danced them with me. I remember my father used to pretend to be a fiddle and sing the songs so that we could practice."

Sylvie chuckled at the thought. Loïc was watching her intently.

"Are you a good dancer?" He asked.

"No! Goodness, no, not like the dancers here at the ballet. I've never seen anything like that."

He was shaking his head. "Obviously not. I mean in the dances you know. We have our own cultural dances that are far less involved than the ballet."

"You dance?"

"Of course I do," he looked offended at the thought, "It's a requirement as a Firstborn. You haven't learned yet for obvious reasons, but you will."

"Do you dance well?" She asked.

"Well enough," he shrugged.

Sylvie glanced around the library, "Will you teach me one?"

"Right now?" He pointed to the ground.

As he spoke, the door to the library opened, and Sir Reynard's towering figure entered.

"Why not teach me right now?" Sylvie pressed. "Who else is going to teach me? I don't have a parent here."

She turned to the centaur.

"Sir Reynard! Shouldn't Loïc teach me a dance? I think it's important for my cultural education."

Sir Reynard continued to approach as he answered. Sylvie could see Loïc shaking his head at her and smiling out of the corner of her eye. "It would certainly be profitable to your Verdélian education, but more than that, it would be entertaining for me."

She glanced towards Loïc and tilted her head towards a slightly less crowded area of the library.

"Alright." He said. "Come along."

He stood and extended his hand, inviting her to join him. Sir Reynard looked on as he replaced books.

"Okay, this dance is called the Pèverelle. In the ancient language, it means 'meadow. ' So it is a very up-and-down pattern, like the rolling hills of a meadow."

"Oh, so not like jumping?"

"No. We rarely jump," he assured her.

She nodded, and very soon, he was guiding her about their little space in the library with his hand firmly on her back. They faced each other, faced away, and he occasionally spun her. "You must let me lead," he said. They ran into each other a few times, prompting a laugh or two from Sir Reynard. Sylvie playfully mocked Loïc's stance every once in a while while he smiled and rolled his eyes. After a half hour, they had almost mastered the choreography.

"Not bad," he complimented, "What do you think?"

"Oh, it's very posh. Stuffy. I like it." Sylvie kept her hands in their place on his shoulder and in his hand.

"Oh, are your dances better? More down to earth?"

"More fun! Here, I'll show you."

"Oh, you're teaching me now?" He asked.

In response, she grabbed his hand and stood him at arm's length. "We start with a skip."

"A skip?" He asked incredulously as if it was an affront to his good name.

"I'm sorry. Let me correct that. It's more of a gallop."

"We're not horses," he reminded her.

"Speak for yourself," Sir Reynard said, poking his head around the corner of a bookshelf. They all laughed, and Sylvie continued teaching. They galloped and hopped and skipped, and *Sylvie* kicked. Loïc refused.

"You two make me miss my youth," Sir Reynard said. "I must go. You two behave yourselves."

They two were alone once again.

"One more round of the Pèverelle? Then we should probably get to bed."

"Yes, please," Sylvie agreed.

They began the dance, and halfway through, Sylvie tripped. Loïc caught her and pulled her in close as they laughed. After Sylvie's giggles had died down, she noticed that Loïc was very quiet and swaying with her. His hand was firmly on her back, his other hand gripping hers. His mouth was near her ear, and she could hear him breathing softly.

Her heart raced as the familiar feeling filled the cavity of her chest, and her breathing sped up. She didn't pull away. After a minute, her breathing slowed to match his. Loïc's breathing was deep and strong, and Sylvie found it incredibly soothing.

Then he sang the words to the lullaby in a smooth, low voice:

*Rocking softly over meadows*
*You can hear the breeze among the waves*
*And the birds of heav'n all songs are singing*
*In the care of Légetoil's Cradle*

*Drifting softly as the wind blows*
*Rain is pattering down; its fall to save*
*And the blades of grass, though earth, are springing*
*Reaching high for Légetoil's Cradle*

It was at this moment that Sylvie sniffled. Loïc stopped singing and pulled her back from him.

"Are you alright?" He asked.

"Yes. I'm just homesick, is all. I missed dancing and, I suppose, lullabies too. Though, it's been longer since then."

He pulled her in close to him again and said nothing.

"You have a very nice voice," she said, her ear against his chest.

"Let me walk you to your room," he offered. He let her go and offered her his arm.

As she sat in her bed that night, she noticed a parchment had slipped beneath her door. The words to the lullaby were carefully written by hand, and a message was scrawled on the bottom: *Mer vivillèn. Loïc.* Sylvie read the last verse.

*As you rise up and your mind grows*
*Let your courage carry you to grave*
*And the good of life your heart keep clinging*
*As you rise from Légetoil's Cradle*

# XXXI

## *A Gift and a Wish*

Nadine had one hand over her mouth. In the other, she held Loïc's note. The sun shone through the drapes, and Sylvie paced anxiously as she waited for Nadine to finish reading.

Nadine slowly lowered the note. A smile crept at the corners of her mouth.

"It seems clear enough to me, Miss," she said.

Sylvie didn't know what to do with her face—her emotions were a whirl.

"What do I do? Thanking him for the note the next time I see him seems so...quaint. And what if someone asks about the note? Do I act like it didn't happen? And anyway, why would he send me this? He plans on marrying Margot."

"What?" She put the note down and turned to Sylvie, who had plopped herself on the bed. "Where did you hear this?"

"He told me himself. That was his plan."

"Because he loves her?"

"I don't think so," Sylvie said, tossing a thread she'd found on her bed into the air.

"Master Loïc would not have sent you this if he was determined to marry Miss Margot."

A rapping at the door broke Nadine and Sylvie from their conversation.

"Who is there?" Sylvie called out.

"Lysandra," came a muted voice from the other side of her door. "The proper procedure would be to send your servant to the door to greet me and allow me passage in to talk to you."

Sylvie rolled her eyes and looked towards the window. "Come in, Lysandra."

The door opened as Nadine began gathering linens.

"Your servant needs to know her place—" Lysandra began.

"Nadine knows her place and excels in it. She is also my very dear friend, and if I catch you speaking to her like this again, you will be dismissed permanently. You can apologize now."

Lysandra stood stiff.

*Apologize? To a servant and an imp no less?*

"Go ahead, please, and then you can tell me the purpose of your call."

Lysandra turned coldly towards Nadine.

"I apologize if my words caused any offense."

"I took no offense," Nadine said with a polite curtsy.

Lysandra turned back to Sylvie.

"The first order of business I've been told is most pressing is that Ancelin arrived this morning."

"Ancelin?" Sylvie's eyes grew wide.

"Yes, he's downstairs."

"Well, the remainder of the orders of business will have to wait. I must see him now," Sylvie said as she stood and walked past Lysandra. *How could I ever mold this girl? She has no respect for my authority or Verdélian culture. I'd like to see Beyern try.*

Her thoughts were loud and angry enough that Sylvie heard them down the hall and glanced back as she reached the end. Lysandra's back was to Sylvie, and she continued to stand still. *Traitor. I knew it,* Sylvie thought.

"Excuse me, do you know where I can find Ancelin?" Sylvie asked as she approached an imp servant at the front door.

The young man looked taken aback as he gazed up the stairs toward her descending figure.

"Ancelin, Madam?" He asked.

"Yes, Ancelin," Sylvie answered, puzzled that he didn't seem to know. "I was told he had arrived this morning."

The young man shook his head. "I'm sorry, Ma'am, I don't know."

Sylvie furrowed her brow but thanked him nonetheless. She summoned her familiar.

"Go find—" Sylvie began.

"Why, Miss Sylvie, my old ward," came a familiar voice to Sylvie's right.

She turned, and Ancelin approached her with a smile.

"Ancelin!" Sylvie called out. She rushed towards him and put her arms around his neck.

"It's very good to see you," Ancelin said warmly, returning her embrace.

Sylvie smiled through tears as a deluge of memories came crashing down on top of her: her departure from Hull, her journey to Verdélys— including her stay in the woods and the discovery of her true name—and her arrival in the Verdélian city, all of which felt to Sylvie like a lifetime ago.

Sylvie heard Ancelin chuckle softly and empathetically.

"My dear Sylvie," he said, "what an adventure you've been on!"

"Oh no," Sylvie choked, "hardly an adventure at all."

Ancelin chuckled again and released Sylvie. She wiped her eyes with the delicate sleeve of her dress and took a deep breath.

"A difficult adventure, to be sure, but an adventure all the same," Ancelin replied.

Sylvie wiped her nose again. "I suppose you're right," she admitted.

"You have much weighing on your mind," Ancelin noted quietly.

Sylvie nodded through another long breath.

Gaëtan and Loïc appeared from around the corner.

"Ancelin, you've found your old friend," Gaëtan said as they approached.

Noticing Sylvie's tear-streaked face, Gaëtan's countenance was suddenly one of concern.

"Are you well, Sylvie?" He asked. "Is something wrong?"

"I...," Sylvie started, "no, nothing's wrong. I've just missed Ancelin, and his return brings many memories."

Gaëtan nodded. "That's very understandable," he said. "Unfortunately," he continued, "I'm afraid we haven't much time to get caught up just now. We have another guest who requires an audience as soon as possible."

"Oh?" Sylvie inquired.

Gaëtan and Loïc looked at each other.

"Sir Reynard's brother is here," Loïc stated.

Sylvie noticed Gaëtan and Loïc's shared expression of unease. Ancelin was his usual cheerful self.

"Why do I get the impression that's not a good thing?" Sylvie asked.

Loïc was the one to reply.

"Sir Reynard and his brother are estranged," he explained. "They don't exactly...agree on things."

Sylvie nodded but was curious to know more. She had never really considered Sir Reynard's upbringing or origins.

"I shall leave you all to it," Ancelin piped in. "You seem very busy."

Sylvie turned to Ancelin quickly.

"Wait," she pleaded, "I need to speak to you!"

"Attend to your duties," Ancelin instructed, "and we will speak later tonight."

With that, he turned and walked away down the palace hallway and disappeared from sight. Sylvie sighed.

"Right," Gaëtan said, bringing Sylvie's attention back to the matter at hand. "Let's meet in the throne room, seeing as we will be handling formal foreign affairs."

Loïc nodded in assent. Gaëtan and Loïc looked as if they were both waiting to ask Sylvie something. After a short silence, Gaëtan spoke.

"Sylvie, could you please invite Sir Reynard to join us?" He asked.

Sylvie raised her eyebrow quizzically. "I suppose so," she answered, "but I thought you said Sir Reynard and his brother are estranged. Why purposefully bring them together? We haven't had Sir Reynard attend previous political matters."

"Fair question," Gaëtan replied, "but even with Sir Reynard's family situation being what it is, he will still be invaluable in discussions with his brother. There's no harm in trying to mend things between them while we're at it, and the first centaur visit to Verdélys in the last eighteen years is a good place to start."

"Very well," Sylvie answered, "I'll extend the invitation. But why me?"

"Thank you, Sylvie," Gaëtan replied, a look of relief on his face. "And given that you're spending time with Sir Reynard regularly, we figured he would take the invitation best if it came from you."

Sylvie shrugged, "We will see," she said with a smile and started for the library. As she glided away on the smooth tile floor, she stole a look over her shoulder. Gaëtan had moved on to other matters, but Loïc stood alone under the vaulted ceiling, his dark eyes looking intently at Sylvie. He did not avert his gaze as she locked eyes with him. Sylvie turned back abruptly and put her head down, quickening her pace on her way to talk to Sir Reynard.

※

"Ah, Sylvie," Sir Reynard said as Sylvie entered the library. "Welcome," he continued. "What brings you to the library today?"

"We would like you to join us in the throne room," Sylvie said. Unsure of what to say next, she opted for candor.

"Your brother is here. We would appreciate your presence as we host him."

"My brother?" Sir Reynard asked, his face showing surprise that was quickly overshadowed by a cloud of somber coldness. "I see," he added.

Sylvie felt an urge to fill the void in the conversation.

"I understand you're not close currently," she started, "but we could use your wisdom in handling this matter."

"I am not certain that my presence will be beneficial," Sir Reynard replied. "My brother—my entire family, in fact—believes me to be a disappointment and failure, as far as centaur culture is concerned."

Sylvie was surprised. Sir Reynard was so wise, well-read, and kind.

"How is that possible?" She protested. "You've taught an entire generation of Firstborn and are the Verdélian palace historian. It seems to me the list of centaurs able to boast as much could be counted on one hand."

Sir Reynard smiled, then chuckled. "You are truly a marvel, Sylvie. Incidentally, you are also correct."

"Come." he continued. "Explaining the circumstances of my relationship with my brother would have us here for much longer than we can afford."

In the throne room, Sylvie took her place between Loïc and Gaëtan. Margot sat on the other side of Loïc. Sir Reynard stood at the base of the stairs leading up to the dais upon which the Firstborns' thrones were located. Palace guards stood at the door as always.

The doors opened, and a guard walked in.

"Sir Johncleave II of Céladon," the guard announced. He stepped aside, and behind him entered a centaur, followed by several others of his kind. The delegation was formal, though not in the same manner as the Verdélia. The centaurs were armed with weapons made primarily of wood and wore scarves and vests patterned after the forest in hues of green and brown. Ornaments and jewelry made of wood and bone adorned most members of the procession.

Johncleave bore a striking resemblance to Sir Reynard, although he was somewhat taller and thinner. His appearance was also wilder, as if either city life had softened Sir Reynard or life among the centaurs had hardened Johncleave. Sylvie could not tell which it was.

Johncleave approached the thrones and bowed low.

"Your majesties," he said in a gruff voice.

"Sir Johncleave, welcome," Gaëtan said.

"Thank you, Master Gaëtan," Johncleave replied.

He looked to his left, directly at Sir Reynard.

"Reynard Bren Octave," he said without so much as a nod of his head. "You have aged."

"As have you, Johncleave," Sir Reynard replied curtly.

Johncleave turned his attention back to the Firstborn.

"I come on behalf of my people," Johncleave began, "and on behalf of all living creatures within our borders. I am aware that you have many pressing matters to attend to, so I will get right to the issue at hand: we are witnessing a sort of universal death within and about the western forests, from at least as far north as the Valley of Dragons down to our southern borders and beyond. In our travels to Verdélys, we witnessed the same thing throughout the land—a loss of vitality in all things living."

Sylvie thought back to her walk in the city with Loïc when he had pointed out the dulling of the colors. This was no illusion.

Johncleave continued, "We are concerned about the implications this may have on Spring plantings and growth. Already, we are suffering significant shortages of food due to the loss of customary hunting in our borders."

Johncleave stopped speaking and looked at the Firstborn, expecting a proposal.

"Thank you, Johncleave, for your report," Gaëtan replied. "I must admit this is the first time we have been made aware of the scope of the effects you mention. We had hoped they might be limited regionally. Unfortunately, that is evidently not the case."

"Indeed not," Johncleave replied. "What do you intend to do to address the situation?" he asked.

"For the time being, we are still investigating its cause," Gaëtan answered, "but we have reason to believe it is linked to a faction of imps seeking to incite insurrection here in Verdélys."

Johncleave thought for a moment before replying.

"If that is the case," he said, "can we trust that the issue is under control? Although treason within your ranks would typically be considered an internal matter into which we would not inquire, if what you say is true, then in this particular instance, it has become a matter of global concern. And, if you would, I would like to hear directly from the Firstborn whose duty it is to keep a relationship with us." His eyes rested on Margot.

She glanced to the others, almost for permission, then spoke. "We are addressing it."

"When?" Johncleave pressed. "We cannot afford delay."

"Presently," she said. Sylvie could tell she was working to keep a positive demeanor despite the Firstborns' plight. They still did not know precisely what they were up against, much less how to resolve this problem.

"Hmph," Johncleave grunted, clearly displeased. "Are we all consigned to die, then, while you lounge about on your thrones, cloaked in a false sense of security behind your tall walls and enchantments?"

Margot did not respond. Gaëtan's lips parted. Loïc sat up in his seat. Sylvie moved her leg slightly over to touch Loïc's, trying to prevent a heated response.

Instead of a Firstborn, though, it was Sir Reynard who spoke.

"I would be careful, brother, to take the role of accuser in matters in which you know so little," he said, addressing Johncleave.

"I did not come to receive admonition from you," Johncleave retorted.

"I imagine you did not," Sir Reynard replied calmly, "but you will receive it when warranted nonetheless. The plague of which you speak is one caused by forces far beyond your control. Those before you, whom you have petitioned for aid, are the only ones in this world capable of providing you the relief you seek. Consequently, I would temper your tongue."

Johncleave was visibly livid, though he did not immediately respond.

"Johncleave," Margot said, "we certainly do not minimize your people's hardships. We are aware of the threat and are taking appropriate measures to locate the source of this evil and root it out. With the help of our recently found Morwenna," she gestured to Sylvie, "we have made significant progress in that regard. All of our faculties are being put to the task. The blight goes deeper than we had hoped, so we ask for your patience."

Although he was visibly still irritated, Johncleave seemed somewhat pacified by Margot's words.

"Very well," he said at last. "We hope our report will assist in your efforts on this. Unfortunately, we may be unable to offer much else in the way of aid."

"Perhaps not for the time being," Margot replied, "though we are encouraged to know we can find allies among the centaurs should the need arise. It does you honor."

Johncleave squared his shoulders and straightened himself further at Margot's words, evidently pleased at the praise from the Firstborn.

"Unless you have other matters to present to us, we ask that you please make yourselves comfortable and stay in Verdélys as long as necessary to recuperate before retaking your journey back west," Margot continued.

Johncleave bowed politely. "Thank you, Miss Margot. We will not burden you long, as we must return before week's end. Your hospitality is greatly appreciated."

With that, Johncleave turned and made his way through the centaurs behind him, who all filed out of the throne room behind their leader.

When the door shut behind them, the Firstborn looked around at each other and then at Sir Reynard. Margot looked frightened, but every other face beamed with pride.

"Margot," said Sylvie, "You should speak up more often."

The boys nodded in agreement. Gaëtan walked towards her and placed a hand on hers. "That was fantastic."

Margot's face slowly slipped into a smile.

"Thank you for your attendance today, Sir Reynard," Loïc said.

"It is my honor to serve the Firstborn," Sir Reynard replied. "My brother forgets his place, coming here asking for help while accusing you in the same breath. Please forgive him."

Gaëtan shook his head. "There's no harm done. I believe he means well, with the good of his people at heart. What we are currently facing is reason enough for us all to be concerned."

Sylvie asked a question that had been on her mind: "Why do they rely so heavily on us? First the Sylph, now the Centaurs?"

Gaëtan spoke first: "At the core, we are their creators, Sylvie. We gave them life. By we, I mean the original Firstborn, of course, not us individually. In the same way we turn to Solaidi for aid through ceremonies, prophecies, and gifts, they turn to us. We are the stewards of all creation. They come to us when the state of the world is out of their hands. Only we have the power, potentially, to control the dark forces. That is why they come to us."

"That is a daunting responsibility," Sylvie noted.

"Indeed it is," Gaëtan agreed.

🏃

Sylvie made her way to the gardens, looking for Ancelin. She found him on the rear patio, leaning over the stone banister. Pockets of snow littered the garden, but the majority had melted over the last two days.

"Hello again, Ancelin," she called, announcing herself.

"Hello, my dear," Ancelin replied without turning around. "I take it your audience went well enough?" He asked.

"I suppose," Sylvie answered half-heartedly.

Sylvie joined Ancelin at the edge of the balcony. The winter sun shone brightly on the gardens, their colors significantly muted. Sylvie knew it wasn't all due to the season.

"I need your help," Sylvie said finally, turning to Ancelin.

"I know," is all Ancelin said in return.

Sylvie smirked. "Well, if you already know, why don't you just give me the answer I'm looking for?"

Ancelin clicked his tongue. "Come now, dear. You know better than that," he reprimanded. "That which is worth learning must be earned."

Sylvie sighed. "Are you going to be able to help me?" She asked.

"I believe so," Ancelin reassured her.

"I need to know if I'm wasting my time," Sylvie said.

"That very much depends," Ancelin answered, a gust of breeze catching his hair and ruffling it about. "What is it that you are doing?"

"Can imps harness éthéra?" Sylvie asked bluntly.

"Well, no, of course, you know that," Ancelin replied with a smile that told Sylvie there was more to his answer.

"Is it possible for imps to harness éthéra?" Sylvie asked, rephrasing her question.

"Now, there is an interesting question," Ancelin grinned. "What do you believe?"

Sylvie sighed as she thought about what she believed was the answer to her own question.

"I don't know," Sylvie said. "I want to believe it's possible. I have some reasons to believe it is and many other reasons to believe the answer is no. I hope it is possible, I suppose."

"Hope is what drives all greatness," Ancelin mused.

"But false hope is a blind guide," Sylvie countered.

"Very true," Ancelin acknowledged, nodding his head.

Sylvie had missed Ancelin, but she had forgotten how circular and evasive his dialogue could be. She decided to cut right to the chase.

"Did you know Zaria's handmaiden?" Sylvie asked.

"I did," Ancelin admitted. "Which one?"

Sylvie hadn't even thought that, as a Firstborn, Zaria would have outlived at least one of her servants.

"The one in the famous painting," Sylvie answered.

"Ah," Ancelin said, a sense of amusement in his voice. "Yes, I knew Amandine."

Sylvie had not found a reference to the handmaiden's name anywhere. Ancelin's wealth of knowledge never ceased to amaze her.

"Was Amandine an imp?" She pressed.

"Yes," Ancelin said.

Sylvie's heart nearly skipped a beat.

"The familiar in the painting, the bird—was it Amandine's?" Sylvie asked hurriedly.

"Yes," Ancelin confirmed.

Sylvie couldn't believe it. She was right. Amandine, the imp handmaiden of Zaria, had been able to harness éthéra.

"But...," Sylvie stuttered excitedly, "how?" The answer she had been searching for was just within her reach.

"It was a gift, just as are all things that are received after they are wished for," Ancelin responded cryptically.

Sylvie felt as if the floor was falling out from underneath her. Not another of Ancelin's mysteries. Not now.

"Wish?" Was all Sylvie could get out.

Ancelin looked at Sylvie compassionately.

"I cannot say more," he said, "Solaidi binds my tongue, but your question has been answered. Its meaning is for you to discover."

With that, Ancelin made his way back into the palace. Knowing him, Sylvie was aware this might be goodbye. She watched him go, mulling his words in her mind.

*A gift*, Sylvie thought, *and a wish*.

# XXXII

*Friendly Fire*

S ylvie walked to the throne room. Lysandra followed close behind, nearly perched on Sylvie's shoulder as she prattled on about upcoming events and what was expected of Sylvie. Or at least what Beyern expected of Sylvie. Sylvie blocked out Lysandra as best she could. Her advisor had become much more intrusive of late now that Sylvie was spending less time on her studies. Loïc's approach with his advisor had emboldened Sylvie to take Lysandra a little less seriously than she otherwise would have.

"After your meeting in the throne room, you'll be needed for trial scheduling. The queue is long, and the prisons are reaching capacity. I suggest you make yourself available for trial most or all days next week."

Sylvie didn't respond but continued walking. As usual, Lysandra had no trouble filling the silence.

"This afternoon is currently free. There's nothing scheduled; I could put together a plan for—"

"I'm afraid not," Sylvie said, "I have something planned for this afternoon. I don't remember what it is at the moment, but it will come to me."

"Why have you not shared your schedule with me?" Lysandra asked, "It is imperative that I know your schedule so that I can help you coordinate your duties."

Sylvie pushed open the doors of the throne room, her lips pursed.

❧

"Good morning," Loïc said with a subdued smile as Sylvie entered the throne room. Perhaps Sylvie wasn't doing as good of a job concealing her frustration with Lysandra as she thought.

Margot and Gaëtan were chatting pleasantly beside the thrones. He was offering her a sweet.

"Good morning, Loïc," Sylvie replied. Sylvie still hadn't had a chance to talk to Loïc since their night dancing in the library. There was much she wanted to ask him, but now was not the time.

Lysandra walked to the side of the throne room alongside the other advisors. Thibault stood beside a woman, who stood beside Lysandra, who stood beside Romain. The one unfamiliar advisor must have been assigned to Margot. Sylvie understood the woman went by Seraphine.

"Why are we meeting with Beyern?" Sylvie asked Loïc.

Loïc seemed slightly surprised.

"Why...," he said, "we're discussing our winter wishes."

"Our what?" Sylvie asked.

"The wishes of winter celebration?" Loïc prompted.

Recognition beamed through Sylvie as if a sunlit window had suddenly been uncovered in her mind.

"Oh! Right!" Sylvie said.

The tumult of recent weeks had pushed the whole ceremony out of her mind, but Sylvie had learned about this event with Sir Reynard. On this day of winter every year, the star Lucentia was at its closest point, uniquely enhancing the éthéra of Winter Verdélia and allowing them to grant the wishes of other Verdélia. Verdélia from everywhere gathered to make their wishes to the Winter Verdélia.

However, another thought held all of Sylvie's attention.

*Wishes! Of course!*

This had to be what Ancelin meant. Surely, this was how Amandine had received her power.

Loïc looked at her with a look of amusement and suspicion.

"What's going on in that head of yours?" He asked, eyes narrowing.

"I was just thinking," Sylvie started, trying to think of something to tell Loïc until she was ready to reveal her plan, "the ceremony isn't for several days. Why are we meeting now?"

The answer seemed to mostly satisfy Loïc. "I'm not sure," he said, "though I suspect he'll be chastising us somehow," Loïc replied with a smirk.

Sylvie giggled. Loïc was probably right.

As if on cue, a guard entered the throne room.

"High Councilman Beyern," he announced.

Beyern walked in swiftly, head held high.

"High Councilman Beyern, welcome," Gaëtan said. The Firstborn made their way to their seats atop the dais. Beyern stood at the foot of the stairs.

"Alondra, Firstborn," Beyern said, more out of custom than respect.

"This audience is at your request; you may speak," Gaëtan announced.

"Thank you, Master Gaëtan," Beyern said, looking at each Firstborn in turn. "I requested this audience to discuss the winter wish ceremony in light of your newest member, for whom this will be the first such ceremony," Beyern said, looking squarely at Sylvie. "And in any event, given the importance of the ceremony, this would be warranted with or without our new Morwenna."

"Very well," Gaëtan said, "what would you like to discuss specifically?"

"I will begin with the admonition given every year to every wishing Verdélia. You two," he said, pointing to Loïc and Gaëtan, "should already know it. Still, it bears repeating. The Winter Verdélia do not grant power, wealth, love, or health. Generally, anything outside of those confines may be wished for. Consider also," he continued, "that unless something forbidden is wished for, the wish *will* be granted, whether the result is as hoped or not. I therefore recommend specificity and clarity."

*The Winter Verdélia do not grant power.* The words struck Sylvie like a rock through glass. That couldn't be right. This had to be the answer.

"Thank you, High Councilman Beyern," Gaëtan said. "Are there any questions for the High Councilman?" Gaëtan asked, turning to his fellow Firstborn.

Sylvie had a question.

"Can you explain exactly how the ceremony is performed?" Sylvie asked Beyern.

*So little knowledge for so much responsibility,* Sylvie heard Beyern think.

"Of course," Beyern said out loud. "Perhaps a demonstration will be best. Come, if you please."

Sylvie stood, made her way down the few steps, and stood in front of Beyern.

"The wisher will take me by the forearms," Beyern explained, putting his arms prominently forward and inviting Sylvie to hold on to them. "The wisher will speak their wish. Assuming the wish is permissible, we will keep our hands clasped until we feel the wish has settled. If the wish spoken is forbidden, I will release the bond, and your wish will be forfeit." Beyern released Sylvie, and she took a step back.

"Is that a common occurrence," Sylvie asked, "forfeiting a wish?"

"It has happened to at least a few Verdélia every year," Beyern affirmed. "Wishing for the return of a deceased loved one is a common one, but one that unfortunately cannot be granted."

Sylvie nodded. She made her way back to her seat between Loïc and Gaëtan.

"I assume," Beyern said, "that you have had many discussions over this occasion and already have a plan for your wishes. I would like to discuss them now."

"We haven't," Gaëtan said.

Beyern crossed his arms.

"How disappointing. Preparation, at least, could perhaps compensate for lack of experience. You would do well to rely more readily on the advice and service of the advisors the Council has appointed you."

Sylvie's eyes narrowed as Beyern continued his scolding.

"The Council has gone to great lengths to select sage and skilled advisors for each of you. Consult with them as you prepare for this ceremony. Your wish is not for you alone but for all of Verdélys."

"While I appreciate your concern," Gaëtan said, "You must remember that Solaidi's deadline is when the star is in its proper place in a few days. Today is nothing but your own arbitrary deadline for us, nothing more."

"As you wish."

Beyern nodded shortly and exited the throne room.

After Beyern had exited the room, Gaëtan turned to the other Firstborn.

"He has a point," Gaëtan said, "it would be good if we all prepared our wishes in advance. This could be a good opportunity to get some answers on the insurrectionists."

Loïc nodded. "Agreed," he said. "And this year, we'll have three wishes."

Sylvie looked at Loïc curiously. "Three wishes?" she asked. "Who isn't getting a wish?"

Margot raised her hand. "Me, obviously," she said, her voice dripping with carelessness and disdain.

"But...," Sylvie protested, "Why not?"

Margot leaned forward and gave Sylvie an incredulous look, one eyebrow raised.

"For the same reason, I don't do anything else like the rest of you. I'm an imp, remember?"

"But why would that prevent you from making a wish?" Sylvie asked.

"The last Winter Verdélia to try granting a wish to an imp died," Margot explained dismissively. "It was banned immediately and has been against Verdélian law for a Winter Verdélia to grant an imp a wish ever since."

"Oh...," was all Sylvie could manage. What had seemed like the obvious answer to her question regarding the imps appeared now to be quite impossible. What else could Ancelin have meant if not this?

Sylvie sat on her throne, deep in thought, her elbows resting on the armrests, her hands linked, and her index fingers against her lips. She looked up as Gaëtan and Margot made their way out of the throne room. Loïc stayed beside Sylvie.

"So," he said finally, "I can see you have a lot on your mind. Are you still going to meet me for your lesson this afternoon?"

*Lesson?* Sylvie thought. She had almost forgotten. Loïc had invited her to receive some training with a weapon to flesh out the combat training she had started.

"Yes, I'll be there," Sylvie answered.

"Great," Loïc replied. "I'll see you soon then."

With that, he, too, walked out of the throne room, leaving Sylvie alone with her thoughts.

※

Sylvie struggled to fasten her sword to her hip. Loïc had insisted that she bring her own.

"You should get used to wielding your sword," Loïc had recommended. "The familiarity will help in a stressful situation." Sylvie had never actually worn her sword before, and she felt awkward with it on.

In retrieving her sword, Sylvie also rediscovered her mother's beautiful blue cloak, which was gifted to her by her father, Remi, that night in Hull. Given the richness of her royal wardrobe, it had sat unused since she had moved into the palace. She decided today was as good a day as any to wear it again. She wrapped the beautiful blue fabric around her and drew it around her body so as to conceal the sword. With that, she went out to meet Loïc.

As she walked, she replayed Ancelin's words in her mind.

*It was a gift, just as are all things that are received after they are wished for.*

The riddle was traditionally Ancelin, but she was convinced that the wish was the key. But how could that be if granting an imp's wish killed the grantor?

*The last Winter Verdélia to try granting a wish to an imp died.*

Margot's words rang through Sylvie's mind. She was missing something.

Sylvie's thoughts had distracted her, and she found herself in the training camp already. As before, the sights and sounds of combat were all about her. The day had turned overcast, and grey clouds loomed low in the sky.

Sylvie made her way to the stables, where she met Loïc. As she entered the familiar scene, she could see the top of Loïc's head over the fence of the stall where she had had her first lesson. She approached and knocked on the open stall door.

334

"Hello," she said.

"Hello Sylvie," Loïc replied with a smile as he looked up from a couple of swords he had placed against the wall. Sylvie noticed a wooden dummy on the stall's far side.

"Ready to get started?" Loïc asked, picking up one sword and turning to face Sylvie.

"I suppose," Sylvie said. Although she felt less out of place following the lesson she had received from Loïc previously, the idea of using a weapon was somewhat frightening. As before, she was also apprehensive about appearing incompetent.

"Great," Loïc replied. "We'll start using this dummy," he said, using his sword to point to the wooden statue. "After which, we'll spar for a bit. I'll use this training sword—the edges and point are blunted—and I'll invite you to use your own sword."

"Shouldn't I use a blunt sword as well?" Sylvie asked, "I don't want to hurt you."

Loïc smiled, a sly look on his face. "There's no risk of that," he said.

Sylvie huffed as she gave him a playful, angry look. She was sure he was right, though.

"Alright," Loïc continued, "let's see this sword of yours."

Sylvie began to draw back her cloak. "It's not mine exactly," she said, drawing the sword from its sheath. Loïc looked at the sword in surprise.

"Woah," he said, drawing closer to get a better view of the weapon. "You don't see these every day. May I?" He asked, putting his hands out to ask Sylvie for the sword.

"Of course," Sylvie answered, feeling an odd sense of pride in Loïc's sudden interest.

"You are full of surprises," Loïc said as he inspected the sword. After a few moments, he returned it to Sylvie.

"Where did you get this sword?" Loïc asked incredulously.

"My adoptive father gave it to me. He said he got it from a Verdélian friend."

"How unusual. This is not just any Verdélian sword," Loïc explained. "These swords were specifically made for a very particular regiment of Verdélian soldiers going back probably over half a century now or more. The soldiers who wielded these swords were the Verdélia's most elite troops, typically the first to engage the enemy or to be sent on special assignments where extreme skill and determination were needed. This particular sword undoubtedly carries a rich history of feats we might be hard-pressed even to imagine."

Loïc's words nurtured several questions in Sylvie's mind about her father, Remi. What had led him to receive this sword as a gift? Remi had mentioned that the Verdélia who had brought Sylvie to Hull so many years ago was his friend—under what circumstances did her father befriend an elite Verdélian soldier? She hoped one day she might get the chance to ask him.

"I didn't know," Sylvie said quietly.

"I wouldn't expect you to," Loïc said kindly. "There are many Verdélia who would not know. But now you can rest assured that you possess a very fine sword. You won't find a better blade anywhere. Now, let's begin!"

Loïc walked towards the wooden dummy.

"This," he said, tapping the flat of his sword against the wood, "is Belthégor." Loïc grinned boyishly as he spoke.

Sylvie giggled, "Great, let's get him!" She said, playing along with Loïc.

"Get him, we shall," Loïc promised, "but we'll do so in a way that won't get you killed. So let's cover basics."

With that, Loïc demonstrated basic sword strikes with his blunted practice sword. Sylvie imitated Loïc, first thrusting at the dummy, then swinging her sword to hit the target with her blade's sharp edge. Loïc watched, advising on how to hold her sword and control and contain her movements.

"Good!" Loïc praised as Sylvie pushed the tip of her blade powerfully into "Belthégor." Sylvie tugged her sword free, ready to continue.

"Is it true that a Winter Verdélia died trying to grant an imp a wish?" Sylvie asked as she readied for another blow to the dummy.

The question seemed to catch Loïc unawares.

"Well, yes," he replied, "although I wasn't there to see it happen. Granting wishes to imps has been illegal for as long as I—or even my parents—have been alive."

Sylvie struck at the dummy again with her sword.

"How do we know that it was the fact that the wisher was an imp that caused the death?" Sylvie pressed.

Loïc thought for a moment. "I guess we don't," he confessed. "Why all this interest in imps and wishes?"

"I guess it's just on my mind since Beyern's visit this morning," Sylvie lied.

"Huh," Loïc breathed skeptically. "Alright," he added, "I think that's enough brutalizing Belthégor for today. Let's talk dueling."

Loïc pushed the wooden figure out of the way and circled back to the center of the stall.

"When facing an armed opponent," Loïc explained to Sylvie as she approached him, "many of the same rules you learned in unarmed combat apply. You want to be grounded and, if possible, strike first. That said," Loïc continued, "you want to exercise more caution not to make a rushed first strike since it can throw you off balance and create an opening for your opponent. You may not get the chance to recover where a blade is involved. Now, take a strike at me, and we'll discuss parrying."

Sylvie made a respectable effort at a lunging thrust at Loïc's chest with her sword. Before the point could get near Loïc, he used his blade to deflect Sylvie's blow with one fluid arm motion.

"Not bad, though you shouldn't let your fear of hurting me hold you back," Loïc coached. "Practice now as if you were facing a true foe so you don't get caught off guard if you find yourself in a situation where your opponent will not be so forgiving. And trust me, you're not going to hurt me—not today, at any rate. Again."

Sylvie attacked again, trying to suppress her urge to temper her strike. She pictured one of the cloaked assailants from the imp district standing in Loïc's place and lashed out with all her might.

"That's better," Loïc said as their swords met with the ringing of metal on metal. Although the contact was jarring, Sylvie was surprised at how well her sword seemed to absorb the shock with Loïc's blade.

Loïc continued to parry Sylvie's attacks, each time explaining his movements and how he was reacting to her assaults.

"Now you try," Loïc said. "I'm going to try to strike you, and you parry the attack."

Sylvie nervously tightened her grip on the hilt of her sword. Loïc swung at her with the edge of his sword. Heart pounding, Sylvie instinctively lifted her sword to block the blow, relieved to hear the sound of metal on metal as Loïc's strike stopped short, blocked on the edge of her blade.

The afternoon continued with Loïc coaching, then showing, and finally requiring Sylvie to practice various techniques for both attack and defense with her blade. Sylvie was soon perspiring profusely. As before, Loïc's appearance suggested he was under little to no physical strain. *It's not fair*, Sylvie thought. Sylvie turned her mind back to the wishes.

"Since the Firstborn can harness the éthéra of all four seasons," Sylvie said through quick breaths, "couldn't they grant wishes as well?"

Loïc looked at Sylvie quizzically.

"I suppose so," Loïc replied slowly. Sylvie was going to have to be careful. She could tell Loïc was getting suspicious, and she knew from experience that he would figure her out if he suspected something.

"Why don't the Firstborn grant any during the winter celebration?" Sylvie asked.

Loïc put the tip of his sword into the dirt.

"Tradition, I guess," he said after a moment.

"That seems to be the answer to many things in Verdélys," Sylvie stated somewhat critically.

Loïc looked Sylvie squarely in the eyes.

"Don't be too critical of tradition," he cautioned. "Tradition carries the combined knowledge of generations of our ancestors behind it. Dismissing tradition is, in a way, proof of a certain level of vanity and pride."

"Maybe so," Sylvie protested, "but not all traditions are rooted in good or truth. If no one were willing to question tradition, there would be no room for innovation and progress."

"True enough," Loïc admitted. "Still, I would be hesitant to deviate from tradition without a good reason for doing so. Now," he said, holding his sword at the ready, "let's finish this lesson, shall we?"

Sylvie's swordsmanship instruction continued at the hand of Loïc, her demanding tutor. The intensity of the exercise increased gradually, and after another hour or so, Sylvie found herself struggling to maintain precise control of her sword. The sweaty hilt of the weapon wasn't helping.

At Loïc's request, she aimed a blow at Loïc. Unsurprisingly, Loïc parried the strike. This time, however, Sylvie's arm faltered. Her sword shot to the left under the force of Loïc's deflection, but as Sylvie's strength failed from exhaustion, she could not prevent it from coming back towards her as well. The honed edge slid along the top of her left thigh, a bolt of pain shooting up into her stomach.

Sylvie let out a cry and dropped her sword, falling to the floor as her leg gave way. The pain was intense, and already Sylvie could feel her pant leg beginning to saturate with her blood.

"Sylvie!" She heard Loïc cry out as he dropped his blunt training sword and knelt beside her. "I am so sorry! I'm such a fool!"

Sylvie was in tears, but through them, she could see Loïc's face, a mixture of deep worry and remorse etched into his dark features.

"How bad is it?" Sylvie asked. She didn't dare look.

She felt Loïc's fingers gingerly on her thigh around the wound.

"It's not too deep," Loïc said, his voice trembling slightly. "I'm going to cut away some of this fabric to see what's going on and get it mended."

Loïc drew a knife from his belt and slid two fingers from his free hand in between Sylvie's leg and her trousers, where they had been cut open. Although he was careful not to disturb the gash on Sylvie's thigh, she winced as his fingers brushed the open wound, and she reflexively grabbed onto Loïc tightly.

"Sorry," Loïc said, his focus on the task in front of him. Using his knife, he cut away a few strips of fabric from her pants, leaving the top of Sylvie's thigh exposed. There was a lot of blood, and the sight sent another wave of pain up Sylvie's leg and into her abdomen. She gripped Loïc tighter.

"Sorry," Loïc apologized again. I'm going to tie this up, and then I need to get some supplies from the barracks to fix this for you."

"Wait," Sylvie said, her voice shaking, "don't leave!"

"I will be right back, I promise," Loïc replied, his eyes full of empathy. "Here, I'll leave you my familiar."

A shimmering dragon appeared and circled about the stall.

"Watch over her while I'm gone," Loïc instructed. The dragon obediently took its place beside Sylvie, its head held high.

Loïc ripped a long strip of cloth from the hem of his tunic and tied it snugly around Sylvie's thigh. Sylvie let out a barely muffled cry at the pressure on her damaged leg.

"I'm sorry," Loïc repeated. "I will be back before you know it." With that, he stood quickly and ran out of the stall.

Sylvie clenched her teeth and breathed sharply through them in short breaths as her leg continued to send daggers up from the cut. Already, Sylvie could hear Loïc racing back towards the stall. His familiar gazed at her with concern.

"I'm back," he said briefly as he took his place beside her on the floor. He had several supplies with him.

"This is going to sting a bit," he said, pulling a bottle of clear liquid out of a pile of clean white cloth.

Without any further warning, Loïc untied Sylvie's leg and poured the fluid out over Sylvie's wound. To her, it felt like he had just set her leg on fire.

Sylvie let out a scream as her muscles tensed involuntarily in response to the pain. She dug her nails into Loïc and heard him wince.

"Sorry," he said again. "I had to clean it."

Loïc took the clean cloth and gently dabbed away the blood as best he could. The wound was still bleeding profusely.

"Try to hold still as best you can for this next part," Loïc requested.

From his supplies, Loïc drew what looked like an iridescent fishtail.

"Tail of pascana," Loïc said as he lined the tail up with Sylvie's cut. In a smooth motion, Loïc placed the tail over the length of Sylvie's wound.

As she watched, the tail began to fuse with her skin, starting with the tail's outside edges. Steadily, the tail took on the appearance of Sylvie's skin. After just a few seconds, the surface of her skin was clean and unbroken, as if she had never been cut at all. She could barely believe her own eyes.

Loïc placed his hand gently on Sylvie's miraculously healed skin, his fingers barely touching her leg. Satisfied that the wound was healed, Loïc sat back and let his shoulders sag while releasing a heavy sigh. He looked at Sylvie.

"I am so sorry," he said again.

Sylvie took a deep breath and wiped the tears from her eyes. She smiled at Loïc.

"It's ok. Apparently, you're a medic as well as a soldier," she joked.

"I'm no medic," Loïc answered, shaking his head, "and you shouldn't have needed one here. I'm such a fool."

Sylvie took Loïc's hand. "It wasn't your fault," she consoled him, "if anything, I should have held onto my sword a little better."

Loïc shook his head. "No. I pushed you too far, and I should have held back. I'm the one that sent that sword onto your leg."

"It doesn't matter at this point," Sylvie replied. "Thanks to you, my leg looks as good as new."

They both looked at Sylvie's leg, which looked utterly unblemished.

Sylvie smiled. "My pants, on the other hand... you'll owe me a new pair."

Loïc forced a smile, but Sylvie could see he still felt entirely responsible for what had happened.

"It's the least I could do," Loïc answered, "but the staff will have as many pairs for you as you could ever need. I'm really sorry."

"Enough of that," Sylvie reproached, "it's behind us now, and it wasn't your fault. If you feel like you need to make it up to me, you can tell me we're done for the day."

Sylvie's comment drew a sliver of a smile from Loïc.

"Yeah," he mumbled, "we're done for today."

He stood and put out his hand to help Sylvie up. She took it and stood, keeping her left foot off the ground. Sylvie went to take a step, but a sharp pain from her now invisible wound made her leg buckle, and she fell right into Loïc. She found herself cradled in his arms, her face awkwardly in his chest.

"Careful, vivillèn," Loïc said.

Sylvie gaze shifted immediately from his chest to his face. "You can't keep calling me that."

"Why not?"

"You know full well why. Your noble obligation to Gaëtan. If you intend to go through with it—well, for Margot's sake..." Sylvie's voice trailed off.

"...and for mine..." she whispered.

He took a deep breath and let go of her. For a while, he said nothing.

*More silence*, Sylvie thought. She could hardly take it.

"I should've warned you. The pascana doesn't get rid of the pain from the wound; it just creates a new skin over the top of the gash. You'll feel it in your leg for at least a few days."

Sylvie straightened herself and nodded. Why wouldn't he say something?

"I'll keep that in mind. Thanks for catching me."

"If only I could," he replied with a whisper. Sylvie watched his hands as he picked up his bag of medicines and remedies.

Sylvie's heart burned in her chest.

"Then catch me if that's what you want!" She blurted out. "You seem so concerned about what Gaëtan wants. What about what you want? What about what *I* want?"

Loïc's eyes betrayed a deep internal struggle.

"I know what I want," he said finally. "But what is right?"

"Can't what you want also be right?"

He sighed.

"I don't know."

With that, he held the stall door open, and she walked back towards the palace.

Sylvie gazed over her left shoulder back at Loïc, who was still visibly struggling with a choice he didn't know how to make.

*If Margot can receive the ability, then maybe...just maybe...*

# XXXIII

## The Wishes of Tradition

I t was the morning of the winter wish ceremony, and Sylvie was awake and focused. She had arisen early, dressed for the day, and reviewed a few of her notes on the winter wishes, which she had been studying intently since Beyern had come to the palace a couple of days prior. She replayed in her mind the technique for the granting of wishes that Beyern had demonstrated.

Sylvie wasn't reciting for her own wish. She had made up her mind: she would offer to grant a wish to Nadine—the wish to receive the ability to channel éthéra. Based on her research, Beyern's caution that the Winter Verdélia did not grant power seemed distinguishable from what she was trying to accomplish. Additionally, she knew the Firstborn had a significantly larger reservoir of éthéra to draw from than ordinary seasonal Verdélia. She hoped this would allow her more flexibility in what wishes she could grant.

Then, there was the matter of the possibility that the exercise could kill her. Sylvie had not found anything additional on that point and had been unable to ascertain precisely what had gone wrong the last time a Winter Verdélia had attempted to grant an imp's wish. From her reading, she learned that even a Verdélia's wish could kill the grantor, depending on its magnitude. There was no way to know for certain that it was the fact that the wisher had been an imp that had led to the Winter Verdélia's death. She had made some vague but related inquiries with Sir Reynard, and based on his answers, she was satisfied that her plan was safe enough. At least, she certainly hoped so.

In any event, Sylvie was confident that this was what Ancelin had meant when they had spoken about the matter. She couldn't explain it, but she was sure that if Nadine wished for the ability to harness éthéra, Sylvie could grant it.

Nadine's familiar knock sounded at the door.

"Come in," Sylvie called without hesitation.

Nadine stepped inside.

"Oh," she said, seeing Sylvie up and ready, "I guess you don't need me this morning."

"I do," Sylvie said. "Come, have a seat."

Nadine looked at Sylvie with an air of curiosity and apprehension, but she obediently sat beside Sylvie on a small day bed.

"Before I say anything, I want you to know that you are free to refuse my request," Sylvie told Nadine.

Nadine nodded in acknowledgment.

"Alright," Sylvie said, sitting up straight and taking a deep breath, "I'd like to grant you a wish today."

Nadine seemed to deflate in front of Sylvie.

*Not this again*, Sylvie could hear Nadine think.

"I know, I know," Sylvie said quickly, "but please hear me out."

"But Sylvie, it's against Verdélian law," Nadine protested.

"On that point," Sylvie rebutted, "it technically is not—though I'm not a lawyer. The law prohibits *Winter Verdélia* from granting imps' wishes. It says nothing of Firstborn."

"That...is a very fine line," Nadine mumbled.

"Perhaps," Sylvie said, continuing with her explanation. "Also, before you tell me that you don't want to try this, listen to this: I confirmed with Ancelin that Zaria's handmaiden from that famous painting—her name was Amandine—she was, in fact, an imp *and* that the bird in the painting was her familiar. In other words, an imp *can* receive the ability to manipulate éthéra. It's been done before."

Nadine was intrigued. She straightened in her chair and looked Sylvie in the face.

"Are you sure?" Nadine asked.

"Yes," Sylvie replied, "Ancelin wouldn't lie to me."

Nadine sat pondering for a moment.

"So you want me to wish for the ability to manipulate éthéra, from you?" Nadine asked.

Sylvie nodded. "Yes."

Nadine considered the idea at length before speaking again.

"Can I think about it?" She asked.

Sylvie let out a short sigh. There wasn't much time to debate this.

"Yes," Sylvie replied, "but I need your answer after breakfast. I'm meeting with Beyern and the other Firstborn later for the formal winter wishes ceremony, and I don't want to miss the opportunity to grant your wish if you choose to make one."

"Thank you," Nadine said with a bow, "I will have my answer when you finish breakfast."

Sylvie sat through breakfast as if in a daydream, her mind consumed by the anticipation of Nadine's decision. The more she thought about it, the more convinced she was that this was the answer. She desperately wanted to prove that this was possible—that imps could receive the gift of éthéra manipulation. She barely noticed as the other Firstborn arrived and was almost too distracted to return Loïc's smile and greeting.

As breakfast drew to a close, Nadine walked into the dining hall. Sylvie sat up, looking straight at her. Nadine made her way over to Sylvie.

*I'll do it*, Sylvie heard Nadine think, *though I hope she'll forgive me*.

Nadine leaned in close beside Sylvie's face.

"I'll do it," she whispered.

"Wonderful," Sylvie said in a hushed tone full of excitement, "let's head back to my suite immediately."

Sylvie stood and, with Nadine, made her way hurriedly away from the breakfast table.

Back in her suite, Sylvie turned to Nadine.

"I'm so glad you decided to accept," Sylvie said. "Here, take my arms."

Sylvie extended her arms, imitating what Beyern had shown her a few days prior.

"Your hands go on my forearms," Sylvie explained as Nadine wrapped her fingers around her wrists.

Their arms firmly interlocked, Sylvie was bursting with anticipation.

"I'm ready," Sylvie said, "you may make your wish."

Nadine looked at Sylvie briefly, then took a deep breath as she looked down at her feet.

"I wish," Nadine began. She paused, and Sylvie gripped her tighter as if to prevent her from rethinking her decision. Sylvie could feel a channel of éthéra opening as Nadine began her wish.

"I wish to know who my parents are."

Sylvie looked at Nadine in shock. Already, she could feel éthéra flowing from her as the wish began to take form. Nadine looked back with a mixed look of guilt and hope.

Sylvie's mind raced. She could break her bond to Nadine and forfeit the wish. They could try again.

Looking at Nadine, Sylvie made up her mind. She held on to Nadine as a vision materialized.

Sylvie and Nadine found themselves in a courtyard. They looked to be in the Summer District, but something was wrong. All around them were the sights and sounds of battle. The vision was hazy as if Sylvie was looking through a lightly frosted window.

There, in the center of the vision, was a young couple. The woman clutched a simple clay vase, a single sprout growing from the black dirt within. Her husband was struggling against several shadowy foes, ferociously trying to prevent them from reaching the woman and her treasure. Sylvie could see that his struggle was hopeless—there were too many foes. They overpowered the man and overtook the woman, from whom they violently pried the vase before leaving her prone on the cobblestones.

The woman cried out in agony. After a few moments, her husband, badly injured, made his way over to her and wrapped his bruised and battered arms around her, trying as he might to console her. He, too, wept.

Sylvie could feel the vision waning.

*Not yet*, she thought, and she maintained her grip on Nadine's arms and willed the vision to continue.

The vision rippled, and Sylvie found herself beside Nadine in the Autumn District. The couple worked in their front garden outside a humble home as two children played in the yard. The weather was pleasant, and the couple smiled. Beneath their happiness, an unfathomable sadness could be sensed.

Suddenly, the vision began receding quickly. Before she realized what was happening, Sylvie watched as the world started to spin before fading to black.

࿊

"Miss Sylvie!" Nadine said through heaving breaths, "Oh, what have I done?"

Sylvie's eyes opened, and she saw Nadine's distraught face streaked in tears, looking down at her.

Nadine's eyes lit up at the sight of Sylvie's open eyes.

"Oh, thank Solaidi!" Nadine cried. "I thought I had killed you!"

Sylvie tried to get her bearings. She was lying on the floor of her suite.

"What happened?" Sylvie asked.

"You did it. You granted my wish," Nadine said, "and then you fainted. I thought you were dead!"

The wish. Nadine's wish. It was all coming back to her now.

"Why...," Sylvie began before stopping herself. Nadine had her reasons. Still, Sylvie felt cheated—Nadine had failed to honor what Sylvie considered Nadine's end of the bargain.

"I needed to know," Nadine replied, her head hanging low to avoid Sylvie's gaze. "I'm sorry. I know it wasn't what you wanted from me."

*I'll surely lose my place at the palace for this*, Nadine thought. *But now I can find my parents. I have to find them. They did not abandon me. They wanted me.*

The tender feelings in Nadine's mind softened Sylvie's demeanor.

"It's alright," Sylvie consoled Nadine. "I'm glad you got your wish. I'll send you with a couple of the palace guards to help you find that house."

Nadine looked up in shock.

"I...you will?" Nadine asked incredulously.

Sylvie nodded, "Yes."

She looked at her desk and then back at Nadine. "Here, help me up, please."

Nadine stood quickly and gave Sylvie her outstretched hand. Sylvie took it and got to her feet, wincing as her healing leg protested against the weight she was putting on it.

Sylvie reached her desk and pulled out a fresh piece of paper. She grabbed her quill and, dipping it into a pot of ink, scribbled out a quick note for Alfric. She signed and sealed it and handed it to Nadine.

"Take that to Alfric," Sylvie instructed. "He'll assign you an escort, and you'll find your family. Do you remember what the house looked like?"

Nadine nodded excitedly, an immense smile on her face. Sylvie saw a replica of the little house shown in the vision inside Nadine's mind. She had captured every detail.

Unexpectedly, Nadine embraced Sylvie forcefully.

"Oh!" Sylvie said, returning Nadine's hug.

"Thank you," Nadine said, maintaining her grip on Sylvie. "No one has ever given me anything like this. I won't forget it."

Sylvie smiled and was glad she had the presence of mind to grant Nadine's wish despite it not being the wish Sylvie had wanted for her.

"Go now," Sylvie said softly, "your family is out there."

Nadine stood, wiped a tear from her eye, and rushed from Sylvie's suite at a dead run.

As she opened the door, Nadine nearly barreled into Loïc.

"Woah!" Loïc called as he stepped back quickly.

"I'm so sorry, Master Loïc!" Nadine exclaimed, turning to face him briefly before continuing down the hall.

Loïc walked into Sylvie's suite, his eyes following Nadine for another second. He turned to Sylvie, his face puzzled.

"What was that about?" He asked. Loïc's eyes narrowed.

"Are you alright?" He asked. "Your eyes are completely bloodshot. You don't look so good." He approached Sylvie and put the back of his hand against her forehead.

Sylvie brushed Loïc's hand aside.

"I'm not sick," she assured him, "but thanks for telling me I look horrible."

Loïc tilted his head and gave Sylvie an exasperated look. "That's not what I meant," he said defensively. "Are you going to tell me what happened? Why was Nadine running out of here like a killer was after her?"

Sylvie considered her options. She figured there was no point lying about what had happened, at least not to Loïc.

"Nadine's going to find her family," Sylvie said calmly.

Loïc leaned back in surprise.

"How is that possible?" Loïc asked. "She's an imp. No one knows who her parents are."

"She knows, and so do I. She wished for it, and I granted it." Sylvie spoke matter-of-factly.

Loïc's eyes grew wide.

"You did *what*?" He asked incredulously.

"I granted Nadine a wish," Sylvie repeated.

Sylvie could see Loïc processing the news. After a few moments, Loïc sat straight, his face composed and calm.

"I would tell you that you're completely reckless, but at this point, what's done is done, and, contrary to popular belief, it didn't kill you," Loïc said.

"Way to *not* tell me," Sylvie said sarcastically.

Loïc smirked, and then his face regained its serious demeanor.

"That aside," he said, "it worked? You granted Nadine a wish?"

"I did," Sylvie nodded.

Loïc put his chin in his hand, his eyes looking down through Sylvie as he considered the implications of what Sylvie had done.

"This is...," he began, "this changes a lot of things. Decidedly, that has been the theme of your arrival in Verdélys."

"I suppose...," Sylvie replied. Where Loïc saw a success, Sylvie still saw a failure. Nadine had not wished for, nor gained, the ability to channel éthéra.

"You suppose?" Loïc questioned. "What gave you the idea to try it anyway, granting Nadine a wish?"

And there was the big question: Should she tell Loïc? She had also told Margot and Nadine. Still, things had not gone as planned so far.

"I...," Sylvie began, "I was hoping Nadine would wish for something else."

Loïc gave Sylvie a querying look that begged for an explanation.

"I wanted her to wish for the ability to harness éthéra," Sylvie admitted with a sigh.

Loïc again looked taken aback.

"You've lost me," Loïc said. "Why on earth would you want that? Imps can't manipulate éthéra. That's power. That's not a wish anyone could grant."

"I wouldn't be so sure," Sylvie countered. "When Ancelin was here, I asked him about Zaria and her handmaiden—you know, from the painting."

Loïc nodded in acknowledgment. "But what does that have to do with Nadine's wish?" He asked.

Sylvie explained herself as best as she could through ragged breaths.

Loïc crossed his arms over his broad chest, one hand held up to his mouth as he considered what Sylvie had revealed.

After several moments of silence, Sylvie spoke.

"I had originally talked to Margot about this," she explained. "Margot didn't want to be seen as an experiment—which I understand. I also think she didn't want to face the disappointment if it didn't work, and to be fair, the odds weren't—aren't—in my favor. So I worked with Nadine instead."

Loïc's eyes were focused. Sylvie could see Loïc's mind racing with the possibilities of Sylvie's discovery.

"Margot," he whispered through his closed fist. He looked at Sylvie. "Did she know you would try to grant Nadine a wish?" He asked.

Sylvie shook her head. "No."

"Right," Loïc said suddenly, rising to his feet. "We need to go. I actually came up here to let you know that Beyern is here for the wishing ceremony. We've kept him waiting too long, as is. Fix your hair and see what you can do about getting some color into your face. We don't want Beyern suspecting anything is amiss."

Under other circumstances, Sylvie might have been hurt by Loïc's blunt comment, but she knew he meant no harm. He was certainly right that they didn't need to give Beyern any additional reasons to see weakness among the Firstborn.

Loïc patiently waited as Sylvie sculpted her hair back into place and pinched her cheeks to get some color into her face. She put a dash of blush-colored powder onto a brush and powdered her face. Her mind was still preoccupied with Nadine's wish. Her quest was still incomplete, and at this point, she had a hard time seeing how she would reach her ends.

Sylvie put the brush she was using to powder her face back in its place.

"I'm ready," Sylvie told Loïc.

"You look wonderful," Loïc said with a smile. "Let's go see Beyern." Sylvie could see that his mind was still elsewhere, scheming, planning.

Loïc and Sylvie entered the throne room arm in arm. Gaëtan was talking to Beyern at the far side of the room. Margot was seated regally on the dais, gazing off towards the ceilings as if detached fully from her surroundings.

"Sorry to keep you waiting," Loïc called as they entered, "High Councilman Beyern, welcome."

"Welcome, Master Loïc and Miss Sylvie," Beyern replied with a short bow.

Before anyone could speak, Loïc continued.

"Let's begin, shall we?" He proposed.

Beyern, Gaëtan, and Margot seemed taken aback by Loïc's urgency.

"I...," Beyern replied, "I suppose there's no reason why not. Who will wish first?"

"I will," Gaëtan said, approaching Beyern.

The Firstborn had previously discussed their wishes. They would wish for information about Belthégor and Rhys and the ills befalling Verdélys and the surrounding lands.

Gaëtan and Beyern grasped arms. Without hesitating, Gaëtan spoke his wish.

"I wish to know if Belthégor is a disciple of Rhys," he said.

A dark cloud fell over Beyern's face as he heard Gaëtan's wish. However, he did not release his grip, and after a few moments, Gaëtan looked at the other Firstborn.

"It's as we feared," Gaëtan said somberly.

"These imp rebels are involved with Rhys? How can that be?" Beyern asked in consternation.

"It would appear so," Loïc confirmed, approaching Beyern. "My turn, High Councilman."

Beyern visibly wanted more answers, but Loïc imposed himself and took Beyern by the arms.

"I wish," he began, "to know the target of Belthégor's next attack."

Another couple of seconds passed, and Loïc released his grip on Beyern.

"It's the Keystone," Loïc told the others.

The ambiance in the room grew cold.

"We must warn the Council at once!" Beyern exclaimed.

"We will," Gaëtan assured Beyern. "First, please be so kind as to grant Sylvie's wish."

Sylvie approached Beyern, slightly intimidated by his agitated state. Beyern took her arms, and Sylvie voiced her wish.

"I wish to know where Belthégor and his followers reside," she said.

Sylvie was swept into a vision, just as she had been when she had granted Nadine's wish. At first, she saw only blackness, but then shapes began to materialize, though their contours were vague, as if seen through a mist or a haze. Leafless trees, their branches and trunks gnarled and twisted, grasped at the fog as they grew from the stony ground. There, behind the trees, a larger shape took form. Emerging from the shadowy mist, a once-formidable fortress emerged. The stones comprising its walls were roughly hewn but enormous, and the entire structure was much larger than the Verdélian palace. The fortress had survived the onslaught of time but had not emerged unscathed as its walls were split and cracked in various places, and battlements that had once been imposing were now crumbling. A distinctive keep rose from behind the walls, and its sight inexplicably filled Sylvie with dread. With that, the vision faded, and Sylvie returned to the throne room.

"Well?" Loïc asked Sylvie.

"I...I'm not sure," Sylvie said.

"What did you see?" Loïc pressed.

"It was a fortress of some kind, a dark place, stony and dead. It looked very old and felt like death. I didn't recognize it."

Loïc and Gaëtan looked at each other.

"The Undying Mountain?" Loïc asked.

Beyern scoffed.

"There is no such place. That is a fool's tale for superstitious children. Something went amiss with the wish," Beyern insisted.

"That has never happened before," Gaëtan countered. Beyern did not address Gaëtan's comment. Instead, he addressed all of the Firstborn.

"These matters need to be addressed immediately," Beyern fumed. "You told me you would keep me apprised of all developments involving this imp rebellion. There is much you have impudently decided to keep to yourselves."

"You're right, of course," Gaëtan replied. "And we are prepared to discuss them with you immediately. Please, sit." Gaëtan gestured to a seat in the gallery of the throne room.

Beyern was caught off guard by Gaëtan's complaisance and took his seat. Gaëtan sat beside him and waved a nearby imp carrying a tray of tall fluted glasses into the room.

"Please," Gaëtan continued, "have a drink to refresh yourself after granting these wishes. Then we will answer any question you have."

"Thank you," Beyern said, maintaining his stern demeanor but taking the proffered glass. He took a long draught, then turned to Gaëtan.

"First, I need to know what you evidently know about how Rhys is involved with all of this," Beyern demanded.

"Quite so," Gaëtan said slowly, eyeing Beyern intently.

Sylvie watched Beyern and saw his brow fluctuate, his lids flutter in a momentary spasm, and his stony facade seem to crack.

"Thank you, High Councilman, for your service here today," Gaëtan said suddenly in an overly accentuated tone.

Beyern seemed confused and mumbled, "thank you, Master Gaëtan."

"Yes, your help is truly invaluable," Gaëtan continued, standing and motioning to Beyern to do the same. "However, we hate to keep you from your family. Please, enjoy the rest of your day with them, and give them our well wishes."

Beyern nodded obligingly. "I will, thank you," he said. He turned and walked out of the throne room.

"Very well executed, my friend," Loïc said, placing a hand on Gaëtan's shoulder.

"Thank you," Gaëtan said with a smug smile.

"What just happened?" Sylvie asked.

Gaëtan kept his eyes on the now-closed throne room doors before turning to Sylvie.

"Bliert berries," he replied. "They cause forgetfulness, beginning with the most recent memories. He only needed a sip of this," Gaëtan said, holding up Beyern's glass, "to forget the better part of the entire morning."

Sylvie's mouth fell open.

"It was Loïc's idea," Gaëtan said defensively.

"Under normal circumstances, I wouldn't be too proud of myself," Loïc said, "but we couldn't afford to have Beyern setting off a panic among the Council that would inevitably spread to the rest of Verdélys. At the same time, we needed the information we wished for. You're the source of the plan, actually, what with your suspicions of our advisors and all. Then, when Beyern insisted we rely on our advisors more, well...I drew my own conclusions and decided it was probably best to keep Beyern in the dark."

Gaëtan just shrugged in agreement.

"Right," Gaëtan said after a moment, "shall we discuss Belthégor, the Keystone, and the Undying Mountain?"

"What's there to discuss?" Margot asked. "We already suspected Belthégor. For the Keystone, the palace guards are already on high alert—I can't even leave or enter the palace without being harassed—and for the Undying Mountain, well," she scoffed and rolled her eyes, "even assuming it exists, there's no recorded mention of its location anywhere."

Gaëtan smiled sarcastically. "Thank you, Margot, for that very constructive summary," he said.

"You're welcome, sir," Margot replied with an excessively formal curtsy.

"If you two are finished flirting," Loïc cut in, "there's something else I think we should all discuss in the study."

Margot gave Loïc a haughty look in response to his comment and turned her nose up in the air.

"Oh?" Gaëtan said curiously, "Very well, I suppose. Let's go then."

The four Firstborn made their way to the study. As Loïc locked the door behind them, Margot settled in one of the oversized armchairs beside the fireplace. Gaëtan took the seat beside her. Loïc and Sylvie sat on the couch.

Gaëtan looked at Loïc expectantly. Margot gazed into the fire in the fireplace, apparently uninterested in whatever Loïc had to say. Sylvie fidgeted with her hands nervously.

"Sylvie has just made a discovery I think we should all be aware of," Loïc said plainly, cutting right to the quick of the matter.

Gaëtan raised an eyebrow. Suddenly, Margot was paying attention. She looked at Sylvie with large, hopeful eyes.

"This morning," Loïc continued, "Sylvie successfully granted Nadine, her imp servant, a wish."

Gaëtan looked at Sylvie wide-eyed, then back to Loïc. Margot's eyes shone with hope, but her face otherwise remained stony as ever.

"Is this true?" Gaëtan asked Sylvie.

"It is," she replied, uncomfortable at the center of all of the attention.

"That is indeed significant news," Gaëtan said, sitting back in his chair. His eyes stared aimlessly ahead of him as he lost himself in his thoughts.

After a moment of silence, Margot spoke.

"Did it work?" She asked, her question directed at Sylvie.

Gaëtan turned to Margot, "She just said she granted the wish."

Margot ignored Gaëtan and kept her gaze fixed on Sylvie.

Sylvie drew a breath before responding.

"No," she said. She saw Margot's hope crumble and stony walls go up in their place.

"I see," is all Margot said.

"But that's because Nadine wished for something else," Sylvie continued.

Sylvie's words seemed to save the last flicker of hope in Margot's countenance.

"Clearly, there's something I'm missing here," Gaëtan voiced.

Loïc turned to Sylvie. "For Gaëtan's sake, some background wouldn't be a bad idea. It should come from you."

Sylvie wished Loïc would explain, but he was probably right. She looked at Gaëtan, who was starving for information. Margot, too, was on the edge of her seat. Sylvie sighed.

"Several weeks ago," she began, "I became curious about the possibility of imps receiving the ability to manipulate éthéra."

Gaëtan expressed surprise at Sylvie's statement but said nothing.

"I thought that if I could discover a way to help the imps harness éthéra, we could heal the contention and contempt between imps and Verdélia. I thought we might be able to avoid fighting, death...I thought maybe we could heal Verdélys."

The other Firstborn listened intently. The pride showing on Loïc's face pushed Sylvie on.

Sylvie explained everything that she had whispered to Nadine and expressed to Loïc. She revealed her secret training sessions with Nadine, everything about Zaria's handmaiden, and her conversation with Ancelin.

Gaëtan's and Margot's eyes widened simultaneously, and both gasped audibly. For the first time Sylvie could remember, Margot wore all her emotions on her face; the perfect porcelain mask dissipated under the hope of Sylvie's words.

"Did Ancelin tell you how it had been done?" Gaëtan asked eagerly.

"You know Ancelin," Sylvie sighed, "so not exactly. What he did say was that the ability had been received as a 'gift,' like 'all things that are received after they are wished for.' At first I didn't understand, until we met to talk about the winter wish ceremony with Beyern a couple days ago. Then it just hit me—I knew that was the answer."

"But you don't know, do you?" Margot contested.

"Well...no," Sylvie admitted.

Loïc, who had been quiet up to now, interrupted.

"We can't dismiss this," he said, looking at Sylvie and Margot. "For as long as we can recall, the idea that an imp could have their wish granted was seen as impossible. Sylvie just proved otherwise. Nadine's particular wish may not have given us the answer to Sylvie's specific question, but the fact her wish was granted makes me believe that what Sylvie is talking about is possible."

Margot seemed to waiver, but Sylvie could see her receding into unbelief.

Gaëtan spoke.

"I agree," he said. Margot seemed slightly taken aback, and her doubts weakened momentarily. "I think you've interpreted Ancelin's answer correctly," he said.

"I agree," Loïc said.

Sylvie had her eyes on her lap.

"I thought so too," she said, "and I was ready to prove it...but I guess fate had other plans."

There was silence, then Loïc spoke.

"Perhaps not," he said. "Margot...," he began.

Margot shook her head and shut her eyes.

"No," she stammered, her voice shaking. "I told Sylvie already that I won't be the subject of this experiment. I've accepted what I am, unpleasant as it may be for me and everybody else who expects me to be what I'm not."

Loïc nodded understandingly. Before he could respond, Gaëtan addressed Margot.

"No one here expects you to be anything other than who you are," he said softly, soothingly. "You are who you are, and you are a Firstborn, same as us. That won't change whether you make this wish or not, and it isn't dependent on the result either."

Margot seemed to ease at Gaëtan's words, but her face was still tightened in anxiety. She looked at Sylvie, her eyes vulnerable and brimming with tears.

"Do you honestly believe this will work?" She asked.

Sylvie felt the weight of Margot's question come down on her like a mountain. Now, a delicate trust was being offered to her.

"I believe it will," Sylvie said, steadfastly returning Margot's gaze.

There was silence for several minutes, save for the crackling of the fire. Margot had folded her hands on her lap and was staring at them as if in a daydream. All eyes were on her.

At last, Margot looked up as she straightened herself in her chair.

"I will make a wish," she whispered, "if Gaëtan will agree to grant it."

Sylvie could barely contain herself, though she now found herself praying Margot's wish would be granted, not for her own sake, but for Margot's.

"I would be honored," Gaëtan said solemnly. His eyes lit up, and he watched her carefully. For a moment, Sylvie realized that perhaps in his eyes, she was seeing adoration—love, even.

Margot's face showed just the hint of a smile.

"Thank you," she said, "let's get this over with then, shall we?"

Sylvie and Loïc looked at each other and chuckled at Margot's familiar personality resurfacing.

Gaëtan presented his arms to Margot, who took them gently. Gaëtan looked at Margot warmly, a reassuring smile on his lips.

"I am ready," he said, "you may make your wish."

Margot looked down at her and Gaëtan's interlocking arms, closed her eyes, and drew a deep breath.

"I wish..."

# XXXIV

## *A Wish of Revolution*

"I wish for the ability to harness éthéra," Margot breathed hopefully.

There was a moment of stillness, and Margot's eyes widened in response to something intangible. Gaëtan, too, looked down at their clasped arms as if watching some invisible event.

Soon, Gaëtan's breathing began to grow heavier. Sylvie noticed his grip on Margot's arms had tightened as the veins in his hands and forearms grew more and more pronounced.

"It's killing you," Margot gasped as she felt Gaëtan's strain. "Let go, release the wish!"

"It's not," Gaëtan grunted, "Don't let go. Loïc," Gaëtan called, "don't let her release the wish."

Loïc stepped up quickly and placed his hands firmly on Margot's, keeping them locked onto Gaëtan's arms.

"No!" Margot insisted, "You're going to kill him! Let me go!"

Margot tried to stand, scrambling in vain to escape Loïc's grasp.

Sylvie's heart hammered inside her as she watched the scene unfold before her. *Please*, she prayed.

Margot began to cry as Gaëtan seemed to grow weaker and weaker. Loïc's face showed fear as he looked at Gaëtan.

"Gaëtan," Loïc said in a steady voice that belied his facial expression, "are you alright?"

Gaëtan only nodded, but his appearance suggested otherwise.

Margot had fallen back into her chair as she cried, her head on her arms and Gaëtan's hands, her copper hair falling in waves that concealed her face.

Gaëtan opened his eyes and looked ready to fall. Loïc quickly released his grip, and as Margot instinctively withdrew her arms beneath her forest of hair, he knelt beside Gaëtan, holding him steady in his chair.

Loïc looked at Sylvie, the same question etched on his face that was now racing through Sylvie's mind.

*Did it work?*

Margot groaned loudly in her chair.

"It's alright, Margot," Loïc said, "Gaëtan is fine."

Margot seemed not to hear Loïc as she gripped the sides of her head tightly with her fingers, groaning loudly as if in pain.

"It's so loud," Margot said through gritted teeth.

Loïc eased Gaëtan back into his seat and looked at Sylvie quizzically. Sylvie shrugged in response. The palace was quiet, save for the soft sounds of the fire.

Suddenly, Margot was clawing at her skin and clothes.

"What's on me?" She gasped. "And why can't I see? It's so bright!"

Loïc hurriedly grabbed Margot's hands as she seemed ready to cut into her skin.

"Margot," he said gently but firmly, "Margot," he repeated as she fought against his grasp.

Margot only let out a long, drawn-out moan in response.

"Margot," Loïc said again, "what's happening?"

"There's too much...," Margot grunted.

"Too much what?" Loïc asked.

Margot continued to squirm in her chair.

"Everything," she replied shakily.

Loïc turned to Sylvie.

"Sylvie, clear the couch," he instructed.

Sylvie jumped up and propped several pillows against the sofa's arm. Loïc lifted Margot, who continued to groan and writhe, and gently placed her down on the couch. He draped one of the nearby decorative blankets over her. Then he stood and turned to Sylvie.

"What's happening?" He asked. His tone was not accusatory but firm.

Sylvie shrugged her shoulders and raised her hands in symbolic innocence.

"I...," she stammered, guilt overcoming her. "I don't know. Nothing like this happened with Nadine..." Her voice trailed off, then broke.

Loïc surveyed the situation, then summoned his familiar. The ethereal dragon roared silently as it stretched its wings.

"Go find Antoine and tell him he's needed at the palace immediately. Tell him to bring as many medical supplies as he can with him. And on your way out, inform Alfric that he is to let Antoine in without delay. Convey to both that this is strictly confidential and not to be discussed with anyone." Loïc's instructions received, the familiar almost instantly vanished from sight as it flew to complete its task.

Gaëtan shifted in his chair.

"How's Margot?" He asked in a faded voice. "Did it work?"

Loïc turned to Gaëtan quickly and encouraged him back into his seat.

"We don't know if it worked yet," Loïc said, "Don't worry about Margot. Get some rest."

Gaëtan tried to sit up, but whether for lack of strength or due to Loïc's insistence, he ultimately fell back against the tall back of his seat. His eyes closed again.

Over by Margot, Sylvie was stroking Margot's hair gently, doing what came naturally to try to ease Margot's obvious discomfort. If Margot was aware of Sylvie's presence, it was not apparent to Sylvie. Margot continued to groan as she shifted this way and that on the couch, clutching at herself as if trying to rid herself of an unseen parasite.

Loïc knelt beside Sylvie.

"Gaëtan's going to be fine," he informed her. "It took a lot out of him, but he should return to himself once he's had the time to rest. Margot, on the other hand..."

He looked at Margot and then at Sylvie.

"I have no idea what is going on. We'll have to wait for Antoine."

They waited for what felt like a lifetime, crouched on the floor beside Margot, who continued to squirm and moan, victim of an unknown ailment.

Finally, Sylvie heard steps on the other side of the door. Loïc stood quickly and rushed to the study entry, unlocking the doors. Before Antoine could knock, Loïc opened the door and pulled him inside.

"Antoine," Loïc said, "thank you for coming on such short notice."

"Of course," Antoine said, "what's going on?"

Loïc looked at Sylvie, who was now standing beside the couch where Margot lay. She looked back at Loïc and to Antoine desperately.

"We don't know," Loïc admitted, turning back to Antoine. "Here, come see." Loïc started back toward the sitting area in front of the fireplace and then turned back to Antoine.

"This," Loïc said, gesturing to the scene around them, "must be kept in absolute confidence at all costs. Until this gets resolved, you cannot mention this to anyone, not even Adelais."

Antoine looked at Loïc suspiciously.

"Adelais is my wife. I don't keep anything from her," he protested.

"This will have to be the exception, for now at least. Can you do that?" Loïc replied.

Antoine studied Loïc's expression momentarily, then looked at Sylvie and Margot's shrouded figure on the couch.

"Fine, alright," Antoine said. "Now, tell me why you summoned me here."

Loïc walked over to Sylvie and motioned to Margot.

"You know Margot, one of the Firstborn," Loïc said to Antoine.

"Yes," Antoine said, kneeling beside her. He looked at Margot and brushed her hair out of her face, placing the back of his hand on her cheek. He made a few more observations, then turned to Loïc.

"What happened to her?" Antoine asked.

"She says she can't see due to excess brightness in her vision, that she's hearing things, and that she can feel things on or under her skin," Loïc explained. "She's effectively incapacitated and has been for probably a half hour or more at this point."

Antoine took Loïc by the shoulder.

"Whatever happened, you need to tell me now if you want answers," Antoine said forcefully.

Loïc sighed. He looked into the fire for a moment, visibly contemplating how to respond.

"Very well," he said, "Margot made a wish, and Gaëtan granted it."

Antoine looked at Loïc in shock as he released his shoulder.

"But...," he asked, "how?"

"We don't have all the details right now," Loïc said, "but it can be done. Sylvie proved it this morning when she also granted her servant a wish."

Antoine shifted his gaze to Sylvie, an expression of amazement on his face.

Loïc continued.

"The point is, Gaëtan granted Margot's wish a little over a half hour ago, and Margot has been like this ever since."

"Any similar symptoms with your servant?" Antoine asked Sylvie.

"No," Sylvie replied, shaking her head.

Antoine looked at Margot, then to Gaëtan, sleeping in his chair.

"What about him?" Antoine asked.

"Gaëtan is alright," Loïc assured him. "He just spent an extraordinary amount of éthéra granting Margot's wish. He'll recover with some rest."

Antoine looked back at Margot and knelt beside her, opening a large leather bag he had brought.

"This is way outside of my realm of expertise," Antoine said as he shuffled through the contents of his bag. "If we're going to be entirely honest, this is way outside of the realm of expertise for any living Verdélian healer," Antoine added.

He looked over his shoulder at Loïc and Sylvie.

"What did Margot wish for?" He asked.

Loïc looked at Sylvie, then back at Antoine.

"For the ability to harness éthéra," Loïc answered.

Antoine, who had returned to looking through his bag, stopped abruptly and turned back to Loïc.

"What?" He asked incredulously.

"Exactly what I just said," Loïc said somewhat impatiently.

"Why would—" Antoine began before suddenly cutting himself off.

*It's not possible...and yet...*, Sylvie heard Antoine think.

Antoine returned to his bag and pulled out a slender glass vial full of a thick liquid. He put the vial on the low table beside the fireplace and wrapped a clean piece of linen over his nose and mouth. He picked up the vial, poured a pea-shaped amount onto his index finger, and rubbed the solution onto Margot's top lip. He stoppered the vial and put it back in his bag, then carefully wiped the remnants of the medicine from his finger.

Very soon, Margot's breathing steadied, and she stopped moving.

"What did you give her?" Loïc asked.

"A basic but potent relaxant," Antoine explained as he rose. "It should let her sleep until tomorrow morning. If her symptoms persist after waking, let me know, but at that point, you may need to consider seeking advice from more experienced sources."

"So, do you know what happened?" Loïc inquired.

Antoine rested his hands on his waist as he looked down on his patient. "No," he said, "not for certain, but my guess is that your arcane ritual worked—somehow. Her symptoms suggest overstimulation of all the senses on a level I haven't seen before."

Sylvie weighed in.

"Is there any way to know for sure?" She asked Antoine.

Antoine shook his head. "Not that I'm aware of until Margot wakes," he replied.

Sylvie looked down at Margot. She seemed so calm now, though a beaded line of sweat on her brow betrayed her recent struggle. Inside Sylvie's sleeping friend lay the answer to the burning question: had she properly understood Ancelin?

Sylvie's mind faded back to the present. Antoine and Loïc discussed Margot and the contingencies if she woke early or her condition worsened.

"Thank you again for coming, Antoine," Loïc said, "and again, please do not breathe a word of this to anyone until we know more."

"Understood," Antoine replied, "though do keep me posted. This is a monumental development regardless—"

Sylvie had begun making her way towards the door and had exited before Loïc and Antoine could finish their conversation. She walked across the cold floor with her bare feet, her red dress swishing across the floor. The palace was growing dark, and Sylvie could see the sun setting out of a window she passed. She fled down the stairs to the basement and finally found peace in the quiet.

# XXXV

## Comfort in the Dark

S ylvie entered the large room dead ahead down the hall at the base of the stairs—the storeroom. The room was extremely dark, and it took Sylvie a moment to find a candle she could light. After a couple more seconds, Sylvie had successfully ignited a couple of sconces against the wall and was taking stock of her surroundings.

The storeroom was huge, and the light of the sconces combined with Sylvie's candle was not strong enough to light the ends of the room in any direction. Rows and rows of shelves stretched out into the darkness in every direction. Here, Sylvie would be able to find anything she could possibly need. Flowers in every form, preserved, dried, or otherwise, were stored in delicate glass containers on the section to her left. Stones, gems, and soil were kept in earthen pots and jars dead ahead. Fishtails, animal horns, fangs of all kinds, and other animal-based ingredients were farther down past the minerals. Cauldrons, beakers, bottles, and more were on the right.

*What were you thinking?* Sylvie scolded herself. She began rummaging through the aisles to distract herself from her thoughts.

Water as a base. *Tranquility. A good place to start.*

Frankincense. *To ease the mind.*

Amethyst. *For balance.*

*And a touch of chamomile.*

Sylvie made her way back to the aisle with all of the flowers. Chamomile was near the top.

Just then, the storeroom door opened, and a white wisp of a dragon floated inside. Loïc followed not a second later.

He looked at her for a moment.

"What are you doing?"

"I'm putting together a solution for Margot. For when she wakes up. To help her feel calm and relaxed."

Sylvie didn't look at Loïc and continued to reach for the chamomile, the rest of her ingredients tucked into her other arm. She heard Loïc approach, but she focused on the task at hand, going up on her tiptoes to try to reach the chamomile. She could barely nick the glass vial through which she could see her objective.

"Sylvie," Loïc said calmly after watching Sylvie struggle and realizing she was ignoring him.

In frustration, Sylvie jumped for the chamomile. She swiped it from its place high on the shelf but could not wrap her fingers around the vial. She watched it fall, waiting for the crash.

Instead, Sylvie saw Loïc's hand extend in a blur as he caught the chamomile in his outstretched hand. Sylvie snatched the jar quickly and made her way towards the front of the storeroom, depositing her ingredients on a nearby table.

"Water, frankincense, amethyst, and chamomile," Sylvie repeated, eyeing her finds.

She heard Loïc approach from behind, then felt his strong hand on her shoulder as he turned her to face him. His dark eyes looked deeply into hers.

"Sylvie," he repeated, "what are you doing?"

"I told you already," Sylvie replied curtly, frustration evident in her voice.

Loïc smiled ever so slightly.

"You know what I meant," he said. "Why are you upset? Margot and Gaëtan are both fine; as far as we can tell, you've uncovered a miracle. You should be proud."

Sylvie tried to jerk out of Loïc's grasp, but he held her firmly.

"We don't know they're fine," she protested. "Besides," she continued, "what if it was all for nothing? What if my true motivation was selfish all along, and it won't even change anything?"

"What are you talking about?"

Sylvie sighed.

"I thought...well, if Margot can harness éthéra now, then she should be able to bear a Verdélian child, should she not? But even so, will that change anything? And even if it does, will this whole plan have been only to satisfy my selfishness?"

Loïc released Sylvie, but she did not move.

"If you're honest with yourself, I think you'll quickly realize that your motivations were, first and foremost, the good of Verdélys as a whole."

"Perhaps at the start, but now?"

Loïc reached out and lifted Sylvie's chin so that she was looking directly at him.

"Give yourself a little credit, *mer vivillen.*"

Sylvie pushed Loïc's hand away from her face.

"Don't," she said, turning away from him and back to her ingredients.

He walked up to the side of the table next to her.

"Do you think this is a game to me? That I would say such things casually?"

"How should I know? You refuse to tell me anything! Every time I think I might get an answer from you, I get silence instead."

Sylvie's heart was racing.

Loïc placed his hand gently over Sylvie's.

"You asked me that night after dinner at my parents' house what had changed since your arrival in Verdélys."

Sylvie looked up at Loïc. He was focused intently on her.

"For the longest time, my romantic future was a matter of duty. I knew a family was important to Gaëtan, so I thought I could do right by him by marrying Margot. Because I was not emotionally attached to anyone, my heart did not protest—that is until I had the chance to get to know you."

Sylvie was barely breathing.

"Sylvie, there is only one future I want: the one with you by my side. And if that is what you want as well...well, I can only wish Gaëtan and Margot the best."

Loïc had both of her hands cradled in his. He was looking at her longingly. They held each other's gaze for several moments.

"Do you share my feelings?" Loïc asked finally.

Sylvie nodded forcefully, an uncontainable smile on her face.

"Yes, I do."

Loïc wrapped his strong arms around Sylvie, holding her close. She could feel his heartbeat and let herself drift to the rhythm of his slow, steady breathing. At that moment, everything else melted away from Sylvie's mind. She was safe. She was loved.

After a while, yet far too soon for her, Loïc released Sylvie. He placed his hands gently on either side of her face.

"Come, let's get back to the others, *mer vivillen.*"

🦌

Sylvie woke to the sound of shuffling fabric.

She and Loïc had spent the rest of the day in the study watching over Margot and Gaëtan. The time had mostly been spent in silence—the most important things had finally been said. They sat close together as the two of them admired the beauty of the fire in the hearth. At some point late into the night, Sylvie had looked up from her place nestled on Loïc's chest and noticed that he had fallen asleep, his rugged features beautifully relaxed in sleep. She had smiled, pulled Loïc's arm tighter around her shoulders, and drifted into a welcome sleep of her own.

Now, though, she awoke as something moved in the dark of the study. The fire had died down to glowing embers, and the moonless night sky was dark.

Sylvie could see Margot's silhouette, a black shape against a black background, sitting upright on the couch. Her head swiveled slowly this way and that as if disoriented.

Sylvie carefully moved Loïc's arm, anxious not to wake him. She rose and made her way quietly to Margot's side.

"Good night, Margot," she breathed almost silently as she sat beside her friend.

Margot exhaled audibly as she groaned quietly.

"I'm not so sure," Margot replied softly.

Sylvie placed her hand on Margot's back tenderly.

"Everything's still so loud," Margot complained in a whisper, "and that fire is so bright..."

Sylvie responded quietly.

"That fire is all but dead, Margot," Sylvie explained.

Margot looked at the few remaining live coals in the fire, raising her hand as if to block out an angry summer sun.

"How can that be...?" She asked aloud.

"I think," Sylvie answered, "it's because your wish was granted. I think you're recognizing the éthéra in the world around you."

Margot looked around at the shadowy study.

"Is this how you experience the world all of the time?" She murmured.

Sylvie thought for a moment.

"I suppose so, though I don't know any other way," Sylvie explained.

"There's so much...everything," Margot marveled quietly.

Sylvie smiled. Then, an idea blossomed within her.

"Would you like to try harnessing it?" Sylvie offered.

Margot hesitated.

"Now?" She asked. "I...I don't know. I'm still a bit overwhelmed by everything. Plus, I don't know how."

"We'll do something simple. I'll teach you!" Sylvie answered in a hurried whisper as she stood and made her way to her desk, careful to avoid the sleeping Gaëtan. She opened a drawer where she had left a small canvas bag full of flower seeds and another containing garden soil—leftovers from her earliest studies under Sir Reynard.

"Here," Sylvie said excitedly as she sat back down next to Margot, "open your hand."

Margot cupped her hand in front of her as instructed, and Sylvie filled Margot's palm with loam.

"What are you doing?" Margot hissed under her breath.

"Just trust me," Sylvie said with a huge smile. She pulled a small handful of seeds from her pouch and sifted through them quickly.

"Here," Sylvie said, "let's do this one." She placed one tiny seed into Margot's hands and buried it into the soil with a poke of her finger. She quickly pulled the drawstring on her pouch and placed it beside her on the couch.

"I can feel it," Margot said in quiet amazement. Sylvie thought she might squeal in delight.

"Isn't it amazing?" She agreed. "It still needs water. Here," Sylvie dipped her finger in her dinner cup and dropped a few tiny drops over where the seed was buried.

"It's ready. Feel your éthéra and channel it into that little seed," Sylvie suggested.

"How?" Margot asked.

Sylvie thought for a moment. It had always been intuitive to her.

"The best way I can describe it is like directing flowing water," Sylvie replied. "The éthéra in you is moving, alive. Guide it."

Margot gazed intently at the little mound of earth in her hand. The study was dead silent and dark, and Sylvie found herself unconsciously holding her breath.

After only a few short seconds, Sylvie saw it—a tiny sprout emerging from the dirt. Its stem poked out, bent and frail, then quickly straightened and spread forth two minuscule leaves.

Sylvie's eyes grew wide in amazement, and she suppressed a cry of excitement. She looked at Margot.

Margot stared at the little plant with the most peculiar expression on her heavily shadowed face. Her eyes glistened, unshed tears reflecting the little light in the study.

"Keep going," Sylvie encouraged.

Margot looked at Sylvie as if she had completely forgotten that Sylvie had been sitting next to her this entire time. After a moment of recognition, Margot smiled big and turned her attention back to her sprout.

Before Sylvie's eyes, the sprout grew into a small plant, putting out several more leaves. Then, a bud appeared. Margot's face showed pleased surprise, and she continued her efforts.

In the dark night of the palace study, a single beautiful bloom appeared in the palm of Margot's hands, the shadows unable to conceal its vibrant violet hue. Margot turned to Sylvie excitedly, her lips upturned into a proud smile.

"Beautiful," came Gaëtan's voice from behind Margot.

Margot turned swiftly, and Sylvie looked over Margot's shoulder to Gaëtan as well. His eyes were fixed on Margot, wonder and a sense of admiration in his eyes. Sylvie couldn't be sure, but she thought he had been awake for some time.

Margot held out the delicate violet towards Gaëtan.

"It worked," she said. She looked him straight in the eyes.

"Thank you," she said, "for granting my wish."

Gaëtan smiled.

"My gift to you."

# XXXVI

## *The Calm Before the Storm*

I t had been ten days since Margot's wish. Margot had taken a few days to recover but was now entirely in her element and quickly acclimated to her new abilities. Sylvie had spent her days with Margot, for the most part, working through basics together. At the same time, Gaëtan and Loïc assumed primary responsibility for the regular and lengthy meetings with Alfric regarding the developing imp situation as well as council and other public audiences. Sylvie's work with Margot had almost caused her to forget that she had not seen Nadine since the winter wish ceremony. Had she found her family? Would she return to the palace?

A sharp prick on her arm jolted Sylvie out of her daydream.

"Ow!" she protested loudly. Margot looked at her with a devious grin, a slender silver needle in her hand.

"Come on, you daydreamer. I'm supposed to be practicing healing éthéra," Margot said innocently. She fidgeted with a beautiful silver ring on her right forefinger, inlaid with a deep, bright emerald cut into a perfect circle.

"Stab yourself next time!" Sylvie said, rubbing at her forearm.

"I'll take that into consideration," Margot replied haughtily. "Now let me see your arm."

A tiny bead of blood sat on Sylvie's skin where Margot had jabbed her. Margot moved her hand over Sylvie's arm, and the blood retreated into Sylvie's skin, and the hole from the needle closed itself, Sylvie's skin appearing as new.

Margot smiled proudly.

"Perfect, if I may say so myself," Margot crowed.

Sylvie smiled. "Well done, Margot," she congratulated.

"Thank you, Sylvie," Margot said. Her tone indicated her thankfulness for Sylvie's support and deeper gratitude for her newfound abilities.

There was a commotion in the hallway.

"The Firstborn are not taking audiences at the moment. I can request an audience on your behalf—"

"You forget who you are speaking to. Out of my way."

Sylvie stood and exited the study as Margot continued her practice. She walked towards the palace entrance, where she saw Beyern berating a member of the staff. Beyern noticed her and fixed his eyes, full of fury, directly on her.

"You, the wayward Firstborn! You and the rest of your would-be royalty owe me answers! What conspiracy did you enter into at my expense? I cannot recall the Winter Wish ceremony or any of your wishes. I confirmed with Councilman Philippe, but he did not take my place as the wish granter this year. And I can recall leaving the palace—but not arriving."

"Beyern, lower your voice," Sylvie said.

Beyern ignored Sylvie's request, whether out of rage or contempt, Sylvie did not know.

"I remember nothing from your wishes. What are you keeping from me? What enchantments have you enacted upon me?"

Sylvie squared herself at the accusation. She wished Loïc or Gaëtan were here to explain themselves. Regardless, she wasn't going to betray them now.

"Hold your tongue, Beyern." Sylvie retorted.

The response visibly incensed Beyern, whose eyes looked like they were about to burst from their orbits.

"Who do you think you are, marching into this palace, berating our staff, and spouting accusations of which you know nothing?" Sylvie continued.

Beyern could barely contain himself.

"You insolent child!"

Sylvie held up her hand to silence Beyern.

"You will address me properly as Miss Sylvie or Morwenna."

Beyern's eyes narrowed.

"You *will* answer me." He seethed.

"I will not," Sylvie replied. "And you will cease any inquiry into the matter at once. I know your secrets, Beyern, just like I knew those of Councilman Victor."

Beyern's features transitioned from anger to apprehension.

"Now leave this palace before I call the guard," Sylvie ordered.

At the punctuation of her last statement, a horn sounded in the distance.

Sylvie looked out the tall palace windows. From down the hall, Margot came and stood at Sylvie's side. The day outside was dark, and Sylvie was sure it was more than just clouds.

"What was that?" Margot said.

Another horn sounded. Suddenly, the doors burst open, and Loïc entered with Gaëtan beside him. "Sorry to interrupt, but something has come up."

Loïc stopped in surprise as he noticed the Councilman.

"Beyern, what are you doing here?" Loïc asked.

"I was just leaving," he replied.

"I'm afraid you won't be. The palace gates are sealed." Loïc said.

"You would make me a prisoner of the palace?"

"Please, Councilman. You are a guest."

With that, Loïc gestured to the palace staff, who escorted Beyern into the palace.

Loïc and Gaëtan made their way towards the throne room without further explanation. Sylvie and Margot followed.

"What's happening?" Sylvie asked Loïc, breaking into a trot to keep up with Loïc's quick pace.

"Commotion in the city," Loïc answered, "we don't know much more now."

Once inside the throne room, Sylvie saw Alfric and a handful of palace guards waiting for them. Based on the sophistication of their uniforms and Durand's presence, Sylvie guessed they were ranking guard officers. Alfric and the other soldiers bowed as the Firstborn entered the room.

"Alfric," Loïc acknowledged, "what news?"

"From what we know, it appears things began in the Summer District, though recent reports indicate similar incidents in all districts occurring more or less simultaneously," Alfric began.

"What incidents?" Margot asked.

"It's unclear—" Alfric started.

The throne room doors suddenly opened, interrupting him. A soldier, whom Sylvie recognized as a scout due to his lighter armor, rushed in and headed straight to Alfric. He relayed a hurried message into Alfric's ear.

The scout's message complete, Alfric grimaced somberly. He turned to the scout.

"Head to the barracks immediately, mobilize all troops. All soldiers are on active duty effective immediately, and leaves of any kind are suspended. Go."

The scout dashed out of the throne room, his light boots beating strongly against the immaculate tile.

"A significant number of imps are converging on the palace from all districts," Alfric said, addressing the Firstborn. "They are armed and are expected to be here within minutes. I will see to the garrisoning of the palace wall and gate immediately."

Alfric made ready to leave, but Loïc held up his hand.

"Alfric, a moment, please. Captain Durand," Loïc said, addressing the Captain, who sported a golden cuirass under his thick green cloak. "See to it that the walls and gates are properly manned."

"Right away, your Majesty," Durand said with a bow before leaving in haste.

"Alfric," Loïc said, turning to the Commander, "we suspect the imps' target is the Keystone."

"The Keystone?" Alfric asked, "But that would require breaching the palace walls or gates. It would be all but impossible for imps to achieve that."

Loïc turned to the rest of the Firstborn.

"There's no purpose in withholding information now," he said, turning back to Alfric.

"These are not imps as we have come to know them. They are under Rhys's influence, and we suspect they are harnessing dark éthéra. The men need to understand the severity of the threat."

Alfric's eyes widened at the news.

"I'll alert them at once," Alfric said.

"One final thing," Loïc added. "I want you and a contingent of your finest men to guard the Keystone. If we cannot hold them at the wall, the Keystone must be preserved."

"But my place is at the front, with the men," Alfric protested.

"Gaëtan and I will worry about the gate and several other competent officers besides. We need someone we can trust absolutely to see to the Keystone's safety. That is an order."

Alfric nodded and exited the throne room.

"I am making for the gate," Loïc said to the other Firstborn.

"I'll join you," Gaëtan said quickly.

"And us?" Sylvie asked, not wanting to be left behind.

Loïc looked at her directly.

"Remain at the palace," he said, "This is a serious threat, Sylvie. See that the staff get safely inside the palace and avoid danger."

Sylvie drew herself up as straight as she could and glared at Loïc.

"I'm a Firstborn, too, and I have every right to fight for the Keystone, just like you! Why would you get to risk your life for your people and prohibit me from doing the same?"

Loïc was about to reply, but Margot stepped in.

"She's right, and you know it. And I'm coming too."

This time, Gaëtan was the one to protest.

"You can help without being on the front line," Gaëtan argued.

"If this is war, all the 'helping' will be done in battle. I'm coming," Margot insisted.

She put her nose in the air to make it clear she would not be entertaining any argument to the contrary.

There was a pause, and Loïc approached Sylvie and took her by the shoulders.

"Sylvie," he said softly yet firmly, "you can, and have, and will serve this people in ways no one else could. But today, people are going to get hurt, and people are going to die. This is not the place to be willing but unprepared."

"I've been willing but unprepared since I left Hull," Sylvie replied, returning Loïc's gaze, "Do you believe I am supposed to be here now?" She asked.

Loïc's dark, nearly black eyes pierced deeply into Sylvie.

"I do," he answered.

"Then believe that I am to fill my station in times of trial also," Sylvie said firmly.

Loïc sighed deeply, his grip on Sylvie's shoulders tightening slightly.

"Very well," he replied, "but see to it that you're properly armored before you leave the palace. Come on, Gaëtan."

Gaëtan, holding Margot by both hands, released his grip slowly, let Margot's hands slide out of his own, then turned and followed Loïc.

Margot turned to Sylvie.

"Let's go show them we mean business," she said with a grin, offering Sylvie a hand.

Margot pulled Sylvie out of the throne room and headed quickly upstairs, ordering a member of the staff to send for her servant as she went.

"And send someone to Sylvie's suite to gather her armor and bring it to my suite," Margot instructed.

Just a few minutes later, Sylvie watched as Margot, standing in her thin, draping undershirt and a pair of heavy green trousers, was getting helped into a thick padded leather jacket and flexible shirt of shining silver mail. A rich green tunic went over the mail, and a breastplate, perfectly fitted to Margot's shape, went over the top of it all, cinching at the sides with thick leather straps. The mail fell down and out from under Margot's tunic in shining rivulets, draping over Margot's thighs.

"Now help Sylvie," Margot ordered as she strapped ornate silver bracers over her forearms. A beautiful helmet, also in silver, sat on Margot's bed.

Sylvie stripped out of her dress, and the staff helped her place a heavy padded jerkin over her undergarment, just like Margot. She put on thick yet surprisingly soft pants tucked into heavy leather boots with a hazelnut hue. With the help of the servants, she donned a glistening shirt of copper mail, followed by a royal blue tunic. Like Margot's, a cuirass went over the top of the blue shirt. The metalwork was immaculately fashioned to Sylvie's size and shape and was wrought over with beautiful motifs of nature, with a heavily aquatic emphasis.

"Here, your bracers," Margot said, handing Sylvie a pair of copper bracers.

As Margot helped Sylvie affix her bracers to her arms, the staff tightened a set of greaves over her boots. The armor was undeniably beautiful, but Sylvie swallowed nervously as she contemplated its intended purpose. A member of the staff approached and handed Sylvie her helm, a gorgeous copper creation with a flowing plume of blue cascading back from its crown.

"Just about ready," Margot said matter-of-factly. Sylvie noticed a beautiful wooden bow leaning against Margot's bed and, beside it, a leather quiver of arrows adorned with silver metalwork. Thickly bunched arrows fletched in green filled the quiver.

A servant buckled a belt around Sylvie's waist. The belt sported an exquisite scabbard containing an equally intricate sword sheathed within.

"Actually," Sylvie said, "I'd prefer my sword if that's alright."

Margot looked at her curiously.

"Your sword? Were you a soldier in your past life in Hull?"

Sylvie chuckled nervously, "No, not remotely. It was a gift."

Before they had finished speaking, a palace staff member reappeared with Sylvie's familiar sword in their hands. The fancy sword was replaced with Sylvie's, and the belt was cinched about Sylvie's waist. Finally, Sylvie took up a beautiful round shield, a large blue stone centered in the polished metal.

Sylvie looked at herself in one of the mirrors in Margot's room. She barely recognized herself. Her hair was tied back tightly, with not a single loose hair about her face as it fell in rivers down her back.

"Let's go meet Gaëtan and Loïc, shall we?" Margot asked. Her fiery red hair was tied back like Sylvie's, and Margot's yellow eyes blazed with determination. Margot and Sylvie instructed the staff to gather everyone inside the palace, then headed down the stairs and into the courtyard.

# XXXVII
## *Rhys Returns*

The sky was dim, though there were fewer clouds overhead. Sylvie saw a detachment of soldiers, with Alfric at their head, standing around the fountain that housed the Keystone. Their weapons were drawn and glinted in the late light of day.

Just then, an ear-splitting explosion sounded from the direction of the palace gate. Sylvie could see no smoke, but the air seemed to ripple in a wave, rushing towards them at an alarming rate. As the shockwave passed, the sky looked like it was suddenly shattering into millions of different shards of glass, which now hung in the air. The soldiers looked around in dismay.

"What's happening?" Sylvie asked Margot.

"I'm not sure," Margot said, "but it doesn't look good. Come on!"

Margot took off at a brisk pace towards the gate; Sylvie followed close behind. From where they were, they could hear the sounds of battle, with metal on metal ringing in the air and the shouts of soldiers gripped in mortal combat.

Before Margot and Sylvie could get very far, they heard Loïc's voice calling out over the commotion.

"Hold the gate! Barricade the entrance!"

What had appeared as a dimness in the sky soon became dark wisps of ethereal smoke, gathering in heavy tendrils along the floor at first but filling up more and more of the sky as they neared the gate. The sound of battle was nearly upon them as they continued to race towards the gate.

Then, suddenly, the fight was all around them. From what Sylvie could see, things were not going well.

The gate had been breached. One of the large metal doors was leaning precariously, its top hinge having come away from the wall. Many Verdélian soldiers lay still on the ground; whether dead or wounded, Sylvie could not tell. A host of Verdélian men still tried to prevent entrance through the broken gate, but they were far too few compared to the host of imps pouring forward wildly. To Sylvie's dismay, many of the Verdélian soldiers were crouched down on the ground, their hands clasped over their heads and faces, tormented by an unseen enemy.

Loïc had taken his position at the very tip of the defense. He and the Verdélia had managed to prevent the gates from coming open completely and had piled debris up as a makeshift barricade, such that, for the time being at least, only a handful of imps could come through the gate at a time. There stood Loïc, taking all on-comers, a heavy round metal shield in one hand, his long and broad sword in the other as he slashed and stabbed at the invaders, death on every stroke. A small number of soldiers stood there with him, trying hopelessly to stem the tide of assailants. As the imps rushed forward, they attacked with spells like the one Sylvie had seen in the basement of the inn in the imp district. Bolts of sickly dark éthéra flashed through the air. Some exploded sharply on shields or missed their mark altogether. Others struck hapless Verdélian soldiers who reeled and succumbed to the attacks.

"They're scaling the wall!" Gaëtan's voice sounded from far up above.

Sylvie saw Gaëtan up on the battlements with several soldiers shooting arrows down on the imp invaders. Suddenly, dark shapes vaulted over the parapet, engaging Gaëtan and his men.

Margot raised her bow and quickly fired an arrow up towards the battlement. An imp, who had just come over the wall, fell with a cry down into the palace courtyard and crashed against the cobblestones with a sickening thud. Sylvie shook herself from the shock of the scene before her and drew her sword.

Another explosion rocked the gate, and the defenders' barricade burst into a thousand splintered fragments of wood and stone. Loïc, who had been standing nearest, had somehow managed to hold his position, crouched behind his shield. Few of the other soldiers nearby were so fortunate.

With the barricade gone, the flow of imps increased dramatically. They poured by the dozens through the gate, swarming onto the road that led to the palace.

Sylvie saw Loïc's head swivel this way and that, quickly taking stock of their situation. With a roar, Loïc raised his hands and launched a wall of flame at the coming invaders. From where she stood, nearly fifty paces back, Sylvie raised her hand to protect her face from the heat. The imp attackers turned to ash as the fire devoured them.

No sooner had the flames faded than another wave of imps came rushing through the smoke and mist.

"Fall back!" Loïc yelled, helping a fallen soldier to his feet and rushing back toward the safety of the nearest buildings. "Archers, cover!"

4020 | *Winter* | *4th Moon* | *21*

Margot joined in as Verdélian soldiers, taking refuge on rooftops and behind buildings, let loose several volleys of arrows into the relentless crowd of attackers. The imps, who were, for the most part, lightly armored at best, fell in droves to the sharp bites of the Verdélian arrows.

"Gaëtan!" Loïc shouted, "The gate is breached! Fall back!"

Gaëtan dispatched another imp who had clambered over the battlements before nodding grimly at Loïc from his perch high up on the wall. He turned to the soldiers with him up on the wall, and they began to descend to the street as more and more imps surged into view.

"Cover the wall!" Loïc barked to a handful of archers to his left.

Arrows flew upwards towards the top of the wall, felling the imps scrambling over the wall and after Gaëtan as he retreated with his men.

The sounds of battle continued as arrows whistled through the air. Try as they might, however, the Verdélia could not loose their arrows quickly enough to stem the tide of invaders. As more and more imps entered the palace gate, Gaëtan and his men found themselves cut off and backed against the guardhouse near the gate. Although Loïc, Margot, and Sylvie were relatively safe for now in a narrow street that funneled the imps to them a small handful at a time, Sylvie knew that would not last forever either.

"Infantry, to me!" Loïc instructed quickly, "We're going to drive a wedge through the enemy and see Gaëtan and his men back to safety. Archers cover! Follow me!"

Loïc put up his shield and charged headlong into the mass of oncoming imps, disciplined soldiers hugging tightly to his sides to form a triangular formation that speared through the attackers. Careful to stay hidden behind their shields, the Verdélia used powerful strokes of their swords and deep, deadly thrusts to cut a path to the palace wall. Arrows continued to rain on the imps as they tried to prevent Loïc and his men from reaching Gaëtan and the other men at the guardhouse.

Sylvie quickly realized that, even if Loïc made it to Gaëtan, the return journey would be even more perilous. Imps continued to flow in through the gate, forcing the Verdélian archers farther and farther back. The distance between Gaëtan and friendly lines was growing.

"We need to keep a path open for them to return," she said urgently to Margot.

Margot nodded.

"You heard her!" She yelled to the Verdélian soldiers. "Keep a path open from the guardhouse!"

Through the madness or battle, Sylvie heard a whisper. A dark, familiar whisper. It grew. *Yes, bring it down.* An image of the Keystone, seen from below, flashed through her mind. *Kill the warrior. Bring him down.* Sylvie turned to glance back down the street towards the palace. Smoke and fog had seeped into the streets. The fragments of broken glass—the shattered enchantments that had kept the palace safe—still hung in the air.

Margot drew from her rapidly dwindling supply of arrows and let loose, her arrow finding its mark as it buried itself into the back of an imp rushing towards Loïc, who had now reached Gaëtan at the guardhouse.

"Sylvie," she called, "the boys aren't going to hold out much longer."

Sylvie snapped back to the situation before her. She took a deep breath. She had to do something. Then she saw Captain Durand.

"Captain Durand!"

The Captain was in the thick of things. At her call, he drew back after dispatching his current foe.

"We need to retake the street as far as the courtyard inside the gate!" Sylvie yelled, "I have entrusted you twice and am doing it again. You cannot fail me. I need to return to the palace."

"By your word," said Captain Durand. His armor, immaculately polished not long before, was now covered in blood and grime, a testament to the Captain's arduous efforts to defend his people.

With that, Sylvie turned and ran headlong towards the palace.

The whispers in Sylvie's mind continued to build, echoes of darkness that dragged Sylvie down. The darkness seemed to crowd around her as she went.

*Crimén bé arment.* Kill the soldier.

The whispers were recognizable now and full of malice.

*The soldier,* she wondered. *Alfric.*

On she ran, towards the palace, towards the pool, and her friend.

*Crimén dèr.* Kill him. *Assaulen.* Attack.

In a moment, another deafening explosion sounded, but this time from the direction of the palace, not the gate. A shockwave, like the one Sylvie had seen when she left the palace, flew past her and out towards the walls.

The blast stopped Sylvie in her tracks as silence fell over the city. The courtyard was in her sights now, though a choking fog obscured all details from view. At the center of the courtyard, where the pool and the Keystone would have been, Sylvie saw a dark, heavy pillar of mist rise as if it were alive.

Through the darkness, she heard a sound like falling rain. It grew louder and louder until she saw a crowd of imps running towards her. In a panic, she dove behind a short stone wall to her right. She hoped she had been quick enough to avoid detection.

The imps swarmed past in their rush towards the palace gates.

Sylvie gazed over the garden wall. The imps had all gone. However, the shadow that had risen from the courtyard was descending the street. Snaking tendrils of darkness writhed along the floor in its wake. From within the shade, Sylvie thought she could make out the form of a creature—no, a person. It drifted past her, and as it did so, she felt as if her very life was being drawn out of her and into a void centered in the darkest part of the shadow.

She shuddered, and the darkness passed from her sight.

# XXXVIII

*A Brief Respite*

S ylvie sat as if frozen in her hiding place.

The sky was darker, heavier. It hung low over the buildings, which appeared somber and lifeless. Sylvie huddled for several moments behind that little garden wall. Then, she saw Loïc run past. His face was firmly set towards the palace, and he was gone from view in an instant. Gaëtan and Margot followed close behind.

Roused from her living nightmare, Sylvie stood and approached the palace. She ran down the cobblestone streets, remembering Alfric and the Keystone. From the corner of her eye, the deepening shadows lunged at her. She shrieked as she jumped out of the way, trying to avoid the shadows' grasp. On she ran. Her foot caught on the cobblestones, but she managed to keep her footing as she continued her frantic dash to the Keystone.

As she came out onto the courtyard in front of the palace, she nearly barreled into Loïc, who was running towards her. His hair hung loosely about his face, heavy with sweat and blood. A dark bruise was forming on his cheek, and a long gash ran the length of his jaw on the right side.

"Sylvie!" He said quickly, "What is it? I heard you yell."

Sylvie looked behind her with wild eyes, checking for pursuers. There were none. She drew breath quickly, trying to respond to Loïc.

"It...it was," Sylvie managed through heaving breaths, "it was nothing...just a shadow..."

Loïc's face was somber, and he sighed in relief.

"But there's more," Sylvie said. "He's back. Rhys. I think I saw him."

Loïc looked at her, his eyes dark.

"You saw him?"

"I think so. It was a shadow. A spirit. It was so dark, and inside...I think it was him."

Loïc hung his head.

"It is possible. The Keystone...it fell."

Sylvie gasped.

"But how?"

"The enchantments on the palace walls were overcome," Loïc answered. "While we were holding the gate, other imps somehow made it over the walls in other locations and attacked the Keystone directly. Alfric—" Loïc choked at the mention of the Commander's name. "Alfric and his men were overrun."

Without thinking, she ran past Loïc towards the fountain, looking for the Keystone that should have been crowning the courtyard. As she approached, more and more fallen soldiers littered the blood-soaked cobblestones. For each Verdélian guard, a half dozen or more imps were strewn on the street. Finally, Sylvie reached the fountain. Gaëtan and Margot stood looking on, their heads bowed in solemn grief.

There, in the fountain, lay Alfric. His armor was rent and torn in several places. He had fallen atop a mound of vanquished enemies. No less than fifty imps lay defeated in the fountain beneath and around Alfric. But even that had not been enough. Beside Alfric was the Keystone, stained red with blood and split into two pieces.

Sylvie put her hand to her mouth. The scene before her took on the air of a vile dream. Alfric had welcomed her to Verdélys on her very first day in the city. Then, and since, he had been the silent and ever-loyal protector of the palace in Sylvie's eyes. More than that, he had been her friend. The thought that any evil could overpower him seemed absurd to Sylvie, even now. Yet there he lay, and Sylvie was confronted with the repugnant reality: the Verdélia had paid more dearly than Sylvie could have ever imagined.

Loïc approached and stood beside Sylvie. Looking up at Loïc, she saw a turmoil of emotions within him. A barbaric fury that raged against silent and unbounded anguish shone through his war-stained face. After only a few moments, Loïc averted his eyes. Tears—of sadness or rage, Sylvie could not tell—trickled down his face.

"We have been fools," Loïc said through clenched teeth.

"We couldn't have known," Sylvie said, trying to comfort him.

Loïc scoffed loudly.

"Oh no?" He retorted, "Even unawares, we should not have paid so dearly an attack by a barely organized mob of untrained imps. But the darkness—Rhys—has been festering among us longer than we suspected. Most of our men succumbed to the darkness before they could even swing their swords at the enemy. We have become weak, and I am a fool for having allowed it to come to this."

Loïc was shaking as he spoke, the muscles in his neck and arms heaving under the strain of his anger.

"We are all to blame," said Gaëtan, who had approached with Margot. "We allowed the Verdélia to wander, and these are the roads they have fallen into. There is blame, but it is to be shared."

The Firstborn stood somberly before the shattered Keystone and their fallen friend, the ever-darkening sky reflecting the shroud they felt within themselves.

𑗉

It was the dead of night, and Sylvie sat in a daze before the fire as it danced in the chimney.

The Firstborn had stood and mourned together at the fountain, for the loss of the Keystone, their friend Alfric and many others, and the loss of the last vestiges of hope for peace in Verdélys. Eventually, with prompting from Gaëtan, they set about to organize the securing of the gate and the gathering of the dead and wounded. Wagon upon wagon of injured soldiers had been shipped to the hospital, which was well over maximum capacity before long. The barracks had been turned into a secondary medical facility, while the palace grounds had been offered a temporary resting place for those who had given their lives in its defense. Though Loïc had overseen preparations in the event of a second assault, reports had soon confirmed that the attackers had all fled the city entirely once the Keystone had fallen.

Their labors had gone on late into the night. Though Spring had formally arrived, the day seemed shorter and darker than any they had had all Winter, and everyone was soon working by lantern light, doing their best to see to the wounded and clear the streets. Finally, after midnight, those soldiers who had not been mobilized in time to participate in the battle took over the night watch at the gate and wall perimeter, relieving those of their comrades who had survived the ordeal. All those who had fought at the gate received commendations from Loïc, who had also offered rotating leaves to the men. The soldiers had refused, insisting instead to stay near the barracks until the wounded had been cared for and the dead buried.

Eventually, Captain Durand, who, with Alfric's death, was now the ranking officer, insisted that the Firstborn return to the palace, tend to their wounds, and take their rest. Loïc protested, but Sylvie convinced him that sleep was needed to prepare for the coming days, which would undoubtedly require all of their faculties. Loïc begrudgingly agreed, and the four Firstborn made their way in silence back to the palace.

As baths were poured for them, the Firstborn had gathered in the study, and Sylvie had started tending to Loïc. The cut on the side of his face had stopped bleeding for the most part, though it had not been adequately cleaned, and Loïc's shoulder-length hair had stuck to the side of his face and been matted into the clotting wound. Sylvie dabbed gingerly at Loïc's face with a steaming hot bandage, trying to clear the gash so that it could be closed appropriately. Loïc shut his eyes and did not react, breathing slowly through his nose.

A short ways away, Margot had done likewise for Gaëtan, who had taken a somewhat more significant beating as he had defended the guardhouse. His most prominent injury was a large and deep cut on the side of his thigh, where an imp's blade had caught just under his mail and sheared through his flesh. The wound had been temporarily bandaged earlier, and now Margot gingerly undid the dressing in preparation for properly healing the damage.

Their baths ready, Loïc had insisted on checking Sylvie's suite before allowing her alone into her room. Even then, he had placed a chair for himself against the inside of her large double doors while she bathed out of the way and behind a metallic, copper folding screen.

"There's no way of knowing if some of our enemies have stayed behind the walls and infiltrated the palace. We're not taking any chances."

Sylvie slipped into the bath and let herself sink beneath the steaming, scented water. As she did so, views of Verdélys under a brighter sun came into view. She saw the water's memories drawn from a well on the palace grounds under a beautiful blue sky. She let herself escape to that past that had been so violently destroyed today. Sylvie resurfaced and slowly wiped the filth of battle from her body, watching it trickle down her skin and into the water.

She stepped from the bath and quickly buried herself in a long, flowing night dress and matching robe, which she tied about herself with a silk sash adorned with embroidered flowers. Her damp hair hung in streams down her shoulders and back.

As she emerged from behind the screen, Sylvie stepped into the central part of her suite to find Loïc staring intently at his hands clasped together in his lap. He noticed her and looked up, his face serious. He forced the corner of his mouth upwards at Sylvie's approach.

"I'm safe," Sylvie said. "Now you go. Get out of this disgusting armor and get clean. I'll meet you in the study."

Loïc had made his way to his suite and Sylvie down to the study. She had no plan as to what she might do once she got to the study, but she knew she would be unable to sleep. She stepped slowly down the opulent palace stairs as an eerie silence permeated the air. At the foot of the steps, Sylvie glided along the smooth tile, the palace silent and dark all around her, until she entered the study. She lit a fire in the hearth and settled on the couch, huddled beneath a blanket. There, she sat still, engulfing herself in the silence of the night. She stared at the flames that flickered in the chimney, watching them as they danced in complete indifference to the day's suffering.

Sylvie turned as she heard the door to the study open. Loïc stepped into view, his silhouette dimly lit by the orange glow of the fire. He wore silk pants that hung close about his legs and a robe tied loosely at his waist. His wet hair hung in waves around his face as it glistened in the firelight. Without a sound, he went to Sylvie and sat beside her.

They sat in silence for some time. The day's events churned through Sylvie's mind, transfixing her. The shock of Sylvie's first glimpse of the breached gate flashed through her mind, as did the death of the imp soldiers at her hand. She relived Loïc fending off hordes of enemies at the gate and watching on as Gaëtan stood surrounded by imps on all sides. She saw Alfric lifeless in the pool beside the toppled Keystone. She heard the whisper of evil floating on the air again:

*At last, I have returned.*

She turned to Loïc.

"I'm so glad you're alive," she said, breaking the silence and grabbing Loïc's arm.

He looked at her as though rousing from a dream. He gazed into her eyes intently without speaking for a few seconds, then his features softened.

"I, too, am happy you are safe," he replied. "We lost much today, but it could have been worse. Losing you—" his voice faded. "Well, all truly could have been lost, but thank Solaidi, it was not so." He took Sylvie into his arms and held her snugly against his chest. Sylvie let herself drift into the comfort of Loïc's embrace, forgetting for a moment the darkness weighing on her heart.

After a long moment, Loïc slowly released Sylvie. She sat up slightly and looked up into Loïc's face.

"What will we do now?" She asked.

Loïc looked at her, his face just a finger's width apart from hers.

"I honestly do not know," he answered. "Waging war against Rhys was never something any of us—or anyone at all—considered possible. We're in no way prepared for the task at hand."

"Indeed," sounded a voice behind them that seemed oddly familiar to Sylvie.

Loïc jumped up and drew a long dagger from his robe as he turned to face the unexpected visitor.

A tall and slender man with flowing white hair stood in the doorway of the study. He had a playful air about him that Sylvie had seen before.

"Ancelin?" She asked.

"Indeed," he replied, "though I do not believe we have met."

He walked towards the Firstborn, and Loïc sheathed his weapon and let out a heavy sigh of relief.

"Next time, consider announcing yourself," Loïc reprimanded.

"And miss seeing you scramble to protect this sweet thing?" Ancelin said, pointing to Sylvie. "Now, where's the fun in that?"

Loïc huffed, and Sylvie blushed slightly.

"You must be Ancelin's brother, then. Why are you here?" Sylvie asked.

Ancelin smiled playfully. "I am Ancelin. Ancelin is my brother."

Decidedly, cryptic turns of phrase were a shared trait between both Ancelins.

"As to the purpose of my visit, can't I just drop by for a visit now that I'm finally off duty? It is finally spring." Ancelin responded as he seated himself in a chair near the fire, with an exaggerated tone of indignation.

Sylvie raised an eyebrow skeptically.

"It doesn't seem in your habit to visit for the sake of the visit alone."

Ancelin tapped the side of his head with one finger.

"Clever girl," he said with a grin. He did not, however, explain his visit and the three of them stood there, listening to the fire in the chimney as the darkness of night blanketed the palace.

"An interesting thing, fire, wouldn't you agree?" Ancelin asked finally.

Sylvie looked at Loïc, hoping he might understand what Ancelin was getting at. Loïc just shrugged.

"I suppose so," Loïc replied aloud.

"Yes...," Ancelin continued as he stared intently at the flames. "Such beauty and warmth are married to a quite impressive potential for destruction. It is a tool and a luxury, but also a weapon and a monster, depending on the circumstances."

Sylvie and Loïc waited silently, anxious for Ancelin to reach his point. He turned in his seat to face them.

"You Verdélia, have feared the fire for too long, treating it like the untamable monster that it can be. In so doing, you have fulfilled your own prophecies. Look at what this day has brought on Verdélys."

"We don't fear fire, in whatever way you intend the symbolism," Loïc answered defensively. As the words left Loïc's mouth, Sylvie realized Ancelin had been speaking symbolically.

Ancelin laughed.

"You *are* tired, aren't you?" he said. "Get some rest, and then perhaps you might be able to understand."

"Or you could explain yourself," Loïc proposed.

Ancelin clicked his tongue.

"You should know better than to expect me to do that. Surely my brother isn't so soft with you souls. Besides," Ancelin added, "I would only be proving my point. No, I think I will not overstay my welcome."

With that, Ancelin stood, nodded slightly in the direction of the two Firstborn, and receded into the shadows of the study before vanishing entirely from sight.

"What did he mean?" Sylvie asked Loïc after Ancelin had gone.

"Evidently, I don't know," Loïc said in resignation as he approached his desk. He pulled some paper and dipped a long, beautiful quill into a pot of ink. He began scribbling on the page.

"What are you doing?" Sylvie asked.

"Writing down what Ancelin said," Loïc answered. "There's a reason for his visit; there always is. Just because we don't have the answer now doesn't mean it won't be needed later. We'll be happy to have this to reference."

Loïc finished writing and put up his quill. He blew on the still-moist ink on the page, then slipped the paper into his pocket. He turned to Sylvie.

"Come, let's get to bed. There will be an emergency council meeting in the morning, and we'll need all the rest we can get."

He offered Sylvie his arm, and she took it gratefully, leaning heavily into him as they made their way from the study. They walked in silence through the shadows of the palace, Sylvie grasping at Loïc's warm skin to ward off the chill of the night air. They reached her room, and Loïc again checked the suite for intruders. As he turned to go, Sylvie hesitantly let her arm slip out of Loïc's. She turned to face him. She could just make out his sharp features in the darkness.

"Good night," she breathed.

She felt Loïc's hands on her hips, and he drew her in slowly but steadily until her body was pressed up against his. She shut her eyes and let the horrors and the grief of that dreadful day melt from her mind as she felt Loïc's heart beating against her chest. She felt his warm breath on her face before his lips pressed against her forehead. He drew back ever so slightly, such that his lips still touched her skin as they traveled down the bridge of her nose. He kissed her again on the tip of her nose, then drew back. He brushed her face with his hand.

"Good night, mèr vivillèn," he whispered. Sylvie basked in the title. Loïc let her out of his grasp and turned to go. Sylvie watched as his frame receded quietly down the empty hallway towards his suite. When Loïc was out of sight, she shut the door and buried herself in her covers.

# XXXIX

## *Treason*

Sylvie sat nervously in her place in the throne room. Her hair was done in a tight but elegant bun, and her crown felt particularly heavy. The other Firstborn sat beside her, all in their formal royal attire, as they waited for the Council to arrive.

Gaëtan turned to one of the guards.

"It's time. Let those who are here in, and show in any latecomers as they arrive."

The guard nodded respectfully and made his way to the large double doors of the throne room. The doors opened, and the Council, headed by Beyern, entered.

As the council members filtered to their seats, Sylvie shifted in her chair. Something was not right. Most of the Council members had vacant expressions, which Sylvie interpreted as the result of exhaustion or shock, but few showed genuine signs of fear and anxiety. Narrowing her eyes, Sylvie focused her thoughts.

As she honed in on the crowd, Sylvie became aware of something that had been obvious but overlooked since the throne room doors had opened: the minds of most of the Council members were largely silent. Although Sylvie could make out a few clear minds, all swimming in thoughts of anxious concern, there was a common cloud over the minds of the remainder of the Council.

Sylvie leaned in towards Loïc.

"Something's not right," she whispered.

Loïc gave her a sideways glance, one eyebrow raised.

"I don't know the details, but be on your guard," she said, answering his inquiring look.

After a few moments, the shuffling of feet on stone died down as the Council members took their seats.

"Thank you for coming on such short notice," Gaëtan began. "Given the gravity of the situation, I hope you won't mind if I skip the formalities and get right to the chase. As most of you know, the palace was attacked yesterday by a considerable force of imps, who we believe were led by Belthégor. In the attack, the Keystone was destroyed."

An underwhelming collective gasp was heard from a few Council members, who began whispering among themselves. Most of the council remained stoic and nodded, acknowledging Gaëtan's words.

"Though our enemy incurred heavy losses in the assault, Belthégor is still at large, and we, too, suffered significant casualties."

Again, Sylvie could distinguish two distinct patterns of thought among the Council: one muted, nearly indifferent to Gaëtan's words, and another, raw in emotion and reaction to the serious news. A hand went up from the audience.

"Yes?" Gaëtan said, pointing to the blonde Council woman whose hand was in the air.

"With the Keystone destroyed, has Rhys returned?"

"We are operating under that assumption," Gaëtan confirmed.

A man on the other side of the room raised his hand. Gaëtan turned and invited him to speak.

"How were the imps able to breach the palace walls and then overpower the palace guard? What are we to make of Verdélys's ability to defend itself?"

"Our enemies harnessed dark éthéra to breach the palace defenses and to incapacitate many of our soldiers," Gaëtan replied. "As you know, our collective understanding of dark éthéra is limited, and we don't have an explanation for how we fell victim to it yesterday. We welcome any knowledge or insight you may have on this issue."

There was renewed mumbling among the Council. One member, a young, stout man with jet-black hair, spoke up.

"It's time to take decisive action," he said. "We've been taking half-measures for too long. All imps need to be interned under armed guard until further notice!"

A collective grumbling arose from the Council, and Sylvie could not determine whether it was in assent or dissent to the Councilman's proposal.

"Drastic measures brought on by paranoia and ignorance are not going to benefit us now," Margot replied firmly.

"With all due respect," the Councilman retorted, "we cannot expect you to view this particular issue objectively."

Gaëtan stepped in.

"If anything, Margot's perspective allows us to consider the interests of all members of the realm. Law-abiding imps are citizens of Verdélys too, and they will not be imprisoned wholesale only to appease the fears of this Council."

The Councilman stood, his face reddening.

"You condemn all of your true subjects, the Verdélia, to death or worse because you do not dare to take the actions necessary to protect them! I am aware that my proposal seems uncivilized to all of us who have become accustomed to easy times. But these are no longer easy times, and we need leaders who can make the difficult decisions for the good of our people!"

It was Loïc's turn to speak.

"The Firstborn will not sanction your proposal, Councilman. Please be seated." Loïc's tone was polite but firm. He stared intently at the Councilman, whose jaw clenched as he debated whether to protest. Finally, the man wilted under Loïc's gaze and sat down.

"Now—," Gaëtan began. Before he could continue, Beyern raised his hand, his face emotionless. Sylvie felt a rustling within Beyern's otherwise obscure mind. She felt transported back to the previous day's battle as she witnessed the rise of a shadow from where the Keystone had once stood. She nudged Loïc with her elbow.

"High Councilman Beyern, please," Gaëtan said, inviting Beyern to speak.

Loïc looked at Sylvie, waiting for an explanation. Sylvie didn't know exactly what to say.

"Something is very wrong with Beyern," was all she could manage.

"Thank you, Master Gaëtan," the High Councilman continued. "If I may, before you continue, I also have a proposal I would like to present to this body," the seasoned Winter Verdélia said in a hollow tone.

Gaëtan nodded, and Beyern continued speaking.

"Esteemed members of the Council," Beyern said ceremoniously, "you are all witness that I have served on this Council for decades, back to a time before these Firstborn," he gestured disdainfully to Margot, Gaëtan, Loïc, and Sylvie, "were placed as infants on their thrones."

"For many years, our people, the Verdélia, have wandered as a flock with no shepherd through rebuilding our society since the last conflict with the imps not twenty years ago. In that time, we have heard many things: that our people are strong, that our people are safe, and that our leaders are capable and trustworthy."

Beyern paused.

"All lies!" he cried.

"Get to your proposal, High Councilman," Loïc interrupted.

Beyern sneered at Loïc.

"Oh, I intend to," he said, malice dripping from his every word. He turned back to the Council.

"We have just been informed by those we look to for leadership that, despite being aware of an imp threat for moons, we were unable to prevent our enemies, mere powerless imps, from striking at the very heart of our kingdom and destroying our most vital protection—the Keystone."

Beyern's voice reverberated high into the vaulted ceilings of the throne room.

"For millennia, the Keystone stood, protecting us from the foulest of evils—but no more. More troubling, however," Beyern continued as he turned back to the Firstborn, "are the circumstances of its demise."

"You see, there remains no living witness of the fall of the Keystone within Verdélys. Those tasked with guarding it—including Commander Alfric himself—were all killed in battle. Reports from our troops, however, generally concur that the imps were held back at the palace gate and never made it much further than the gate's inner courtyard."

Loïc sat forward, indignant.

"Refrain from perjuring yourself, Councilman. The palace was surrounded by imps that reached the Keystone from several directions."

"So you would have us believe! But everyone who witnessed the scene unfold is now dead." Beyern exclaimed, an accusatory finger pointed directly at Loïc. Beyern's eyes were filled with a calculating madness. "All are dead except me. You see, I was there that day, upstairs in the palace, watching the battle unfold."

"Any number of soldiers can confirm that what I am saying is true. Speak with Captain Durand before you continue making a fool of yourself," Loïc retorted.

"On the contrary," Beyern replied loudly, "we have made fools of ourselves for twenty years, believing you children—two little boys, an imp, and a straggler raised by animals in the wilderness—could lead this people. But no more!"

Beyern turned to the Council.

"Councilmembers! Today, the fate of Verdélys is in your hands! These four," he made a sweeping gesture with his arm towards the Firstborn, "have shown not only that they cannot lead but that they would go so far as to betray the Verdélia and conspire to bring about the downfall of the Keystone! At best, these four were negligent in protecting our most valued treasure. At worst, they orchestrated its demise. You can stand idly by and allow these agents of Rhys to sow chaos in our midst, or you can stand now with me to put an end to this treason!"

A thunderous clamor of voices echoed against the stone walls as several people spoke up at once in response to Beyern's fiery speech.

"The only one guilty of treason here is you, Beyern!" shouted Loïc as he stood to his feet, his eyes blazing.

"We stand with you, High Councilman!" yelled several members of the Council, some also standing to show their support.

"Well said! For the safety of our people, the Firstborn must abdicate!" cried another Councilmember.

"I present the motion to the Council," Beyern continued loudly over the tumult. "All in favor of transitioning ruling authority from the Firstborn to this Council, so indicate!"

Beyern raised his hand high in the air in support of his motion. Several other Councilmembers immediately raised their hands in assent. The majority of the Council followed suit in the couple seconds that followed. A few folded their arms across their chest in objection to Beyern's motion.

"This is not right!" a powerfully built man from the Summer District called out. "This Council lacks the authority to effectuate your motion, Beyern. Withdraw it!"

"Desperate times, you naive fool," Beyern replied derisively. "We no longer can afford the luxury of playing everything 'by the book.' If we do not take action, there will be no Verdélys left to argue about." He kept his hand straight up, holding it like a banner against the Firstborn.

"Do not yield to Beyern's fear-mongering," Gaëtan said in a strong, steady voice. "We have faced enough chaos from without; we do not need to allow it into the very heart of Verdélys."

Beyern turned to the Firstborn and lifted his face proudly, self-importance emanating from his expression.

"Your time of uninspiring puffery is at an end," he said smugly. "The Council has decided. You are unfit to rule and are guilty of treason."

"Your Council is divided, Beyern. No decision has been made!" Loïc exclaimed.

Beyern ignored him and turned to address the guards stationed at the throne room doors.

"Soldier, arrest these four and ensure their imprisonment until they can stand trial for their crimes."

Three of the guards began to approach the Firstborn at Beyern's orders. Sylvie recognized the same obscurity in their minds that was infecting the majority of the Council.

The fourth guard stood still, evidently unsure what his next action should be.

"Stand down," Loïc ordered the four guards. The three continued towards the dais without a word.

"You," Loïc called to the guard who had kept his post at the door. "Go find Captain Durand and bring him here immediately. Go!"

"Any individual assisting these four will be guilty of treason, just as they are!" Beyern screamed, his voice reaching a fevered pitch.

"Go, that's an order!" Loïc repeated. The soldier nodded and burst out of the throne room at a dead run.

"Arrest them!" Beyern yelled at the remaining soldiers, who had reached the foot of the dais.

"This is your last chance to stand down," Loïc said steadily. "I don't want to hurt you, but if you insist on following Beyern in his madness, you will leave me no choice."

The soldiers wavered at the foot of the steps, but an unseen force pushed them on, and they began to make their way up the stairs. Another group of soldiers arrived at the throne room.

"Finally!" Beyern yelled, "Go, seize them!"

The newcomers marched purposefully towards the Firstborn, and Sylvie's heart sank as she realized they, too, were taken by whatever madness had seized Beyern.

Before the first guard could make it up the final step, Loïc lashed out with the heel of his boot and landed a heavy kick into the soldier's stomach. The blow caught the man off guard and sent him careening down the stairs, his metal armor making a thunderous noise as it bounced and scraped along the stone.

Suddenly, the throne room was an explosion of commotion. The soldiers who had just entered the throne room, about a dozen strong, rushed the stairs towards Loïc. With a flurry of quick punches, Loïc sent the two foremost guards tumbling back into their comrades who struggled to make their way up the steps.

"Halt!" A booming voice sounded from the entrance to the throne room.

All eyes turned to see Captain Durand storming into the throne room, his face twisted in rage. The loyal guard followed quickly in his footsteps.

"What is this?!" Captain Durand demanded, marching towards the group of soldiers on the throne room steps. "Surely I am not witnessing what my eyes tell me I am witnessing. Have you all lost your minds?!"

For a moment, the soldiers cowered before Captain Durand's imposing fury. Sylvie noticed more soldiers arriving at the throne room doors.

"Captain Durand," Beyern stated, "your duty, and that of these soldiers, is to Verdélys. This Council has just assumed stewardship of the city; therefore, your loyalty and that of these men is to the Council. The Firstborn are charged with treason, and as such, you are all ordered to take these four into custody so that they may be tried."

Sylvie thought Captain Durand might bound over to Beyern and strike him down on the spot. Soldiers at the doorway began crowding into the throne room.

"You've taken this too far, Beyern," Gaëtan said.

"I'm only getting started!" Beyern cackled. "Enough pleasantries. Soldiers, take them, and Captain Durand too, if he cannot obey orders!"

More than two dozen soldiers were in the throne room, and Sylvie could see more descending the hall toward the throne room's open doors.

Captain Durand drew his sword with a sharp metallic ring.

"The next one of you to take another step forward will pay for it with their life."

The soldiers stood anxiously in place, looking for courage among their peers. Eventually, one soldier growled and shouted as he reached for his sword.

"Alright, I'll do it then!"

The soldier drew his sword and advanced on the Firstborn.

In a flash, Captain Durand made good on his threat. Before the guard could take his second step, he was stopped by the point of Captain Durand's sword, cutting deep into the soldier's chest. Captain Durand withdrew his sword, and the soldier collapsed onto the floor in a clamor of crunching metal. Then, the throne room was eerily silent.

Captain Durand turned to the Firstborn.

"Run," he said firmly.

The throne room was once again turned into a battlefield in a single instant. Soldiers rushed forward, trying to get to the Firstborn and Captain Durand. Captain Durand ruthlessly dealt blows of his sword to all oncomers, littering the stairs with soldiers.

"Run!" He bellowed as he dispatched another soldier.

Sylvie stared in shock at the scene before her. Loïc's forceful grip on her arm roused her from her waking nightmare.

"We have to go!" Loïc shouted. He pulled her away towards a side door behind Margot and Gaëtan, who were already escaping.

"After them!" Beyern screeched, his demonic voice filling the room.

Sylvie stole one last glance over her shoulder.

Captain Durand stood at the top of the stairs leading up to the four thrones. The one loyal Verdélian soldier stood at his side. Together, they beat back the waves of those who once had been their comrades but were now twisted shells of their former selves and agents of chaos.

Sylvie felt Loïc pulling her forcefully along. She turned to face forward again, put her head down, and ran.

# XL

## *Flight of Friends*

The beauties of the palace flew past in a blur as Sylvie ran, the pounding of heavy boots behind them as soldiers gave chase. As they rounded a corner, ten or so guards appeared in front of them, cutting off their escape. Margot and Gaëtan ground to a halt in front of Sylvie.

*We're not getting out of this,* Sylvie thought to herself.

Loïc, on the other hand, didn't slacken his pace. He swiped an old, polished shield hanging decoratively on the wall and placed it in front of himself as he ran head-on at the guards.

"Come on!" Loïc shouted to the other Firstborn. Sylvie followed closely behind, and Gaëtan and Margot did likewise.

"Halt!" one of the guards yelled. A moment later, Loïc made contact, sending several guards crashing to the floor. Gaëtan, who had drawn his sword, slashed at a guard whose hand was grasping at Margot. The guard howled in pain as he held onto what was left of his hand. The Firstborn slipped through the breach opened by Loïc and continued their sprint out of the palace and towards freedom.

The four of them ran, dashing past familiar scenes that Sylvie had just begun to call home. Soon, they were out of the palace gate and in the city itself. The palace guards were still hot on their heels, and Sylvie could hear them shouting amongst themselves.

"Come on! They're not far now!"

Gaëtan had taken the rear, and he pushed a merchant cart into the street as they ran past, temporarily blocking the road.

"Hey!" The unlucky retailer shouted as his wares were sent rolling into the roadway.

The guards cursed as they came upon the obstruction and its owner while the Firstborn continued their escape.

"Get this out of the way! Come on, move!"

The soldiers' voices receded slightly.

"Where are we going?" Sylvie called out after Loïc.

"Away. I hadn't exactly thought of a destination," Loïc admitted, slowing slightly.

Just then, an idea came to Sylvie's mind.

"Follow me," she said as she continued to run towards the Winter District.

The Firstborn wound through the city, taking small streets and alleyways to lose their pursuers. Sylvie slowed down. "We should shape-shift. We don't want anyone to recognize us. Margot, get between us."

They walked as a group. By now, the streets were silent. Eventually, Sylvie found herself in a familiar cul-de-sac. She slowed as she approached the worn iron gate at the end of the street.

"Where are we?" Loïc asked, looking at their surroundings curiously.

"This house belongs to Thaddeus," Sylvie explained, her chest rising and falling quickly as she breathed heavily to catch her breath.

Loïc pushed firmly and sharply on the gate, and it gave way with a horrendous screech.

"Who's Thaddeus?" Margot asked as she slipped into the gate after Sylvie. Margot, too, was out of breath, and her hair was sticky and slick at her hairline and around her ears.

"He was formerly an adviser to the Firstborn on matters of dark éthéra," Sylvie answered.

Margot raised an inquisitive eyebrow.

"Who else knows about this place?"

The memory of her day here swept back into her mind, and she remembered Alfric but didn't think now was the time for the full story. "No one."

"How did you know him?"

"We met in the Winter District a while ago."

On the front doorstep, Sylvie knocked twice before trying the doorknob. It was unlocked.

"Hello, Thaddeus?" Sylvie called out as she stepped into the ramshackle house. The place was just as dark, dusty, and dreary as she remembered it. Margot, Gaëtan, and Loïc followed after Sylvie, and they soon found themselves standing in the parlor together. Loïc shut and locked the door behind them.

"Thaddeus?" Sylvie tried again as she ventured into another room full of clutter.

The house was silent.

"Doesn't seem like he's home," Loïc observed, looking over the contents of the house that were thrown haphazardly about every available space.

"Maybe it's for the better," Gaëtan suggested.

"You might be right," Sylvie agreed.

Loïc spoke up. "Now that we're temporarily out of danger, we need to get messages to a few people. I'm thinking of Sir Reynard and my family... Beyern is likely to go after anyone with ties to us, and I don't think it will be for a pleasant conversation over tea."

"Nadine," Sylvie said.

"Yes, she knows too much."

Gaëtan said, "But we need to be careful. It appears Beyern has somehow swayed the majority of the guard to his side."

Sylvie interjected.

"It's Rhys," she said. Looking back, she recognized what she had felt within Beyern and the Council.

The other Firstborn looked at her intently, confusion and concern on their faces.

"When the Council entered the throne room this morning, something was off." Sylvie tapped her head with one finger. "Their minds—there were no thoughts, just darkness and confusion. Most of the Council felt the same, and most of the guards, too. I felt the same thing to a much greater degree in Belthégor."

"So he's controlling them?" Gaëtan asked.

"Not exactly, I don't think," Sylvie answered, "but they're under some kind of influence."

"That seems to be a phenomenon," Loïc said somberly. "The dark éthéra takes hold of those susceptible to it, and soon it becomes their master. I read about it after we found out Belthégor was involved with Rhys. I'm assuming that's what happened to many of the soldiers during the attack yesterday as well."

"How do we know who's susceptible?" Margot asked.

Loïc shrugged.

"I didn't find an answer to that question, unfortunately."

The four Firstborn stood quietly in the shadows of the derelict house. To Sylvie, it felt like they were alone in the world against a towering evil that filled the space all around them.

"So where do we go from here?" Margot asked. "We can't stay holed up in this crumbling dump forever."

"We can't stay in Verdélys at all," Loïc replied.

"What do you mean? We can't leave now!" Gaëtan countered.

"We have no choice," Loïc answered back. "Best case scenario if we stay is a civil war that would likely see the complete ruin of the city. Worst case...well, I'll leave that to your imagination. Besides, think back to the prophecies: 'thrown from throne.' I'd say we're right about there now."

"But that doesn't mean we're meant to leave Verdélys," Gaëtan said.

"No, but how about 'you'll travel far' in my prophecy, 'man and merfolk' in yours, and 'your road to former home will lead' for Sylvie? I think our path is marked."

Gaëtan was quiet.

"How can we leave the city in the hands of Beyern? Who knows to what fate we'd be condemning those who remain." Sylvie said.

"There's nothing we can do about that now," Loïc replied. "We must find a way to break Rhys' grasp on the Verdélia, especially the Council. As of now, I think that means destroying Rhys."

"And how exactly are the four of us supposed to do that?" Margot asked.

Loïc shook his head. "I don't know. But we can't stay here."

"Do you think we're supposed to go to Hull?" Sylvie wondered aloud.

Loïc shrugged. "That's my best guess, based on everyone's prophecy. Plus, it's one of the last places Rhys would consider looking for us. We'll be safe for a while, at least while we plan to retake Verdélys."

"What about Sir Reynard? Your family? Nadine, even?" Sylvie asked.

"I was planning to see my family tonight and have them leave the city," Loïc answered. "I'm hoping Sir Reynard was able to make his way out of the palace. He should leave Verdélys as well, as should Nadine—she knows enough to be valuable to Beyern."

"I haven't seen Nadine since the winter wishes ceremony," Sylvie lamented.

"Send your familiar," Loïc suggested, "but have it be discreet and don't meet here. And don't go to meet her alone."

"We can't risk the same for Sir Reynard," Gaëtan pointed out. "If he didn't escape the palace, sending a familiar to him would lead Beyern's minions right to us."

Gaëtan had a point. The Firstborn stood silently in the dusty parlor, trying to find possible solutions.

"We could send a familiar Beyern wouldn't recognize as one of ours," Margot suggested.

"Good idea," Loïc agreed. "I'll have someone from my family send for him. They can head west together and stay with Sir Reynard's family for now."

"What about Nadine?" Sylvie asked.

"Assuming we find her, we can send her with them, I suppose," Loïc proposed. "In the meantime, we need to gather supplies for our journey. It's a full moon to Hull on foot under normal circumstances, and we don't have more than the clothes on our backs."

Sylvie and her exiled friends spent the rest of the day planning their escape. That afternoon, Sylvie sent her familiar out to look for Nadine, with precise instructions to stay hidden and have Nadine meet at Loïc's family home that night.

Over a dusty table that the Firstborn had cleared of its contents, Sylvie, Loïc, Gaëtan, and Margot had decided that Loïc and Sylvie would meet with Loïc's family and Sir Reynard and see them out of the city. In the meantime, Gaëtan and Margot would gather supplies for their journey to Hull. They would be ready to leave Verdélys the next night if everything went according to plan.

⚘

It was dark in Verdélys. The night was cold, colder than most that Sylvie could remember, even though winter was behind them. The sliver of moon hanging in the sky gave off a dim and sickly light. The stars, which Sylvie had compared to diamonds strung in the fabric of the night when she had first arrived in Verdélys, were now little more than flecks of white caught on the dark expanse of sky overhead.

Loïc and Sylvie huddled close together and out of sight just across the bridge from Loïc's family home. Sylvie's teeth chattered—she hadn't had time to take cloaks or other belongings with her when she had fled the palace with the other Firstborn.

"You stay here," Loïc said. "I'll head to the house. If it's safe, I'll send one of my brothers out for you."

Sylvie barely had time to nod before Loïc went over the bridge and through the front yard gate. She watched as he walked briskly up to the door and disappeared inside.

She waited what felt far too long before she saw a smaller figure leave the house and come jogging towards her.

"Miss Sylvie!" She heard Loïc's brother call in a sort of hushed shout.

"I'm here," Sylvie said softly. "Let's go!"

The boy nodded, and they walked back to the house together.

Once inside, Sylvie was welcomed by a bustle of bodies going this way and that, and the house in a general state of disarray. Loïc was speaking to his father in the dining room. Both wore solemn expressions on their faces.

"Oh, hello, dear!" Bergita called out when she saw Sylvie. "Dreadful times, I'm afraid. I'm just glad you all made it out of the palace!"

"Thank you," Sylvie said, unsure of how much Loïc had conveyed. She approached Loïc in the next room.

"I don't know how long it's going to be," Sylvie heard Loïc say bluntly, "but you'll hear from us as soon as we have a plan."

Loïc and his father noticed Sylvie.

"Hello, Sylvie," Loïc's father said with a nod.

"Welcome," Loïc added with a smile. "My father sent for Sir Reynard. If he escaped the palace, he should be here soon. We'll meet Adelais, Antoine, and Felicity on the way out of the city."

There was a knock at the door.

"Sylvie, it's for you, dear," Bergita called.

At the door, Nadine stepped into the house, her jet-black hair tumbling in waves out of her hood.

"Nadine!" Sylvie cried as she threw her arms around the girl's neck.

"Miss Sylvie," Nadine said in her customary soft tone, a smile on her face.

"Where have you been?" Sylvie asked. "Well, never mind that for now. I have so much to tell you."

Sylvie explained the events of the prior days, culminating in the Council's betrayal and their escape from the palace.

"There's no telling what Beyern might resort to. We think it's best if those close to us leave the city."

Nadine nodded solemnly. "I understand."

"Loïc and his family are going west with Sir Reynard. I figured you could join them."

Nadine didn't immediately respond. Loïc approached from the other room, standing behind Sylvie's shoulder.

"Welcome, Nadine," he said. "If you need anything for the journey, talk to my mother. I'm sure there are plenty of my sisters' things for you."

Nadine bowed respectfully.

"Thank you, Master Loïc," she said, "that's very kind."

Sylvie could tell from Nadine's demeanor that she was holding something back.

*How can I refuse? They're being so kind, and I owe Miss Sylvie this much, at least.*

"Nadine, is everything alright?" Sylvie asked.

Nadine looked over Sylvie's shoulder, visibly uncomfortable to hold Sylvie's gaze.

Suddenly, Sylvie had a thought.

"Oh my goodness, I never even asked. Did you..." Sylvie thought carefully about how to phrase her question. "Did you find out anything about your family?"

Nadine's countenance told Sylvie that she had broached the correct topic.

"Yes and no," Nadine answered.

Sylvie let the silence prompt a more complete response out of Nadine. Behind them, the house continued to churn with people going this way and that, packing food and other belongings into bags and satchels of all sizes.

"I found the house," Nadine explained.

"You did?" Sylvie asked excitedly. "And?"

"My family wasn't there. The current resident has been living there for over ten years."

"Oh...," Sylvie sighed. "Nadine, I'm sorry."

Nadine looked disappointed but not disheartened.

"I talked to the neighbors. They said that the couple who had lived in the house before—my parents—had moved to Lumivale many years ago to make a new start and get away from the memories of that house."

"So you want to go find them," Sylvie concluded.

Nadine nodded.

"You can't go alone," Loïc interrupted. "Even under normal circumstances, it would be a bad idea, but with things the way they are, it would be completely reckless."

Nadine lowered her eyes compliantly. Sylvie didn't need to read her mind to see that she was crushed. Then, a thought came to Sylvie.

"Maybe she doesn't have to go alone," Sylvie said, turning to Loïc.

"Maya, Gaëtan's friend, is from Lumivale. Her whole family lives down there. We could send Nadine down with Maya. Fredrich could accompany them, too. That way, Nadine gets to go look for her family, and we get two more of our friends out of Verdélys."

Loïc looked impressed.

"That's a fair idea," he acknowledged.

Sylvie smiled and blushed slightly at the compliment.

"Thank you, Miss Sylvie," Nadine said, taking her by the hands.

"You can thank us when you're on your way to Lumivale," Loïc said dryly. "For now, we should pack you a travel bag. We obviously won't be able to get your things from the palace."

Nadine nodded.

"Come on," Sylvie said, "let's see what we can find you."

Sylvie worked with Bergita to find Nadine a few changes of clothes from some of Adelais' old things that were still in the house. Sylvie didn't know what Maya and Friedrich might have available regarding supplies, so she helped Nadine pack extra rations of food in her pack, as well as cooking and other camp gear.

Finally, the preparations died down, and the family and friends gathered near the rear door. Bergita and Lionel's faces showed concern and determination. Loïc's siblings expressed a mixture of excitement and sadness. As always, Loïc was difficult to read, but Sylvie could sense great turmoil beneath his stoic features as he watched his family preparing to leave their lifelong home.

"May we all reunite here again under peaceful times," Lionel wished aloud at last.

Sylvie's heart pinched as she echoed Lionel's prayer within herself.

Following their father's lead, the children exited quietly into the dark of the night. As planned, the group split into two: one group comprised of Bergita, Lionel, and the girls crept west towards the outskirts of the city. They would meet with Adelais, Antoine, and Felicity before making their way out of Verdélys. Sylvie, Loïc, Nadine, and Loïc's brothers headed north. The whole family would exit the city and meet back up on the outskirts of Verdélys before Sylvie, Loïc, and Nadine would see everyone off with Sir Reynard.

The streets they walked were buried in blackness, and Sylvie barely recognized the once-vibrant and beautiful neighborhoods of carefully crafted homes and shops that had been bursting full of life just weeks prior. There was no wind and no other Verdélia outside. Their procession marched on.

Eventually, the buildings grew increasingly sparse, and they turned west to rendezvous with the rest of their party.

"I hope Sir Reynard made it," Loïc whispered to Sylvie.

They would know soon enough.

After another lengthy walk through ragged, brittle grasses that should have been the beginnings of a spring meadow, Sylvie and her group approached a small thicket of trees. They engulfed themselves in the shadow of the canopy and let down their packs.

"I'm glad you could make it," a familiarly gruff voice said from deeper in the copse.

"Sir Reynard!" Sylvie called in subdued excitement.

Sir Reynard's large frame approached them from the shadows.

"And we are very happy to see you made it," Loïc replied, visibly relieved. "Have you seen the rest of my family?"

"Not yet," Sir Reynard said.

The six stood just at the edge of the little forest, staying within the shadow of the trees as they strained their eyes, hoping to pick up any movement from the city's western edge. It wasn't long before a handful of figures could be seen trekking through the fields towards them. A few minutes later, the group was gathered all together deep in the heart of the thicket. Adelais cradled a fussy Felicity while Antoine and Lionel reviewed their provisions and plans. Loïc was hugging his siblings tightly, each in turn. Finally, those who were to depart were gathered together, their few essential belongings on their backs. They stood opposite Loïc, Sylvie, and Nadine, who would soon return to the hostile city.

"Be safe," Loïc said. Now, even he could not keep the emotion from his voice.

"We are going to safer places than you, son," Lionel assured him. "Be careful, and be smart."

"I will," Loïc promised.

Sir Reynard stepped forward.

"It has been an honor and a privilege for me to serve you both," he said, "and as I have served you until now, so I vow on my life to keep your family safe."

Sylvie noticed for the first time that a frighteningly large sword hung from Sir Reynard's back.

"Thank you, Sir Reynard. It has been an honor for us to learn at your hand," Loïc replied.

Bergita approached and gave her son a final embrace. She turned to Sylvie.

"See to it that he behaves, will you please, Sylvie?" Bergita said, smiling through tears.

"I promise," Sylvie managed through tears of her own. Bergita gave her a big hug and returned to join the departing family.

With a final wave, Loïc's family followed Sir Reynard into the blackness of the thicket until they were lost from sight. Sylvie watched a pale moonbeam glisten on Loïc's wet cheek as he watched his family flee the evil that had taken their home.

꩜

Sylvie knocked gingerly on Maya's door, trying to be loud enough to get Maya to notice without drawing unwanted attention to the trio standing alone in the empty street.

Sylvie, Loïc, and Nadine had made it back into Verdélys without significant trouble. They had avoided a few patrolling guards, but the roads had been mostly devoid of life, and the oppressive darkness had made it easy to stay concealed. Sylvie's had followed her gliding familiar through the streets until she reached an unassuming apartment.

Sylvie heard feet shuffling on the wooden floorboards behind the door. She heard Maya moving about inside, presumably trying to see who could be at her door at this unusual hour.

*Is that Sylvie?*

With a metallic click, the latch opened, and the door opened slightly.

"Sylvie, is that you?" Sylvie heard Maya whisper incredulously.

"Yes, can we come in?"

"I...," Maya began. "Yes, of course. Come in. But what...I mean...," Maya mumbled.

Sylvie and her companions slipped through the opening before quickly closing out the darkness behind them. They found themselves in a cozy little entryway, heavily decorated with flowers and living things and a prominent shelf covered in beautiful awards and trophies. One particular sculpture was a rendering of a dancing Maya carved out of a beautiful lavender crystal. Maya was wearing a short green nightdress, and her hair—curled earlier that day— was a tousled jumble falling from her head down about her shoulders.

"Thank you, Maya," Sylvie said.

"You're welcome, of course," Maya said with a smile. She looked at her other guests with an apprehensive smile.

"Master Loïc," she said with a polite curtsy. Loïc nodded back politely. "I don't think I've met you before," she said, addressing Nadine.

"This is Nadine, she's a friend," Sylvie explained.

"Then welcome, Nadine," Maya said with another small curtsy.

Nadine returned the gesture.

"We're sorry to disturb you, Maya, but things in Verdélys have taken a turn for the worse," Sylvie began.

Maya's features sobered, "I imagined. This district was spared any fighting yesterday, but I heard what happened at the palace!"

Maya's eyes widened as she realized only two of the Firstborn were present.

"Oh my goodness...Gaëtan and Margot, are they...?"

"Oh! No, no, thank Solaidi," Sylvie answered reassuringly, putting her hands on her heart in symbolic reassurance. "They're alright."

Maya dropped her shoulders in relief.

"However," Sylvie continued, "we're all exiled from the palace. Beyern has orchestrated a coup."

Maya was stunned, speechless for a moment.

"The High Councilman? Really?" She asked finally.

Sylvie nodded. "I'm afraid so. He and the majority of the Council are under the influence of Rhys. We were lucky to make it out of the palace."

Maya gasped.

"Rhys? I thought that was a story we were told as children to teach us about evil. He's real?"

"He's real. And he's back." Loïc said seriously.

Maya looked down pensively at her feet.

"So, how can I help?" She said, looking back up at her visitors.

Sylvie looked at Loïc, then at Nadine. She turned back to Maya and sighed.

"I know this is a lot to ask, but...will you go with Nadine to Lumivale? We thought Fredrich could go with you."

Maya's eyes grew wide again.

"Leave Verdélys? When?"

"Tonight," Sylvie said.

Maya's eyebrows jumped. She looked to Loïc as if to verify that Sylvie was being serious. Loïc looked right back at her, his eyes set and unwavering.

"We're afraid Beyern might try to reach us through friends and family," Sylvie explained. "It's safer to get you out now, so that can't happen. I know you have family in Lumivale. We thought they could take you in until things in Verdélys return to normal. Nadine's also looking for her family, and she thinks they may live in Lumivale."

"I'm always welcome in Lumivale, but...what about my studies? If I leave Verdélys now, I may never be permitted to reincorporate the theater program. Fredrich either, if he did come with me."

Sylvie had been so focused on seeing their plan through to completion that she hadn't even considered what they were asking their friends to relinquish. Looking at Maya's face now, she could see the sacrifice it would be for Maya to give up what she had worked so hard to achieve.

"We don't know what life in Verdélys under Beyern—under Rhys—will be like, but I'm willing to wager it won't be pleasant," Loïc interjected. "If you stay, there's no guarantee that you'll be able to continue your program anyway. Worse still, you could be in serious danger."

Maya's face darkened as she began to realize the implications for the future of Verdélys.

"I can say, though, that once this mess is sorted, I will personally see to it that you are reinstated at the theater," Loïc promised.

Sylvie smiled. Loïc was no fan of the theater, but he cared about his friends and those he felt responsible for as a Firstborn.

A timid smile crept back onto Maya's face.

"Thank you, Loïc," she said. She put her hands on her face as she mulled her decision over in her mind.

Sylvie held her breath instinctively. The night was oppressively quiet.

"I guess I don't have much choice," Maya said, looking at her friends with a look that mingled resignation and good-natured optimism for the adventure ahead. "I'll go to Lumivale."

"Thank you," Nadine whispered.

Maya nodded.

"Time to call for Fredrich then, right?" she said with a grin.

Loïc and Sylvie nodded, and Maya's luna moth familiar whisked out into the darkness to summon their friend.

※

While waiting for Fredrich to arrive, Sylvie and Nadine helped Maya pack her things for the trip to Lumivale. Nadine had brought several things from Loïc's parents' home that were redistributed into other bags, and Maya packed clothes, bedding, and other essentials into a large backpack.

Friedrich arrived just as Maya had finished packing up her things. Sylvie could sense his mind was full of questions, but he had come at Maya's request nonetheless and with his own bag, ready to leave Verdélys.

"You know, he must be fond of you to come on a whim in the middle of the night, ready to follow you on such a wild journey," Sylvie prodded Maya. Maya smiled as she looked affectionately at Fredrich as he and Loïc discussed the planned trip to Lumivale.

"He is quite a gentleman, isn't he?" Maya replied.

"He is," Sylvie said with a smile before welcoming Fredrich.

Loïc had asked if Fredrich or Maya had swords. When both replied that they did not, Loïc pulled his purse off his belt and dropped a few gold coins into Fredrich's palm, along with instructions to visit a certain blacksmith, a man by the name of Braun, in the Summer district.

"Tell him I sent you and that you each need one of his finest swords," Loïc instructed the journey-bound trio.

"It's the middle of the night. Surely he won't be accepting customers," Fredrich had protested.

"He'll accept you," Loïc had assured them.

Fredrich, Maya, and Nadine hoisted their packs onto their backs, each slinging additional satchels over their shoulders to accommodate their gear and supplies.

"I can hardly believe this," Maya said softly. "I suppose we should go before I give myself too much time to think about it."

"Everything's going to be alright," Fredrich replied comfortingly, placing a hand on Maya's shoulder. "Let's consider this a vacation to Lumivale to see your family. We'll be there in no time."

Reassured, Maya smiled and drew a deep breath. She left the key to her humble house with Sylvie, "just in case," according to Maya. Nadine and Sylvie embraced tightly.

"Thank you for everything," Sylvie told Nadine. "I don't know how I could have managed Verdélys without you." Tears had flowed silently down Sylvie's cheeks as she prepared to leave her dear friend.

"We'll meet again soon, Miss Sylvie," Nadine replied. "Thank you again for your gift."

The three travelers said their final goodbyes to Sylvie and Loïc, who watched them vanish down the cobblestone streets and around the corner of a wooden-beamed flower shop.

"We'd better get back to the others," Loïc said, offering Sylvie his arm.

Sylvie nodded and gratefully took Loïc's arm, following him into the blackness of the city.

# XLI

### *Gaëtan's Capture*

L oïc knocked twice on the faded and scuffed iron door of Thaddeus's
weather-torn home before pushing his way through the entry, the old
and forgotten hinges protesting loudly as the door swung open and shut again
behind them. Sylvie squinted as she tried to make out the contours of her
surroundings, which were buried in blackness. From the other room, she
thought she heard sniffling. She heard someone get up as a chair scraped
against the old tile flooring and rush towards them. Loïc placed himself in
front of Sylvie and put his hand on the hilt of his sword.

"Where have you been?!" Margot said hysterically as her silhouette burst into
view. Even in the darkness of the old abode, Sylvie could see Margot's hair was
in shambles, and from her voice, she had been weeping forcefully.

Loïc approached Margot quickly and placed his hands on her shoulders.

"What's wrong? Where's Gaëtan?" He asked.

At the mention of Gaëtan's name, Margot broke down into sobbing.

"They...," she managed through tears, "they...took him..."

"Who took him? Where did this happen?"

"We were...," Margot forced out as she tried to compose herself, "we were
getting supplies. We were almost done when we ran into a patrol. We kept our
heads down and almost got away, but they recognized me. Gaëtan was
shifted...I wasn't. It's all my fault."

Margot heaved another massive sigh as she began to recover her regular
breathing pattern.

"Gaëtan told me to run...so I did. I thought he would be right behind me,
but...," her voice trailed off, and Sylvie could tell she was about to lose her
composure again.

Loïc tried to keep the conversation on track by cutting in quickly.

"How long ago was this? Where were you when it happened?"

Margot continued to struggle through ragged breaths.

"A little under an hour ago? I don't know; it feels like forever. We were in the Autumn district when it happened."

Loïc stood and made for the other room. Based on his determination, Sylvie could tell he had already decided on a course of action. She rushed after him.

"What are we going to do?" She asked.

"We're going to get Gaëtan, obviously," Loïc replied.

"Margot!" He called over his shoulder, "What did you manage to get together regarding supplies?"

Margot made her way to the doorway of the cluttered living room, wiping her nose with the back of her sleeve.

"Most everything, honestly," Margot called out hoarsely. "We were out for a second trip after gathering food, a tent, bedding, and clothes. Gaëtan had cookware, tools, and rope when the guards got him."

"Good. Most of that I got from my parents, or we can do without," Loïc answered, looking over the supplies piled beside a dusty sofa. He rifled through what looked to Sylvie like heavy folded cloaks or blankets, food rations, and waterskins. He stopped at a pile of delicate fabric.

"Where did you get your hands on this?" Loïc asked Margot incredulously as he held up a large sack made of silvery white fabric. It was so light that it danced this way and that as it caught every draft of air.

"Gaëtan knew someone," was all Margot replied.

"What is it?" Sylvie asked, puzzled.

"It's légetoil silk. It's weightless, and when fashioned into a bag, its contents are also rendered weightless," Loïc explained.

"Like the lullaby?" Sylvie asked.

"Yes. That's why the cradle is floating... it's made of Légetoil silk. Spider's silk, in human terms. That makes things easier," he continued, beginning to divide their supplies. "Margot, you're going to take all our supplies and meet us outside the city." Loïc began packing the silk bag with supplies, starting with a thick bedroll. "There's a spot just past where the treeline begins. If you take the East road, you'll see a little basin with a large outcropping of stone on the right side through the trees. Wait for us there." Loïc packed quickly and efficiently, working with the confidence that comes from habit.

"I'm coming to get Gaëtan too!" Margot protested.

"No," Loïc cut her off firmly, "you're not. Once we get Gaëtan, we must head straight out of Verdélys and on to Hull without worrying about stopping inside the city."

"Then have Sylvie do it. I'm going to get Gaëtan!"

"No, you're not," Loïc repeated.

Sylvie heard an undertone of rising frustration in Loïc's voice.

"Sylvie can shift, and you can't yet. Plus, I need Sylvie's mind-reading ability to help me locate Gaëtan and slip through the palace undetected. Please, just take these supplies like I asked, and trust me to get Gaëtan. Can you do that?"

Loïc stood and looked squarely at Margot, his arms outstretched as he offered the four large silk bags, now full of provisions and supplies, to his fellow Firstborn. Margot, who was typically always composed, barely looked like herself, her thick red hair hanging in a chaotic mess about her face and her common dress wrinkled and dirtied as it brushed the floor.

"Yes," Margot replied dejectedly as she took hold of the bags.

"Thank you," Loïc said. "Let's go."

Loïc led the girls out of Thaddeus's now-abandoned home. The silence outside was stifling. The three friends walked down the street and paused.

"Remember," Loïc said to Margot, "take the East road to the treeline. You'll see..."

"Some rocks and a gully. I know," Margot said.

*Back to her usual self*, Sylvie thought to herself.

"Right," Loïc said with a nod. "See you soon. I'm sending my familiar with you just in case something happens, but be careful."

A white wisp of a dragon materialized in the air.

"Keep an eye on Margot and guide her out of the city. Come get me if there's trouble," Loïc instructed his familiar.

Margot looked Loïc and Sylvie squarely in the face, her golden eyes burning.

"Bring him back."

"We will. Now go," Loïc answered.

Margot turned and made her way off into the shadows. High above, just below the eaves of the buildings that lined the street, the ethereal form of Loïc's familiar followed closely behind Margot.

"Let's go," Loïc said, turning to Sylvie before heading towards the palace.

Sylvie ran to catch up to Loïc.

"What's the plan?" She asked.

"First, shift yourself into an imp," he said as his face warped into an unrecognizable imp man with a broad, square nose and pronounced cheekbones.

Sylvie focused her own éthéra and felt her features change and shift.

"To be frank, I prefer your natural hair," Loïc said with a smile behind his disguise.

Sylvie couldn't help but smile.

"Oh, come off it," she said, "now's not the time."

Loïc shrugged.

"It's always the time."

Sylvie rolled her eyes.

"Are you going to tell me your plan, or are we just going to improvise?"

"There's not much in the way of a plan," Loïc admitted as he continued to walk quickly through the night towards the palace. "We'll enter through the servants' kitchen, try to figure out where they're keeping Gaëtan, and break him out. The details will depend largely on what we find inside the palace."

Sylvie raised one eyebrow skeptically.

"You call that a plan??"

"We're a bit short on information, so all things considered, yes."

Loïc pulled Sylvie into the deep shadows beneath a low-hanging balcony. At the crossroads just ahead, two guards marched purposefully down the street, their heads pivoting this way and that. As their footsteps faded, Loïc and Sylvie continued their journey.

Before long, they found themselves at the palace gate.

"I don't recall your 'plan' mentioning anything about getting through the gate," Sylvie chided.

"We're just going to walk in," Loïc whispered confidently without slowing his pace.

Sylvie felt her chest tighten as they approached the gate and guardhouse. Just a few paces later, she could make out the features of the guards stationed at the gate.

Loïc and Sylvie walked through the gate without so much as a nod to the guards. Sylvie tried to contain her surprise as she kept pace with Loïc.

"Told you," Loïc said quietly as they turned left and away from the main entrance towards the servants' kitchen. "To them, we're just another set of imps—servants or allies; it doesn't matter." Sylvie moved quickly to keep up with Loïc's purposeful pace.

"Once we're inside, follow my lead," Loïc said to Sylvie as they neared the palace. "We'll need to get our hands on someone who knows where Gaëtan is, and they'll either tell me or you can get it out of their head. We will be in real trouble if discovered, so keep a low profile. Just in case things go wrong, though," he handed her a straight, simple dagger in a plain sheath, "take this and stick it somewhere it won't show."

Sylvie did her best to conceal the weapon somewhere it would still be accessible if she needed it.

They reached the heavy wooden door that was the entrance to the servants' kitchen. Loïc tried the worn iron door handle. It was unlocked.

Loïc turned to Sylvie and gestured to have her follow him inside. Sylvie followed Loïc through a short, dark entryway. Sylvie barely had time to enter the kitchen before Loïc pulled her down behind a stack of crates full of potatoes and other vegetables pushed up against a long stretch of counters. From a crack between the boxes, Sylvie could see a member of the kitchen staff walk into the kitchen from the far right side of the long room with an armful of dishes. She walked the fifteen paces to a table directly in front of the Firstborns' hiding place and dropped her load down on the table with a thud, her back to Sylvie and Loïc. As the girl turned to leave, four men burst into the room, laughing and shouting boisterously at each other as they went. They were not wearing palace uniforms, and Sylvie did not recognize them.

"Well, well, what have we here?" one of them called out as he saw the servant girl standing near the table.

He approached his friends in tow.

"Hello dear," said the man who seemed to be the little gang's leader, a crooked smile adorning his face. His deep-set eyes glinted with ill intent beneath a set of long but slim eyebrows.

"Hello," the girl said timidly. Her exit blocked, she stood quietly, her hands held together in front of her.

"What's a lovely girl like yourself doing all alone down here? Care for some company?" the man raised a dirty hand to brush the girl's face. His companions chuckled and jeered in encouragement.

"Just doing the dishes," the girl replied, her voice trembling. "I need to get on with my work, please."

"Aww," the man replied, "come on now, I'm sure you can spare a few minutes." He pushed himself forward into the girl and grabbed at her waist.

"Please," she was begging him now and pushing his hands off of her.

Sylvie turned to Loïc to push him to action, but by the time she had done so, he was already moving.

In one motion, Loïc stood and grabbed a heavy glass pitcher sitting on the counter beside them and hurled it forcefully into the side of the leading man's head. It shattered with a crash against his skull, and he fell to the ground while the servant girl let out a scream.

Before the three other men could react, Loïc had hurdled the crates he had been hiding behind and landed a heavy punch to the second man's jaw, dropping him to the floor to join his comrade. One of the remaining men tried to strike Loïc with an awkward jab, but Loïc blocked the attack before kicking the man in the stomach. Sylvie heard the air leave the man's body as he doubled over before Loïc sent him, too, to the floor with a heavy strike to the exposed rear of his head. Sylvie heard footsteps before she looked to see the fourth man running out of the kitchen.

In the blink of an eye, Loïc swiped a knife from the pile of dishes the servant girl had left on the table and sent it flashing through the air towards the fleeing man. The blade whirled through the air for a split second before lodging itself deeply between the man's shoulder blades. The deserter fell to the ground without another sound besides that of his body hitting the kitchen tile, like that of a heavy bag being dropped to the floor.

Sylvie stood slowly out from behind her hiding place. She looked at the body of the fallen man at the far side of the room. Loïc turned to the imp girl.

"Do you know where they're keeping the Firstborn?"

The girl was in shock and was leaning away from Loïc in fear.

"Who—" she started with a gulp, "who are you?"

"A friend," Loïc replied quickly, "now answer my question. Do you know where they're keeping the Firstborn?"

The girl looked to Sylvie, then back to Loïc.

"I...I'm not sure. I heard some talk about him being kept in one of the suites upstairs, but I don't know if he's there for sure."

Loïc turned to Sylvie, one eyebrow raised as if asking for confirmation.

Sylvie nodded.

Loïc turned back to the servant girl.

"Thank you," Loïc said, turning to leave. As he stepped over one of the fallen bodies, he looked down at it before turning to Sylvie and then to the servant girl.

"We need to get these out of sight."

With the help of the imp girl, Loïc and Sylvie tied up the four men with some twine from the kitchen pantry and shoved them into a large closet full of mops, brooms, and other cleaning and kitchen equipment.

"Once we're gone, they're going to look for someone to blame, and there's a good chance it will be you," Loïc said to the servant girl. "If you can, you should leave the palace for the foreseeable future."

"I don't have anywhere to go...," the girl lamented.

Loïc had already started making his way out of the kitchen, but he paused and turned to the girl. He reached into his pocket, grabbed something, and stretched out his hand.

"Make a new start for yourself," he said, placing what he held in the girl's hand.

As she opened her fingers, the girl's eyes widened at the sight of three bright gold coins. She looked up at Loïc, then to Sylvie, tears in her eyes.

"Thank you!" she said emotionally.

"Go!" Loïc prompted gently but firmly.

The girl nodded and made for the door that Sylvie and Loïc had just used to enter the palace.

Loïc looked at Sylvie.

"Let's go get Gaëtan."

Sylvie followed as Loïc walked out of the kitchen, turned a sharp corner, and came to a secluded and tightly wound spiral staircase. If Loïc hadn't walked right to it, Sylvie would have missed it completely.

The two of them worked their way up the cramped steps. There was little light in the tiny stairwell, and Sylvie began feeling claustrophobic. Before long, she found herself behind Loïc in a remote alcove on the second floor somewhere she didn't recognize. She followed Loïc as he walked cautiously but swiftly along the wall towards the main hallway.

At the juncture, Loïc stopped and motioned for Sylvie to stop as well.

"Any thoughts ahead?"

Sylvie reached out with her mind.

*Thomas better not be late for his watch.*

Sylvie looked to Loïc and nodded.

"Guards. Thinking about the turning of the watch."

Loïc gripped his jaw and stroked his chin.

"Alright, we're servants on assignment from Beyern. He wants us to make Gaëtan presentable for an audience with the High Councilman in just a few minutes. Follow my lead."

Loïc walked out confidently into the hallway's light and approached a pair of guards on either side of Sylvie's suite. Sylvie followed Loïc nervously.

*Where did this one come from?* Sylvie heard one of the guards think to himself.

*And would you look at the new girl?*

Loïc walked right up to the doors of Sylvie's suite.

"What do you think you're doing, boy?" one of the guards asked gruffly. *And who's your friend?* he thought. Sylvie tried to ignore the guard and focus on the task at hand.

"Beyern sent us. We're to get the Firstborn cleaned up for an audience with Beyern."

The guards looked at each other.

"I didn't hear anything about any audience."

"I'm telling you now," Loïc insisted.

*Where's Thomas? Beyern wouldn't send two servants unaccompanied up here for this one.*

Sylvie could feel things unraveling quickly. She walked slowly but purposefully up to one of the guards and smiled bashfully.

"Alright...it was my idea. I just...I heard the Firstborn had left the palace, and I thought I could come to look at some of the dresses and jewelry the ladies had left behind...maybe even try some on..."

Sylvie looked up at the guard, a mask of innocence on her face.

"Could you, maybe...escort us inside, just for a few minutes?"

Sylvie put her hands on the man's forearms.

The guard looked at his companion, then back at Sylvie.

"For you, sweetheart, just a few minutes," the guard said.

He turned to the other guard.

"You stay here; I'll take her inside."

"Oh no, you don't! I'm joining you!" the soldier protested.

"Fine, just keep an eye on that one," the first guard said, nodding towards Loïc as he opened the door to Sylvie's suite.

As the doors peeled away to reveal the interior of the suite, Sylvie clenched her jaw and worked to keep her expression from betraying her. Gaëtan sat in the middle of the room, tied to a chair, his face bruised and bloodied. His dark blond hair hung in cords across his face. Two guards stood on either side of him. Their faces hardened at the sight of Sylvie and Loïc and their escort.

"What are you doing?" One of them said gruffly to the soldier closest to Sylvie.

"I'm Giving the little lady a tour of the royal suites," the soldier replied. "She wants to try on a dress for me."

"Forget about it," the first guard responded. "Beyern will have our heads for this. Get out."

Sylvie's escort waved him off with a dismissive gesture of his hand.

"Shove off. Alright now," he said, turning to Sylvie, "let's see you get into one of those dresses."

Sylvie tried to block out the filth coming from the soldier's mind.

"Alright, but shut the doors," Sylvie replied, keeping up the facade.

The soldier nodded to his colleague, who walked over to the suite doors and closed them with a quiet click of the latch, leaving Loïc and Sylvie alone in her suite with Gaëtan and his four guards.

Sylvie walked over to her wardrobe. She could feel eyes and minds all over her. She picked a faded emerald dress—one of her favorites—out of the wardrobe and turned around, holding it tight against her chest.

She looked at Loïc. With a slight grin, he nodded, turned in an instant to the guard beside him, and drew the soldier's sword from its sheath. With his other hand, Loïc grabbed the soldier by the throat. Under Loïc's crushing grip, Sylvie watched the man turn a deep shade of red.

Loïc used his captive as a shield as he advanced on the guards framing Gaëtan. Unable to attack without wounding their comrade, the guards watched helplessly as Loïc came into striking distance.

"Don't just stand there, you imbeciles; cut him down!" the guard closest to Sylvie shouted.

The sound of steel on steel rang out loudly as Loïc engaged Gaëtan's guards.

"You," the fourth guard said, turning to Sylvie, a twisted smirk on his face, "thought you could make a fool out of me, did you? Well, just wait until I'm done with you."

The guard approached but did not draw his sword. Sylvie could sense he had plans other than killing her right then and there.

*Strike first.* Loïc's advice came through her mind strong and clear.

Sylvie was still holding the green dress in front of her. She slipped one hand into her skirt's waistband and drew the dagger that Loïc had given her, keeping it concealed behind the beautiful dress. In one motion, she threw the dress over her attacker's face and lunged at the guard with her other hand, the dagger aimed directly at the soldier's throat. Before the guard had time to brush the flowy green fabric out of his face, Sylvie felt her blade find its mark through the beautiful dress. The guard made a gurgling noise as he fell, and Sylvie watched the green dress, which still covered the dying man's face, turn a sickly red. Sylvie shuddered violently.

Regaining her composure as best she could, Sylvie looked up to see Loïc cutting Gaëtan loose. The three other soldiers lay immobile on the floor.

"Come on, old friend, let's get you out of here," Loïc said as he put one of Gaëtan's arms over his shoulder. Loïc temporarily dropped his disguise, and Gaëtan's eyes shone in recognition.

"I thought those voices sounded familiar. I'm ok. I can walk," Gaëtan insisted.

Sylvie instinctively rushed to Gaëtan and wrapped her arms around him.

"Gaëtan, I'm so glad we found you!"

Gaëtan coughed, then chuckled.

"I'm glad you found me, too. It would probably be best if we postpone the festivities until later, though."

Sylvie stepped back sheepishly.

Loïc turned to Sylvie.

"Is the hallway clear? Can we leave the way we came?"

Sylvie approached the large, familiar doors and reached out with her mind.

"It's clear, there's no one outside," she said, turning to Loïc and Gaëtan. As she did, something caught her eye.

Loïc and Gaëtan were making their way to the door as Sylvie ran back to her desk.

"Sylvie!" Loïc hissed, "What are you doing? We need to go!"

Sylvie reached beneath her desk and whirled around, returning to her friends. In her hands, she held the sword her father had gifted her before she had left Hull.

"I figured we could use it…and I'd hate to leave it behind," Sylvie said.

"Fair enough," Loïc conceded, "but keep it out of sight. Now let's go."

Sylvie took the lead, reaching ahead with her mind for the thoughts of anyone walking the palace halls ahead of them. Gaëtan went next, with Loïc bringing up the rear. Sylvie traced back their steps towards the small servants' staircase that led down to the kitchens.

"Let me go first," Loïc said in a hushed voice as they reached the stairs. Sylvie watched as Loïc sunk out of sight down the dark spiral stairwell, and followed Gaëtan as they made their way single-file down the narrow steps.

There was no one in the kitchen. The three Firstborn made their way swiftly across the tile floor to the back door and into the cold night air.

Sylvie breathed a sigh of pent-up relief she hadn't even realized she was holding in. She looked at Loïc with a foolish grin. Loïc's mouth was slightly upturned, too, but his face was still serious.

"We're not out of here yet," he said soberly. "Gaëtan, can you shift?"

Gaëtan nodded, and before long, his blonde hair had been replaced by a tangle of ashy black waves, and his irises were shown with a vibrant sunflower hue.

"Great. Let's keep moving," Loïc said as he approached the gate.

Just like on their way in, the guards barely noticed the three walk out through the gate. Sylvie couldn't even sense a sidelong thought concerning them in the minds of the guards.

*I suppose just three more servants leaving the palace*, Sylvie thought to herself as she kept pace with Loïc.

"Is Margot alright?" Gaëtan asked as they walked north up one of the city's main thoroughfares. The sky to the east was turning from an unfathomable black to a rich navy blue. Sylvie knew that, given the chance to stop, she would be exhausted, but the intensity of their situation galvanized her forward. Her heart beat quickly, and she felt her blood coursing wildly through her veins.

"Margot is fine; she's meeting us outside the city," Loïc replied quietly.

They marched on, and Sylvie barely noticed as the crowded streets gave way to yarded homes, then the occasional farmhouse bordered by spacious fields, neatly plowed and showing the first signs of springtime growth.

Before long, Verdélys was behind them.

# XLII

*Farewell Verdélys*

"How far did you send her?" Sylvie asked Loïc as she, Loïc, and Gaëtan continued down the road. Verdélys continued to recede behind them.

"Far enough. I didn't want her stopping just outside of the city."

The night, or what was left of it, was still dark, though blue was creeping higher and higher into the sky.

The three Firstborn continued down the road, a well-worn dirt path that wound its way east among gently rolling hills. In the darkness, Sylvie tried to look ahead for a treeline, indicating they were getting close to their rendezvous site. It was a bit longer than Sylvie had anticipated before she could make out the first signs of a leafy canopy protruding over the tops of the hills ahead.

Before too long, they were approaching the treeline. The sky had lightened further, but the undergrowth was buried in utter darkness, and Sylvie couldn't make out anything beneath the trees.

"Send your familiar," Loïc instructed, "let's make sure she's there, and we're not running into a trap."

Sylvie summoned her familiar.

"Go look for Margot in those woods."

The mermaid's billowy tail swished this way and that as it receded into the darkness. A few moments later, it returned with Loïc's familiar in tow.

"She's waiting for us. Let's go."

Gaëtan was the first one into the trees. Loïc and Sylvie followed, a shared look of relief on their faces.

Sylvie peered into the shadows as she crossed the forest's threshold, trying desperately to make out anything in front of her. Slowly, her eyes adjusted to the dark, and she could make out the rock outcropping Loïc had set as their meeting place.

Margot and Gaëtan were already wrapped in a tight embrace at the base of a large, smooth boulder covered in moss. Margot pulled away and stroked Gaëtan's face gingerly, tears running down her face at the sight of his battered visage.

"I told you I'd get him," Loïc said as they reached Margot.

"Thank you," Margot said, her eyes conveying gratitude more fully than her words ever could have.

"*We* got Gaëtan. I'll remind you," Sylvie said. "If it wasn't for me, the two of you might be sharing the same fate back in the palace."

Loïc chuckled nervously.

"Yes. We couldn't have done it without your feminine wiles," he said through a snicker.

Sylvie just turned up her face and smiled, taking Loïc's sarcasm as a trophy.

Margot tilted her head questioningly. "Do I even want to know?" She asked. "In any event, thank you," Margot nodded.

"Yes, a very sincere thank you to both of you," Gaëtan added.

The four friends stood there a moment, breathing deeply the fresh night air beneath a canopy of trees, grateful to be free and together.

Of course, Loïc was the first to break the peace.

"Right. Unfortunately, that's all the rest we can afford at the moment. We must put as much distance between us and Verdélys as possible. Margot, where are our things?"

Margot pointed to a large fallen log that leaned, pitted and worn, against the rock outcropping. In the shadows beneath, Sylvie spied four silvery bags.

"Great," Loïc said, walking over and picking them up. "One for each—not that it matters much; they're weightless." As he spoke, he handed the bags to Sylvie, Margot, and Gaëtan before shouldering his own.

"But...," Sylvie said hesitantly, "none of us have slept all night. Wouldn't we be better off getting on the road after a little sleep? Look at Gaëtan."

Gaëtan was doing his best to look stoic and ready for a long trek to Hull, but it was apparent his captivity had left him in a rough way.

Loïc looked at the group, then towards the road, then back to his friends.

"We can't stay here. It's too close to Verdélys. We can stop around midday for a rest, but we can't stay within reach of a search party from the city now. I'm sorry." Loïc did look genuinely sorry to push the others on, but Sylvie knew he had their best interest at heart.

"You're right, of course," Gaëtan replied. "A search party equipped to follow us long distance will take time to assemble, giving us time to put some distance behind us. A light search party could reach us here from Verdélys relatively quickly. We can't risk that."

Loïc nodded and led the way back to the road. Gaëtan and Margot followed, Gaëtan leaning on Margot's arm, with Sylvie trailing behind. Tiredness was setting into her muscles, but she pushed on behind her companions.

Back on the road, the Firstborn took a final look west towards Verdélys. Then, as one, they turned resolutely east and marched towards their fate.

🐾

Travel that day had been uneventful. They had eaten breakfast on the road, not daring to stop as they shared bites of what little perishables they had brought. Loïc kept them moving at a very brisk pace, and Sylvie had hurried to his side to take his arm, partly to help her keep up and partly in the hopes that she might be able to slow him down, if even only a little, for her sake and Gaëtan's. The sun rose a few hours later, illuminating their path and the beautiful trees and meadows surrounding them. Sylvie's trip to Verdélys came flooding back to her as they walked.

As promised, Loïc ended their march around noon. The sun was high in the sky, bright and warm, though Sylvie was still chilled under the shade of the trees. The friends shared a meal and settled down for a deserved rest deep in the thicket, concealed by the heavy undergrowth. Loïc took the first watch.

🐾

Their journey continued for several weeks. The scenery passed in a blur as the four Firstborn continued north and east, making for the pass that would lead them into the valley that Sylvie had once called home. As they went, Margot honed her skills in éthéra manipulation and even managed to summon her familiar—a chamigua, a strange, lizard-like creature. The spring days were gorgeous, and the nights were still cold. During the day, the friends shared thoughts and stories, laughing and smiling as they went. There would be time to discuss more serious things soon enough. At night, Sylvie cherished the moments spent cuddling beside Loïc around the fire and the beauty of the nights spent under the stars, the only sound that of the wind in the branches and blades of grass. Sylvie was happy.

🐾

The days were noticeably longer when they reached the mountains that separated them from Hull.

"Tomorrow, we'll start up through the pass," Loïc said, shuffling off his pack in a small clearing among the trees. "Not long to go now." As had become routine, Loïc set off in search of firewood. Sylvie and Margot also dropped

434

their packs and went off hunting mushrooms and berries, leaving Gaëtan to keep watch over their small camp.

Spring was in full bloom all around Sylvie as she wandered through the forest, her eyes peeled for anything edible. The deep and bright greens of the forest were dotted with the bright colors of blooms and their attendant butterflies. Birds sang gayly among the tree boughs, providing a symphonic accompaniment to the renewal of the season.

"So...," Margot said as they walked along, not taking her eyes off the forest floor, "what's Hull really like? What are humans like?"

Margot's question made Sylvie pause. Now that she thought of it, her memory of Hull seemed so distant she felt as though she had to fish deep into her mind to remember what life in Hull really had been like.

"Hull is...quiet," Sylvie said finally, "It's plain. A few handfuls of cottages clustered together in the middle of nothing. It's a whole other world compared to Verdélys."

"How...quaint," Margot said sarcastically, a smirking grin on her face. "And the people?"

"I never got along all that closely with anyone other than my parents in Hull, I suppose," Sylvie said, half to herself. "They're nice enough, though superstitious and not much for excitement or adventure. They know Hull, which seems to be enough for them."

"I'm sure they're going to love an impromptu visit from four Verdélian strangers, aren't they?" Margot asked with a wicked smile.

Sylvie huffed in mock frustration.

"Margot!" she scolded, "as far as they're concerned, you're as human as the rest of them!"

"Now, where's the fun in that?" Margot asked, not ready to drop her act just yet.

Sylvie shook her head.

"The fun is that you don't get ostracized—or worse—burned as a witch or heretic. Is that good enough for you?"

"Fine," Margot complained in a playfully defeatist tone. "Hey, look! Mushrooms!"

❧

Sylvie and Margot made their way back into camp. Sylvie's skirt was held out in front of her as a makeshift basket filled with a modest amount of mushrooms, berries, and nuts. The sun had not set yet, but a small fire was already casting dancing shadows around the clearing, the flames flickering quietly from a bramble of branches that Loïc was tending.

Sylvie approached Gaëtan and dropped what she and Margot had managed to gather gingerly beside him.

"Impressive as always, ladies," Gaëtan said as he began to sort through the mushrooms and fruit. Margot sat beside him, basking in the compliment.

"Thank you," Sylvie said as she walked over the fire and crouched beside Loïc. He looked up at her.

"Did you find enough? I could go out and see if I could add meat to the menu."

"I think there'll be enough," Sylvie said, wrapping her arm around Loïc's. "Besides, we still have some rations left in our packs. We'll be alright."

Across the fire, Gaëtan and Margot worked together to cut up the mushrooms and season them with what they could find in their packs. The two of them smiled and laughed, caught up in a game Sylvie was not privy to.

Night came, and the four friends sat around the dying embers of their fire. The nights were growing warmer, but the breeze through the trees was still cool. Sylvie pulled a blanket out of her pack and drew it around her, sinking into Loïc's shoulder as she did so. He lifted his arm and draped it around her shoulders, pulling her in tight.

"Would you look at us?" Loïc said quietly to no one in particular. "I'd have called anyone a fool who would have tried to tell me two moons ago that this is where we'd be today."

"Too true," Gaëtan agreed from across the fire. "Though honestly, I have fewer complaints than anticipated." Margot rested her head on Gaëtan's shoulder as she nodded in agreement.

"Is that so?" Loïc said with a smile. "Ready to give up ruling for the life of a vagabond?"

Gaëtan chuckled.

"Duty says otherwise, but I can think of worse things."

There was no response as the four watched the last coals smolder on the ground before them.

*So can I*, Sylvie thought to herself as she felt Loïc's heartbeat on her cheek.

※

The Firstborn had been up before the sun and started on the road early, taking breakfast to go. Their path had begun to incline almost immediately, and Sylvie had wholly forgotten how steep the road had been. Even with a weightless pack, Sylvie's breathing soon came sharp and fast, and the warming spring sun poking between the mountain peaks sent beads of sweat trickling down her face. Despite the arduous journey, Sylvie felt a gust of nostalgia in the sweet mountain air. They would be in Hull in about two days at their current pace, and an anxious longing was growing inside of Sylvie.

Around midday Sylvie, Loïc, Gaëtan, and Margot paused under the shade of a lonely tree on the banks of a splashing mountain brook cascading down the hillside. They refilled their waterskins and paused for a bite to eat. As Sylvie prepared to bite into a piece of dried meat, she heard Loïc, who was standing and surveying the valley behind them, curse under his breath.

"What's wrong?" Sylvie asked as Loïc began rifling through his pack.

"See for yourself," Loïc replied as Gaëtan and Margot took notice, walking over to where Loïc was crouched, rearranging his pack and shuffling items between his and Sylvie's bags.

"A party of imps, down on the road less than a half day's journey behind us."

Sylvie's pulse quickened and she walked over to the edge of a large rock overhang that overlooked the plains they had left behind just that morning. It took her a minute, but sure enough, down the road, she could see about two dozen tiny figures behind them. She couldn't make them out as imps, but here and there, a helmet or a spearhead caught the sun and glinted in the distance.

Sylvie turned to see Margot and Gaëtan beside her, looking down at the company of pursuers.

"Are you sure they're imps?" Sylvie asked.

"Sure enough," Loïc said. "That's Verdélian armor down there. Last time I was in Verdélys, people wearing that weren't our friends."

Sylvie drew in her lips in a tight grimace.

Gaëtan walked over and shouldered his pack. Loïc did the same, though he now carried his sword on his hip.

"So what do we do?" Sylvie asked. She had hoped and believed that they had managed to leave Verdélys unnoticed.

"We're going to keep heading for Hull," Loïc explained. "When we reach the other side of the pass, you three will keep for Hull. I'll draw our little welcome party off north, and once I've dealt with them, I'll join you in Hull. Margot, how many arrows do you have left?"

Margot opened her bag in search of her quiver.

"But there are thirty imps down there!" Sylvie protested, "We can help; don't do this alone."

Margot offered her quiver to Loïc, which contained about twenty arrows. Loïc grabbed half of the arrows and put them in his quiver, his bow slung across his back.

"I appreciate the sentiment, Sylvie, but we don't want to give away our head start, and we certainly don't want to lead them to Hull. Besides, I can easily lose thirty undertrained rebels out here. There's nothing to worry about. Let's head out."

Loïc started briskly up the trail as if to cut off any further protest from Sylvie.

"I wish he wouldn't do that," Sylvie grumbled to Margot as they followed Loïc and Gaëtan up the mountainside.

"Do what, be such a man?" Margot said with a smile.

"He can be a man without being such a tough guy," Sylvie complained.

Margot laughed through labored breaths. She looked over at Sylvie, her flushed face almost matching her red locks.

"Can he, though? This is Loïc we're talking about."

Sylvie expelled a breath with a growl of frustration.

"He could at least try," Sylvie answered.

"But deep down, don't you love that about him?"

Margot's eyes were teasing but also sincere.

She wasn't wrong.

Sylvie trudged up the mountain with her friends.

⚘

There hadn't been much talk as they made their way through the pass. The sun had moved up and behind them as the day progressed, and they reached the far side of the pass. The Firstborn chased their shadows on their way to Hull and away from their pursuers. Each step towards the opening in the cliffs before them had filled Sylvie with dread—she wasn't ready for Loïc to leave.

All too soon, for Sylvie's liking, the four friends looked down onto the forested downhill slope, which led them to Hull. A narrow path scribbled into the cliffside wandered down to their right.

"This is where we split," Loïc said without indication of any emotion in his voice. Sylvie couldn't tell if she was going to cry or scream.

"Don't go," she pleaded, looking deeply into Loïc's face.

"I won't be gone long," Loïc said, taking Sylvie by the shoulders. "Go see your family; I'll be there soon!"

She knew she could not talk him out of this. She fell into his arms, embracing him tightly around the middle. Loïc wrapped his arms around her for a moment, then released her. Sylvie hesitantly let go of Loïc, but as she stepped back, he took her face in his strong, warm hands. His dark and serious eyes stared into her own.

"I will return to you, *mer vivillen*. On my honor."

Sylvie felt Loïc's hands draw her in. She closed her eyes, and a moment later, their lips touched. Loïc's kiss was tender, and her heart soared. Her hands tightened on his arms as she returned his kiss.

438

Loïc drew away, but only just. Their noses were still touching.

"Now go with Gaëtan and Margot. You don't want to lose your head start."

Loïc turned to Gaëtan.

"Get into the woods as soon as you can, and stay off the road from here on out."

Gaëtan nodded. "Will do."

Gaëtan gently placed his arm around Sylvie's shoulders and shepherded her away from Loïc and onto the path that led down into the forest. Sylvie kept her eyes on Loïc, tears obscuring her view. Loïc smiled and blew her a kiss, then turned and settled himself onto a large boulder jutting out into the pass.

"Come on now," Gaëtan insisted, prodding Sylvie along. "He'll be fine. You've seen him get through worse."

Sylvie obediently turned towards the sloping path ahead of them, the road now obscured by the shadows of the coming night. The chill of the mountain breeze reflected a coldness she felt within as she turned to see Loïc, perched nonchalantly on his rock, recede behind her.

*Goodbye, my love,* she thought as she sank below a rise and lost Loïc from view.

*More magic...*

# *Glossary*

**Alimout** [ah-lee-moo] *noun* mountain goat found in the north-eastern mountain ranges; the wool is edible

**Alondra** [ah-lohn-drah] *interjection* "hello" in the ancient tongue

**Ancelin** [ahn-seh-lahn] *proper noun* the given name for the brothers born to bring the seasonal cycles and thus the seasonal Verdélia

**Aritené** [ah-ree-teh-nay] *proper noun* the largest theater in the city of Verdélys

**Assaulen** [ah-so-lahn] *verb* "attack" in the ancient tongue

**Bliert** [ble-yairt] *noun* green berries that cause forgetfulness when eaten

**Céladon** [say-lah-dohn] *proper noun* the northern city of the Sylphs

**Crimén bé ardent** [kree-mehn bay air-dahn] *phrase* "kill the soldier" in the ancient tongue

**Crimén dèr** [kree-mehn dair] *phrase* "kill him" in the ancient tongue

**Enclave** [ahn-klahv] *noun* a plant with sap that can be used as invisible ink; the petals can be rubbed over the ink to reveal the writing

**Éthéra** *common.* [eth-ee-rah] *ancient.* [ay-tay-rah] *noun* the ancient word for Verdélias' energy source or form of magic

**Frimédia** [free-may-dee-ah] *proper noun* the title of the premiere dance company of Verdélys

**Gaëtan** [gay-tahn] *proper noun* one of the four Firstborn

**Gnattire** [nyah-teer] *noun* a burrowing plant often used in gardens to attract gnomes

**Grisdon** *common.* [griz-dun] *ancient.* [gree-dohn] *proper name* the name of the largest dwarven city in the northern mountain ranges

**Im haritelle pou tilent** [emm ah-ree-tel poo tee-lahn] *phrase* "all things for the good" in the ancient tongue

**Litel parchon** [lee-tel par-shohn] *phrase* "like lightning" in the ancient tongue

**Loïc** *common.* [loh-ick] *ancient.* [loh-eek] *proper name* one of the four Firstborn

Lumivale [loo-mee-vahl] *proper name* the southern city of the imps, found in the swamplands

Lunardé [loo-nar-day] *interjection* "good evening" in the ancient language

Mielaleur [mee-el-ah-loor] *noun* a honeybee with wings of fire; the honey from this bee can be stirred into tea and elicit a warming and relaxing sensation

Mistralle [mees-trahl] *proper noun* the title for the south-eastern peninsula

Nèmor [nay-mor] *noun* "foe" in the ancient tongue

Orpap [or-pahp] *noun* a tree with leaves of gold commonly found in the northern mountain ranges;

Piscana [pee-skah-nah] *noun* a fish with a long transparent streaming tail that can be used to cover lacerated skin to heal injury

Pés kiren rhati jet [pay kee-ren rah-tee zhay] *phrase* "by reason, not force" in the ancient tongue

Pèverelle [peh-vuh-rehl] *noun* a dance popular during Verdélian events that means meadow; it is most recognized by its lilting quality

Rangdèf [rahng-def] *noun* a tusked crocodile that guards the merpeople; its tusks cause visions of the dead when they pierce skin

Sébelle pou fecil haritelle [say-bell poo feh-seel ah-red-tel] *phrase* "hope for better things" in the ancient tongue

Sovrène [sohv-rehn] *interjection* "good evening" in the ancient tongue

Tembré [tahm-bray] *noun* "time" in the ancient tongue; recognized as a popular musical style in Verdélian culture

Verdélia [vehr-day-lee-ah] *noun* the species to first be planted and subsequently create the remaining known magical creations

Verdélys [vehr-day-lees] *proper noun* the city of the Verdélia

Vivillèn (mèr) [vee-vee-yen (mehr)] *phrase* "my daughter of water" in the ancient language; a pet name

## Alina and Samuel Dampt

Alina was born and raised in Henderson, Nevada. Samuel was born in France and moved to Mesa, Arizona (and across the street from Alina's relatives) during elementary school. After a brief long-distance relationship, Alina and Samuel got married and moved to Utah to attend law school, before moving back to Mesa, Arizona where they're currently settled with their four children.

Throughout all of this, the idea for "Daughter of Water" grew in Alina's mind, and eventually developed into a rough draft that Samuel helped finalize into the novel it is today. The story reflects both Alina and Samuel's love of nature and fantastic tales of good versus evil.

Alina and Samuel are keeping busy with the next installments of the Verdélian Chronicles, and with raising their four young children amongst the endless soccer practices and games, ballet lessons, and music rehearsals.